TRAIN-WRECKED HEARTS

NORFOLK SOUTHERN SERIES #1

JENNIFER SIENES

I'd like to dedicate this book, my first self-published endeavor, to my amazing husband Chris. Your unending support, encouragement, and love allows me to spend my days creating the stories God puts on my heart. Thank you.
And as always, none of this would be possible without the One for whom I write—my Lord and Savior, Jesus Christ.

Chapter 1

Sarah Beth

No one likes to hear, "I told you so", but it would be a whole lot easier coming from anyone other than Mama. The four-day drive from Los Angeles, California to Rossville, Georgia wasn't near enough time to build the layer of skin I needed to deflect her criticism. Especially since my confidence had taken a beating for the last eight years.

"Are we almost there, Mama?" Gracie Lynn's voice broke into my mental tirade, reminding me why I was putting myself through this in the first place. I'd face a firing squad for my sweet girl.

"Yes, baby. Another hour or so." I cut a glance at the rearview mirror to see her reflection. With my old clunker loaded right up to the headliner, it was really the only view available. "You need to go potty?" Anything to delay the confrontation with Mama.

"I'm hungry."

Like one of Pavlov's dogs, my stomach rumbled in response to her declaration. It'd been hours since we hit the road with only a meager continental breakfast in our bellies. Jasper was coming up right quick, the last easy stop before the always-busy Chattanooga traffic. "How 'bout a Sonic burger?"

"Sonic?" I didn't need to see her reflection to know that lit up her eyes some. "I wanna blast." Just what I needed—a four-year-old on a sugar high. Mama's first meeting with her only grandchild would be challenging enough without Gracie Lynn bouncing off the walls.

"You eat at least half a burger, and I'll share a small blast with you."

One of the things I liked about Sonic was not having to get out of the car. It had that fifties' drive-in-restaurant vibe. When we finished our meal, I drove across the street and parked at the Dollar General so we could get out for a bit. It was good to stretch the cramps from my legs and back. I closed my eyes as my face was drawn to the sun like bees to a blossom. A little sunshine therapy was just what my soul needed—a refreshing shot of filling my senses.

Although it was warm, there was just enough of a breeze to remind me it wasn't quite spring yet. Living in Los Angeles all those years, I'd almost forgotten the precarious nature of Tennessee weather. If I was remembering correctly, the first little winter hadn't hit yet, and there'd be four more to follow before June. I did miss the seasons.

Glancing up at the sky as Gracie Lynn climbed out of the car, it struck me just how clear it was. No yellow cast from all the cars clogging up the streets of L.A. Just pure blue with some wispy clouds to make it a touch more interesting.

"You smell that, Gracie Lynn?" I closed the passenger door and took hold of her free hand—the other was holding tight to the Sonic Blast cup.

Gracie stuck her little nose in the air and sniffed. "Smell what?"

"Sunshine, baby girl. Just pure sunshine." The therapy was already working on my spirit. I fingered a wisp of curly, blond hair from her cheek.

"Oh, look, Mama." Gracie Lynn shoved her ice cream at me and started running for the front walk of the Dollar General.

I nearly fumbled the icy cup in my haste to keep up with her. As I glanced ahead, the sight of a cardboard box full of wriggling fur-covered bodies pulled a groan from me. Puppies were my baby girl's Kryptonite.

Gracie Lynn dropped to her knees at the side of the box. "Ahhh. They're so cute." Her voice rose to a squeal as one of the puppies reached over the top of the box and licked her hand. "Can we get one, Mama?"

I offered an apologetic grimace to the old man sitting in a lawn chair beside the box. "I'm afraid not, sweetie. Now isn't the right time."

She lifted heartbroken eyes at me. "That's what Daddy always says. When *is* it gonna be the right time?" *Ready, aim, fire!* Gracie Lynn's words struck to the core of my heart. Guilt was a powerful motivator.

"Free to a good home," the old man said, his eyes twinkling. He knew an easy target when he saw one. "My granddaughter's mini poodle went carousing when she was in heat, and the neighbor's terrier took advantage." With a shake of his head, he clucked his tongue. "Ain't they the sweetest things you ever did see?"

Well, he was right about that. Gracie Lynn had one in her arms now, and it looked up at me through big black eyes in a cloud of tan and white fur. But cute and sweet would dissipate like fog in the holler with every whine and potty mishap that was sure to come. And it wouldn't earn me any favors with Mama, either.

The closer I came to Rossville, the tighter my belly clenched. If I didn't know better, I'd have blamed it on the Sonic Blast or spoiled cheese on my burger. But it was the same ache that had become a regular part of my day up until last month, only this time it was on account of Mama instead of Jason. And no amount of sunshine therapy was going to fix it.

If I could sit quietly at the feet of Jesus for a week, His presence might could calm my spirit, but I didn't have that kind of time. Maybe I should've let Mama know I was coming. She never was a big fan of surprises. If she told me to stay away, I'd be lost. There was nowhere else for me to go.

What was I thinking springing her granddaughter on her like this? If she was fixing to be ugly about me coming home, Gracie Lynn would pay the price. The child had already lived with enough rejection; a guest spot on a trashy, daytime talk show was surely in her future.

Drawing in a breath deep enough to reach my toes, I turned the car just before the Pickett's Mill Motel sign and drove beneath the massive, ancient magnolias. The place never was all that cheerful, but its once yellow color had faded to nothingness—or maybe it was just covered in grime. The gutters were sagging like an old woman's bosom, and the boxwoods on either side of the front office doors were scraggly and weed-infested.

Mama might be opinionated and cantankerous, but she was hard-working and took great pride in the business she'd inherited from her mama when I was no bigger than a thought. How often had she badgered me near to death about keeping the weeds clear of the flower beds? And boy, if she didn't give every room I cleaned the white glove test as if we were preparing it for royalty. Now it was neglected and eerily quiet.

"Are we here, Mama?" Gracie scrambled out of her car seat and poked her head next to mine to look out the windshield as I put the car in park.

"We are, baby." There wasn't a soul in sight and uneasiness had me clenching the steering wheel. What if something awful had happened to Mama? She could've died of a heart attack or some aggressive form of cancer, and no one would've known where to find me.

Pressing a hand to the ache in my chest, I blinked back the sudden tears. Just the thought of Mama dying all alone was enough to have me bawling like a baby. One minute I was dreading the thought of seeing her, and the next I was dreading the thought of not. Mother-daughter relationships were as twisted as a mess of knots in a necklace.

"Can you wait here in the car for me for a couple minutes, baby?" If I found Mama lying dead in her room, it would be enough to give me nightmares. I surely didn't want Gracie Lynn to be traumatized, too.

"But I wanna meet my nana. Never had me one before."

"Just a few minutes, okay? I'm not even sure she's home." Or alive. "And keep the door locked 'til I get back." I got her settled in her seat before climbing from the car.

My heart was beating a crazy staccato as I neared the glass doors to the front office. Mama and me had lived in the small, two-bedroom apartment in the back of the office for as long as I could remember. Growing up, I wanted to be like my friends who lived in real houses with space enough to have a private thought, and no stragglers wandering in at all hours of the night.

I tugged on the door handle, expecting it to be locked, and was surprised when it gave. The room didn't look much different, aside from the mail stacked on the counter and the empty coffee pot on the side table. Not just empty, but dusty as well. And the place smelled musty, as if it had been shut up for weeks without a lick of fresh air.

I leaned across the reception counter. "Anyone here?"

Nothing.

Maybe Mama had sold the motel. If so, I had no business walking into the back apartment uninvited. I shifted down the counter close enough to check the name on the top piece of mail in the stack. *Georgina Pickett*. Mama's name, so she was still living here.

"Hello?" I tapped the service bell with enough force to wake the dead.

"We're closed." The weak voice floated from the back, but there was no doubt it was Mama's. Even a whisper from her would set my pulse to racing.

Squaring my shoulders, I stepped through the *Employee Only* door and headed for the apartment. The kitchen sink was filled near to the brim with dirty dishes, and there were discarded frozen dinner boxes scattered across the counter and stacked in the trash can.

Mama *was* sick. Long as I could remember, she'd told me frozen dinners were the work of the devil. Made people lazy and unhealthy.

I made my way down the short hallway to the room at the end. "Mama? It's me, Sarah Beth."

"Who?" The sharpness of her tone nearly had me running in the opposite direction. What was I going to find waiting for me?

I took a deep breath and stuck my head into the room. Mama lay on the bed, pillows propping her up, eyes glassy with what I imagined was pain. A stack of books, opened mail, and a half-full water glass were on the end table.

"It's me, Mama. Sarah Beth."

A frown marred her brow as she struggled to sit up. "So, the baby chick finally comes home to roost, huh?" With a cluck of her tongue, she narrowed her eyes. "What took you so long?"

Aaron

The Bible commands Christ followers to care for the widows and orphans. I didn't know if the cranky lady who owned the motel next to my house was a widow, but she was for sure alone. Might be why she was so grouchy whenever I saw her. Nothing worse than having no one to give a rat's nest about you.

After hauling the groceries from the back of my Jeep to the kitchen, I separated out the frozen dinners I'd picked up for her. Best to get that chore done with before I crashed. Hadn't slept in more than forty-eight hours, and there was no telling when I'd come to once my head hit the pillow.

I hooked the four plastic grocery bags over one arm and stepped out the kitchen door to the back patio—if you could call it that. More like a patch of stained concrete with weeds growing up through the cracks. The whole place needed lot of work—which was the only reason right there I could afford it. More important was the location. Out in the country but only minutes from Chattanooga's DeButts rail yard.

My plan was to flip it. I was hesitant to put much into a house with a motel only a stone's throw away. The noise alone would be a deterrent for would-be buyers. But my realtor assured me it was as good as dead as far as businesses go. And it appeared she was right. Hadn't seen even one guest since I'd moved in.

Could hear a mockingbird chattering overhead as I made my way to the motel. Didn't know if the owner would be up and about, but it didn't matter. I'd leave the food in her freezer, like always, and she could pretend it miraculously appeared like manna from heaven. It was just easier on the both of us that way.

As I rounded to the east end of the long, L-shaped building, I spotted an old, rusted car parked out front, like someone was actually checking in. *Huh*. Could be a visitor. Or maybe someone was lost and looking for directions.

"Come back here, puppy!" The child's voice coincided with the appearance of a small tan and white ball of fluff heading my way.

With some fancy footwork and quick reflexes, I was able to scoop up the puppy before it could evade my reach. The child came running from around the corner, curly blond hair fanning her red cheeks. The moment she spotted me, she came to a screeching halt. Someone taught her Stranger Danger. So, where was that responsible person?

"Hey, there." Crouching down, I held out the wriggling puppy. "This must be yours." She looked to be the size of my niece, Sadie, so that would make her about three or four. Way too young to be on her own.

She glanced around, clearly looking for whoever had brought her here. The last thing I wanted to do was scare her. Being six-foot-three, it kind of came with the territory until kids got to know me.

"Is your mama or daddy with you?"

She clasped her hands together and frowned. "I'm not s'posed to talk to strangers."

"That's a good rule." I held out the puppy again. "What d'you want me to do with this little rascal? If I put"—I shifted it to see its sex—"her down, she might run off again."

The little girl moved forward, arms outstretched, and I transferred the puppy to her then moved back so she wouldn't feel threatened.

"Mama said to stay in the car, but I thought the puppy might wanna go potty."

"You know where she is? Your mama?" The kid didn't drive herself to the motel.

"Seein' if my nana is home." She hugged the puppy to her little chest. "I never had me a nana before."

Nana? Was she talking about my crotchety neighbor? Wasn't what I'd call grandma material. But maybe it was just me she didn't care for. I was hoping to change that over time.

"Gracie Lynn!" The frantic woman storming from the motel moved faster than the pup had only moments before. "Didn't I tell you to stay in the car?" It wasn't anger shooting from her wide eyes; it was fear. She reached the little girl, knelt at her feet, and pulled her close.

"Sorry, Mama." The little girl—Gracie Lynn—didn't seem the least put out with the scolding. "But I think the puppy has to go potty."

The woman's gaze flicked up to me as she stood, her arm still around Gracie Lynn's shoulders. Her big, blue eyes seemed to dwarf her narrow face, as did her long, honey-blond hair. Gracie Lynn's mama. So, did that make her the neighbor lady's daughter? "Sorry if she bothered you," she threw over her shoulder as they walked away.

It took a beat to collect my wits. "Hold on a sec." When she twisted around to look at me, I rushed on. "Are you kin to the woman at the motel?"

She straightened her spine some and turned to face me again. "Why do you wanna know?" Suspicion fairly oozed from her tone.

Like mother, like daughter. The two of them could use a lesson in common curtesy. I held up the grocery bags. "These are for her. They need to go into the freezer before much longer. Thought if you were kin, you could deliver them for me."

The wariness in her eyes eased some. "Do you work for the grocery store?"

"No, ma'am. Just trying to be neighborly." I aimed the zinger her way, but no telling if she caught it. I tilted my head toward my place. "Moved in about three months ago. You're the first person I've seen here."

She frowned. "Mama said she was closed, but I didn't think..." Could barely catch her words, but I had me a feeling she wasn't talking to me anyway.

"Am I gonna meet my nana now?" Gracie Lynn shifted the puppy and tilted her head back to look at her mama.

"In a minute, baby girl." She flicked a glance my way. "I'm her daughter. Do you know what's going on with her?"

A grunt escaped. "We're not exactly on friendly terms. I don't even know her name."

A grimace marred her lips. "She can be a little...standoffish."

"That's one word for it," I mumbled.

"Georgina," she said. "Mama's name is Georgina Pickett."

I pointed to the sign barely peeking through a huge magnolia tree. "Pickett's Mill Motel. That makes sense."

Smoothing Gracie Lynn's hair, the woman frowned. "It doesn't appear you know Mama at all, so why are you bringing her groceries?"

"Like I said before, just being neighborly." A pang of shame heated my ears some. Neighborly, yes. But I was also being a touch opportunistic. If Miss Pickett was fixing to sell the motel, I wanted first crack at it. I'd raze it and maybe build another house.

Rather than tell her the whole truth, I hedged. "Came over one day to introduce myself, and it appeared she didn't have anyone to help."

"Well, I'm sure she appreciates it." She reached out to take the grocery bags, and I noticed the gold band on her ring finger. Was her husband visiting, too? "And if there's something we can do in return, just let me know." Was that actually a smile on her face?

I handed off the bags. "There is one thing."

Wariness clouded her eyes once again. "What's that?"

"You can tell me your name."

Her lips twitched. "Sarah Beth McAllister. And you?"

I offered my hand. "Aaron Cooper." She hesitated a beat before placing her small, soft one in mine. "Are you going to be visiting for a while?"

Lips twisting, she glanced at the motel. "Only time will tell."

Chapter 2

Sarah Beth

There was a time I thought Mama hung the moon and stars. Never having a daddy, she was the center of my world. That is until I got old enough to see there was more to life than she could provide. There was a whole world out there just waiting for me, and I wanted to experience it.

College was the first step toward independence, even if living on campus wasn't an option. Classes at the University of Tennessee at Chattanooga opened my eyes to the possibilities. I didn't have to live small, like Mama did, and she didn't take to the notion that I had aspirations bigger than owning her family legacy. It caused more than a few heated discussions.

Then I met Jason.

Now here I was, a single mama with a daughter of my own. I'd lay down in front of a moving train to spare her life. I could see why Mama was so protective when she feared she'd lose me, but it didn't make it any easier to come crawling back to her. In fact, it was downright embarrassing.

I was just fixing to tell her about Gracie Lynn when I looked out her bedroom window to see the car door was open—and my daughter wasn't in her seat. My heart dropped to my toes, and I rushed out in the middle of Mama's tirade. You couldn't go a week without hearing about some child gone missing, and I would've had no one to blame but myself for leaving Gracie Lynn in the car.

Then to find her conversing with that very tall stranger. Aaron Cooper seemed nice enough, but unless Jesus Himself came down from heaven and offered His approval, I wasn't of a mind to ever trust another man—especially with my precious child. Might account for why I was so short with him, even if he did bring Mama bags of food.

With my back to Aaron and my free arm around Gracie Lynn's shoulders, I walked her toward the motel as my heart settled some. I couldn't let her disobedience go unchecked, even if I was kicking myself for telling her to stay in the first place. "When I tell you to do something, I expect you to listen." A lingering fear had my words coming out sharper than intended. "You can't just go running off like you did."

"I didn't want the puppy to pee in the car."

How could I argue with that? "Well, let's get her leash and take her for a quick walk before we go inside. We don't want her messing on your nana's carpet." Not that it would make much of a difference. Mama had obviously let the place go to pot over the last eight years.

I set the grocery bags on the front walk in the shade then led Gracie Lynn and the pup to the small playground on the west side of the building. It was in worse shape than the motel. The swings were hanging all cattywampus-like on rusted chains and the slide looked like a stiff wind would topple it. I'd spent my childhood playing on this exact equipment, but I didn't dare let Gracie Lynn near it for fear she'd get hurt. It was a lawsuit waiting to happen. Patchy weeds and stickers had grown through the now-thin layer of rubber mulch making it about as appealing as a bed of snakes.

"There's a swimming pool?" Gracie Lynn shoved the puppy's leash into my hand and raced ahead.

"Stay behind the fence," I cautioned. Not that there was any chance of drowning, since there wasn't but an inch of green water skimming the bottom. Still, a fall into that pit could do serious damage.

How had things gotten so bad in such a short amount of time? Surely, Mama hadn't just given up after I left. If so, how did she survive? She wasn't old enough for Social Security, and unless she had some secret fortune hidden away somewhere, she didn't have much to live on.

I walked the puppy to a patch of weeds to do her business then called Gracie Lynn back. "Before I take you in to meet your nana, I want you to know she's been laid up some."

Gracie Lynn wrinkled her nose. "What's that mean?"

I fingered a strand of fine hair from her sweaty forehead. How did I explain to her what I wasn't sure of myself? "Well, she's in bed for starters. Might've hurt her hip or leg." If the walker was any kind of clue. "I didn't get a chance to find out before coming to search for you."

"Is she 'tagious?"

Despite the nerves strumming throughout my body, a smile tugged at my lips. "I think you mean *con*tagious, and I don't believe so. But if she's grouchy, I don't want you to think it's on account of you, okay?"

She shrugged her narrow shoulders. "'Kay."

I watched the puppy dancing around on the end of her leash for a moment with enough energy to power a locomotive. "On second thought, let's leave your puppy in the car for now. I don't want your nana to be overwhelmed." One surprise at a time.

"What's that sound?" Gracie Lynn tilted her head, and I did the same. The faint wail of a train whistle blew in on a breeze, bringing with it a pang of melancholy. Growing up, it was a reminder of a daddy I never knew.

"That's a horn. Whenever a train goes through town, the conductor blows it to warn people it's coming." Had Gracie Lynn ever seen a train before? There weren't many railroads in L.A. "When we get settled, I'll take you to the rail yard in Chattanooga."

After being outside in the bright sunlight, the front office seemed even darker than when I first went in. "Wait here while I put the food away." Mama's freezer was all but empty, if one didn't count a couple of ice packs and a stack of four ice trays. I peeked inside the fridge. Not much there either, aside from crusty bottles of condiments. If not for Aaron Cooper, she might've starved to death.

I took Gracie Lynn's hand and led her down the short hallway toward Mama's bedroom.

"Sarah Beth?" Mama called.

We came to the doorway, and I took myself a deep breath. "Yes, Mama, I'm back. And I have—"

"What in the world got you so worked up you had to run outta here like your tail was on..." Her voice faded away and her eyes went wide as she caught sight of Gracie Lynn. A smile softened her pinched lips. "Who have we here?"

Placing my hand on Gracie Lynn's upper back, I guided her toward the bed. "Mama, this is Gracie Lynn." When Mama's eyes caught mine, I said, "Your granddaughter."

"Why..." Her eyes welled as they flitted to Gracie Lynn. "Come here, young'un."

Gracie Lynn stayed rooted where she was. "How come you're in bed? Are you sick?"

Mama huffed out a soft laugh and her eyes lit up a bit. It appeared Gracie Lynn had the power to perform miracles. "Not sick. Just hurt my hip some time back, and it's not healing properly."

Gracie Lynn approached the bed. "Whenever I get hurt, Mama kisses it and makes it better. You want me to kiss it for you?" *Bless my baby's heart.*

Mama put a finger to her chin, like she was giving the idea serious consideration. "I don't think that's gonna work, but you know what will?"

"Huh?"

"A hug." She held out her arms. "That's bound to make me feel a whole lot better."

Gracie Lynn didn't even hesitate. She tumbled into Mama's arms and held tight while a lump the size of Georgia lodged in my throat. I pressed a hand to my heart. *Thank You, Jesus.* One hurdle down and about a dozen to go.

"Mama?" I waited until she lifted her eyes to mine. "We need to talk."

Her mouth pinched again as she loosened her hold on Gracie Lynn. "How long are you planning to stay?" Her shoulders went stiff as if she was preparing for a blow.

"That's one of the things we need to talk about."

Mama shifted to peer out the window. "Is it just you and the child?" Fair question.

"Yes, ma'am." I wasn't of a mind to discuss Jason in front of Gracie Lynn, and I gave Mama a look that told her so.

Mama rubbed a gentle hand down Gracie Lynn's back. "You might wanna get the two of you settled in your old bedroom. Could be Gracie Lynn would like to take a little rest or watch some T.V."

Gracie Lynn's eyes lit up. "I can play with my puppy."

I swallowed a groan as Mama said, "Puppy?" A frown marred her face, and her eyes shot my way. "You're not meaning a real one, are you?"

Gracie Lynn bobbed her head up and down. "Yep. You can help us name her. She's so cute!"

Mama sighed. "Well, let's get you situated first, then we'll get a good look at your puppy and see what we can come up with." Gracie Lynn was with Mama five minutes and had her heart softened more than I'd accomplished in nearly thirty years.

Sophomore year of high school, my English teacher assigned Charles Dickens *Great Expectations*. I was never a fan of classic literature, and finishing it was purely an act of determination. There was no way some geezer-author was going to bring down my grade. The one thing about that book that stayed with me was the theme. Miss Haversham was the archetype of disappointment and revenge. She was like a ghost who stopped living the day her fiancé left her at the altar, never even taking off her wedding gown.

When I stepped into my old bedroom, I was reminded of that book and how empty it left me feeling. Mama hadn't changed a thing. Everything was the same, right down to my class schedule at University of Tennessee, still wedged in the mirror above my dresser.

Had she kept it as a shrine, or had she just not cared enough to come in once I was gone?

"Was this your room, Mama?" Gracie Lynn tugged her hand out of mine and sat in my desk chair. She set it to swiveling back and forth like the pendulum of a clock.

"Yes, baby girl. And now it's ours." The double bed would be snug, but it was a whole lot better than a twin. As long as the puppy didn't share it with us. "Let's go get your stuff out of the car and see if we can't find something to use as a crate for your puppy."

Twenty minutes later, I had Gracie Lynn settled in the room, my cell phone in her hands to keep her occupied. I wasn't a fan of babysitting-by-screen, but I'd make an exception if it would give Mama and me time enough to hash out the particulars of my so-called visit.

I found her right where I left her and was again struck by reminders of Miss Haversham. An implausible fictional character inspired by someone just like Mama, no doubt. I couldn't help but feel some guilty that my leaving might've caused her undue pain.

"I met your neighbor outside," I said, shifting the small, wood chair from the corner to Mama's bedside.

Mama harrumphed. "A busy body is what he is."

"Maybe so, but he was kind enough to stock your freezer." I dropped into the chair and crossed my arms. Taking off like I did, and never even giving Mama the courtesy of a phone call, I didn't have any right to question her. But it wasn't going to stop me. "What would you have done without him?"

Mama clucked her tongue. "There's plenty of grocery stores delivering food these days. But since he was offering, why go to the extra expense?" How ironic Mama had spent my entire life warning me of the evils of men, and here she was depending on the kindness of one, a virtual stranger, to care for her.

"Mama—"

She held up her hand like a traffic cop and glared at me. "First things first, Sarah Beth." There was no arguing with her when she jutted out her jaw like so. "You wanna tell me what's going on here? Haven't heard one word from you in years. Didn't know if you were dead, and I certainly didn't know you had yourself a baby. And now you show up out of the blue like nothing's happened"— she narrowed her eyes— "with that precious little girl." She waved a hand toward the hallway as if I wouldn't know who she was talking about otherwise. "Where's that husband of yours? Did he up and leave you like I said he would?"

Even though I had it coming, it was still a bitter pill to swallow. "No, Mama. He's dead." That ought to give her pause. I waited a beat to ensure full impact. "Was killed in a car accident." No reason to add fuel to the fire by admitting he was drunk and nearly took out an innocent family in the process. At least not yet. No doubt, the time for truth speaking would come sooner or later. I voted for later.

Mama's gaze slid from mine, her jaw working like she was fighting against whatever words were flittering through her mind. I would've been a fool to expect condolences. Jason was the enemy as far as Mama was concerned. Good riddance to bad rubbish. It would've hurt some if I wasn't of a mind to agree with her on some level.

"So, now you've come crawling home like the prodigal." It wasn't bitterness lacing her tone; it was resignation. Should I point out that the prodigal was welcomed with open arms and unconditional love? Then again, he'd been repentant. Might could take a lesson from his playbook.

"I know I've failed you, Mama." Failed myself, too, if I was going to be brutally honest. "But I can't be sorry I left. If I hadn't, I wouldn't have Gracie Lynn, and she's the best thing I've ever done." If only Mama could feel the same about me.

Mama's face softened. "She's beautiful, Sarah Beth. The spittin' image of you at that age." It was a comfort to know Mama wasn't going to take out her disappointment in me on her granddaughter. "So, you plannin' on stayin'?" Was that hope I heard in her voice?

"Depends on you, I suppose" I drew in a deep breath and spit out the question that laid like a rock in my gut. "Are we welcome?"

Fingering the blanket laid across her lap, she nodded once. "Reckon we can work something out." It was clear Mama need me as much as I needed her, but the both of us clung to a pride we had no right to.

We sat in silence for a moment while I worked out the best way to approach the elephant in the room. "How long have you been laid up?"

She shrugged. "A couple months or so. Was outside doing chores when I took a fall."

"You saw a doctor, right?"

She snorted. "A fat lot of good that did me. Like I can afford physical therapy, even if I could get myself there."

"So, you didn't break anything?" That would be a blessing for sure.

Mama waved her hand like she was dismissing the question. "Don't you be concerned about me, chil'. You got enough problems of your own." Wasn't that the truth?

"I'm here now, and unless you plan on sending me packing, I'm not going anywhere." Her silence spoke volumes. Didn't she say, "What took you so long?" when I walked in earlier? A plea for help if I ever heard one.

"How long's it been since you had paying guests, Mama?"

Eyes downcast, she grunted. "It's been slow. No one wants to stay in an old motel when there's so many better choices in Chattanooga."

I hesitated to push, but it was best to get everything out into the open. "Then how're you paying the bills?"

"I get by." Was there a reason her eyes didn't quite meet mine? "Right now, I need to use the bathroom, then I'll see what we got for supper." She scooted to swing her feet off the bed and motioned toward the walker. "You wanna get that for me?" The subject was as good as closed for the moment. At least she didn't tell me to mind my own business.

"Sure, Mama. But since I'm here, why don't you let me take care of supper?"

As she stood, a low groan escaped her lips. "Suit yourself."

I watched with bated breath as Mama moved to the attached bathroom. She looked thin, which was unexpected since she'd been living off high-sodium frozen meals and didn't appear to be at all active.

Once Mama closed herself into the bathroom, I looked in on Gracie Lynn. She was asleep on the bed with the puppy snuggled to her side. It had been a long month, topped off with four days of travel, and it was catching up with the both of us. What I wouldn't give to lay down next to my daughter and take a quick nap.

But there was no rest for the wicked.

Chapter 3

Aaron

A moment of reverence always comes over me in the pitch dark and quiet of the predawn morning as I leave for work. For that brief moment, the world is at a standstill, and I can almost take hold of the Lord's presence. But it's thin as a wisp of smoke and just as fleeting.

I made the short drive from the house to the DeButts rail yard in Chattanooga under a blanket of stars. Prayed myself up for the work ahead. *Please, Lord, keep the train on her tracks and the freight free from complications.* The rote prayer was more superstition than faith. God would do as He saw fit, but it didn't hurt to put in my request.

I parked the truck, grabbed my gear, and climbed out. A gust of wind nearly whipped the coat from my grasp and chilled me to the bone. That old saying March comes in like a lion and goes out like a lamb doesn't hold true for Tennessee. Might be a teaser of warm weather for a day or two, but here it was the last day of the month and close to freezing when you factored in the wind chill.

As I made my way to the rail office, I glanced toward the north where Lookout Mountain was shrouded in darkness. The crunch of gravel underfoot was barely audible over the chug of train engines as some pulled into the yard, and others pulled out. Never a dull moment. More than a hundred locomotives a day ran through this yard to get the freight where it needed to go.

Being a train engineer was in my blood. Started with my great-granddaddy and was passed down from generation to generation. As the oldest son of a railroad man, my career was chosen the moment Mama heard the words, "It's a boy." Couldn't complain, though. Wouldn't want it any other way.

I stepped out of the cold and into the relative warmth of the office—more like a warehouse—where people were gathered in groups of two and three. Spotted Billy Jones off to the side, waving his arm to get my attention. I returned his wave and made my way to his side. The train was my responsibility, but its contents were on Billy. By the furrow in his forehead, I guessed we had us a "special dangerous" load. Chemicals of some sort. The thought of it had my gut clenching. *Okay, Lord, I'm depending on You to keep us safe.*

Wasn't an hour later, the dispatcher announced the all-clear to head out. Billy laced the air hoses, inspected the wheels and brake shoes, and checked on the cargo. He was my eyes and ears.

"We all set?" I asked as a matter of course when he slipped into the box. "Freight cars secured?" It turned out my instincts were right—we were carrying chlorine and ammonia. One leak could create havoc and put the communities on our route in danger. Last thing we wanted was to cause harm, and Norfolk Southern didn't need the bad press.

"She's ready to go." Billy dropped into the engineer's seat to my left and scratched at the scruffy hair he called a beard. "It's gonna be a long day." The way his eyes and shoulders drooped, I guessed it wasn't his first of the week.

We headed out of Chattanooga, keeping the speed below the required 35 miles per hour, as the sun began to peak. Once we were clear of town, I'd up the speed. "We'll be okay." I glanced over at him. "Haven't seen you in a while. Stayin' busy?"

He grunted. "Busier than a one-legged cat in a sandbox. Haven't been home more than a couple days in the last three weeks. Missed Kyle's birthday."

I felt for the guy. Being low man on the totem pole was hard enough without a family. "That's rough. But hey, you can take some comfort knowing he'll never remember."

Billy scowled. "A kid only turns two but one time. There'll come a day he's gonna realize I'm missing from all the pictures."

I could relate. "Maybe Missy can photoshop you in." I flashed him a grin to lighten the heaviness in the cab. "It's only a matter of time before you make it to the Pool."

He barked out a laugh, but there was no humor in it. "You hear they're fixin' to revisit the idea of one-man crews again? They get their way, and I'll be lucky to have a job at all."

Same story, different day. At least that what I told myself. No job was truly secure. "You know they're just making noise. It'll never happen. Not after the backlash they got the last time they tried it." The way Billy stressed about the job, he might be better off finding something more to his liking. Of course, for a guy with nothing more than a high school-diploma, the pay and benefits were pretty good.

"Easy for you to say. Maybe I should do like you and get myself trained up as an engineer. Be a smart career move, don't you think?" This was a repeat of every conversation we had when working together.

"Yep. If you're willing to put the time in." My standard response. He didn't see Missy and the kids enough as it was, adding another six months of training would make it that much harder. Then again, if he could beef up his resume, it would be that much easier to get assigned a regular time and train station.

Billy was one of the best Extra Board conductors I ever worked with, but his heart wasn't in it. Couldn't say I blamed him. I rarely saw my own dad before he got himself a set schedule. Working the railroad was like being on a rock tour—without the money, fame, or groupies. Or pictures, for that matter. Didn't hardly know what my dad looked like until I was near eight.

I kept my focus on the controls and track ahead. End of March, and the trees were just starting to show some new life. Another month, I wouldn't be able to see anything past the thick foliage along both sides of the track—at least not in this particular stretch. Right now, rolling hills, ancient barns, and a lot of farmlands passed by my vision.

It wasn't until we were coming up on Varnell that Billy and me could take a breath. Some people thought all we did was ride the train from one station to the next, but that wasn't near accurate. We had slow orders and signals to attend to at all times, and our eyes and ears had to be engaged. One slip up could cause an accident, and it'd follow us our entire career.

Billy chanced a glance my way. "So, what've you been up to since I last saw you?" His question immediately had me thinking about Sarah Beth showing up on the scene. Prettiest thing I'd seen in a coon's age. "Still working on that place you bought?"

"Fix 'er and flip 'er," I said. "That is if the rundown motel next door doesn't chase off potential buyers." It was a wonder Georgina Pickett was still hanging on. Maybe now that her daughter was visiting—

Billy snorted. "You'd think being single and all, you'd find a better way to spend your time. You can bet I would."

It took a beat for me to get my mind off Sarah Beth McAllister's blue eyes and catch up to the conversation. "Yeah? Like what?"

"I don't know. Go out and meet yourself some fine women. Play the field." He shook his head. "Wouldn't be hammering nails, that's for sure." Billy talked a good game, but I didn't buy it. He'd be lost without Missy. If I remembered correctly, they'd been together since high school.

Wasn't a woman I'd ever dated I could see myself with forever. Every time I got close enough to even think about getting serious, a wall went up, and I couldn't get out of the relationship fast enough. Perplexing as it was, I figured God would bring the right person at the right time—if He had it in His mind I'd marry at all. Maybe that wall was His way of keeping me single.

"I'm no player," I finally said. No point trying to explain to Billy what I didn't understand myself.

"Funny you should say that." He shifted in the cracked and sagging conductor's seat to face me. "Missy's got a sister that might could be the perfect—"

"Nope."

"But—"

"Uh-uh." I shot a glare across the few feet separating us. "That's not gonna happen." Every setup I'd been subjected to turned out to be worse than the last. And then there was that whole wall thing. Disappointing her sister was a sure-fire way to get on Missy's bad side.

Billy grunted. "You don't wanna hit the singles scene, you don't wanna be set up. How you figure to find yourself a wife? One of them online dating apps?"

I fiddled with the control panel in front of me. "Who says I'm looking?" It was time to nip this conversation in the bud, as Barney Fife might say. When had Billy turned into the redneck marriage broker?

I was holding out for God's best—or at least that's what I told myself.

Sara Beth

Never in my life had I thought of Mama as being old. All the time I was living at home, she was up with the roosters cleaning rooms, tending to the vegetable garden out back, and keeping up with whatever activities I had going on. Now, she couldn't even make it to the bathroom without her walker.

Mama was only fifty-seven, but she moved like someone thirty years older. Something had to be done, and if I had to take her to the doctor kicking and screaming, that's what I'd do.

"I already told you, I can't afford no doctor," she said when I brought it up again. Why was she so determined to stay stuck in her sorry circumstances?

With teeth gritted, I sat on the edge of her bed. Trading attitude with Mama would get me nowhere. Instead, I relaxed my jaw, took a deep breath, and covered her hand with mine. "That's where you're wrong, Mama. There's a place in Chattanooga that'll treat you, but we gotta fill out the proper form to prove you're eligible. Once we do that, you can meet with someone who can get you the help you need."

"Eligible?" Her mouth slid into a sneer. "You mean I gotta jump through a bunch of pointless hoops just so they can tell me I don't qualify." She pulled her hand from underneath mine and waved it in the air to encompass the room. "I got a business, Sarah Beth. No one's gonna believe I'm indigent." Some business. A bunch of empty rooms slowly deteriorating.

Mama had always teetered on the edge of stubborn, but now she was like to drown in it. "Owning this place and having an income are two different things. You don't get a regular paycheck. If I can just get a copy of your tax returns—"

"No, ma'am." Her eyes shot enough heat to start a fire. "You don't need to be going through my private records." I swear, Mama could try the patience of a Baptist preacher.

I stood and glared down at her. "So, what's your plan? Waste away in this bed like someone who doesn't have the sense God gave a rock?" Tears burned at the back of my eyes. "Don't you wanna watch your grandbaby grow up, Mama? See her graduate high school someday, maybe get married?"

Mama turned away, but not before I saw her chin tremble. If anything was going to make her want to fight for her life, it was Gracie Lynn. "There's a storage box tucked under that old desk of your granddaddy's in the office. Tax returns are there."

Between tending to the puppy—or rather, Jazzy, as she was finally named—Mama, and Gracie Lynn, it took me almost three hours to get the required forms filled out. It didn't help that I had to fight Mama every step of the way. *Why do they need a copy of my driver's license? And bank statements? Really? You'd think my tax returns would be enough.* Every question was met with suspicion.

I heated a can of tomato soup and opened a box of saltines for lunch, then convinced Mama to eat at the kitchen table with Gracie Lynn and me.

"After I get these dishes washed up, I'll head into town and drop the forms off at the clinic." I held my breath, waiting for an argument from Mama.

She swallowed a spoonful of soup. "Why don't you just fax them in? Can't see wasting the gas and time to drive to Chattanooga."

"It's five miles, Mama," I pointed out. "Besides, this extravagant lunch we're having is the cumulation of just about everything left in the pantry. No sense having your neighbor drop off frozen dinners when I can fix us something a sight better." And healthier. But that argument wouldn't get me far.

Mama dipped a cracker into her soup. "I'm not altogether sure how much money I got in my checking account." Maybe she wasn't aware, but since I had to make copies of her bank statements for the application, I knew there wasn't enough to pay this month's bills. How had she been getting by?

"Don't worry, Mama. I'll take care of the groceries. After all, Gracie Lynn and me are the ones eating most of the food." Mama didn't eat enough to keep a bird alive.

"Can we get ice cream?" Gracie Lynn chimed in.

"We'll see, baby." I wiped a drip of soup off her chin with a finger. "Finish up so we can get going." An urgency thrummed through my nerves worrying over whether Mama was going to put a halt to the tiniest bit of progress we'd made.

A cold storm from the north had kicked up, making the spring-like weather of two days ago seem like a dream. Still, I was grateful for the fresh air as I slipped behind the wheel of the car. I didn't recall the motel apartment being so stuffy, and if it wasn't so chilly, I'd have opened up the windows to air it out.

"You all buckled up?" Twisting around, I watched as Gracie Lynn clicked the seat belt into place. It'd been months since she let me help her. Maybe that stubborn streak came from Mama. Or me. It'd been so long since I'd put up a fight, I'd nearly forgotten I once had a rigid backbone of my own.

The drive to Chattanooga wasn't much more than ten minutes. After living in L.A. for years, this traffic was a breeze. I first stopped off at Volunteers in Medicine on Marlin Road. I was hoping to speak with someone about Mama's application—see if I couldn't finagle some encouraging information. But the best I could get was a receptionist promising someone would contact Mama directly to get her an appointment with a coordinator—if she qualified. She explained HIPAA wouldn't allow anyone to talk to me anyway. I supposed all these steps were necessary, but it seemed like a whole lot of wasted time and energy.

As Gracie Lynn and me stepped out of the clinic, a gust of wind slapped me in the face. Ice cream didn't sound the least bit appealing, but it could be thirty below, and Gracie Lynn would still want it.

"Let's go get your ice cream, and then we'll hit the market for some groceries, okay?"

Gracie Lynn hopped on her tippy toes. "Bubblegum?" The thought of it made my teeth ache.

"We'll see what they have, baby."

Clumpies Ice Cream had been around when I was little, although the owners had expanded over the years. Was it three locations now or four? I pulled into the lot as memories of Mama and me sharing the newest flavors washed over me. It was our special treat whenever I did something worthy of a celebration. Didn't take much back then—acing a spelling test, cleaning my room to her liking, or even being extra kind to a guest.

I could still picture the two of us in our special booth—back corner of the parlor. Mama always encouraged me to try something other than plain ol' chocolate. But afraid of being disappointed, I stuck to my usual. Then she offered me a bite of her mint chocolate chunk. A life-changing experience for an eight-year-old.

I blew out a breath and unbuckled my seatbelt as I heard Gracie Lynn do the same. She poked her head between the front seats. "If they don't got bubblegum, can I have chocolate?"

I planted a quick kiss on her cheek. "Absolutely." The girl was an easy pleaser, that was for sure. Maybe it was due to the fact she'd had to settle so much in her young life, she didn't have much in the way of expectations.

When we got to the door, she slipped her hand from mine. While I scanned the menu board, she ran up to the counter where a few other customers waited. It didn't appear she'd get her bubblegum, but there were a lot of flavors that would be a sight more exciting than chocolate. Of course, had Mama not pushed, I might still be stuck in that rut.

"Sarah Beth?"

I twirled around to see who was talking to me, and it took a moment to put a name to the face. Jenna Wright. The last time I saw her was right out of high school, and she'd changed. A lot. If it wasn't for her honey-smooth drawl and vibrant green eyes, I would've never recognized her.

"Jenna?" Could hardly keep the shock from my voice. She pulled me in for a hug, and the smell of her shampoo or perfume tickled my nose. Back in the day, Jenna wasn't much for cosmetics, but now she could be the poster child for Estee Lauder. Not that I'd know the difference between that and Maybelline.

Jenna stepped back and beamed at me. "Where have you been all these years? I heard from someone, though I can't for the life of me remember who, that you'd gotten yourself married. You just visiting or you back for good?" Same old Jenna, even if she was twenty pounds lighter and appeared to have walked from the pages of a glamour magazine.

Her questions were a whole lot simpler than my answers. "Long story, but for now I'm back."

"Mama?" Gracie Lynn tugged on the sleeve of my sweater. "Can I get my ice cream cone now?"

I smoothed my hand over Gracie Lynn's hair. "First, I'd like you to meet someone. This is Miss Jenna. We went to school together. Jenna, this is Gracie Lynn."

Jenna's eyes widened. "You have yourself a little girl?" She crouched down to eye level with Gracie Lynn, though how she managed it in three-inch heels was a wonder. "Well, hey there, Gracie Lynn. It's a pure pleasure to meet you." She fingered one of Gracie Lynn's curls. "You're the spittin' image of your mama."

"Hi." Gracie Lynn smiled. "Are you a movie star?"

Jenna's face lit up as she let out a soft laugh. "Aren't you the sweetest thing this side of the Mississippi?" She tapped Gracie Lynn's chest with a manicured nail. "I'm just a real estate agent, but you sure make me feel like a movie star." She popped up again and pressed a hand to her chest. "This must be a God thing, because I was just thinking about you the other day." With a quick glance at her watch, she grimaced. "I'm gonna be late for an appointment if I don't leave straight away, but is there a time we can meet? I'd sure like to run something by you."

We exchanged numbers then I watched as she strolled out of the ice cream parlor with a little wave. I had the strangest feeling she was right—our meeting was a God thing. I hadn't thought of Jenna in years. We'd become friends out of necessity. I was the awkward motel-living girl, and she was the chubby nerd. We were misfits, and we needed each other.

Here it was, ten years later, and I was once again the motel-living girl, but no one would ever mistake Jenna for a chubby nerd. So, what in the world could she want to talk to me about?

Chapter 4

Aaron

A cool wind tugged at the flannel shirt I'd slipped over my tee for warmth. I could gripe about the cold, but in no time, heat and humidity would take its place, and I'd whine about that, too. Never content. Wasn't that human nature?

Birds were twittering and flitting from branch to branch in the trees canopying the backyard as Dad, Linc, and me trenched around the cracked patio. If the day went as planned, I'd have it prepped and formed to pour a new one before suppertime. Figured it wouldn't increase the value of the place, but it'd be a whole lot more attractive to potential buyers.

"I don't know why you don't just build yourself a wood deck on top of this mess," Linc said. "Might be more expensive, but it'd look a sight better."

I shook my head. Hadn't he been listening when I shared my house-flip plan? "Why would I do that if I'm just gonna turn around and sell the place?"

Linc stopped chipping away at the scruffy lawn that bordered the patio and looked at me. "Sell it? Since when?" That answered my question. It was a wonder we had the same parents.

I barked out a laugh. "Since the day I bought it. Where've you been?" This is what happened when you had a genius for a little brother. He formed equations in his head like a savant, but he couldn't keep track of a conversation that didn't include numbers.

Dad leaned his shovel against a tree and reached for his water bottle. "Linc doesn't accept things that just don't compute." He took a swig then wiped his mouth on the back of his glove. "Don't you think it's time you settle down? Stay in one place and grow some roots? Your mama's wondering if you're ever gonna give us grandkids."

Not this again. I slammed the shovel point into the shallow trench hard enough to send a zing up my arm. "Cassie's already given you two, and the professor here"—I waved a hand to indicate Linc—"is fixing to give you another. Isn't that enough?"

Linc's grin about took up his whole face. You'd think he'd solved the world's energy crisis instead of just getting his new wife pregnant. Had to admit, there was a pang of envy deep inside of me.

"Yeah, well, you're the oldest," Dad grumbled. "Almost thirty-four and still not a prospect in sight."

It was time to lighten the mood. "Don't you worry, Dad. Abraham was almost a hundred before he had Isaac. I still have plenty of time." He scowled, but it got Linc snickering. At least that was something.

"Don't be so sure about that." Dad worked a rock from the trench with the shovel. "It goes by quick as a lick. Before you know it, you'll be my age, wondering where it went." Dad talked like he was some old guy, but he could still run circles around men half his age—me included. "Just don't get so focused on making money that you miss what's important."

I swallowed a groan. "It's *one* fixer-upper, not a career choice."

He arched a brow and planted that "I'm not buying what you're selling" look on me. "One? Didn't you say you plan on acquiring the property next door so you can build a spec home?"

I snorted. "Gotta convince Miss Pickett into selling it first, and at this point, that doesn't appear likely." Not with the way she chased off my realtor. I glanced toward the property in question but couldn't make out much through the trees. "Her daughter showed up a few days ago for a visit. Was hoping I could talk to her about what they're planning to do with the place." I hadn't gotten anywhere with the mama. The woman could hardly stand the sight of me, even after plying her with food. Most people liked me just fine, so I didn't know what her problem was.

Then again, I didn't even know if Sarah Beth and the little girl were still around. Most likely, Miss Pickett had already scared them away with her winning personality.

Sarah Beth

It was pretty clear right quick that I had bitten off a whole lot more than I could chew. Gracie Lynn was a handful at times, but she had nothing on Mama. I'd made the colossal mistake of giving her a bell to ring whenever she needed something. I thought it would be less irritating than her yelling at me from the bedroom. Boy was I wrong. I didn't know it was possible to hate an inanimate object. Of course, in Mama's hands, that old cowbell was anything but lifeless. The clanging from the back room made a ruckus clear to the kitchen.

"Nana's calling, Mama." Gracie Lynn didn't bother to look up from her plate of mac and cheese.

I swallowed a sigh and attacked the baked-on mess that clung to the casserole dish. "She can wait a bit." The bell should've been given with a promise from Mama to use it no more than twice in a half-hour period.

I glanced at Gracie Lynn as she slipped a piece of macaroni to Jazzy. "That's not dog food, baby girl. You don't wanna make her sick, do you?"

"No, ma'am." Gracie Lynn patted the puppy's head. "But she's hungry."

"Sarah Beth!" Mama's screech cut off my response. Talk about being impatient.

Drying my hands on the seat of my jeans, I crossed the kitchen with a growl as pinpricks of irritation climbed up my spine. "You finish up your lunch, baby. I'll see what Mama wants, and then we'll take Jazzy out for a potty break." Who was I kidding? I was the one who needed a break.

With every step toward Mama's closed door, the bell got louder, and my temper grew hotter. I was never one to raise my voice, but I was fixing to lay into Mama real good. You'd think after being bedridden and alone for a few weeks, she'd be more self-sufficient.

"What is it, Mama?" I said through gritted teeth as I pushed the door open. It only took a split second for my stomach to drop clear to my shoes. Mama was on the floor, her back against the bedframe, ringing that ol' bell for all it was worth. How in the world—

"For pity's sake, Sarah Beth. What took you so long? I been sitting here forever." If I hadn't been so concerned, I would've pointed out that it wasn't but ten minutes since the last time I was there, fluffing her pillows like she was the Duchess of York.

"What happened? Did you fall?"

Mama grimaced. "I was trying to get to the bathroom, and my foot caught on the blanket."

I dropped to my knees next to her. "Did you hurt your hip?" Not sure where it was safe to touch, my hands hovered over her like a healer at a tent revival.

"No, just my pride." She grabbed hold of my wrist. "Help me up before I wet myself."

"You sure it's okay to stand? What if you aggravated your injury?" One more reason to get Mama to a doctor. Without knowing how badly she'd been hurt all those weeks ago, I could do more harm than good.

"I'm fine, Sarah Beth. Don't go fussing over me." Seriously? She'd been asking me to do just that since I'd come home three days ago. Now that I had something to worry about, she changed her tune.

"Well then, let's get you up." Even though Mama didn't weigh much, it took all my strength to haul her from the floor to a standing position. We shuffled to the bathroom where she did her business, then shuffled back again.

"Mommy!" Gracie Lynn came barreling down the hall. "Jazzy got out."

"Got out?" I eased Mama down onto the bed. "How'd that happen?" It wasn't like the puppy could open the door on her own.

Gracie Lynn tugged at my arm. "Please, Mommy. You gotta get her."

Swallowing a sigh, I patted her back. "You stay with Nana." It was fixing to be one of those days.

A gust of wind nearly ripped the sweater from my hands as I stepped outside to scan the yard and motel lot for Jazzy. Nothing. As small as she was, I couldn't help but wonder if she might've been carried away like Toto in the *Wizard of Oz*. The thought of it made my stomach flip. Now, if I were a puppy, where would I go?

Deep voices came from somewhere in the vicinity of Aaron Cooper's property. If I could hear them, no doubt Jazzy did, too. I blew out a breath and headed toward the bank of woods that separated the two properties. I would've rather faced the man with a little feminine armor. Maybe pulled my hair back so it wasn't whipping about my face and swiped a little mascara on my eyelashes. Not that I cared what Aaron Cooper thought of me—or any man, for that matter—but a girl had her pride.

The house Aaron lived in was at least as old as the motel. I used to play in the forest of hackberry, maples, hickory, and ash separating the two properties when I was no bigger than Gracie Lynn. A person couldn't see through the thick foliage once spring hit, but now the leaves were sparse as stubble on a teenage boy's chin.

I gingerly made my way through what appeared to be a pathway—most likely from Aaron going back and forth with Mama's groceries—trying to avoid ankle-biting prickly bushes. If Jazzy had come this way, she was sure to have suffered a scratch or two. *Please, let me find her. Gracie Lynn doesn't need any more disappointments in her young life.*

I recognized Aaron's voice as I moved closer to the house. It looked the way I remembered it—one story, red brick exterior, brown shingle roof, and not much else for color. The only thing that made it stand out was being in the middle of a couple of tree-filled acres. Scraggly boxwoods and a bunch of weeds were the extent of the landscaping.

"Well, look who we got here." For a moment, I thought Aaron was talking to me. But I hadn't yet spotted him, so chances were, he hadn't spotted me, either. That meant...Jazzy?

Picking up my pace, I rounded the back end of the house. Aaron, hands covered in buff-colored gloves, held Jazzy up at eye level. The breath *whooshed* from my lungs as I slapped my chest. *Thank God.* It wasn't until then I noticed the two men with him—one young, the other going gray. Still, they resembled each other enough to be related, although Aaron was a head taller than both of them.

I cleared my throat and called out, "You found her." Three pairs of eyes glanced my way—four if you counted Jazzy's. She either saw me or recognized my voice, because it wasn't until that moment she started squirming like a fish out of water.

"Sarah Beth." Aaron shifted the puppy under one arm and grinned. Laugh lines crinkled around his eyes—were they gray or blue?—and a perfect row of white teeth stood out against his tanned skin. "We gotta stop meeting like this." His light brown hair kicked up a bit with the breeze as he moved toward me.

I reached for Jazzy and cut a glance at the other two men. "Sorry to disturb y'all. It seems my daughter's puppy is fixin' to be an escape artist." Although I knew good and well Gracie Lynn was the accomplice. I ignored the weeds stuck to Jazzy's fur, tucked her under one arm, and offered an apologetic smile. Being the center of attention had never been comfortable for me. And seeing as I was the only woman made it almost unbearable.

"Don't you give it another thought," the older man said. He stripped off a glove and strode toward me, hand out. "Paul Cooper. I'm Aaron's daddy." Did I know how to call it or what? He hitched a thumb toward the other man. "And this is his brother, Linc."

"Hey," Linc said with a nod. "You staying at the motel next door?"

"You could say that. I'm Sarah Beth, and my mama owns the place."

He laid aside the shovel he'd been leaning on and offered a hand, just like his daddy. "Good to meet'cha. Aaron mentioned you were visiting for a spell."

So focused on returning his handshake and thinking up a graceful exit, it took my brain a moment to catch up to what he said. What could they have been discussing that my name would even come into play? There was a long-forgotten part of me that was itching to find out.

"Actually, I'm here to stay for the foreseeable future." I watched Aaron to gauge his reaction. His eyes widened, but it took a beat too long for a smile to follow. That told me he was surprised, and not in a good way.

Red flags popped up like a frantic rip current warning.

Aaron

It took a full five seconds to come up with an appropriate response to Sarah Beth's announcement. Lucky for me, I was quick enough to plaster an innocuous smile onto my face.

"I'm sure your mama's pleased you're staying on." My charitable, Christian side should be pleased, too. Miss Pickett obviously needed the help. Wasn't that why I'd been taking food to her the past few weeks?

But then there was that other side of me—not so Christian. The one that had an ulterior motive. Hoping to ease my way into her good graces so she'd give me first dibs on purchasing her dump-of-a-motel. No doubt, Sarah Beth would see right through me, like a cheap piece of glass. Then again, she might be an ally. Maybe she'd want her mama to sell as badly as I did.

Dad's deep voice cut into my thoughts. "Where've you been living, if you don't mind me asking?"

Sarah Beth hugged the puppy to her chest to get the wiggles under control. "L.A." Short and sweet. She wasn't any chattier than her mama.

"What's your daughter's name?" Linc cut in.

Sarah Beth's smile transformed her face into something worthy of a magazine cover. It was easy to see what got her going every day. "Gracie Lynn." She rubbed her cheek on the puppy's head. A maternal move that only made her more attractive.

"My wife's gonna have our first baby in a few months. A girl." Was Linc even aware that whenever he brought up Ashley's pregnancy, he got a goofy grin?

"Congratulations." Sarah Beth took a step back like she was making her escape.

Dad tugged his glove back on. "How old's your girl?"

Sarah Beth glanced toward the motel and then back at Dad. I could practically see the tug-of-war in her mind. Southern hospitality versus familial duty. No doubt she didn't have time for idle chitchat with a demanding mama and young girl to take care of.

"She's four," Sarah Beth said with a sigh. "Goin' on thirty."

"What about your husband?" Dad prodded. "What's he do that he can take time away from work?"

"Dad." The reprimand would undoubtedly go in one ear and out the other, but I had to try. "Sarah Beth's gonna think you're working for the Feds." Humor often had a way of diffusing a situation. At least that was my hope.

Sarah Beth glanced at me with a shrug. "It's fine." Then she looked at Dad. "My husband died, so it's just Gracie Lynn and me."

Why did that bit of news lighten my mood? Another strike against me, I supposed. But oddly, Sarah Beth didn't come across as a grieving widow. Unhappy? Yes. Untrusting? Definitely. But I didn't see her wearing sackcloth and ashes. Still, she wore the man's ring. Wasn't that a sign of grief?

Dad frowned. "I'm sorry to hear that. Didn't mean to be insensitive." No truer words had ever been said. Even though Dad might seem nosy to those who didn't know him, he genuinely cared about people. If he had a clue I was harboring some questionable motives of my own, he'd lecture me from here to Sunday.

Sarah Beth offered Dad a soft smile. "You're fine, Mr. Cooper. I appreciate you caring enough to ask."

Dad rubbed his chin. "Then maybe you won't mind me asking just one more thing."

I rolled my eyes at Linc who grinned and shrugged as if saying, "What're you gonna do? It's who he is."

She straightened her shoulders as if bracing for a hit. "What's that?"

"You haven't mentioned your daddy. How long has your mama been running that place on her own?"

Sarah Beth readjusted her hold on the puppy. "Long as I've been around. He walked out on Mama before I was born." Though there was no more emotion than if she'd been reading off a grocery list, there was a tremble to her chin.

Dad shook his head and blew out a sigh. "I'm real sorry to hear that, young lady. Seems you've weathered a whole lot of loss in your young life."

"You can't hardly miss what you didn't ever have." Sarah Beth tilted her head toward her mama's place. "I gotta get back now, but it's been real nice meeting y'all."

I kept my eyes on Sarah Beth until she disappeared into the thicket of trees. How strange that the more Dad probed, the more questions came to mind regarding her. Questions that were none of my concern. As hard as it was to resist a mystery, this was one I'd best stay clear of.

Chapter 5

Sarah Beth

When I was little bitty, one of the first things Mama drilled into me was the difference between a want and a need. I didn't dare eye something frivolous at the store for fear she'd ask, "Is that something you can live without?" When I got older, her go-to line was, "Money don't grow on trees, chil'. You'd best learn that right quick."

It was downright aggravating, but it stuck. I could pinch a penny with the best of them. So why was my bank account melting away like a snow cone in August? I needed to find myself a job, but how could I juggle Mama, Gracie Lynn, and work? Mama could mind Gracie Lynn for me if she was in better shape. That didn't seem likely anytime soon if she couldn't even get herself from the motel apartment to the car without leaning on me.

We shuffled out the door while Gracie Lynn skipped ahead. She was always excited for an outing, even if all we were fixing to do was sit around in the waiting room while Mama worked with her physical therapist.

After I got Mama situated in the passenger seat, she glanced up at me. "I don't want you gettin' your hopes up, Sarah Beth." She'd been saying that all morning, and I was beginning to understand it wasn't *my* hopes she was concerned about.

Gracie Lynn slid into the car seat behind Mama. "Can we get an ice cream after Nana sees the doctor?"

Money don't grow on trees, chil'. But I wasn't going to do her the way Mama did me, even if money was tight. "Let's see how Nana feels afterward, okay?"

As I rounded the front of the car, my phone rang, and I glanced at the screen—Unknown Caller. *Ignore it.* But what if it was the doctor's office? Appointments got shuffled around all the time, and it'd be best to know before driving into Chattanooga.

"Hello?"

"Sarah Beth? It's me, Jenna."

"Oh, hey." Although I'd halfway been waiting for her call since we ran into each other, I hadn't thought to save her number in my phone.

"I've been meaning to touch base since last week, but the days sort of got away from me. You have time to meet up for coffee?"

I opened the car door and slipped behind the wheel. "When?"

"How 'bout now? I could meet you wherever you like."

Mama's sigh was big enough to fill a balloon. "We gotta get going, Sarah Beth, or we're gonna be late." A half hour ago, she was complaining that we had to go at all, and now she was worried about being late?

With a shake of my head, I glared at her. "I'm fixin' to take Mama to the doctor, so I can't right now. Why don't you come over later this afternoon?" I wrangled my seatbelt on before starting the engine. It sputtered like an indignant old woman before it caught. There was always a fifty-fifty chance it'd cough and die. One more thing to be worrying over when I already couldn't sleep at night. "You still there?"

"Yes, Sarah Beth. I'm here." Throat-clearing came over the line. "I'd rather meet you somewhere, if it's all the same to you."

It wasn't all the same. I'd have to make arrangements for Gracie Lynn and Mama, which would take a God-sized miracle to pull off.

"Bring Gracie Lynn along, if you'd like," Jenna said, as if she'd read my thoughts. "We could meet at Puckett's at say 1:00? I'll treat y'all to lunch."

A friendly face and a free meal. What more could I ask for? "Sounds good. See you then." I disconnected the call with my thumb and slid the phone onto the console between Mama and me.

"Who was that?" Suspicion laced Mama's question, and with it a flood of memories. When I was in high school, I couldn't leave the house without her giving me the third degree. It was like she was just waiting for me to disappoint her—until the day I actually did.

"A friend from school. I ran into her the other day when I was in town buying groceries." I was about to ask if she remembered Jenna Wright, but it would set off a load of questions I didn't have answers to quite yet.

When I'd agree to meet Jenna at Puckett's, I didn't take into account the parking situation. If it weren't for Gracie Lynn and my desire to be on time, I would've found myself a spot far enough from the downtown hub that it'd be free. Resigned to the $10 charge, I pulled into the lot across from the restaurant. Pure highway robbery.

Gracie Lynn hopped out of the car and scanned the lot. "Where's the robber, Mama?"

"What?" I took hold of her hand.

"You said there's a robber." She tilted her head to look at me and squinted against the sun's glare. "I don't see nobody."

A flood of warmth soothed my irritation, and I couldn't help but chuckle. Mumbling to myself could get me in hot water if I wasn't careful. "I was talking about the cost of parking, baby girl, not a real person. It's what you call a figure of speech."

"Does that mean you don't got enough money for ice cream?" No four-year-old should be concerned about their mama's financial situation.

"There's always enough money for ice cream." I leaned down, planted a kiss on her head, and breathed in the sweet scent of her baby shampoo. *Count your blessings.*

As we crossed the street, a verse from the Bible came to mind—don't worry about tomorrow. Each day has enough trouble of its own—or something like that. I didn't recollect what book it was in or where I'd heard it, but it was true. There were surely enough problems to focus on for today. I'd be paralyzed if I started fretting about what would come tomorrow.

It appeared half the population of Chattanooga was having lunch at Puckett's, and it took a minute to spot Jenna standing in the back corner, waving us over. Gracie Lynn's hand in mine, we weaved through tables filled with boisterous patrons. How anyone could hold a conversation was beyond me.

"I got us a nice, cozy table." Jenna reached over Gracie Lynn to give me a hug. "I'm so glad y'all could make it on such short notice." As if she was willing to take no for an answer.

I couldn't help but admire Jenna's cropped yellow jacket and designer jeans as we sat down. She didn't buy her clothes at Walmart, that was for darn sure. "Thanks for inviting us." I tucked my bag beneath my chair. "And for including Gracie Lynn."

Gracie Lynn could've used a booster seat, but she sat so tall and proud, I didn't have the heart to suggest it. I couldn't recall the last time she'd been in a restaurant that didn't require us to order from the counter before sitting on plastic benches. Maybe never.

Before Jenna could respond, a waitress showed up with menus. Her arms were tatted, and she had a row of five or six earrings on one ear. She must've had a higher pain threshold than me. "What can I get y'all to drink?"

"Sweet tea for me," Jenna said. "And can you put this on one ticket, please?"

"Sure thing."

"I'll have a sweet tea, too." I turned to Gracie Lynn. "You wanna Coke, baby girl?"

Gracie Lynn's eyes went wide. "Can I?" Soda was reserved for special occasions, and I figured this was one of those times.

"Yes, but you gotta make it last through lunch."

Once the waitress was gone, Jenna folded her arms on the table. "So, tell me how you've been. I wanna hear everything." Back when we were in school together, Jenna and me didn't have secret between us. It hit me right then how much I'd missed our friendship.

I glanced at Gracie Lynn who was unpacking the few crayons from the box the waitress left for her along with a coloring menu. It wasn't like she didn't know her daddy was gone, but the details weren't something she needed to learn. At least not until she was old enough to understand.

"Gracie Lynn and me are good." I tilted my head toward my daughter and raised my brows at Jenna. Hopefully, she'd get the message. "We're on our own, which is why we've come home. I didn't know Mama was in a bad way until I got here, so there are a few unexpected challenges."

Jenna's eyes went soft, and she nodded. "I can imagine. Her bein' laid up like she is can't be easy."

How'd she know about Mama's injury? I thought back to our conversation last week. Had I mentioned it then? "Yes, well she saw the doctor this morning, and they scheduled her for some x-rays and a CT scan. I'm hoping she'll recover with some physical therapy."

The waitress materialized with a tray of drinks. "Y'all decide what you're gonna have for lunch?"

While Jenna ordered, I quickly perused the menu, mindful of the cost. I didn't want to take advantage of Jenna's generosity.

"Gracie Lynn will have the PB&J with fruit, and I'll get a small strawberry spinach salad, please." What I wanted was a thick, juicy burger and sweet potato fries. Just the thought of it had my stomach growling.

Once we were alone again—or as alone as one can be in a roomful of people—Jenna leaned forward. "Business can't be goin' well what with your Mama out of commission."

I grimaced. "You're right about that. I need to find myself a job, but with Gracie Lynn and Mama needing to be looked after..." I shrugged.

"You're in a pickle, that's for sure." Jenna focused on unwrapping the napkin from her utensils, and my belly clenched. Was there more to this lunch invitation than rekindling an old friendship? No. I was just being paranoid. Married to a master manipulator for six years will do that to a person.

I moved Gracie Lynn's Coke away from the edge of the table. "We'll get it figured out."

"Oh, I'm sure it'll be fine." She ran a finger up the condensation on her glass of iced tea. "But have you considered selling the motel?" She cut me a quick glance like she was assessing my reaction.

Selling? It was Mama's legacy. Been in the family for decades.

"I mean, the business probably isn't worth anything at this point, but the land has value." The uneasiness from before grew sharp edges that poked old wounds.

"Is this why you asked me to lunch, Jenna?" My heart kicked up so fast, it put a quiver in my voice. "So you can make a real estate deal?" The thought of her betraying me in such a way caused a lump to form in my throat.

"Of course not." But a tell-tale flush stole up her neck, as she fidgeted with her napkin. "It's merely a suggestion, Sarah Beth." She was lying. It was as obvious as Pinocchio's long nose.

Shaking from head to foot, I grabbed my bag from beneath the chair and scooped Gracie Lynn into my arms. "You can keep your suggestions to yourself. I don't appreciate bein' used." Jenna's appearance hadn't been the only thing that changed over the years.

Blinded by tears, I stumbled through the restaurant to make my escape.

Aaron

Yesterday's haul down to Atlanta was wracked with all sorts of issues. A tree had gone down on the tracks between Plainville and Forestville, a knuckle had come loose and had to be replaced, and we had a key load that needed to be specially monitored. To top it off, the motel guests in the room next to mine last night had themselves a real knockdown-dragout at one this morning.

I was bleary-eyed and desperate for a strong cup of coffee as I made my way to the Atlanta railyard for the return trip home.

Mid-afternoon, I got a text message from my realtor. She wanted to see me as soon as I got back into town. It was nearing eight before I arrived in Chattanooga, and I was hungry and tired. A quick meal and a good night's sleep was all I had energy for. If Billy hadn't been yacking beside me all yesterday, filling my head with impending doom and gloom over the stability of my job, I would've put my realtor off until another time.

But a little good news would make it easier to sleep tonight.

I threw my bag on the back seat of my truck, climbed into the cab, and pulled out my phone. A text later, I was heading for the real estate office. It seemed late to be conducting business, but that's why they made the big bucks.

Simpson & Wright Realtors was located on a side street, making it some easier to find a place to park. Every year, the population of Chattanooga grew—or maybe it was more of a tourist draw. Can't say I ever paid attention to the census. Either way, traffic was a nightmare and parking a challenge.

The office lights were on, but the door was locked. I rapped my knuckle on the glass and peered inside to see if there was any activity. A few seconds later, Jenna Wright appeared, phone stuck to her ear. She tucked it between her chin and shoulder, unlocked the door, and waved me inside.

"Come on back," she whispered before leading the way. "Yes, Mr. Robbins, I understand your concern."

I kept a respectable distance as I followed her down the long hall. How she could walk on those stilts was a mystery. It had to be painful, not to mention bad for her back. What was it with women? Carrie was the same way. Before she hit puberty, my little sister was spending every bit of her babysitting earnings on makeup and clothes. Both of which inevitably created battles with Mama.

"Look, Mr. Robbins"—she reached her office and waved a hand toward the two client seats—"we can iron out those details once they accept our offer." Rounding her desk, she rolled her eyes at me before dropping into her white, leather chair. "Yes, I promise to let you know the minute I hear from their agent."

As I sat, I glanced around the small office. Two framed certificates were on the wall behind her—a testament to her legitimacy as a real estate agent. A couple of colorful prints in shades that matched the brightly painted walls. Orange? Or maybe it had some exotic name like coral reef. Sounded a lot better than plain, old orange.

"Thanks for coming in, Aaron."

I turned my attention to Jenna, unaware until this moment that she was off the phone. "Your text made it sound urgent." If the occasional all-caps weren't enough of a clue, the two exclamation points did the trick. Figured Miss Pickett finally agreed to talk turkey.

Jenna folded her hands on her desk and drew in a deep breath. "I can't help you with the acquisition of the motel property."

It took a moment for me to process what she said, and another to read her expression. Brows drawn together, eyes downcast...and were those tears hovering on her lashes?

"I don't understand." I couldn't help but glance at the door, hoping for an escape. I didn't do tears.

Sniffing, she reached inside her desk drawer and pulled out a tissue. She dabbed her eyes and nose, cleared her throat, and drew her shoulders back with a sigh. It didn't appear she was going to have a meltdown after all, and I could breathe again. "As you know Miss. Pickett made it pretty clear she wasn't interested in selling the place."

I rapped the desk with a knuckle. "And you thought in time, you might could talk her into it." Why were we rehashing old information?

"Well, I should've given it more time. But then Sarah Beth came home, and I figured the two of us being friends would give me some leverage."

"Wait. What?" This was news. "You never mentioned knowing Miss Pickett's daughter when we talked before."

"She's been gone so long, I didn't think it would make a difference." Jenna wadded up the tissue. "I assume y'all have met?"

I nodded. "Yeah. I was hoping she might be willing to talk her mama into selling the place."

Her mouth twisted into a grimace. "That's what I was thinking, too." She sighed. "I invited her to lunch today. But the moment I hinted at selling the motel, she got so upset that she walked out."

"Why? It's not like it's doing them any good the way things are."

She slumped back in her chair. "Her reaction might not have anything to do with the property and everything to do with thinking I was using her to make a sale. Which I suppose I was." Rubbing her forehead, she sighed. "She's been gone for years, but we were real close at one time. Who knows what's happened since? She's got herself a sweet little girl and no husband." She looked at me. "Do you know anything about her?"

I shook my head. "Said her dad left before she was born. Other than that, she's a pure mystery." *One I wouldn't mind unraveling.* The thought caught me off guard. Wasn't it just the other day I was thinking I needed to steer clear of her?

"Yeah, her mama didn't miss a chance to rub that in. Sarah Beth didn't dare bring a boy home for fear he'd get painted with the same brush as her daddy. I think Miss Pickett hates men."

That right there explained a few things. Maybe it wasn't me that rubbed her wrong, but the entire male population.

"He was a railroad man," Jenna said.

"Who?"

"Sarah Beth's daddy." Jenna sat up and leaned her elbows on the desk.

Wonder if Dad knew him. "Last name of Pickett?"

Jenna shook her head. "Pickett's her mama's family name. I don't know what his name was. She was always Sarah Beth Pickett."

"You mean Sarah Beth didn't even have her dad's last name to remember him by?"

"Nope."

I couldn't imagine not knowing my dad. He was a huge part of what made me who I was.

"Do me a favor, Aaron?"

"Sure."

"If you decide to talk to Sarah Beth about selling the motel, don't let on that you were my client. I don't want her thinking we were conspiring against her."

I nodded. "Sounds like Sarah Beth might have a few ghosts she's battling without us adding to them."

Chapter 6

Sarah Beth

Mama would say I got up on the wrong side of the bed, but it didn't much matter which side I climbed out of, I would've still been in a sour mood. Lying awake all night, seething, will do that to a person. I was hurt, pure and simple, and it didn't make a whole lot of sense. So, what if Jenna had an ulterior motive for inviting me to lunch? It wasn't like we were still in high school—BFFs or some such. Once we'd graduated, we hardly even saw each other.

But that didn't smooth the sharp edges of betrayal. I could count my friends on one hand, and I just lost one.

It wasn't only Jenna's shenanigans that made me feel ugly. It was Aaron's daddy. Well, not his daddy, exactly. It had more to do with what I told him the other day when he said something about it being rough that I never knew mine. *You can't hardly miss what you didn't ever have.* That was an outright lie, and it had been niggling at me from the moment I said it. My entire life, I wondered if things would've been different if I'd had a daddy. Would *I* have been different?

Then again, if my daddy was anything like Jason, I should be counting my blessings. I only prayed Gracie Lynn wouldn't end up needing therapy someday because of him. Not that he ever laid a hand on her, but as much as I tried to protect her, there was no hiding the bruises. And she heard enough to cause trauma. Mama might be a tad on the difficult side, but her bark was a whole lot worse than her bite. The same couldn't be said for my late husband.

Mama and Gracie Lynn were still sleeping when I took Jazzy out to potty. It was fixing to be a beautiful spring day with the sun peeking from behind the rolling hills. The air was still and fragrant with the sweet scent of forsythia growing wild alongside the edge of the property.

After Jazzy did her business, and we had ourselves a little potty party, I walked her around to the back of the motel. A gravel path led to where Mama used to keep picture-perfect garden beds for vegetables, strawberries, and blueberries. Now, the eight-foot field fencing—tall enough to keep the deer out—sagged something awful in places, and it appeared she hadn't sown anything more than a patch of weeds in quite a while. I couldn't even make out where one bed started and another ended.

The rusted latch hung loose from the tall, weathered-wood gate that creaked when I opened it. Mama had been so proud of this garden. She'd planted rosebushes, lavender, and rosemary along the fence line—barely recognizable now.

"Oh, Mama," I whispered, breaking off a dead branch from a rosemary bush. "Why?"

"Sarah Beth?"

I whirled around, nearly losing my balance as Jazzy's high-pitched barking disturbed a flock of birds from the limbs of an old hackberry tree and set off my nerves like nails to a chalkboard. Jenna was standing outside the fence not twenty yards away. She was almost as unrecognizable as Mama's garden dressed in an overlarge black sweatshirt, faded jeans, and Keds. Her big hair was pulled back tight accentuating her thin face and high cheekbones.

I scooped Jazzy into one arm and shushed her before turning my attention to Jenna. "You're out and about early. How'd you know I was back here?"

She hitched a thumb over her shoulder. "When I pulled into the motel, I saw you headin' this way."

Yesterday's confrontation played like a tug-of-war in my mind. I was angry at Jenna, but when I thought of walking out the way I did, my face went warm and a knot fisted in my belly. Not my finest moment. "I don't have time to talk with you right now. You should've called first." I stepped around her and headed back to the motel.

"I was afraid you wouldn't answer if I did."

Turning, I glared at her. "I'm not gonna talk Mama into selling this place just so you can walk away with a big commission."

With a shake of her head, Jenna put both hands up as if to stem my tirade. "That's not why I'm here, Sarah Beth. I feel bad that I brought it up yesterday, and I came to apologize. I know how it must've hurt, me asking you to lunch and then springing that on you." Her chin trembled as tears swam in her eyes. "It was shameful, and I'm mighty sorry."

This was the Jenna I remembered. Would it be foolish of me to trust her? God certainly didn't bless me with the gift of discernment. Rather than respond, I put Jazzy on the ground and let her wander as far as the leash would allow.

"Will you forgive me, Sarah Beth?" She worried the corner of her lip and pleaded with her eyes.

A lump rose in my throat, and I swallowed it down. Who was I to hold a grudge when I'd made a mess of mistakes myself? "Sure, Jenna."

The words were barely past my lips when she closed the distance and pulled me in for a hug. "Thank you."

I couldn't remember the last time anyone but Gracie Lynn had touched me in such a way, and I'd forgotten what a powerful comfort it could be. It took a few beats for my brain to connect to my arms and return the hug.

When we pulled apart, Jenna swiped tears from her eyes. "I don't have myself a slew of friends, and I was praying you'd give me another chance."

How could that be? Surely, she had realtor buddies and was friendly with some of the girls we'd known in school. They wouldn't be looking down their thin noses at her anymore.

Jenna turned her focus on Mama's garden, her mouth falling open. "Oh, my word. I remember this being your mama's pride and joy."

"Funny. I was thinking the exact same thing a few minutes ago." I tugged Jazzy back as she lurched toward Jenna like she was aiming to jump on her. "Just about the only good memories I had of living here was tending to the beds alongside Mama." There was something miraculous about watching food grow from a tiny seed. God's creation in the making, even if I didn't appreciate it like I should've at the time.

Jenna planted her hands on her hips and perused the back of the motel. "Have you thought about tryin' to revitalize this place? If your mama's not gonna sell, and you're needing a job...it's not like you don't have experience."

That was true. I'd only ever worked at the motel, if I didn't count the piddly, minimum-wage job I'd had in L.A. before Gracie Lynn was born. But then reality reared its ugly head. "Look at this place, Jenna. Why would anyone stay here with all the fancy hotels in Chattanooga?"

Jenna squinted her eyes like she was thinking real hard. "You find yourself a niche. Kind of like what they did in Chattanooga with the Choo Choo hotel. But something different—affordable. And then you figure out how to market it."

I snorted out a laugh. "Oh, this place is unique, all right. Right down to the dumpy furniture and peeling wallpaper." I shook my head. "I might've taken offense yesterday, but you were right. It's not worth anything except the land it sits on."

Jenna sighed. "I don't wanna get you upset again, but if that's how you feel, why don't you convince your mama to sell?" She held up her hand, palm out. "And forget I'm a realtor. I'm just asking as your friend." Jenna was going to be walking on eggshells around me for a while.

"There's no talking Mama into doing anything she doesn't want to. She'd let this place rot around her and die destitute before she'd let it go. She thinks it's her legacy." I nodded toward the motel. "Speaking of which, I need to check in on her and Gracie Lynn. You wanna come with?"

Jenna wrinkled her nose. "Your mama isn't my biggest fan. I'd rather not set her off."

It didn't take a genius to put two and two together. I groaned. "I take it you pitched the idea of selling to her before I came along."

She nodded. "If she hadn't been hobbling on one leg, she'd've thrown me out on my hiney."

The image Jenna's words brought to mind had me grinning. "Well, girl, if we're fixing to be friends again, you're gonna have to mend fences with her eventually. Might as well get it over with."

Aaron

Nothing ruder than someone pounding the heck out of my front door when I was in a dead sleep. It took a good bit for me to realize it wasn't part of the dream I was having. I got the sheet untangled from my legs and stumbled down the hall in nothing more than my boxers and t-shirt. If my visitor was shocked by my appearance, it would serve him right for showing up so early.

"Hold up," I muttered. Head throbbing, eyes gritty, I reached the entryway. Dad was on the other side of the window-topped door, scratching his brow and peering inside.

I yanked the door open and glared at him. "You know what time it is?" My words came out froggy, and I cleared my throat. I needed four more hours of sleep or a strong cup of coffee.

"Yeah. It's the time you asked me to come by and help get the back patio finished up." He narrowed his eyes. "You still in bed?"

I rubbed my face. "Not anymore."

"You did say eight o'clock, didn't you?" He headed for the kitchen. "Got any coffee?"

Yawning, I shuffled behind him. "Didn't get much sleep last night." Instead, I tossed and turned half the night while God did a number on my conscience. Couldn't help but feel some guilt over causing a rift between Jenna and Sarah Beth. There were days I wondered why the good Lord didn't throw His hands up in despair of me ever maturing in my faith.

While Dad sat at the kitchen table, I filled a kettle with water and put it on the gas stove. Collecting a paper filter, the ceramic pour-over coffee maker, and two mugs, I situated them on the counter.

"Why don't you just buy yourself one of them Keurig thingies? It's a lot faster. Or one of them fancy espresso machines like your sister's got that foams the milk and everything in less than a minute."

I stared at him through bleary eyes. "You can't rush good coffee, Dad. There's a process."

He snorted. "I can't tell the difference between instant and drip. Coffee's coffee, far as I'm concerned." He tapped his fingers on the table. "So, how come you didn't sleep well? Everything going okay at the railyard?"

The sun was pouring through the window above the sink. Since my work routine required me to be up before dawn, it was rare I slept past six. But it'd been close to that before I fell asleep.

"Got a few things on my mind is all." Like Sarah Beth McAllister. A few weeks ago, I didn't know her from a hole in the wall, and now thoughts of her were keeping me awake. Well, not *her* specifically. It wasn't like I was mooning over the woman. Well, maybe a little. There was something vulnerable about her that drew me in. A brokenness I wanted to somehow fix, as if I didn't have enough issues of my own.

"You're not fretting over talk about Norfolk Southern cutting back to one-man crews, are you?"

"Not—" The kettle whistle cut in, and I turned the burner off. "I'm not worried for myself." I scooped ground beans into the filter and started the pour-over process while the smell of coffee wafted up. "That's one reason I got certified for both positions. But I've been luckier than most."

Dad scoffed. "It's not luck, son. You worked hard to get where you are."

"Maybe." Okay, so there was no maybe about it. I did work hard. But so had a lot of guys. "You know Billy Jones."

Dad nodded. "From what I hear, he's fixin' to be a fine engineer."

"He's been covering for Cecil James the last couple of weeks, so I've been working alongside him."

"Cecil James? Didn't he have some kind of heart surgery?" It was amazing Dad kept abreast of everything that went on, even being retired.

"Triple bypass." I set his mug down on the kitchen table and sat across from him. "Billy's been filling my head with all the what-if scenarios. I take it with a grain of salt, but it's hard not to be some concerned over where the railroad's heading."

Dad blew on his coffee before taking a sip. "Worrying never did nobody a bit of good. You do what's right, keep your eyes on the Lord, and the rest will take care of itself."

It was the "keep your eyes on the Lord" that tripped me up at times. It wasn't like I was doing anything *wrong*, exactly. But even when I went out of my way to help someone out—like Miss Pickett—there was a less-than-noble motivation attached.

That got me thinking again about Sarah Beth. Why was it all roads seemed to lead straight back to her?

"I heard that Sarah Beth's dad worked for the railroad." I took a sip of coffee and could swear the caffeine jolt fired up my brain. "You might've known him. Only problem is, his last name's a mystery."

"Well, that's easy enough to rectify. Just ask Sarah Beth." His lips twitched into a grin. "Give you something to talk to the gal about."

"From what I hear, she doesn't know his name, either."

Dad frowned. "Guess that makes sense seeing as how he skipped out on her mama before she was born." He narrowed his eyes on me. "You sweet on this girl?"

I snorted. "Of course not. I hardly know her."

"Uh-huh." His grunt spoke volumes. "If that's true, what d'you care if her daddy worked for the railroad?"

"I'm just curious, is all. You've known everyone who's worked for Norfolk Southern, so I'd bet my last dime the two of you crossed paths. I can't imagine my life without you and Mama. It seems Sarah Beth might feel she's missing a huge part of her family puzzle."

Dad's mouth turned down as he shook his head. "Can't imagine that she doesn't. Even if the man didn't contribute one thing to her life, he's still a part of her." He focused on the mug between his hands. "I imagine there's some brokenness in you from what your mama and me did right after you were born. That kind of thing goes deep."

Couldn't decide whether I was shocked or annoyed Dad dredged up that ancient history. "You're wrong. I'm not the least bit broken."

His head snapped up, and he quirked a brow at me. "No? Then hows come you're pushing thirty-four and still haven't had one serious relationship?"

If the same question hadn't been running through my head recently, I might've been offended. All I could offer by way of a defense was my pat answer. "Haven't met the right woman yet, is all. When God brings her around, then—"

Dad's rude snort cut me off. "You don't think what we did to you had any effect?" Even with his head down, I could see the tightness of his lips. The idea of him holding back his emotions had mine on shaky ground.

"Dad." I waited until his eyes met mine. "You and Mama didn't *do* anything to me. Why are you bringing this up now?"

He shrugged. "I don't know. Suppose it's because your mama and me were talking just last night about how you seem a little disconnected at times. Figure what we did...or what happened back then plays a part in it."

Disconnected. That's what I'd felt lots of times, but I didn't figure I'd let on in any way to Dad and Mama. That wall I tended to put up—it was normal, wasn't it? "I'm sure Linc and Cassie have been a little standoffish sometimes, too. I mean, maybe not Cassie, seeing as how she's a girl, but Linc..."

Dad rubbed his brow. "It's not an accusation, son. Just an observation." He looked at me. "You gonna tell me you don't feel it?"

I was too tired for a conversation that went any deeper than a puddle. Wasn't in the mood to psychoanalyze my issues, either.

I pushed up from the table. "I'm gonna get changed then we can get to work on the patio." As I walked out of the kitchen, I could sense Dad's eyes boring a hole in the back of my head. Could be I wasn't cut out to be a husband and father, but I wasn't about to talk to him about it—not when he was carrying a boatload of guilt over something that couldn't be changed.

Chapter 7

Sarah Beth

Having a list of exercises from Mama's physical therapist was useful as a phone without a charger. Twice a day, I had to push, prod, and threaten to get her to work through the regimen. You'd think she liked being bedridden and helpless the way she carried on.

"That physical therapist is already torturing me three times a week, Sarah Beth. Isn't that enough?" The woman could try the patience of Job.

"You know it's not." I helped ease her onto the kitchen chair. "If you wanna get full mobility again, we need to do what your PT says." It was a wonder I could speak at all with my teeth clenched. They were going to be ground down to nothing before I hit thirty if Mama kept acting like a child.

"Mama?" Gracie Lynn stood at the kitchen entrance, the puppy squiggling in her arms. "Can me and Jazzy go outside and play?"

I tamped down the automatic "No." It was time I loosened those apron strings a tad. "Make sure you keep ahold of her leash, don't wander further than the parking lot, and stay off the playground." One of these days, I was going to get that equipment fixed.

"Okay." She scampered off before I could add any more rules.

I turned my focus to Mama. "We're gonna do ten extensions on each leg."

Mama harumphed. "You keep saying 'we' like you're havin' to do all this work alongside of me."

She had no idea.

After squatting down in front of her, I placed my hand behind her ankle and twisted so I could look her in the eye. "It's called *supervised* exercises. Believe me, there are about a hundred things I'd much rather be doing right now. So, why don't you stop your griping so we can get started? The sooner we do, the sooner we can be done." It was pathetic that I had to use the same stern tone with her that I did with Gracie Lynn when she was acting up. But it must've done the trick, because Mama clamped her mouth shut and focused on extending her leg.

If I'd had a daddy, he'd be the one helping Mama right now. She probably wouldn't have gotten hurt in the first place if she had someone taking care of the heavy lifting. And maybe I wouldn't have been desperate enough to believe the lies Jason told me. Then again, Daddy had run out on Mama and me, and all my wishing and dreaming wouldn't change that fact.

We finished up with the last set of exercises, and I helped Mama to the recliner in the front room. I'd say her not wanting to lay in bed all day was progress.

"Hey, Mama." I perched on the edge of the sofa facing her. "Can I ask you a question?"

She grabbed ahold of the remote and pointed it at the T.V. "Uh-huh."

"I was just—" The blare of the television cut me off. I glared at it before focusing on Mama again. "Can you turn that down?"

She sighed, but fiddled with the remote until the soap opera drama was tolerable. "What is it, Sarah Beth? I'm missing my program." Her being distracted might could give me an edge.

"I want to know something about my daddy. Like what kind of man he was."

Furrows appeared in Mama's brow, and she scowled at me. "What? Why're you asking about him after all these years? I done told you everything I know ages ago."

"Remind me." I almost groaned at the near pleading in my tone. Mama might not have both oars in the water at times, but she could sniff out desperation like a hound dog on a hunt. "The only thing you told me is that he took off before I was born. How'd you two meet? What was he like?"

She snatched up the remote again, and I figured that was that. Then she lowered it with a sigh. Eyes still glued to the television, she said, "It was at a church picnic. Your nana dragged me to it nearly kicking and screaming. She thought it was high time I met myself a nice feller and got married." With a quick glance at me, she twisted her mouth. "Your granddaddy had passed away a couple years before, and your nana figured we needed a man around seein' as how it was just us." She clucked her tongue. "I don't know why. We've been cursed with the men in our family dying young for the last four generations." Her gaze met mine. "Including your husband." While I was still trying to untangle my thoughts, she continued. "Who'd wanna step into that?" And just like that, she turned once again to the television and whatever fake drama was unfolding in that make-believe world.

When I was little, Mama refocusing her attention was all it took to hush me up. I wouldn't be so easily dismissed now. "What was he like?"

"Who? Your granddaddy?" I'd have thought she was being dense if not for the twitch of her eye. If Mama were a poker player, that would be her tell.

"My daddy. Where was he from? What'd he look like? What was his name?" It wasn't until that last question popped out of my mouth it hit me how pathetic it was that my own daddy was basically an anonymous sperm donor.

"You only need to fix your face in the mirror to see what he looked like." Her mouth softened, and it appeared she almost smiled. "You got his blue eyes and sharp features. Same hair color, too."

"I do?" How strange. But then, no one would guess Mama and me were related, so I had to resemble *someone*. Could it be that looking like my daddy is what had her scowling half the time she looked at me? Gracie Lynn didn't resemble Jason the least little bit, although that could change. But I couldn't imagine I'd love her less because she reminded me of him.

"Course, that's not to say he was feminine looking. 'Cause he wasn't." She fiddled with the remote. "And you're not the least bit masculine, neither. Gracie Lynn favors you a good bit, and she's a beautiful little girl."

It took a full ten seconds for me to wrap my head around the fact Mama just said I was beautiful. Of course, she did it indirectly, but the result was the same. It brought back a long, almost-forgotten, memory of her fingering the curls off my cheek when I wasn't much older than Gracie Lynn. "You're pretty as an angel," she'd murmured.

Now, tears burned at the back of my eyes, and I had to swallow the sudden lump that grew big as a rock in my throat. I'd learned long ago the old adage beauty's only skin deep, but it didn't change the truth of needing to feel pretty, nonetheless. And Mama hadn't ever been one to heap on the praise.

Of course, Jason had told me I was beautiful—right up to the day I married him. After that, it seemed like a switch had been turned off, and I couldn't do anything to please him. The thought of it had my stomach knotting up like a mess of worms. Why did life have to be so gosh darn complicated?

Before she could raise the television volume, I said, "Remind me of his name."

Her mouth went all tight again. "Why? You thinkin' of tryin' to find him?"

The idea hadn't even occurred to me. "No, I just—"

"He's dead." Her brown eyes met mine. "You hear me, Sarah Beth? No sense getting your hopes up, 'cause he's been dead and gone for years now. Gracie Lynn and me is the only kin you got left."

The harshness of Mama's words struck me dumb. Why'd she have to be so ugly? What had I done to cause her to feel the need to turn most every conversation into a sparring match?

I was about to ask that very question when I caught something in her eyes—aside from another twitch. Fear. A cold tingle shot up my spine ending in a shudder. Now, why would talking about my father make her afraid? If he was dead and gone, like she said...or was he? Hadn't her eye twitched earlier in the same way when she'd lied?

Aaron

Last three days I had off, the rain made it impossible to get anything done outside. Instead, I'd chipped away at the kitchen tile counters to prep them for granite slabs. Once those went in, I'd repaint the cabinets—got me a clean, crisp white. Who knew there were so many shades? Over a hundred at least. Took days to narrow it down, even though it shouldn't have mattered. Was planning to sell the house soon as it was done.

This morning, the sun was shining, and it was fixing to be a perfect day to do some planting. Had a couple of crepe myrtles I'd picked up on my last day off along with some five-gallon boxwoods to go along the west side of the house. If I wasn't careful, I'd find myself getting attached to the old place.

I'd just gotten the first hole dug when I heard a yipping behind me. The puppy that belonged to Sarah Beth's daughter—Gracie Lynn—was giving me what for like I'd invaded her territory instead of the other way around. Feisty little thing, considering she couldn't weigh more than three pounds. Quick, too. If it weren't for the leash trailing behind her, I would've never caught her.

Had my whole day planned out, and it didn't include playing dog catcher. Course, the idea of seeing Sarah Beth again took some of the edge off my irritation. Might be Dad was right—I was a little sweet on the lady. But neither was he wrong about the walls I'd erected. If she dared to get close enough, no doubt she'd see them firsthand.

I tucked the puppy under one arm and tromped through the wooded section between the two properties. In the last couple of weeks, the sparse leaves had filled in, and I had to swat some branches out of the way to pass by. The parking lot was empty, except for Sarah Beth's beater-of-a-car. The thing didn't look like it could get to Chattanooga and back, let alone across the country.

Some noises came from the far side of the L-shaped building, and I headed that way. Rounding the corner, I stopped short. Gracie Lynn was sitting on one end of a rotting teeter-totter like she was waiting for someone to join her. The rest of the playground equipment was in the same sad shape. A swing set with a cattywampus glider on one side and a swing with the seat hanging off one chain on the other. There was a wide metal slide attached to an elevated platform covered by a high-pitched roof in serious need of repair. The whole kit and caboodle was a lawsuit waiting to happen.

The puppy barked, and Gracie Lynn turned. Her eyes went wide as saucers. "Jazzy! You was supposed to stay here." She struggled to get off the teeter-totter and ran to me, hands out. "I tied her to the slide, but she musta got loose."

"It's a good thing she didn't go too far." I shifted the puppy from my arms to hers. Had Jazzy gone out to the street instead of my property, there was no telling what could've happened to her. "Are you out here all alone?" I glanced around. Was no one watching out for the little girl?

"Mama's fixin' Nana's legs." Gracie Lynn kissed Jazzy's head then put her on the ground. I snatched up the leash before she could take off again. The two of them needed a fenced yard and some serious training.

"Aaron. What're you doing here?"

I twisted around to see Sarah Beth crossing the weedy patch of lawn. Just the sight of her had my heart rate kicking up a notch or two like it had a life of its own. But as she drew closer, I could see wariness shadowing her eyes. Was she afraid of me or afraid of life in general? Someone did a number on her, and I'd bet my last dime it was her husband.

And there it was again—that almost instinctive desire to fix make everything better. But I'd need to move real slow if I didn't want to spook her. "Rescue mission." I flicked a hand toward Jazzy who was sniffing at something near the teeter-totter. "The puppy got loose and came over for a visit."

Sara Beth's eyes went as wide as Gracie Lynn's had earlier. Why were they so surprised Jazzy would do what dog's do—escape every chance she got?

"I'm sorry if she bothered you." She hitched a thumb over her shoulder. "I was putting Mama through her PT exercises. Told Gracie Lynn to stay off the playground." She shot the girl a glare as she said this. "Still, I shouldn't have left her alone so long." She grimaced and hugged her chest like she was literally holding herself together. "You must think I'm an awful mother." She was talking to me, but I got the strangest sensation she wasn't all there. Had a faraway look about her, and a frown marring her pretty face.

"No, of course not." I shifted so I was between her and Gracie Lynn. "You okay?" I whispered. Wanted to offer some comfort—a pat on the back, maybe a hug—but chances were, she'd mistrust my motivations. And why not? Even if I hadn't a clue there was some abuse in her past, we were virtually strangers.

She blinked, and her eyes seemed to refocus. "Oh, yes. Sorry. My mind was on something else. Thank you for bringing Jazzy back." She waved for Gracie Lynn to come to her. "You go on inside and wash up for lunch, baby girl. And make sure you put Jazzy in her crate. We don't need her messin' on Nana's carpet again."

Gracie Lynn blew out a big sigh and marched up to us. "Can Mr. Aaron stay for lunch?"

Before I could answer one way or the other, Sarah Beth jumped in. "I doubt Mr. Aaron's a big fan of PB&J." She smoothed Gracie Lynn's hair off her sweaty forehead. "Besides, I'm sure he has lots to do, and we've already wasted enough of his time."

Scrunching her nose, Gracie Lynn looked up at me. "Don't you like peanut butter?"

I was tempted to accept her lunch offer, just to see how Sarah Beth would react. But that'd be the *opposite* of treading softly. "I like it just fine, Gracie Lynn. But your mama's right; I've got some trees and bushes to plant. Maybe another day."

"Okay." Gracie Lynn tugged on Jazzy's leash. "Come on, baby girl, we gotta get ready for lunch." She sounded just like her mama.

A soft laugh escaped Sarah Beth's lips as we watched the two of them cross the scruffy lawn. "That child is the best thing I've ever done," she said so quietly, I had me a feeling she was talking to herself.

"How're things going with your mama?" Anyone privy to our conversation might think I was concerned for Miss Pickett. I sort of was, but it was more like I was searching for something to keep Sarah Beth talking a bit longer.

Sarah Beth waited until Gracie Lynn was out of sight before she turned to me. There was a sparkle to her eyes, and a smile had replaced the earlier frown. The magic of a child's love.

"I think you know Mama well enough to guess." She glanced at the ground and scuffed a thick weed with the toe of her sandal. "It was nice meeting your brother and daddy the other day." Was she now the one prolonging our conversation?

"Sorry my dad was so nosy. He can't seem to help himself."

Her lips twitched, and she shrugged. "You're fortunate to have such a sweet family."

A laugh escaped. "You think my dad's sweet, you'll go into sugar shock if you meet my mama and sister." As she turned to walk away, I scrambled for something more to say. "Sarah Beth." Her name popped out before anything more profound came to mind.

She stopped and glanced over her shoulder. "Yeah?"

"Is it true you've never even met your dad?" *Smooth move—question the lady's honesty.* "I mean, I know you said he left before you were born, but I thought maybe..." I blew out a breath. "Forget it." I waved a hand for her to go. "I'm butting in where I don't rightly belong. It's just..."

A few steps, and she was standing close enough I could see a shadow of sadness pass over her eyes. "It's funny you'd ask me this now." With a shake of her head, she folded her arms.

"Why's that?"

Her gaze narrowed on me. "I just had me a conversation with Mama over that very thing. And, yes, it's true. I never met my daddy." She barked out a humorless laugh that ended on a sob. Blinking rapidly, she focused her eyes on something over my shoulder. "I don't even know his name. Can you believe that? It never occurred to me that I ought to search for him. I mean, why would I? He didn't want any part of me, so what do I care?"

I held my breath, afraid that if I said anything, she'd clam up. On the other hand, if I let the silence linger too long, she'd walk away. "But you do care." I offered the words in the same low voice I'd use to assure a wild animal that I meant no harm.

"Yes, I suppose so." Tenting her eyes from the sun, she stared at me. "When I asked Mama who he was, she told me to just forget about him. He's dead and gone."

I couldn't imagine Miss Pickett softened the blow any. "That must've been hard to hear."

She jutted her chin out. "I don't think it's true."

"No?"

"Believe it or not, Mama's good at a lot of things; lying's not one of them."

She worried the corner of her lip for a moment then shook her head. "I don't know why I'm unloading all this on you. I'm sorry. You do a good deed for Mama, and you get yourself all mixed up in our mess." Waving her hands in the air, she turned and walked away.

There was something about Sarah Beth McAllister that made me want to slay her dragons. I've never been the knight-in-shining-armor-type. Then again, I'd never remodeled a house, either. Until I tried.

Chapter 8

Sarah Beth

It was a pure miracle that Mama got through all her PT exercises without once making a fuss. It was important to reward good behavior. All the parenting magazines said so. I just never thought it'd be Mama I'd need to train. It was the only reason I was willing to leave Gracie Lynn in her care while I met Jenna for lunch. That, and the fact she and Gracie Lynn both begged me to.

"Don't forget to take Jazzy out to pee every hour, Mama." I tucked my bag to my side and pecked a kiss on Gracie Lynn's head.

"Gracious, Sarah Beth, you've only told me about ten times. You talk like I'm dumb as a stump." I was prepared for a scowl to accompany her comment, but it didn't make an appearance. Two Mama miracles in one day? Had to be a world record.

"I'm sorry, Mama. It's just I forget myself sometimes, and you're not used to looking after a puppy." Or a four-year-old, for that matter. But before I could launch into any more instructions, a honking horn snatched the words clear from my brain.

"That's your friend, I reckon." Mama refusing to use Jenna's name was her passive-aggressive way of letting me know she didn't approve. Jenna could apologize from here to Sunday, and it wouldn't do her any good. "She must be in a hurry to be leaning on the horn that-a-way."

I literally had to bite my tongue to keep the peace. Fact was, I'd been doing a lot of that since Mama said my daddy was dead. She was hiding something, but it wouldn't do me a bit of good to bully it out of her.

"Try and stay off your feet best you can, Mama. Gracie Lynn loves to be a help, don't you, baby girl?"

Gracie Lynn beamed. "Yes, ma'am. I can do all kinds of things."

One last kiss on Gracie Lynn's head, and I slipped out the door with a sigh. *Please, God, don't let this be a mistake.*

Jenna insisted on picking me up, which was a blessing for sure. My gas tank was hovering on empty, and I'd need to take Mama to Chattanooga for PT the next day. I was pinching pennies tighter than King Miser, and it was flat wearing me out.

The skies opened up just as I slipped into the passenger side of Jenna's Infiniti. It still had that new car smell, even though she'd had it almost a year. Maybe it was the leather interior or could be that's just how luxury cars smelled. I practically melted into the butter-soft seat.

"Hey there, girl. You look nice." Jenna patted my knee before putting the car into gear. "You doin' okay?"

"Just fine." Aside from Mama's lie and the flood of envy I battled when I was around Jenna. What would it be like to ride in style every day? Wear designer clothes and cosmetics that came from somewhere other than Walmart? My shirt might've been a Drew Barrymore original, but it sure didn't come from Nordstrom's, where I was sure Jenna shopped.

Jenna's chipper voice broke into my pity party. "I've got the perfect place for lunch. And just so you know, it's on me."

I was becoming her personal charity project. "Oh, Jenna, that's sweet, but—"

"No arguments." She waved a hand in the air like a queen dismissing her subjects. "I closed on a million-dollar listing this morning, and I wanna celebrate with my friend."

Maybe I should consider getting myself a realtor's license. I didn't need a fancy car or even fancy clothes. It'd just be nice to feed Gracie Lynn something better than mac and cheese or peanut butter.

"After lunch, I thought we'd pop over to Dirty Jane's. Have you ever been?"

That got my attention. "Dirty Jane's?" Was that one of those places Mama used to warn me about?

Jenna cut a quick glance my way and giggled. "I guess not, by the look on your face. It's an antique store, Sarah Beth, so you can take yourself a breath and relax."

Pressing a hand to my heart, I huffed out a laugh. "You had me worried there for a sec." Antiquing wasn't my thing, but the least I could do was keep Jenna company while she shopped. She was treating me to lunch, after all.

I was expecting to stop somewhere near downtown Chattanooga, but Jenna jumped on 127 North and skirted around town instead. "Where're we going?"

"Old Man Rivers," she said. "It's a tavern that sits at the base of Signal Mountain. Only been opened for a couple of years."

By the time she'd pulled into the small parking lot, the rain let up, and the clouds parted enough that a ray of sunlight beamed down like some angelic sign. I breathed in the clean, humid air as I climbed out of the car. Determined to enjoy this rare outing, I pushed aside all my doubts and fears for the future. There were worse things than living with Mama indefinitely, although for the life of me, I couldn't think what that might be. Except maybe prison.

The restaurant was situated in a small historic building on Cross Street. Jenna was right about it being out of the way, but gauging by the number of people seated inside, it wasn't a deterrent. And when I read through the menu, I could see why. If the food tasted half as good as it sounded, this would be my new favorite place.

The chatty hostess seated us, took our drink orders, and handed us each a menu. There was a tug-of-war going on inside me. Spending grown-up time with my friend on one end and worrying over leaving Gracie Lynn in Mama's care on the other. Was this how a working parent felt?

"What're you gonna order?" Jenna slapped her menu closed and looked at me. "I thought I'd get the Seared Catfish Po Boy this time, but everything is delish."

After salivating over the options, I finally decided on the Fall Harvest Turkey Sandwich. "You think that's a good choice?" I asked Jenna as she took a sip from her water glass.

"Absolutely. Can't go wrong with brie, green apples, and fig jam."

The waitress showed up with our drinks, jotted down our orders, and collected our menus. "Y'all let me know if you decide on something other than sweet tea to drink, you hear?"

After she was gone, I folded my elbows on the table. "So, antiques, huh? Searching for anything special?"

Jenna arched a brow and grinned. "We're going to Dirty Jane's for you, Sarah Beth, not me."

A bark of laughter escaped before I could stop it. "I don't even like antiques."

She cocked her head. "Think vintage." Still couldn't connect the dots.

"You lost me." I ran a finger down the condensation on my water glass. "Antiques, vintage, post-modern. I know nothing about interior decorating."

She leaned toward me like she was fixing to tell me a secret. "But I do. And once we walk through Dirty Jane's, you'll have yourself an education."

I frowned. "What's the point? It's not like I have me a place of my own. Even if I did, I wouldn't be filling it with fancy furniture."

"But that's where you're wrong." With a shake of her head, she sighed. "You already have that fancy furniture. It's gathering a whole lot of dust in those musty, old motel rooms at your mama's place."

Either Jenna hit her head and was suffering from a concussion, or I was. Nothing she said was making sense. Before I could tell her so, the waitress appeared with our orders.

"Enjoy," she said as she placed a heap of yummy-smelling food in front of us.

As I picked a piece of turkey from the roll and popped it into my mouth, the fog lifted from my slow-as-molasses-brain, and Jenna's meaning became clear. "Ohhh." It was a wonder I could function some days. "You're talking about repurposing the junk at Mama's to fix up the rooms."

She laughed and rolled her eyes. "Give the girl a prize. Took you long enough."

I threw her a scowl that'd make Mama proud. "Even if by some miracle, I could use every bit of that old junk and talk Mama into it, it still wouldn't be enough. What's that old saying about putting lipstick on a pig? There's carpeting that needs to be replaced, and yellowed wallpaper that would have to be removed."

"Elbow grease is all," Jenna said.

I couldn't help the snort that broke loose. "Elbow grease and a whole lot of money. Which I don't have." *But that's not exactly true.* The thought had me clamping my mouth tight.

"I have some savings set aside I can loan you."

It took a sec for me to process Jenna's words. "Oh, no." I put my hands up to stop her from saying any more. "You have any idea how hard it is for me to let you buy me a sandwich? There's no way I'm gonna take your money. If the whole thing were to fall apart, which I expect would be the case, then I'd be floating in debt." It was crazy talk. Still, Jenna's generous offer was enough to get me choked up some.

But what if I *could* do it without borrowing money? If Jenna was willing to take a risk on me, shouldn't I be willing to take a risk on myself? Except I had Gracie Lynn to think about. If I lost it all, she'd be the one to pay the price.

Aaron

I liked me a good rain as much as anyone, but it botched the plans for my day off. The house was coming along right nice, and if all went well, I'd be ready to put it on the market come fall. September was the perfect month, according to Jenna. Summer heat would be about gone, and the autumn colors would be making an appearance. Buyers would be able to picture the holidays in their new home—fat pumpkins on the porch, lights hung along the eaves, maybe a Christmas tree in the front window.

Rather than work outside like I'd planned, I gathered a list of supplies needed at Lowes. Fixing to leave, I opened the front door to find Linc standing there, fist raised like he was about to knock. Looked like a drowned rat with his hair plastered to his head and his t-shirt and jeans soaked through.

"Hey, bro. Was I expectin' you?" The way my days blended together, it wouldn't be the first time I'd blanked on an appointment.

He shook his head hard like a dog coming out of the river, showering me with water droplets. "Nope. I was just driving around and sort of ended up here."

I backed up so he could enter. "Let me get you a towel. Don't worry about dripping on the tile floor, it needs a good cleaning anyway." I left Linc in the entryway and collected dry clothes from my bedroom.

"You headin' somewhere?" he called out.

I snatched a towel from the linen closet at the end of the hallway and jogged back to him. "Lowes." I tossed the towel at him and set the t-shirt and jeans on the sofa. "Was hoping to finish planting today, but with the weather..." I waved a hand at the rumble of thunder to make my point. "How come you're not at work? Everything okay with Ashley?"

He emerged from under the towel and handed it to me. "Everything's fine. Just had me a day off and was restless. Guess I'm a little edgy, is all." He yanked the wet shirt off and held that out, too.

Shaking my head, I chuckled. "What am I, your personal maid?" But I took it from him and waited for the sopping jeans to follow. "I'll stick these in the dryer. Wanna come to Lowes with me?" Maybe he'd tell me what had him feeling anxious, although I could guess. With a baby on the way, everything in his life was about to shift. Linc never did take to change.

"Sure. But can we make a detour? I got something I wanna check out." He scraped his fingers through his damp hair.

"No problem. Let me throw these in the dryer, and we'll get going."

Rather than tell me where we were headed, Linc directed me to 153 North toward the Chattanooga Quarry. "Needing a load of gravel?" I teased. He and Ashley lived in a second-floor condominium, so I knew for a fact that wasn't our destination.

"Course not." Subtle humor was lost on him. He peered through the rain spattered windshield, arms folded across his chest.

"You cold? I can turn on the heat," I offered.

"Nah. I'm okay." I could feel his eyes on me. "So, anything new with you?" His too casual tone had me stiffening my spine. Whatever he was fishing for, I had a sinking feeling Dad provided the bait.

"Not since we talked like two days ago." I cut him a quick glance. "You?"

He shrugged. "Ashley had a sonogram yesterday. Everything's going as expected."

"You know the baby's gender?" It blew my mind the docs could make a picture clear enough to see if it was a boy or girl. I was beginning to wonder if I'd have a kid of my own someday.

"Told you before, we want it to be a surprise." He squirmed a bit and tugged on the shoulder harness of the seat belt. When he cleared his throat for the second time, it was proof I was right. He hadn't just stopped by; there was an agenda. "You see much of the gal that moved in with her mama next door?" And there it was. He was definitely fishing with Dad's bait.

"That you askin' or Dad?"

"He thinks you're sweet on her." Guess that was answer enough.

"Hardly know the lady." I shut off the windshield wipers. "And it wouldn't make a difference one way or the other if I was. She's got her hands full without the likes of me buttin' in."

He rolled the window down just enough to let in a whiff of fresh air. "You've had yourself a lot of girlfriends."

His definition of "a lot" and mine were two different things. He and Ashley had been together since high school. His first and only. "A few, maybe. Not so many." Of course, every one of them was now married and had a kid or two.

I blew out a breath. "You payin' attention to where we're going? I don't want you getting so caught up in snooping for Dad, you get us lost."

"When you come to Jersey Pike, take a right and follow it for a couple miles. And just so you know, it's Mama that sent me snooping, not Dad."

I grunted. "They're tag-teaming me, and you got stuck in the middle."

"Didn't get stuck. I volunteered." He tossed me a glare. "Anything wrong with your family worryin' over you some? They just want you to be happy. Not spend all your time working."

A snort escaped. "I do things other than work."

He cut me a glance and grunted. "Yeah? Like what?"

Every response I came up with slipped away quick as a greased pig. Remodeling the house never was a hobby, although it was what I spent most every waking hour doing when I wasn't at the railroad.

"Okay, so I work a lot. There are worse things."

"They think it's on account of what happened when you were a baby." Linc pointed to remind me Jersey Pike was coming up.

Not this again. "Why can't they leave it alone? I told Dad last time we talked he was making something outta nothing." I slowed the truck to make the turn. "Maybe he isn't so far off base, though." I sped back up and threw a look at Linc. "But I need you to keep that between us. You hear? They don't need to carry that guilt with them."

"I agree." He leaned forward, drawing my attention. "But they're not gonna let it go until you do."

Couldn't hold back the scowl. "What're you talkin' about? I'm not the one beating this old horse to death. They are."

Linc blew out a breath loud enough to fill the cab. "You don't get it, Aaron. As long as it's keepin' you down, they're gonna feel bad. Parents are only as happy as their kids."

It took a minute for that to sink in. "When'd you get so wise?"

He chuckled. "Well, I *am* almost a father, you know." He pointed ahead. "Turn right on Enterprise. We're almost there."

There ended up being Creative Cedar Designs, a playground equipment company. I slowed the truck and glanced at Linc. "Aren't you getting a little ahead of yourself, bro?"

He shrugged. "It's never too soon to plan."

Huffing out a laugh, I turned off the engine. "First off, your baby isn't even born yet. And secondly, y'all live in a condo. Where're you gonna put a playground? In your front room?"

"Just so happens we put an offer in on a place in Collegedale yesterday. Three bed, two bath on a quarter acre not far from where Mama and Dad's place is. Plenty of room for a playground out back." A grin split his face and pulled one from me.

I nudged his shoulder. "Way to bury the lead. When will you hear if it's accepted?"

Unlatching his seat belt, he shrugged. "Today, I hope. Guess that's what has me a little nervous. A mortgage, a kid...grown-up stuff, you know?"

"Well, professor, if anyone can handle the stress of being an adult, it's you." I climbed out of the truck and met him by the hood. "But don't you think it's still a bit early to buy a playground? The kid won't be able to use it for at least a couple years."

He led the way toward the outdoor display where several sets of expensive-looking equipment were set up. "I'm not buying—just planning. Every kid deserves to have a dream playground, don't you think?"

I couldn't help but picture Gracie Lynn sitting alone on the broken-down teeter-totter. A knight-in-shining-armor would also be a hero to the damsel's little girl, wouldn't he? But even if Sarah Beth never gave me the time of day, Linc was right—every kid deserved to be given a dream.

I backhanded Linc's arm. "How 'bout I make you a deal?"

His eyes were glued on the towering displays. "What's that?"

"You work with me on a little renovation project, and I'll help you build one of these beauties from scratch."

And just maybe, it could be the first step in putting a chink in that wall I'd built around my heart.

Chapter 9

Sarah Beth

Crazy as Jenna's idea to remodel the motel was, it sparked something in me that had been missing in my life for some time. Hope. After Gracie Lynn and Mama went down last night, I riffled through a couple of drawers at the front desk until I came across a ring of keys for the rooms.

The rainy day had given way to a clear sky, and there was enough of a moon to light my way to the farthest room from the office. The exterior paint, once a cheery yellow, was now faded and peeling in places like an invasive skin disease. What shrubs planted in the beds along the front that had survived the years were now scraggly and anemic. Compared to all the fancy hotels that had gone up in the area over the last several years, the Pickett's Mill Motel would've been unimpressive even in its heyday. Now, it was downright pathetic.

It took a few attempts before I could get the key into the lock—moon or no moon. I should've brought my phone for light. I threw the door open and felt along the wall for a switch while my nose twitched at the musty smell that wafted up. Mold? With humidity and no ventilation, that would be my guess.

A weak glow came from a lamp on the nightstand between the two queen-sized beds, chasing shadows to the perimeter of the room. I stretched the limits of my imagination to picture how new carpeting (or maybe a more practical flooring), refinished walls, fresh bedding, and a gallon of Mr. Clean might could make a difference.

After spending an hour at Dirty Janes with Jenna educating me, I could now see the furniture in this room wasn't cheap—just old. Dark and nicked up. But apparently, old was now good. The wood was solid oak or maybe mahogany. I didn't know one from the other. Either way, it didn't have lick of veneer marring its surfaces, which meant I could sand refinish them if I chose.

It took me an hour to go through all twelve rooms, and by the time I finally got into bed, my head was spinning with possibilities. I could research popular colors of the 50s and 60s. What if each room had a different theme? Jenna had been right—it would take a lot of elbow grease. But what couldn't be cleaned up or refurbished would need to be replaced, and that would take money.

And then there was the whole niche idea. People weren't going to stay at the motel unless we had something unique to offer. *What could that be, Lord?* I fell asleep with that whispered prayer on my lips. Even though I woke without an answer, I figured there were times we had to step out in faith and let Him do the heavy lifting.

If only I could convince Mama to dream along with me.

The morning started off early, since Mama had a nine-o'clock PT appointment at the hospital. I hooked Jazzy to her leash and sent her out with Gracie Lynn.

"Be sure she goes potty before you give her a treat," I said as she tugged the puppy out the door. "And give her enough time to poop, too."

I put a pot on the stove for oatmeal and took out a couple pieces of bread to toast. "Mama?" I yelled down the hall. "You about ready for breakfast?"

"Don't fix me nothing, Sarah Beth," came the muffled response from behind her closed door. "Ain't hungry." Nothing new there; Mama was never hungry. It's why she was wasting away like some homeless waif.

A quick peek out the window as Gracie Lynn handed Jazzy a treat, I then headed for Mama's room. With a quick tap, I poked my head in. She was making the bed, fully dressed. It struck me how different things were from when I first arrived a month before. I'd been so busy worrying over what had to get done, I didn't take time to be thankful for the little miracles along the way. *Thank You, Jesus. Forgive me for taking You for granted.*

"Hey, Mama? I'm gonna make some oatmeal. If you're not hungry enough for that, maybe a piece of toast? I even got a jar of that peach jam you like."

Mama smoothed the wrinkles from the bedspread. "Don't fuss at me, chil'. I told you I don't want no breakfast."

I sighed. "How 'bout a banana?"

Expecting her to lash out, I was taken back when she chuckled. "Sarah Beth Pickett, you could nag a body to death before they'd die of starvation."

I wasn't about to sour her good mood by pointing out my last name was McAllister—not Pickett. Although if it weren't for Gracie Lynn, I'd dump my married name in a flat second. "Whatever it takes to get you to eat something, Mama." I kept a close watch as she pivoted and sat on the bed.

"You're healing up pretty good." I pushed the door wide and entered. "You got much pain?"

She wrinkled her nose. "Fair to middlin'. Hoping we can stop going to the hospital for PT after this week. You do just fine takin' care of me. No sense in that sadistic therapist torturing me no more." Another of Mama's compliments couched in a complaint.

Since Mama was feeling kindly toward me, now might be the best time to ease into the idea about the motel. "I was thinking I'll have to find myself a job pretty soon. And, of course, some kind of daycare or preschool for Gracie Lynn."

She harrumphed. "Daycare?" Her gaze flickered with disappointment—as expected. "I can watch Gracie Lynn just fine if you're set on goin' to work. She's no more trouble than that puppy of hers." Gracie Lynn brought out Mama's maternal side. She might tolerate me, but she adored her granddaughter. "It's not like I got nothing else to do."

God handed me the perfect segue. "I've been here over a month, and we haven't talked about your plans for the motel."

Mama picked at a loose cuticle and shrugged. "There's lots of things we haven't discussed, Sarah Beth." Her eyes slid my way. "Like what happened to Gracie Lynn's daddy. You wanna tell me about that? Other than him being dead."

I should've known better than to try and manipulate the conversation with Mama. Best to get it all out in the open and deal with the consequences. I pushed off the bed and crossed to the one chair in the room where I might could breathe easier. Plus, I could keep an eye down the hall for Gracie Lynn. "He got himself killed driving drunk." I dared to look at her. "You were right about him all along."

Mama shook her head, eyes focused on the floor. "He ever lay a hand on you?"

My throat went dry, and I couldn't collect enough spit to swallow. "Let's just say he was a mean drunk and leave it at that," I finally croaked out. She didn't need to know the details. The shame of it heated my face and had damped my palms as flashes of his abuse flitted through my mind. The bruises I had to hide with long sleeves, even in the dead of summer. The black eye and split cheek that kept me housebound for nearly two weeks.

"He ever lay a hand on Gracie Lynn?" Her tone was sharp, but it broke at the end.

"No, ma'am. I wouldn't let him." But there were a whole lot of ways to hurt a child other than physical.

She ran a hand over her face. "Lordy, Sarah Beth. Why'd you stay? Didn't you know you could've come home any time?" A sheen of tears glistened in her eyes, and just seeing them got mine to watering, too. I wasn't a crybaby—unless someone else started up first.

"I was fixin' to leave him when I found out I was pregnant. He made all sorts of promises, and things seemed good for a time." I glanced down the hallway just as Gracie Lynn passed through to the kitchen.

"Mama?" she yelled.

I cleared my throat. "I'm in with Nana," I called out. "Why don't you get yourself a banana and I'll be right out?"

"Okay."

Taking a deep breath, I locked eyes with Mama. "I don't want Gracie Lynn to hear us talking about her daddy."

Mama waved her hands in the air. "Don't you worry about me saying a word. I wouldn't do anything to hurt the child."

I nodded and got up to leave.

"Sarah Beth?"

One hand on the doorknob, I turned back to her. "Yes?"

"About the motel. I don't rightly know what I'm gonna do. Maybe you got yourself some thoughts. If so, I'd like to hear them."

Mama's words shocked me speechless for a moment. Not only kind, but a mind-reader to boot. "Nothing concrete. Just a pipe dream, really."

She nodded once. "Everyone's gotta have a dream now and again. Why don't you get Gracie Lynn's breakfast together, then me and you can sit a spell and talk about it?"

A rush of joy laced with a whole lot of gratitude came over me so powerful, I couldn't help but cross the room and wrap her in a hug. "Thanks, Mama. I'll be back right quick."

By the slack jaw and size of her eyes, I'd say she was as shocked by the gesture as I was. There were too many secrets between us for me to trust in my emotions, but it was a start for sure.

Aaron

Family was complicated. Had me a few buddies who moved as far away from theirs as possible the second they graduated high school. Others stayed so entangled, they couldn't think for themselves.

I fell somewhere in the middle. Recent evidence to the contrary, Mama and Dad kept to the hands-off approach to parenting us adult kids. They offered help where they could—paid for Carrie to go to college when she didn't get the full ride Linc did—but they didn't beat us over the head with their opinions.

So, I would've been a hypocrite if I took offense when three different people working the train yard told me Dad had signed on with the Federal Train Association as an inspector. It was news to me. When Rick Baxter said something,

I figured he had his wires crossed. He was all the time spreading rumors that turned out to be false. The next guy who said something about it got me thinking Rick was right. But it was the train master, Keith Danvers, who sealed it.

If I was the last to know, I had no one to blame but myself. Since Dad's last visit, I kept my distance. It came natural as breathing, which I was coming to find out wasn't necessarily good. Only one way to change that.

As soon as Mama and Dad became empty nesters, they sold the two-story brick house we grew up in and bought themselves a single level on half an acre. While Dad said he didn't want to fuss with the stairs in his old age, Mama was happy to have a lot less to clean. It made sense, although it never felt like I was coming home when I stopped by. Instead, I was a visitor.

I pulled into the long driveway and parked by the garage under the shadow of an ancient black walnut tree. It was fixing to be suppertime. Although I didn't call ahead, Mama always cooked up enough food to feed a small gathering at a Baptist church.

Dad was waiting on me at the garage door before I was out of my truck. He had the hearing of a hound dog—or maybe it was the instincts. Either way, he always seemed to know when I showed up.

"Hey, Dad." I slammed the truck door and headed toward him.

"Well, ain't this a surprise." He pushed the door open wide enough for me to pass by. "You stayin' for supper?"

"Long as I'm not taking food from your mouth."

He snorted. "You know better 'an that."

I followed him past the laundry room and half bath and into the kitchen where Mama was taking a dish from the oven. Potato casserole would be my guess. Mama didn't think a meal was complete without it. Wasn't sure how she cooked like she did and kept the weight off.

"Aaron's here," Dad announced, snatching a slice of red pepper from a cutting board. There was a platter of fried chicken and a dish of collard greens besides. "Wants to know if you fixed enough to feed another mouth."

Mama slid the hot dish onto the stovetop and turned to me, a bright smile lighting her face. Or maybe it was the steam wafting from the casserole that had her face glowing. "Always." She came around the counter to hug me. Stepping out of my arms, she patted my cheek. "About time you stopped by. Was starting to wonder if you forgot where we lived." Her tone was light, but I sensed an underlying reprimand.

"Busy, is all." I inhaled and patted my belly. "Smells like heaven in here." I wasn't above using flattery to get back on Mama's good side. "Can I get the drinks?"

"You know where everything is," Mama said. "Paul, you wanna set out the good dishes? We're gonna put on the dog tonight."

When our plates were full, we sat at the kitchen table and held hands while Dad said the blessing. "Thank You, Lord, for this daily bread. May it nourish our bodies and fuel our minds that we may serve You in whatever we do. We pray this in Jesus' name. Amen."

"Amen," I mumbled along with Mama. Couldn't remember the last time I bothered to say a blessing before digging into a meal. Maybe that was part of my problem—too focused on myself and not enough on the Lord.

I forked a bite of potato casserole. "Heard some surprising news today."

"Yeah?" said Dad. "What's that?"

Mama clucked her tongue. "You know good and well what Aaron's referrin' to, Paul. Thought you were gonna tell him yourself."

He cocked his head my way and raised his brows. "Was just waiting for him to return a phone call or stop by. He's been scarcer than hen's teeth lately."

Didn't care for the stab of guilt that hit me with that remark. "Well, I'm here now."

He grunted. "Only because you heard tell I was going back to work. Didn't feel good getting it second-hand, did it?"

Couldn't deny that. "No, sir. Don't guess it did."

Mama reached over and slapped Dad's arm with the back of her hand. "You happy now that you got one up on the boy?"

Frowning, Dad looked down. Only Mama could shame him with a few pointed words. "Reckon that was small of me. Sorry, Aaron," he mumbled.

My lips twitched at Dad's sudden humbleness. "No apology necessary. It's no one's fault but my own." I cut my eyes to Mama. "Figure if you gotta sic Linc on me, you must be feeling desperate."

Mama squirmed. "I didn't *sic* him on you, exactly. Just was hopin' for a little news."

I set my fork on the plate and leaned on the table. "All you gotta do is ask." When her eyes didn't meet mine, I sighed. "Okay, I haven't been...approachable lately."

Dad barked out a laugh. "Lately? Try never. Unless it comes to work. Everything else is hands off with you."

I sighed. "You're right. It's just easier to stay focused on work and not take stock of other things." Personal things. "Y'all are the most important people in my life, and I've been pushing you away for a long time."

The two of them could've been bookends with their wide eyes and open mouths. I was so focused on their response, it took a beat for me to realize just how good it felt to come clean. How long had I been carrying around tension in my shoulders?

Mama cut a glance at Dad before speaking. "Then it wasn't all in our minds? We haven't been transferrin' our feelings onto you?"

"Transferring?" Strange word for her to use.

Dad cleared his throat. "Your mama's been seein' a shrink."

Mama huffed out a breath and glared at Dad. "I haven't, either. She's just a *counselor*, Paul." Her gaze slid over to me. "It's no big deal, really. She's a Christian woman who specializes in family stuff."

Great. My issues were such, Mama needed to talk to someone about them. Someone other than me or Dad.

Mama patted my hand. "You just wipe that stricken look off your face, Aaron. It's not just this stuff with you that's got me feeling a mite lost." She tilted her head toward Dad. "Your daddy's retirement hasn't exactly been a picnic for me, either. That's one reason he's decided to go back to work." She shot a look at Dad. "Isn't that right, Paul?"

"It seems I get underfoot," he said with a grimace.

"Bored is what he is," Mama corrected. "Turns out if he doesn't have a purpose of his own, he's focused on finding me one. But that's not what we were discussing. Let's get back to this problem of yours, Aaron. What can we do to help?"

I took me a deep breath. "For starters, you can stop feeling guilty over something that happened over thirty years ago." Emotions welled up in my chest, making my words harsher than intended. Or maybe it was frustration that we kept having this same conversation without anything changing.

Mama grunted. "Now you sound like my counselor."

Relief pulled a smile from me. "Sounds like a smart woman. Maybe I need to start seein' her," I joked.

"Maybe you do." But Mama's tone was dead serious. "She says it doesn't matter that you were too young to remember back then, it can still affect you just the same. Leaving you like we did—"

"Stop!" I raised up my hand. "You're right, Mama. I don't remember anything. Wouldn't even have a clue it happened if y'all didn't tell me about it. But you feeling bad over it isn't gonna fix things. In fact, it makes it harder for me." Appetite clear gone, I pushed my plate back. "I don't know what the answer is but talking to someone I don't know isn't it."

Dad cleared his throat. "Suppose until you have a reason to want things to change, you ain't likely to take that step." His eyes caught mine.

Breaking eye contact, I couldn't help but squirm as images of Sarah Beth came to mind. The way she moved, graceful like. How she tended to Gracie Lynn with a gentle touch. Her shy smile that got my heart to pounding. A vulnerability that made me want to protect her.

Hard to be a lady's knight while battling demons.

"A good start might be to pray on it some, don't you think?" Dad pressed.

First thing I learned in Sunday school was Jesus is always the answer. Just never figured quite figured out how.

Chapter 10

Sarah Beth

There was a quote Jason used to throw at me when I dared to voice the slightest complaint against him. "Change the way you look at things and the things you look at change." It was his arrogant attempt to twist my thinking around, so I'd believe his wretched behavior was all in my mind.

I detested that saying.

But as I stood alongside Jenna, staring at the old motel, the quote suddenly made sense. It hadn't helped my disastrous marriage, but I was beginning to trust that God had a plan. He could spin anything to work for me, couldn't He? Even a sad excuse for a man like Jason and a quote from someone I'd never even heard of.

Jenna glanced at me. "Your mama's really okay with the reno idea?"

I squinted at the building as if doing so would pretty up the picture some. "Shocking, isn't it?" At least it was for me.

"You have any ideas about the direction you wanna go?" She swiped at a bead of sweat above her lip. It'd rained for an entire week, and now that the sun was out, the humidity kicked up a good bit. Spring had sprung for sure.

"I think so." I waved her to follow me to the front office. "Let's go inside and I'll show you what I found."

"Is Gracie Lynn with your mama?" Jenna glanced around the lot as if searching for her.

"Dropped her off at preschool this morning. I'll pick her up before lunch." If I could wait that long. Didn't matter that Brianna, the teacher, came highly recommended; I'd never left Gracie Lynn with anyone before, so my nerves were a bit tender.

Of course, it didn't help that she'd cried like I was abandoning her for good. Made it nearly impossible to leave. But she'd been glued to my side from the day she was born. That couldn't be good for her social growth, could it? And it was only three days a week. Brianna assured me it was perfectly normal for Gracie Lynn to carry on like she did, and the sooner I left, the easier it'd be on my baby girl. Much easier on Brianna and her assistant, too, I supposed.

After the glare of the sun, the motel office seemed downright dark. I was hoping once Jenna and me got to work, some of my edginess would smooth out some. "You go into the kitchen, and I'll collect my notes from Mama's desk. Want some sweet tea?"

Jenna poked her head into the kitchen like she was unsure what she'd find.

"Mama's at physical therapy, so you can quit your worrying." I went the opposite direction to the office where Jazzy was snoozing away in her crate. Amazing how much dogs could sleep.

"Someone take her for you?" Jenna's voice floated down the hall to me.

I hugged Mama's laptop to my chest and joined her in the kitchen. "Nope. She carried herself. Just hope my car doesn't give her fits." Especially since I needed it to pick up Gracie Lynn.

"Wow." She took the computer from me and set it on the table. "Wondered why your car wasn't out front. You must be tickled to death things are going that good."

While pouring the tea, I went through a mental inventory of what all I was feeling. "Tickled might be an overstatement." I set our glasses on the table and sat next to her. "Cautiously optimistic, maybe."

Rather than jump into my plans for the motel as expected, Jenna folded her arms on the table and looked at me. "I get that. I mean, it hasn't been easy with your mama. It takes time to rebuild things."

That, and the fact she lied to me about my daddy. I almost said as much, but something held me back. Why I could blurt such a personal thing to Aaron, who I barely knew, and not to Jenna made about as much sense as a screen door in a submarine.

Jenna broke into my thoughts. "I've been seein' this man for a little while, and I'm kinda like you. Cautiously optimistic." She shrugged and flipped the laptop open, like she hadn't shared anything more personal than her grocery list.

"That's it?" I slapped my hand on the table. "You drop a bomb like that, and then nothing?" Could be the both of us were holding back.

"It's no big deal, Sarah Beth." If that was true, then why did she bring it up? Why couldn't she look me in the eye? Instead, she was focused on the laptop screen, and I'd bet she didn't see that, either.

"How long you been dating?"

She turned to me with a sigh. "Look, I didn't say anything because I was afraid it'd come across as insensitive."

"Insensitive?" I tangled with that idea for a moment. "You mean because my husband's dead?"

Her eyes went wide, and she stammered. "What? He...what? I thought you were divorced."

"If I was divorced, would I still be wearing this?" I held up my left hand to point out the wedding band.

She shrugged. "Didn't give it much thought, I suppose. You never said one way or the other."

"I'm sure I told you—" Slapping a hand to my forehead, I huffed out a laugh. "I didn't, did I?" It struck me right then that our conversations had stayed in the shallow end of things. She didn't ask anything about my past, and I didn't ask anything about hers. "We aren't acting much like friends. Instead, it's like we're cautious acquaintances."

Jenna twisted her mouth in a grimace. "Ain't we a pair? So busy worrying over whether we're gonna overstep, we don't share anything important." She flicked a strand of hair from her face. "Didn't used to be this way."

"It doesn't have to be, Jenna." It was about time I took a chance and jumped into the deep end. I took me a deep breath as if I truly was fixing to dive into a pool of water and fixed my eyes on my clasped hands. "If it makes you feel any better, it was only the other day I told Mama the truth about Jason. He got himself in an accident because he was drunk. That's how he died. A drunk. A mean, abusive drunk." My voice caught on the last word, and I blinked real hard to keep the tears back.

Her eyes filled as she covered her mouth as if to hold in whatever words were teetering there.

"It's hard for me to say out loud, because I'm ashamed." I couldn't look her in the face while confessing the truth. "Ashamed that I married him in the first place and ashamed that I stayed after he became abusive." But saying it somehow eased the weight a bit. Maybe because I didn't have to carry it alone anymore.

Jenna reached over and squeezed my hand. "I'm sorry, Sarah Beth. I wish I'd known. I was afraid if I asked too many questions, you'd think I was prying."

I offered a weak smile. "It's what friends do, right?"

"I suppose." She hesitated for a moment then reached out and tapped my wedding ring. "So, if I could be so bold," she ventured, "why're you still wearing this? I mean, if you're not grievin' over the loss and all."

I stared at the gold band. A worthless symbol. "It keeps the men at arm's length, not that they're crawling out of the woodwork." I fixed my eyes on her. "Although, I'd like to hear some about your guy."

A grin split her face. "I promise to share more about Chad later. Right now, I wanna see your ideas for the motel."

"Chad, huh?" I slid the laptop in front of me with a grin, suddenly feeling tons lighter. "Okay, but you gotta tell me what you really think about it. No sugar-coating."

"Pinky swear." She held out her pinky finger like we used to do when we were kids, and I hooked mine into it. We both giggled as if we were still eleven. Maybe it was relief over the earlier tension having dissipated like summer fog in a holler.

I blew out a sigh. "Okay, let's get this done before Mama comes home. There's only so much drama I can take at one time." I pulled up the website

I'd bookmarked the day before. "You said we needed a niche—something to set us apart."

"Absolutely. What'd you find?"

"Well, it's really on account of you I got this idea in the first place." Feeling a little unsure of her reaction had me stalling.

Lines formed between her brows, and she frowned. "What'd I do?"

"Took me to Dirty Janes." I turned the laptop so she could see the screen. "What d'you think of this?"

Her eyes scanned the article, her lips silently mouthing the words. When she let out a hoot, I knew she caught my vision. "This is genius."

"Really?"

"Retro chic. Why didn't I think of it?"

I laughed. "Maybe because you weren't raised in a motel built in the 50s. When you said vintage was making a comeback, it got me thinking. Why not use what's already retro and make it work for us instead of against us?"

Jenna swept a hand toward the computer. "Obviously, it's working for these business owners."

"It's still gonna take some money," I said. "And some creativity to make each room unique."

She bit her lip and eyed me. "Listen, I'm serious about floatin' you a loan. I know you don't want to take that risk, but—"

"No." I held up a hand and shook my head. "I appreciate it, Jenna, more than you can know." No one had ever been willing to bet on me before. That alone boosted my confidence. "I have the money." I wrinkled my nose. "A life insurance policy I put in an account for Gracie Lynn's future."

Her face lit up. "But that's great. I thought you didn't have anything."

It was blood money, but I was due. "I swore I'd never touch it, but after everything Jason put Gracie Lynn and me through, his death ought to account for something."

And if it all went to hell in a handbasket, then so be it.

Aaron

Showing up at the Pickett's Mill Motel without running it by Sarah Beth first was kind of a chicken move. I didn't want her to shoot down my plans or have to get her mama's permission. Figured if they weren't too happy with me, having Linc as my partner in crime might could help. He had a way of softening the hardest of hearts—even that of Georgina Pickett.

Linc had dismissed his classes for the day and was even able to wrangle a couple of his students to help with the project. Two strapping boys—Tyler and Rick. Looked more like body builders than math majors. We got the truck loaded up by mid-morning and I drove it next door while the crew walked through the woods. Best possible scenario would be if Sarah Beth and her mama were gone for the day. Then we'd be anonymous donors that swooped in and worked a little magic.

Although, I didn't want to be *too* anonymous. Wasn't going to win any points with Sarah Beth if she didn't know I was in the mix. That was the tricky part of the hero balancing act. Put myself out there without coming across as cocky or prideful.

I didn't spot Sarah Beth's beater-car in the motel parking lot as I drove in, but there was another vehicle sitting out front. Looked like a late model Infiniti. Either Miss Pickett had herself a visitor or Sarah Beth won the lottery.

The lawn stretching across the yard wasn't more than a patch of weeds, so I didn't figure it would hurt any to back the truck over it. Stopped just shy of the railroad ties used to border the playground and jumped out just as the guys showed up.

Linc lowered the truck bed before joining me, and the boys got to unloading.

"So, what's the plan?" Linc watched as Tyler hefted a stack of sanded and stained two-by-eights over his head like they weighed nothing.

"First off, we're gonna check all the bolts holding this thing together and replace any that's defective. Got a couple new swing belts, plenty of chain, and other parts that might come in handy. Also got a couple rolls of weed matting."

"What's with the wood?"

"To rebuild the seesaw. Did the prep work at home; now we just gotta put it together." I reached into the truck cab and pulled out a few sheets of paper. "Got the directions right here. Figure with the four of us working, we can get most of it together before suppertime. Whatever's left, I'll knock out as time permits."

Linc grinned. "Dad's right. You've got a thing for the lady."

Rather than argue, I merely shrugged and glanced at the inground pool at the far end of the yard. Best thing they could do was get it filled before someone got hurt messing around.

"What's going on out here?"

Sarah Beth's voice had me whipping around. She and Jenna Wright were standing not twenty feet away—close enough I could see the furrow between Sarah Beth's brows and a spark of humor in the Jenna's eyes.

"Hey, Sarah Beth." I nodded at Jenna, not quite sure how to address her. She'd asked me to keep our working relationship quiet, but did that mean I should act like I didn't know her? Instead, I focused on Sarah Beth. "You remember my brother Linc."

Her smile was so quick, I almost missed it. "Yes, of course. But what're y'all doing here? And what's this?" She waved a hand toward the boys unloading the truck.

In hindsight, it might've been better had I asked for permission after all. It struck me right then how presumptuous this would look—especially since I hardly knew her.

"I thought I'd surprise you... I mean, Gracie Lynn, by fixin' up the playground. Just so she can be out here without you worryin' if she'll get hurt." I watched for some reaction other than wariness and confusion. They seemed to be her go-to responses toward me.

"Aren't you sweet, Aaron?" Jenna planted her hands on her hips with a grin.

Sarah Beth turned to her and flicked a hand from Jenna to me and back again. "You two know each other?"

Jenna let out a laugh. "Girl, this is Rossville. There isn't a person that's lived here for more than a year I don't know. Fact is, I was the one who sold the house next door to Aaron."

Quick as that, the tension eased from my shoulders. At least where Jenna was concerned. Couldn't say the same for Sarah Beth. "I was only trying to be neighborly," I assured her. Didn't want her thinking I was working an angle, even though I sort of was.

Sarah Beth eyed me with suspicion. Might could be she had a harder shell around her heart than I did. "Bringing Mama food is being neighborly." She blew out a breath. "This is going above and beyond. I can't imagine what it's costing you, but whatever it is, I'll pay you back. It might take me some—"

"No, ma'am," I snapped, well aware that Linc, Jenna, and the boys were watching our interaction like we were the next big thing in reality T.V. "You mind if we talk over there where it's not quite so... crowded." I glared at Linc who had the nerve to snicker.

Arms crossed, Sarah Beth followed me as I moved toward the edge of the motel. It was becoming clear right quick that I was making a mess of things. Forget about cocky and prideful; she was going to start thinking I was a creeper.

When we were out of earshot, I stopped, took me a breath, and faced her. "Okay, I should've asked before jumping into this project."

Her blue eyes narrowed on mine. "Why are you doing this, Aaron?" Before I could speak, she held a hand up. "And don't say you're just being neighborly, because I don't buy it."

If I told her the God's honest truth—that I was honing my skills as a knight in shining armor—she'd hightail it so fast, it'd make my head spin. But there was more to it, so I focused on that instead.

"The other day when I brought that puppy of yours back here, I saw Gracie Lynn fussin' around on that dilapidated seesaw." I waved toward the offensive piece of equipment. "It didn't seem right your little girl doesn't have anywhere safe to play while y'all are here."

She chewed on her lower lip, eyes drawn to the playground. "I'm aware it's a hazard, but it's only temporary." So, she planned to leave. Had to admit, it was a disappointment.

"Even if y'all are only gonna be here a couple months—"

"We aren't," she cut in. "We're fixin' to stay indefinitely. What I meant was the *hazard's* only temporary. Mama and me are gonna reopen the motel, but there's a lot of work that needs to get done first. And the playground's on that list." Her gaze landed back on the boys as they got to work. "Or it was on the list."

There went my plans for Miss Pickett's property. I pondered that piece of news, expecting some irritation over my long-range goal being blown to smithereens. But it didn't come. At least not in the moment.

Her gaze slid back to me, and she smiled. It lit up her whole face, turning what was pretty into downright beautiful. About took my breath away. "I do appreciate your thoughtfulness, Aaron. I didn't mean to sound ungrateful, and I intend to repay you."

I barked out a laugh. "You're kiddin, right? It'd be like me sneaking over to paint your house 'cause I don't like the color and then expectin' you to foot the bill for it."

She frowned like she was trying to make sense of what I just said. Before she could answer, a car came rumbling down the drive—Sarah Beth's car.

My spine stiffened when I recognized Miss Pickett behind the wheel, and she didn't look none too pleased.

"Great," I said under my breath. I turned to catch Linc's attention, hoping he'd rescue me. Pathetic, I know. But he had a way with mamas. Soon as he glanced my way, I waved him over.

Miss Pickett got out of the car and hobbled around back of it. "What in the Sam Hill is goin' on here?" Her mouth was set, chin jutted. Reminded me of Saul 'Canelo' Alvarez facing his fiercest opponent.

"Hey, Miss Pickett. It's good to see you out and about." Linc stopped beside me, and I put a hand to his back and pushed him forward. "I don't believe you've met my brother Linc."

Linc glanced at me like I was throwing him to the lions but recovered quick enough to stick out his hand. "Pleased to meet you."

Miss Pickett ignored him. "Ya didn't answer my question. What are y'all doin' here?"

Linc didn't seem the least putt off. He clapped me on the back. "My big brother here thought Sarah Beth could use a little help getting the playground in working order."

She narrowed her eyes. "You don't say."

Sarah Beth stepped in—an unexpected alliance—and put an arm around her mama's shoulder. "He was concerned for Gracie Lynn, Mama. Isn't that thoughtful of him?" I wasn't sure if she was trying to sell me on Miss Pickett or herself. Either way, the older lady's face softened.

"Appreciate it. Aaron, is it?"

"Yes, ma'am." At least she remembered my name. That was progress right there.

"Suppose y'all should get to it, then." Moving toward the motel, she threw over her shoulder, "Speaking of Gracie Lynn. Ain't it time for you to collect her from preschool?"

Sarah Beth rolled her eyes and let out a soft laugh. "Don't let her get to you. Kindness doesn't come natural to her."

As Linc and me rejoined the guys, Sarah Beth and Jenna followed behind Miss Pickett. It didn't appear Sarah Beth had been given a whole lot of love in her life, but she showered it on her daughter, just the same. God's grace worked in mysterious ways. Maybe He'd do the same for me.

Chapter 11

Sarah Beth

Years of mistrust had a way of wearing a person down. I couldn't take anything at face value for fear I was being lied to or used. It would be easy enough to lay the blame for my paranoia on Jason, but it started way before he came into the picture. Desperation causes a body to overlook the obvious, and I was feeling pretty desperate when I met him.

He was a charmer who could switch his story quick as a lick to explain away his lies. He had no family to speak of—a daddy he never saw and a half-brother who landed himself in prison before he turned twenty. The combination of those facts is what a discerning person would call "red flags."

Knowing how gullible I'd been in the past made it hard to trust in the kindness of others. I didn't care for that particular trait, especially when I saw it mirrored in Mama. The way she was with Aaron was downright embarrassing. Imagine my humiliation when I realized I hadn't been much better.

As I watched Gracie Lynn and Jazzy running around the "new" playground, I had myself an epiphany. If I was going to do better than Mama, I'd need to make a few changes. First off, Gracie Lynn and me needed to find ourselves a church. Mama used to drop me off at a little Baptist one on Sunday mornings until I asked her one day why I had to go if she didn't. That put a stop to it, which was fine by me, because I got to sleep in.

But every now and again, one of those Bible stories I learned in Sunday school came to mind, and it got me thinking there was a whole lot more to knowing the Lord than saying a prayer when things weren't going my way. After all, if He could protect Daniel from a bunch of lions and save his three friends from being roasted in a furnace, He could certainly fix whatever was broken in me.

Another thing that needed changing was me seeing everyone through suspicious eyes. Maybe Aaron had himself an agenda attached to fixing the playground, but why couldn't I just trust it was like he said—making it safe for Gracie Lynn?

And it was high time I stood up to Mama. Oh, I was doing some better since I'd come home, but if we were going to work together, I couldn't kowtow to her any longer. The worst she could do was throw me out, but she'd lose Gracie Lynn in the process, so I knew that wasn't going to happen.

"You sure that boy checked to be sure everything's good and tight?" Speak of the devil.

I turned to find Mama crossing the yard. It surely didn't take long for me to put my money where my mouth—or rather mind—was. "Yes, ma'am. He wouldn't have told her she could play on it if he hadn't."

She tented her eyes against the morning sun. "That black weed cloth on the ground's a sight, isn't it?"

Drawing in a deep breath, I sent up a little prayer for patience. Mentally sparring with Mama didn't come with a set of directions. "He's fixing to bring a load of something to cover it up later this week. Mulch, I think he said."

"If Gracie Lynn falls on that, she might skin up her knee something awful," Mama grumbled.

Hands on hips, I turned to her. "Oh, Mama, can't you just be grateful he went to all this expense and trouble? I swear, you look for things to complain about."

She clucked her tongue. "Yeah, well, you gotta wonder what he's after."

And I'd be right back where I started, mistrusting everyone and everything. "No, actually, I don't."

Gracie Lynn's shriek of laughter cut into what was fixing to be an argument. "Hey, Mama, look at what Jazzy got."

The puppy was running in circles, a plastic Coke bottle, almost as big as her, clamped in her mouth while Gracie Lynn chased her.

"You be careful, baby girl, you hear? Nana's afraid you might skin your knee if you fall." Mama may have a glass-half-empty attitude, but she wasn't wrong about that particular concern. It didn't mean she was right about Aaron, though.

I glanced at Mama. "When Aaron was carting food over here while you were laid up, did you think he was after something then?" Let's see her turn that kindness into a self-centered agenda.

She twisted her mouth into a grimace. "Probably workin' his way into my good graces in case I decided to sell the motel."

Talk about ungrateful. And paranoid to boot. "You're kidding, right?"

She jutted out her chin. "No, child, I'm serious as can be. That friend of yours was over here trying to talk me into selling for some client. I'd bet my bank account it was your Aaron."

I snorted. "You're way off base." Jenna would've told me if that were true. Besides, Mama's bank account didn't amount to a hill of beans, so it wasn't much of a bet. Still, I couldn't quite tamp down the slightest niggle of doubt. After all, Jenna was Aaron's realtor—she said so herself. "What would he want with this ol' place?"

At the same time a thought popped into my head, Mama voiced it. "The land."

So much for my newfound decision to not be like her. "Why do you all the time have to be so suspicious of everyone?" I was asking the question as much to myself as I was to her.

"Not everyone. Just those that ain't truthful 'bout their motives. Can't help it if the good Lord blessed me with the gift to read people. I was right 'bout that no-count husband of yours, wasn't I?" And she'd never let me forget it, either.

Even though the sun was warm on my shoulders, a sudden chill skittered up my spine. I wanted to ask her if she was so gifted, why she married my daddy. But that would only fuel a fire that was best left alone. I needed to stay focused on moving forward, not living in the past. Although, I wasn't quite ready to let loose of the idea my daddy might still be alive. Could be Mama wasn't the only one with a sense about things. Only time would tell. Until then, I needed to get along with her.

I waved my hand for Mama to follow me. "Let's go take a look at the garden, see what all we'd need to do if we're fixin' to make use of it this year."

She cut a quick glance at me, like she was surprised at the change of subject. "I don't know, Sarah Beth. It's been years since I've set foot down there. Wouldn't be surprised if kudzu and alligator weed's taken over."

"Well, it can't hurt to check it out." The garden wasn't a high priority—except it was the one thing Mama and I did together when I was growing up that had good memories attached. I needed to find my way back to something sweet and pure. Although, if memory served, we should be planting by Mother's Day, and that was coming up right quick.

I called out to Gracie Lynn. "Baby, why don't you and Jazzy come down to the garden with Nana and me?"

Gracie Lynn glanced up from where she and Jazzy were playing tug-of-war with the Coke bottle. "Okay." She hefted the puppy and bottle into her little arms and skipped across the playground to us.

With a hand on her shoulder, I guided the two of them down behind the motel building while Mama followed at a slower pace. She was getting better, for sure, but she was cautious in her steps. I suppose if I'd taken a fall like she did, I'd be a little hesitant, too.

"You do know, even if we were to get all them weeds pulled up, it'd cost a pretty penny to get the soil in decent shape, let alone buying a bunch of plants," she said to my back.

"Yes, ma'am." I'd been crunching numbers for the last couple nights, trying to figure out how to stretch Jason's life insurance twelve ways to Sunday. I was hoping Mama would offer to kick in some, too. After all, it was her business. Hadn't talked to her about her finances, though, other than what I needed to get the forms filled out for her doctor's office. But she was living off something, so maybe she had money stashed away somewhere.

When we got to the garden gate, I glanced down at Gracie Lynn and Jazzy. "I think it's best if you two stay out here, baby girl. I'm worried you might get bug bites." Ticks were high on my list of the creepiest insects. Of course, the grasses all over the property were growing thick and tall, so there was really nowhere but the playground that was safe.

"Okay." She put Jazzy on the ground and wriggled the Coke bottle at her. The two of them got back to tug-of-war like I hadn't put the least little hitch in their game.

Mama scowled at the mess of weeds that had overtaken the beds. No kudzu, but plenty of oxalis and ragweed. "If we were gonna plant, it'd have to be in the next little bit. With the garden lookin' like it does, it ain't likely to happen this year. What we can do is fire up the mower and knock some of this down."

I thought about the John Deere Mama had ever since I could remember. "You still got that thing?" It had to be more than thirty years old. "Thought you'd have replaced it by now."

She huffed out a laugh. "I ain't made of money, Sarah Beth." As if I thought she was.

If we were going to launch into this remodel project, I'd need to know if there was a snowball's chance of Mama pitching in the least little bit. "Speaking of money." I drew in a deep breath and asked the question that had been on my mind from the first day I'd arrived. "How're you paying your bills with this place shut down like it is?"

She pushed open the garden gate and stepped through it. "I get by. Have a little income that tides me over."

"Yeah? You mind me asking where it comes from?" What I wanted to know more than that was how much she had coming in.

"Two things you don't ask a person, Sarah Beth. How old they are and how much they make." She hitched her brows at me before turning away. "Thought I taught you better 'an that."

Aaron

The railroad had been a part of my life from my earliest memories. In fact, Dad was down in Atlanta the day I was born, stuck in some motel after his ten-hour stretch—not that I could possibly remember. Heard about it when I got older. I knew going in, working as a conductor wasn't the best career choice for someone who wanted a family. Dad did okay, but Mama basically raised us kids. Hadn't thought much about it, until recently.

What was it about Sarah Beth that had me yearning for more than work? Or maybe it was Linc with his baby coming. Or my sister Carrie announcing last weekend that she and Russell were fixing to try for a third kid. Seemed like everyone's life was moving forward except mine. Even Dad was changing course by going to work as a train inspector.

With the days getting longer, I got home before the sun set. Had me a whole thirty-six hours before I had to report back. A month ago—heck, a week ago—I would've grabbed a quick bite and gotten in a good four or five hours working on the house before calling it a night. Instead, I found myself glancing toward the motel, even though I couldn't see it anymore through the dense foliage. Hoped maybe that puppy of Gracie Lynn's would break free and find her way over, giving me an excuse to see Sarah Beth. Maybe even ask her out. The thought of it had my gut clenching in a way I'd not experienced before. *Chicken.*

I microwaved a Hungry Man dinner and downed it with a glass of sweet tea, all the time searching for a reason to go next door. Had a load of mulch coming in the morning, so I could wait until then. Or not. Could be Sarah Beth wouldn't be around the next day. I wasn't into Latin—fact was, I barely passed high school English—but I liked the saying *carpe diem*. Seize the day. No time like the present.

If I was fixing to make an impression, the least I could do was splash some water on my face, run a comb through my hair, and change into clean jeans and a t-shirt. Tried out a smile in the mirror, but it quickly shifted into a scowl. Maybe this right here was why I didn't pursue the ladies. Twisted me into trying to be someone I wasn't.

Pocketed my phone so I'd have a flashlight to find my way back—that is if Miss Pickett didn't send me packing the minute she laid eyes on me. Decided tromping through the scrubby weeds wasn't the best idea unless I wanted the chiggers to feast on me. Instead, I walked the road where trees arched overhead, and a couple mockingbirds caused a ruckus. Took in the sweet scent of some flowering shrub mixed with the rich soil as a few insects chirped away. If I ever saw a more perfect spring evening, I couldn't recall.

The gravel drive going into the motel was more dirt than not. A couple potholes my truck found the other day needed to be repaired if they planned to reopen for business. Fixed my thoughts on that rather than the sudden uptick of my heart. Last time I asked a girl out on a date was high school. Since, it seemed the women did the asking. Wasn't sure if that was progress or not.

Even though it was barely dusk, lights shown through the motel office windows and what I figured was the living space for Miss Pickett and Sarah Beth. Not enough room to have a thought. A whole lot different than the house I grew up in.

Before I had a chance to knock, the puppy's yip started up from the other side of the office door. Jazzy might not be able to do more than take a small chunk from a person's ankle, but I had to give her points for being a good alert dog.

"Gracie Lynn." Sarah Beth's voice. "Don't you open that door until we know who it is." The sheers covering the window rustled a bit before they were pulled aside to reveal Sarah Beth's expressionless face. No smile, but she wasn't scowling, either.

The doorknob twisted back and forth for a moment before Gracie Lynn got it open. First thing I noticed was her huge grin. At least I had one Pickett on my team. Her blonde curls were damp, and she was wearing pink pajamas.

"Hey, Mister Aaron."

I bent down and scooped up the puppy before she got past my feet. "Hey there, Gracie Lynn. You fixin' to go to bed?" Jazzy squirmed her way up my shoulder and bathed my face with kisses. Make that two for Team Aaron.

"Yes, she is." Sarah Beth opened the door fully and reached over Gracie Lynn to rescue me from being licked to death. "And it's time for Jazzy to go into her crate for the night."

"Who's there, Sarah Beth?" Miss Pickett called from the depths of the apartment.

Sarah Beth rolled her eyes and called out, "It's okay, Mama. It's just Aaron."

"Well, for Cripe's sake. Don't he know what time of night it is?" Wouldn't surprise me if she appeared with a loaded shotgun pointed at my chest.

"Don't mind her." Sarah Beth tucked the puppy under one arm and put her other hand on Gracie Lynn's head to steer her out of the doorway. "She's just cranky because... well, because she's Mama. What can I do for you?"

I made myself a mental note to never show up this time of night again. It appeared to be the witching hour. So much for asking her out. "Nothing important. Just wanted to let you know I have that mulch being delivered tomorrow. I'm off work, so I can—"

"Is that Aaron fella still here?" Miss Pickett's screech could be heard clear to Chattanooga.

Sarah Beth touched my arm with an apologetic smile. "Give me five minutes to get everyone settled, and we can talk then." Before I could respond, she closed the door.

Even with all the negative attitude coming from Miss Pickett, I couldn't stop the grin that tugged at my mouth as I wandered to the playground. If I stood the least little chance with Sarah Beth, I was gonna have to get into her mama's good graces.

Although the sun was fixing to set, there were a couple of spotlights coming off the side of the motel chasing all but the deepest shadows away from the swing set. Once the mulch was laid out, all that would be left to finish was the canopy cover for the slide. I had it sitting in my garage, mostly ready to install. This playground didn't look fancy like the one Linc wanted us to build, but it was safe and functional. Sarah Beth could always add to it later if she wanted.

"There you are." Sarah Beth's voice had me spinning around. "Thought maybe you'd given up on us and went back home where it's nice and quiet." She shrugged into a black sweatshirt while closing the distance between us. With the spotlight on her hair, it almost looked like she was wearing a halo. "I'm sorry about my mama."

I tucked my hands into the front pockets of my jeans. "Not your fault." I tilted my head toward the swings. "Wanna sit for a minute?"

She quirked an eyebrow and grinned. "Why not?" As she passed me, I caught the faintest hint of a flowery scent. Shampoo maybe? She sat in one of the two swings, wrapped her hands around the chains, and pushed off slightly with the toe of her shoe.

I sat in the other and twisted enough that I could see her. "Just curious, but has your mama always been so..."

"Ornery?" Sarah Beth supplied with a snort. "She's had her pleasant moments. Although they seem to be rare as hen's teeth these days."

"Is she the reason you took off like you did?" The question was out before I thought better of it. She might not appreciate me asking about her past. At least not this early in the game.

Her sigh filled the air. "Honestly, I have no one to blame but myself. Was Mama difficult to live with? Absolutely. I had it in my head that anything was better than living with her harping and griping. But the truth is, she warned me about Jason, and I chose to ignore her."

Had me a feeling that living with that constant clanging would cause a person to go stone deaf after a spell, but Sarah Beth didn't need me pointing it out. "Then I shouldn't take her dislike of me personally?" I said with a chuckle. I figured when she said no, then I could follow it up with an invitation to a picnic or dinner out.

Sarah Beth leaned her head on the swing chain. "Mama thinks everyone has an angle. You do a nice turn, she's gonna accuse you of wanting something for it."

Her words were like a bucket of ice-cold water. Wasn't that exactly what I'd been doing? Bringing groceries to Miss Pickett to soften her up about selling the motel to me. Fixing the playground for Gracie Lynn to work my way into Sarah Beth's good graces.

Miss Pickett wasn't nearly as crazy as she seemed.

Chapter 12

Sarah Beth

Life with Mama was a series of slow steps. Two forward, three back at times. She was downright ugly for a couple days after Aaron's little visit. She wasn't much better with Jenna, either. It had me some concerned about going into business with her.

So, I prayed. But when I remembered how God answered my last prayer—to get me away from Jason's abuse—I added a few conditions. *I don't want Mama dead, Lord. Just maybe soften her heart some. Otherwise, I'm fixing to pull out of this whole deal with her. I'm kind of stuck here, not knowing what to do, so if you could give me an answer right quick, I'd surely appreciate it.*

I hadn't found a church for Gracie Lynn and me yet, but I did find an old devotional tucked away on the top shelf in my bedroom. I had a vague recollection of one of my Sunday school teachers giving it to me years ago, but I don't think I ever bothered to open it. Flipping through the pages now, I landed on a passage that was so perfectly timed, I knew God was in the mix.

I didn't have any idea who J.B. Meyer was, but he referenced Psalm 78:72 which said, "He guided them by the skillfulness of his hands." I liked the idea of God guiding me. Even if I *hadn't* made a mess of my life following my own ideas, He would've done a whole lot better. But this J.B. person had something to say about it that was a direct answer to my prayer. "Ask Him to shut against you every door but the right one...Meanwhile keep on as you are, and consider the absence of indication to be the indication of God's will that you are on His track."

I was sitting on my bed pondering the wonder of God, when Mama appeared in the doorway. "We gonna get to my PT or what? You said we'd start soon as you dropped Gracie Lynn off at preschool, and that was an hour ago." She glanced around the room before narrowing her eyes on me—like homing in on her prey. "What're you doin' in here, anyway? Thought you said you had a mess of work to get done."

I slapped the devotional closed and hugged it to my chest. We could all do with a little more God around here. "If you must know, I'm praying."

She snapped her mouth shut. Even backed up a step, like she was rocked by the admission. "Oh." Glancing down at her feet, she crossed her arms. "You think when y'all get done talkin', we might could get started on my exercises? Gracie Lynn's gonna need picking up before you know it."

Nodding, I set the book aside and stood. "Let's get going." I shooed her forward with a wave of my hands and followed her to the kitchen. It wasn't near the professional setup the hospital had, but the dining chairs were sturdy and easy for me to maneuver.

I steadied Mama as she sat. "How've you been feeling this mornin'? Any pain?" Squatting beside her, I tapped her right leg.

Mama grunted as she extended it. "None to speak of."

"That's good." Maybe it was time I started wading into deeper conversational waters with her. "You've been a touch...cranky lately." Usually, Mama excused her ugly behavior on feeling poorly. I was curious to see where she'd lay the blame when she didn't have that to fall back on.

She grimaced, but I wasn't sure if it was a reaction to what I said or a twinge of discomfort from the exercise. "Just don't like my routine bein' upset. You got that fella comin' here all hours of the night."

I hitched my brows at Mama. "All hours of the night? Don't you think that's a bit of an exaggeration? Gracie Lynn wasn't even in bed yet." It was all I could do to not roll my eyes. "Besides which, Aaron was stopping over to let us know he was having that mulch delivered." I parroted back his excuse, even if I didn't quite buy it. "He was just being neighborly."

"Which never came, now did it?" Mama fairly crowed, as if it proved Aaron was just like all the other men she was quick to bash.

"I'm sure something came up. Maybe he had to work..." That made sense, although I had no idea what he did. Construction, I guessed, since he was remodeling his house and was handy with tools.

"And then you're gone half the weekend with that friend of yours," Mama grumbled like a petulant child. She even looked the part, crossing her arms and sticking out her lower lip far enough to catch herself a fly.

"You mean *Jenna*?" I put one hand below her knee and the other under her foot as we transitioned into the next exercise. "It was one afternoon, Mama. And, just like Aaron, she did us a huge favor." Truth was, it was Jenna's connections and guidance that was going to make the motel remodel a success. I never would've thought of estate sales—and if I had, I wouldn't have known how to find them. Thanks to her, we now had two retro chairs along with some vintage artwork. It wasn't much, but it was a start.

Why was Mama so threatened by me having friends? It was like she was jealous of the time I spent with them, which sort of made sense in a peculiar way. What she needed was a friend of her own. Someone who might could teach her a thing or two about gratitude.

And I knew just the place to meet such a person.

"Hey, Mama? I've been thinking it'd be good for Gracie Lynn and me to go to church. You wanna come with us?" It might be a whole lot easier for God to soften her heart if she was hanging out in His house.

"Church?" She said it like I'd asked her to come hang out at a honky tonk. With a flick of her wrist, she brushed my hand aside and scowled. "Don't see no reason for it." If I had a mind to get on her bad side, I could list a few for her. "God and me had words the day my mama died, and we ain't spoken since." Her chin was set hard as granite, and I figured her heart wasn't much softer.

"Well, Gracie Lynn and me are going." Which meant I had to find one real quick, or else I'd be a liar. "You change your mind, you're always welcome to join us." I patted her leg to show her we were finished. "Now I gotta pick Gracie Lynn up from preschool. When I get home, I'll get to that research on stripping wallpaper." And flooring. And painting. The thought of all we'd have to get done to make this work was enough to scare me off the whole idea, if not for Jenna. Her enthusiasm was better than a shot of adrenaline.

Mama brushed at a piece of fuzz on her jeans and glanced at the clock. "I'll fetch Gracie Lynn from preschool, if that'll help."

I wasn't about to question her intentions, even though they were suspect. Mama looking after Gracie Lynn would keep both of them out of my hair for a spell. "Thanks, Mama. I appreciate it."

She collected her bag from the kitchen counter. "If you don't mind, I was thinkin' of gettin' her ice cream on the way home."

"That's fine." Even better. I'd give me more time to get some work done.

Soon as Mama was gone, I took Jazzy out to potty then locked her in the office with me where I could keep an eye on her. Seemed as if she was always getting into some sort of trouble, just like a toddler.

I powered up the computer then searched through Mama's desk for a notepad and something to write with. Found old receipts, three pens that didn't work, and a stack of empty file folders. Use to be, she had a dresser at the back of the closet where she stored office supplies. Mama never did strike me as organized, but if she'd been there, I had no doubt she'd know where to find what I needed. Maybe it was another of those gifts the Lord bestowed on her along with her sense about people. Couldn't help the snicker that erupted with that thought.

Sure enough, there was a dresser tucked into the back corner of the closet. Another piece of retro furniture we might could use in one of the renovated rooms. Would Mama be willing to swap it with a file cabinet or a few boxes?

The top drawer was stuffed with old pictures, which I made a mental note to come back to when I had more time. I caught a photo of the two of us on some beach when I was near Gracie Lynn's age. Maybe going through these together would loosen Mama up a bit.

The second drawer was full of junk, which I sifted through before finding a mechanical pencil. And miracle of miracles, there was lead in it. Now for a notepad. Or at least a blank piece of paper or two. The bottom drawer had an unopened ream of copy paper. Hallelujah! As I lifted it out, an envelope dropped onto the closet floor. Probably trash. What I needed to do was dump the whole mess into the garbage. It was time for a good purging.

I left the paper on the desk and returned to the closet for the envelope, which had yellowed with age. Hand-addressed to Mama, the writing was in all caps, masculine and bold. But the return address was so smudged, I couldn't quite read it. Moving closer to the window, I held it in the light and squinted. Garrett Marshall.

Huh. I wonder—

"Sarah Beth!" Mama's voice carried into the office. "We're back. Turns out, my wallet wasn't in my purse, so we didn't go for ice cream." Which also meant she'd been driving without her license. Good thing the preschool was so close.

"I'll be right there, Mama." I folded the envelope in half and tucked it into my back pocket. If Gracie Lynn had her heart set on ice cream, there'd be no living with her. There might be a partial carton in the freezer, which would have to do.

"Mama." Gracie Lynn threw the office door open. "Guess what we got to do at school today?" Between her jabbering and Jazzy's barking, I didn't have the time to give Garrett Marshall another thought.#

Aaron

The best laid plans don't take into account unexpected issues with a freight train. Like when the air brakes kicked in and we got stuck south of Sugar Valley for three hours. Put me into my run time, and I ended up having to be taxied to the next yard and wait it out at a motel until I could clock in again. There was nothing for it but to reschedule the mulch delivery. Sarah Beth would understand. If I hadn't been practically tripping all over myself the last time I saw her, I might've remembered to get her number. Would've been considerate to give her a heads up. I thought about texting Jenna for it but decided it'd be best to keep the two relationships separate.

It was nearing suppertime when I got back home, and I was scheduled to report to DeButts first thing in the morning. I was still recovering from Miss Pickett's sharp tongue after my last visit to the motel, but unless I wanted to put Sarah Beth off another twenty-four hours or more, there was nothing to do but man up.

As I approached the motel, what sounded like Gracie Lynn's giggles floated from the playground area. She was one happy kid. If God was looking favorably on me, it'd be Sarah Beth out with the little girl instead of her nana. If anyone saw me sneaking along the edge of the building like a lily-livered chicken, they would get themselves a good laugh, but I wasn't taking any chances.

I didn't reckon on Jazzy having the instincts of a hound dog. She started barking her fool head off and came running at me before I could peer around the side of the building. I bent down to pet her, and when I came back up, Sarah Beth was waiting for me, not twenty feet away.

"Hey, there." She flashed a smile bright enough to warm the darkest heart. "Gracie Lynn was just asking when she'd see you again. And here you are."

I swear every time I saw Sarah Beth, she was a sight prettier than the time before. Then again, maybe I just noticed more—like how her cornsilk-colored hair glistened in the sunlight or the depth and sparkle of her blue eyes. I shook my head to clear it of the romantic nonsense. If this kept up, I'd be writing poetry and strumming a mandolin beneath her bedroom window like a lovesick fool.

"You okay?" Her smile wavered a bit as a crease formed between her brows.

I huffed out a laugh. "Fine. It's been a long couple of days is all, and—"

"Hey, Mister Aaron." Gracie Lynn flew at me with every bit as much energy as her puppy and wrapped my legs a quick hug. "You gonna stay for supper? Nana's fixin' hot dogs and beans."

I ruffled her hair—so much like her mama's. "I'm sorry, sweet girl, but I gotta catch up on some rest before heading back to work tomorrow. Maybe another time." I glanced at Sarah Beth. "Just wanted to apologize for the mulch not getting delivered. We got stuck between Sugar Valley and Oostanaula yesterday."

Sarah Beth stared at me like I'd grown horns. "Stuck...where? How?" She shook her head. "I'm sorry, but it only just occurred to me this morning that I don't even know what you do for a living. I was thinking construction. Am I wrong?"

Construction? I laughed. "Guess we haven't had many real conversations, have we?"

"Guess not." She bent down to look Gracie Lynn in the eyes. "You got about fifteen minutes before we need to scoot inside for supper. Why don't you go play on the swings while Mr. Aaron and me talk?"

"Okay, Mama." She picked Jazzy up and marched over to the playground, the puppy flopping in her arms.

Sarah Beth watched her for a moment then turned back to me. "So, what *do* you do?"

"The short answer is I'm a train conductor for Norfolk Southern. I have a run between Chattanooga and Atlanta—Debutts station and Inman. Long answer will take a little more time than what we got right now."

She turned to glance at Gracie Lynn before stepping a bit closer to me and lowering her voice to a near whisper. "My daddy worked for the railroad." Of course, I already knew that, but only because Jenna shared it with me when we met in her office weeks ago. Crossing her arms, she tilted her head as her eyes caught mine. "If I was gonna look for him, that's where I should start, don't you think?"

Was she asking for my help? Mama was all the time saying that Dad never just listened—he was too busy working out how to fix whatever situation she needed to discuss. I didn't want to make the same mistake. Still, I couldn't stand silent as a tree stump, either.

"But you don't know his name, do you? I mean, that's what you told me last time we talked about it." The day Miss Pickett told Sarah Beth her daddy was dead and gone.

She chewed on the corner of her lip like she was undecided. Then with a shake of her head, she pulled a slip of paper from her back pocket. No, not a slip of paper—an envelope. "This might could be nothing." After a quick glance at Gracie Lynn, she drew a little closer to me. "I found this in Mama's office. Purely by accident, mind you. It wasn't like I was snooping or anything." She handed it to me.

I took it from her and unfolded it. It was addressed to Georgina Pickett. Squinting at the return address, I saw it was from someone named Garrett Marshall, but I couldn't make out the entire address—only that it was in Atlanta, Georgia. "This your dad?"

She shrugged. "Honestly, it could be anyone. There was no letter inside. It's just..." She clamped her mouth tight.

"What?" A sort of tingle went up my spine like my body knew whatever Sarah Beth was going to share was important. Last time that happened was when I got the call confirming my job with the railroad.

Flicking a strand of hair from her face, she huffed out a nervous laugh. "You're gonna think I'm crazy."

Quirking a brow, I waited while a mockingbird filled the silence. A breeze kicked up, and the rustle of leaves in the trees overhead played backup.

"The thing is, I sort of prayed about my situation with Mama not long before I found this." She took the envelope from me and shrugged. "It feels like this is God's doing."

I might not have bothered to open my Bible in a coon's age, but I didn't hold to coincidences. Not for those of us who believed in God. Everything worked together for whatever master plan He had going on, even if I didn't live like it at times. My gut—or maybe something a might more reliable—told me this guy was Sarah Beth's father.

"You know what railroad company your dad worked for?" There were about a dozen different freight train companies in Tennessee alone.

Sarah Beth shook her head. "Afraid not." Rubbing her forehead, she let out a sigh. "This is pointless. I mean, for all I know, Mama was telling the truth about him being dead, and looking for him could be a waste of time and energy." She returned the envelope to the back pocket of her jeans. "I should stay focused on doing what I can to get this place reopened so we can bring in some kind of income." If I hadn't seen the dejection in her eyes, I might've thought she bought into her own words.

"Look. Why don't you talk to your mama again? Maybe if you bring up his name, it might soften her enough to talk about it." Sarah Beth searching out this guy on her own might open a can of worms she wasn't ready for.

She snorted. "You obviously don't know her." Crossing her arms, she dropped her head.

The thought of Sarah Beth being hurt had my chest constricting. The girl was getting under my skin for sure, and I couldn't just stand by and watch. Not when I could do something to fix it. Guess I wasn't much different than Dad. I touched her arm. When she lifted her head, I said, "I've only been with the railroad for twelve years, but my dad worked for Norfolk more than thirty before he retired. He knows everyone. And he just agreed to take an inspector position, so that's gonna widen his pool even more."

The shadows in her eyes cleared when she smiled. "You think he might ask around for me?"

I chuckled. "Are you kidding? Snooping is in his job description." Literally, now that he was an inspector. It was going to cause more than a little tension with the crews. "I'll give him this guy's name, and we'll see what he can come up with."

I only caught a quick glimpse of her grin before she launched herself at me. "Thank you, Aaron." She hugged my neck and pecked me on the cheek. "You're the best." Couldn't remember when a kiss that simple set my heart to racing.

"Sarah Beth!" Miss Pickett's sharp reprimand had Sarah Beth jumping away so fast, you'd think we were doing something inappropriate. Then again, maybe Miss Cranky Pants thought a hug was indecent. "Supper's ready." The slam of the door had the both of us cringing.

Sarah Beth's face was flush clear to her hairline. "Don't mind Mama, she's just—"

"Bein' Mama." I couldn't help but finger a strand of hair from her red cheek. "No worries. Her intense dislike of me will toughen my hide a good bit."

An unexpected burst of laughter shot out of Sarah Beth. "The way she's going, you'll be wearing armor in no time."

The perfect attire for a knight.

Chapter 13

Sarah Beth

Ever since I'd thrown my arms around Aaron, I kept reliving the warmth of his hug. It was downright silly, really. I hardly knew the man. Although he'd done more for me and Gracie Lynn in the last six weeks than Jason ever had. And Aaron was even kind to Mama. That alone earned him extra points, seeing as how Mama treated him like he was no better than dirt.

Jenna had us a full Saturday scheduled for garage sales and another estate sale. It'd be good to be away from Mama for a day, even if she'd fuss later over me being gone. She might think she was tough as shoe leather, but I'd dealt with a whole lot worse during my marriage. I thought about taking Gracie Lynn, but Mama shamed me into leaving her behind. The two of them were practically inseparable, and I hadn't yet decided if that was good or bad. If things didn't work out with Mama, it would be Gracie Lynn who paid the price. She'd already lost enough; she didn't need to lose her nana, too.

I slipped out the door just as Jenna's car rumbled into the drive. It was supposed to be a cool day, with lots of clouds overhead and possible thunder showers. I always loved the weather in the South. So different from L.A., where it never thundered, and rain showers were sparse as the hairs on a teenage boy's chin.

Jenna stopped long enough for me to climb into the passenger seat then she was off again. "You ready to shop till you drop?" It appeared she was. Had on loose jeans and shoes that looked comfy enough to actually walk in. Even had her big hair pulled up into a clip like it'd reduce drag so she could move quicker.

Buckling the seatbelt, I glanced at her. "I'm halfway to dropping already. I peeled wallpaper until midnight. What a tedious chore that is. I think the tips of my fingers are growing calluses."

"I told you I'd come help. All you gotta do is—hey." She slowed the car and patted my hand. "You took off the wedding band. Not wantin' to chase off the men anymore?"

I rubbed the naked finger with my thumb. "Hardly. It just seemed deceitful to wear a symbol that should mean something when it doesn't." There were enough lies going around without me adding another one. The whole time I was spraying and scraping wallpaper, my mind created different scenarios that involved Mama and the possibility of having a daddy. If he wasn't dead, like Mama claimed, then what good would come of finding him? He didn't give a lick for me while I was growing up, so why would he care about me now? And why would Mama lie about it? Was she protecting me or punishing him?

Jenna broke into my internal rant. "You're awful quiet over there. Everything okay?"

If I told her things were fine, it'd be another lie. Didn't we just the other day vow to be open with each other? "Got me a little dilemma, and I'm not sure what to do about it." I should've told her when it first happened. Now she might think I didn't trust her.

Jenna cut me a quick look. "You and your mama having more troubles?"

Crossing my arms, I shrugged. "I think she lied to me about my daddy being dead."

She whipped around so fast, her hair clip slipped a bit. "Are you for real? Why d'you say that?"

"She acted all squirrely-like when I asked her about him. Got defensive, and her eye sort of twitched."

"Twitched?" She frowned. "What does that even mean?" She probably thought I was nuttier than a pecan pie.

I threw my hands up. "Never mind. You're right, I'm crazy." I fixed my eyes out the windshield as we drove under a tunnel of trees.

"Whoa, there, Sarah Beth." Jenna eased the car to the side of the road and cut off the engine. "I never said anything about you bein' crazy. Didn't think it, either. It's just…" She blew out a breath. "Guess my first thought was worry for you."

Thunder rumbled overhead, and I pushed the button to roll down the window some so I could hear it better. "Well, I half think I'm crazy, so I wouldn't blame you for thinkin' it, too." Crazy for wanting a daddy who didn't want me.

She reached over and rubbed my arm. "I don't wanna see you get hurt again. Mercy, girl, you've had worse luck than most anyone I know. Hate to see you bringin' on more disappointment. Haven't you had enough?"

Tears bit at the back of my eyes and grew a rock in my throat. "What if I told you I think God's working this out?" I dared a peek at her.

Wrinkling her nose, she said, "God, huh?" She slumped back in her seat and stared out the window as fat raindrops pelted it. "Did you get a word directly or is it more a feeling?" There wasn't even the slightest smirk on her lips.

"You believe me?" If I was remembering rightly, Jenna went to church when we were growing up. But that didn't mean much. Just about everyone in the South went to church—it was the thing to do on Sundays and Wednesday nights. More a social gathering than an act of worship.

"Course I believe you." She let out a rude snort. So un-Jenna-like. "I'd be the last person to undermine your belief in God. If you only knew what Jesus has done for me."

Relief pulled a grin from me. "Okay then. I suppose we still have a lot to catch up on."

"And we will. But right now, finish what you were sayin' about why you think your daddy might still be alive." The rain was now coming down so hard, I had to strain to catch Jenna's words.

I thought about the order of things before launching into an explanation. I told her about the devotional I'd read and finding the envelope. "Purely by accident," I pointed out at the end.

"So, now what? You gonna ask your mama about this Garrett fella?"

I twisted my mouth. "Can you imagine how she'll react if she thinks I was going through her stuff? Which she will. No way she's gonna believe otherwise." Shaking my head, I let out a groan. "She'd like to skin me alive."

Jenna sighed. "Then what *are* you gonna do?"

"Well, Aaron said he'd ask his daddy if he might know the man since he's been with the railroad for years. If not—"

"Aaron?" Jenna's eyebrows went so high, it's a wonder they didn't slide right off the top of her head. "I didn't know the two of you were that cozy."

I squirmed a bit. "We're not, really."

She clucked her tongue. "Obviously you trusted him enough to share about this Garrett Marshall and ask if he could talk to his daddy about it." Pouting didn't sit well on her. Exactly what I was afraid of. Jenna's nose was out of joint, and she thought I didn't trust her.

"Oh, Jenna, don't you start fussing over this." It ached my heart some to think I'd hurt her. "He just happened by right after Mama lied about it, and I was feeling a little raw."

She huffed out a breath and swiped at a strand of hair that had come out of the clip. "So, there's nothin' going on between the two of you?"

I thought about that hug we shared. It wasn't anything more than me being grateful for his kindness. Although, it did remind me I was a woman. "Friends, is all."

She sniffed. "Friends, huh? You don't think he's fine as frog hair split four ways?"

A bark of laughter escaped before I could control it. "Do you?"

Her mouth slid into a crooked grin. "I do like tall men, and he's easy on the eyes. If I didn't have my heart set on Chad..."

And if I hadn't had my heart broken by Jason. No doubt Jenna would've thought he was easy on the eyes, too. But I'd heard once the same could be said of Ted Bundy. Looks weren't worth a hill of beans if the man was a louse—or a serial killer.

Then something Jenna said connected with my slow brain. "Wait a minute." I narrowed my eyes on her. "I thought you were takin' things slow with Chad." The boyfriend I still hadn't met yet. "Cautiously optimistic, I think you said. Now you got your heart set on him?"

She wriggled her brows and grinned. "He started attendin' church with me a couple weeks ago." That was good as an engagement in some Southern circles. "I think he might be the one."

I mirrored Jenna's earlier pout. "I can't believe you. Fixin' to marry this guy, and you haven't even introduced us yet."

Jenna grabbed hold of my arm, eyes wide. "Come to church with us tomorrow. You and Gracie Lynn. Then y'all can go to lunch with us. I really would love to get your take on him, Sarah Beth."

I shook my head. "You forget, I'm not the best judge of men." Which was a reason right there I'd probably never get involved again, let alone married.

"You like Aaron, don't you?" She had me there. "So, that means you're not completely lacking in discernment."

Hadn't I been fixing to find a church for Gracie Lynn and me to start attending? Ask and you shall receive. It was enough to give me goosebumps.

Aaron

I would sooner be hung by my toes than attend a baby shower. A *couple's* baby shower, no less. What lame brain came up with that idea? Had to be a woman. No sane man would think games that included diapers and baby bottles was any kind of fun. And if that wasn't bad enough, I was the only single man there.

If it hadn't been for Sarah Beth, I would've begged off the whole event. Between my work schedule and Dad taking the inspector position, it was going to be tough to find a time in the next few days to talk. As it was, I hid out in Carrie's kitchen and waited for an opportunity to do just that. Mama had me mixing ice cream punch and lining platters with crustless sandwiches. Cucumber and cream cheese, she'd said. I'd need to stop by Smokey Bones for some real food on my way home. Couldn't be soon enough for me.

"You know, son,"—Mama said, handing me a carton of orange sherbet—"this is supposed to be a joyous occasion. You think it's too much bother to smile a little?"

I offered a grimace—the best I could do under the circumstances. "When's Dad gonna get here?" Figured he'd come with Mama, and I'd get to business right away. No such luck.

"Soon as he can. There was a problem with the cake. It had the wrong colors." She clucked her tongue with a shake of her head like it was some great tragedy. "Your daddy's waitin' on them to fix it."

I flung a scoop of ice cream into the punch bowl half-full of 7-Up, while Mama's eyes bored into me. Partygoers in the front room were competing over who could diaper a doll quickest. Every now and again, a cheer was raised, like they were watching a sporting event.

"You wanna tell me what's got you in a mood?" Mama took the scooper from my hand and eased me aside.

"Nothing." At least not that I could pinpoint. "Why?"

"You're a tad aggressive with the ice cream. Got more punch on the counter than in the bowl."

"Sorry." I snatched up a dish towel and wiped my hands.

Mama took a large spoon and stirred the concoction. "You havin' problems at work? Is that why you're itchin' to talk to your daddy?"

Crossing my arms, I rested my hip on the counter next to her. "You mean because he took that job with the FRA?" Federal Railroad Association. Basically, a railroad snitch for the government.

She nodded.

"Why would that be a problem?" Sarcasm dripped from my tone. Lowest form of humor, but there were times it was all I had.

"You gettin' hassled some?" She eased the towel still clutched in my hand and wiped the mess I'd made on the counter.

I let out a snort. "No one would dare for fear Dad might retaliate." Not that he would. "But it's not exactly makin' me friends, either." There wasn't a railroad man alive who wanted an inspector on his tail. "So, why did Dad go back to work, really? Y'all having some financial troubles?"

A soft laugh escaped Mama's lips. "On what your daddy's made over the years? Hardly." She opened one of the drawers and moved things around until she came up with a soup ladle. "It's like we told you; he's bored. Doesn't have enough to occupy himself."

"Maybe he should take up golf."

Another laugh. "Lumberjackin' would be more his speed."

My thoughts went back to when we were younger, and Dad was never around. It was tough on Mama, basically raising us kids by herself. "Isn't it hard havin' him gone so much?" It was one of the reasons I didn't take to getting married and having a family.

"It was when y'all were little." She sighed. "And especially when I was pregnant with Linc." She touched my arm. "Well, you know that better 'an anyone. But if you're thinkin' I regret the life I've had with your daddy, you'd be wrong. He's a godly man, and he's always been a great father. You do what you have to." She patted my cheek. "You'd make some girl a fine husband, and I have no doubt, you'd be a good daddy, too. Don't you let your job dictate your future."

Before I could latch onto her advice, Dad walked into the kitchen carrying a bakery box. "You'd think decoratin' a cake was brain surgery, the way those girls fussed around." He slid the box onto the counter and threw me a smile. "Hey, son."

"Dad. You're just in time for the stroller races."

He put an arm around Mama's shoulders and gave her a squeeze. "Think I'm a better go-fer than player. What's your excuse?"

Mama kissed his cheek and stepped away. "Says he's hanging out in the kitchen to help me with the food and such, but I have a sneakin' suspicion he's wanting to talk to you. So, I'll leave you to it." She hefted the punch bowl and glared at the both of us when we tried to help her with it.

Dad watched her until she was out of sight, a half-smile on his face. It hit me right then how much they loved each other. Nearly forty years of marriage, and he couldn't take his eyes off her.

"What's your secret?" I blurted.

A crease separated Dad's eyebrows. "To what?"

"Marital bliss." I shrugged. "Or whatever you call it. Seems like you and Mama have it down."

He tilted his head like he was giving the question serious thought. "It's the Lord," he finally said. "That's all there is to it. Can't love like we're called to on our own. I can't be everythin' your mama needs, and she can't be that for me, neither. But when you give it all to Him"—he pointed upward—"He'll take you through the hard times."

It sounded cliché, but I knew better.

"So, is your mama right? You need to talk to me?" He leaned over and rested his elbows on the counter. All ears. That right there was one of the things I admired most about him—other than his faith.

"Yeah." I glanced past him to be sure no one was within hearing distance. Sarah Beth's personal stuff didn't need to be fodder for gossip. "It's about Sarah Beth."

He grinned wide enough to split his face in two. "Yeah? You two gettin' on real good?" Leave it to Dad to jump right to it. So much for being all ears.

"Dial it back a notch, Dad," I said with a chuckle. Had to give him points for enthusiasm. "It's about her dad. You remember me telling you a month or so back that he worked for the railroad?"

"Yep. Said she didn't know his name, though."

I nodded. "Then you probably remember me sayin' that he's dead." I lowered my voice on the last word, like it was dirty or something. Fact was, pronouncing death on someone who might still be kicking made me uneasy.

Dad straightened, eyes widening. "You sayin' different now?"

"Don't know for sure." I reached into my back pocket for the scratch paper I'd stuck there before leaving my house. "She came across an envelope sent to her mama. This name was at the top." I slid it over to him. "That's all that was readable on it except a smudged return address in Atlanta."

"Garrett Marshall." He frowned. "Was there anythin' in the envelope? A letter or something that makes her think he's her daddy?"

That's where it went off the rails a bit. "No. Just the name." I blew out a breath. "And a feeling he's the one."

"A feeling?" His eyebrows shot up. "What? Like a gut-thing?"

"More like a God thing." If anyone was going to believe God was leading the way, it'd be Dad. "Said she'd prayed right before stumbling onto this name." I tapped the paper.

He scowled. "So, why is she thinking he's not dead? Another feeling?" Not the least bit of derision in his tone.

"Sort of." I snatched the paper and stuffed it back in my pocket. "She thinks her mama lied about that." It sounded a whole lot crazier out loud than it did in my head. "Anyway, just thought I'd run it by you. What are the chances this random envelope holds the key to her dad? I mean, really? She doesn't even know what rail line he worked for, or his position, or even what his name is." I was so busy pondering the incredulity of it all, it took a beat for me to realize Dad hadn't responded.

Instead, he was chewing on the inside of his cheek, his eyes fixed ahead.

"Dad? Did you hear what I just said?"

Blowing out a breath, he looked at me. "If I'm remembering correctly, there was a fella by the name of Garrett Marshall who worked for Norfolk some thirty years or so ago. Didn't know him well, since I'd just signed on when he left."

The hairs on the back of my neck prickled. This could be Sarah Beth's dad. "Where'd he go?"

He shrugged. "Don't rightly know. I can check around and see if he still works for the railroad, but if he doesn't, I can't be much help." Frowning, he scratched his head. "Did you see this envelope Sarah Beth found?"

"Yeah."

"If you had to hazard a guess, how old would you say it was?"

"I don't know. Anywhere from a year to twenty, I suppose."

Blowing out a sigh, he thumped the counter. "Like searchin' for a needle in a haystack."

Unless Sarah Beth was right, and God was in the middle of the whole thing. Then it'd be a piece of cake.

Chapter 14

Sarah Beth

Too poor to paint and too proud to whitewash was something I'd heard growing up. But until I had to dress myself for church, it never hit so close to home. Taking a last look in the mirror, I cringed at the thought of sitting next to Jenna in her swanky clothes. My tank dress was decent, and it was clean—aside from one itty bitty stain that even I had to strain to see. But it was old as sin and not the least bit stylish. Of course, Gracie Lynn looked sweet as lemon pie in a pink flowered tunic and striped leggings, so she was golden.

I hustled her to the front room and snatched my bag from where I'd left it on the couch the evening before. Mama was sitting in her recliner with her nose in a book. Pouting, most likely.

"I took Jazzy out to pee just before we got ourselves dressed, and she's in her crate. So, unless she takes to fussing real loud, she'll be fine until we get home."

Mama didn't even bother to look at me. "Gone all day yesterday, and now you're fixin' to be gone again today."

Eyes closed, I breathed slow until I got control of my tongue. "You could come with us," I reminded her. Only asked her three times. Of course, if she took me up on the invitation now, we'd be late for sure seeing as how she was still in her housecoat.

"Yeah, Nana." Gracie Lynn rested her elbows on the arms of Mama's chair and leaned in close. "Come with us."

Mama's smile took ten years off her face as she lowered the book. "You go on ahead, chil'." She touched Gracie Lynn's cheek. "I've got a few things to get done here. Besides, if I'm with you, who's gonna take your puppy out to pee?"

"Come on, baby girl. We gotta get going or we're gonna be late." I waved Gracie Lynn to me. "You need me to pick anything up for you before we head home, Mama?"

She went back to her book. "Reckon I'll be fine."

"Okay then. We'll be back after lunch. There's leftovers from supper last night if you get hungry." I didn't wait for her reply but took hold of Gracie Lynn's hand and marched out to the car.

It was fixing to be a hot day. Mid-May, and it felt more like end of June. Already had sweat popping up on my forehead, and it wasn't yet eight-thirty.

Gracie Lynn got herself buckled into her car seat while I started the car. It coughed and sputtered some. *Come on, Lord. If you want me in church today, you're gonna have to get the car running.* Then engine caught, and I looked up and whispered, "Thank You."

"Who you talking to, Mama?" Gracie Lynn piped up.

"Was just thanking Jesus for getting the car going." I needed to do more of that—thanking instead of griping.

We were halfway to church when a thought hit me clear between the eyes. It was Mother's Day. *Mother's Day.* Even when Mama and me were estranged, I always sent her a card for the Hallmark holiday. And now that I was with her, I'd completely forgotten about it.

"Stupid, stupid, stupid," I muttered.

"You talking to Jesus again?"

"No, baby girl." I blew out a sigh. "Just remembered something that was kind of important, and I'm angry with myself." Mama might not be the picture of maternal love, but she was the only one I had. Was *she* aware it was Mother's Day?

There was but one way to fix it. I glanced at Gracie Lynn's reflection in the rearview mirror. "We're not gonna be able to go out to lunch with Miss Jenna and her friend after church like we planned."

"Why?"

"I forgot today's Mother's Day, and it wouldn't be right to go without Nana. Why don't we pick up something special and take it to her instead? Won't that be fun?" There was a good chance Mama wouldn't show her appreciation, but then again, she'd surprised me before.

I half expected Gracie Lynn would ask what Mother's Day was, but I was spared for the time being. Not having a mama of his own since he was a kid, Jason didn't give the holiday a thought. It wasn't like I could celebrate myself once Gracie Lynn was born.

We arrived at Shiloh Baptist Church, which wasn't anything like the tiny one Mama dropped me at when I was young. This building was modern and spread out, and the parking lot alone was big enough to get lost in. I pulled into an empty space while a bunch of butterflies took off in my belly. I never was one for crowds and walking into one where I didn't know but one person—two, if I counted Gracie Lynn—made me feel sort of naked. *Sorry, God, I shouldn't use the word naked at church.*

"Are we here?" The level of excitement in Gracie Lynn's voice made up for my jangling nerves. You'd think she was fixing to enter an amusement park rather than a church.

"We're here." My heart was thudding so hard, I had to catch my breath. "Let's see if we can find Miss Jenna."

We crossed the lot filled with cars and strangers while sweat pooled in my armpits. Good thing I was wearing a tank dress, or I'd be showing perspiration stains for sure. My hand was so slick, I could hardly keep ahold of Gracie Lynn's.

Just breathe.

We passed couples and families, all offering smiles of welcome, as we approached the front door.

"Sarah Beth?"

It was a man's voice, and since I didn't know any men, other than Aaron, I figured there was another Sarah Beth in the crowd he was talking to. Still, I glanced behind me and spotted an older couple arm-in-arm. I knew him, but from where?

He grinned and offered his hand. "This is a pleasant surprise." His grip was firm but not crushing. It was a wonder he could hold onto my sweaty palm. "This must be your little girl," he said while giving Gracie Lynn a little wave.

"Yes." And then it struck me in the absolute nick of time. Aaron's daddy. How could I have forgotten? "Gracie Lynn, can you say hello to Mr. Cooper? He's Mr. Aaron's daddy."

Gracie Lynn leaned against my hip, head tucked down with a sudden case of shyness. "Hello."

"It's nice to meet you, Gracie Lynn." The woman with Mr. Cooper bent down to look her in the eyes. "I'm Aaron's mama. He's told us a lot about you." When Gracie Lynn buried her face further in the folds of my dress, Mrs. Cooper stood up, smiled at me, and offered her hand. "I'm Janice."

"It's nice to meet you, Mrs. Cooper." I wiped my hand on my dress before accepting the handshake. She appeared just as sweet as Aaron said she was. Her short brown hair framed high cheekbones. Aaron favored her a good bit—same striking green eyes and narrow nose.

"Please, call me Janice." She tilted her head toward her husband. "And he's Paul."

"Of course." I peered around them to see if they had any other family with them.

"Aaron's not here," Paul said. "He's workin' today."

Janice clucked her tongue. "We can't go usin' that as an excuse for him. It's been years since he's stepped foot in church."

The same could be said about me, but here I was.

"Sarah Beth." Jenna's voice drew my attention from Aaron's parents as she approached with a man on her arm. He didn't look the least little bit like I'd expected. Rather than tall and handsome—which would match Jenna to a T—this guy was a tad shorter than Jenna, balding, and a bit nerdy in his wire-rimmed glasses. I couldn't help but glance at his thin chest to see if he was wearing a pocket protector.

"We won't keep you," Janice said, touching my arm. "It's nice to put a face to a name. Oh, and Happy Mother's Day."

"Happy Mother's Day to you, too."

There were random thoughts bombarding me from every side. What had Aaron said about me? She'd said it was nice to put a face to the name—*my* name. And what had he told his parents about Gracie Lynn, seeing as how Mrs. Cooper... Janice... said they'd heard a lot about her? And most important, had Aaron's daddy done any digging yet into the name I gave Aaron?

Then there was Jenna with this man who could've been a body-double for Barney Fife. Life was full of the unexpected.

Church was a whole lot different from what I remembered. Of course, I'd been a child the last time I set foot into God's house. Even though there were some memories left over from Sunday school, I never soaked up a thing the pastor said. Now here I was, a grownup without excuse. If I hadn't remembered Mother's Day all on my own, I would've been reminded at the service. The entire message was a tribute to a mama's love, and it got me thinking.

Honor your mother and father. It was commanded in the Bible, and I'd failed it something awful. Oh, I was respectful to Mama when I was growing up—at least to her face. But I spent a lot of those years grumbling about her failures rather than being grateful that she was there. Unlike my daddy.

When the service was over, I took hold of Gracie Lynn's hand and followed behind Chad and Jenna. I glanced around for Mr. Cooper, even though this wasn't the time or place to ask about him searching for my daddy. It would give me some comfort, though, if I knew Aaron had talked to him about it, and he was willing to help out.

"Where would you ladies like to go to lunch?" Chad asked when we got outside. He earned points by crouching down to include Gracie Lynn. I was ashamed for judging him based on his looks without knowing a thing about him. Talk about shallow. I should know better than most how unfair that was, since Jason's good looks proved to be the extent of his character.

"We're gonna have to beg off lunch, Chad." I wrinkled my nose at Jenna. "I plumb forgot today was Mother's Day. It wouldn't be right for me to go off with y'all and leave Mama to herself."

"She's welcome to come along," Chad offered. He had pure kindness in his brown eyes, which reflected confusion when Jenna nudged him. "What'd I say?"

I laughed. "You didn't say anything wrong. Jenna has an unholy fear of Mama, is all."

Jenna's mouth dropped open. "Not true." Then she grimaced. "Well, maybe a little. But I can see why you'd wanna spend this day with her. If my parents hadn't retired to Florida last year, I'd wanna be with my mama, too."

I turned to Chad. "Where do your parents live?"

"Dad's in Texas, which is where I was born and raised. My mom passed away a couple of years ago. Ovarian cancer." Tears welled up in his eyes, and he cleared his throat.

My heart ached for his loss. "I'm so sorry." Here I was, fussing half the time about Mama when I should be thanking God she was still alive.

After we said our goodbyes and Jenna hugged both Gracie Lynn and me, I watched them walk hand-in-hand to his car. I liked Chad, and after only a short conversation with him, I could see the attraction Jenna had to him. He was kind and stable. I was proud for her. If I'd chosen better... well, I supposed I wouldn't have Gracie Lynn, and I wouldn't trade her for anything this world had to offer.

"Well, baby girl, what d'you think we should get Nana for lunch?" Few places in Rossville were open on Sundays, but if necessary, we could drive into Chattanooga. The least I could do for Mama was weather a little bad traffic.

"How 'bout ice cream?"

Chuckling, I was fixing to nix the idea when I heard my name called. I turned to find Aaron's parents walking toward us. The church parking lot had thinned out while I was talking with Jenna and Chad, but there were still a few cars maneuvering out of the lot. I pulled Gracie Lynn to the side and waited for the Coopers to catch up.

"We just wanted to welcome you again to the church," Paul said when they drew near.

Janice smiled at Gracie Lynn. "There's children's church during the second service, which is at eleven. Just in case y'all wanna come back another Sunday. I think Gracie Lynn might like that." Then she shook her head and chuckled. "Here I go, buttin' in where I don't rightly belong."

Aaron was right—his mama was pretty sweet. "Not at all. It's good to know." I squeezed Gracie Lynn's hand and looked down at her. "You'd like children's church, baby girl. You could learn more about Jesus. When I was little, I didn't understand anything they said in the big church. But Sunday school was different."

"Sarah Beth," Paul said, drawing my attention. "Aaron talked to me about..." He glanced Gracie Lynn. "Well, you know."

"Yes, sir." My heart kicked up something awful, and I pressed a hand to my chest where they could surely see it beating.

"Don't know nothing yet, but I'm lookin' into it."

"Thank you. I appreciate it so much." It was all I could do to keep from throwing my arms around him, like I'd done with Aaron when he agreed to ask his daddy about Garrett Marshall. The thought of it had my face heating.

"We hope to see you back next Sunday," Miss Janice said, touching my arm. "You have yourself a blessed Mother's Day."

"You, too, ma'am." I fairly skipped beside Gracie Lynn back to the car. Even if my daddy was dead and gone, like Mama said, it was a pure pleasure knowing there were people like the Coopers willing to walk it out with me.

The warmth of their kindness stayed with me while I picked us up some lunch to take home to Mama—and it wasn't ice cream. Mama liked herself a roast beef sandwich with horseradish and cheese, which I was able to order at the deli in the grocery store. It wasn't fancy, but I was hoping she would see the thought behind it and consider it a worthy gift.

I found a Mother's Day card from daughter and another from granddaughter at the back of the store. Gracie Lynn and me signed them—or I signed and Gracie Lynn printed—while we sat in the parking lot, sweat trickling into our hairlines and down our necks.

"D'you think Nana will like my card?" Gracie Lynn held it up so I could see her name printed in a mix of different size capitals and lowercase letters. It was perfect.

"She'll love it, baby girl, because it came from you." I put the cards in their respective envelopes and set them aside. "You need to climb in back and buckle up now."

Gracie Lynn scrambled over the top of the front seat, her dress hiking up to show off her ruffled undies. "You think she'll like the samich?"

A laugh escaped. The child was pure joy. "Yes. Now get yourself buckled up so we can get home before we melt."

With every minute we drove back to the motel, the joy that had taken hold was being suffocated by unease. I never knew what to expect when I went home. Most often, Mama was in a mood. But I replayed the church message in my head—or at least the parts that stuck. It wasn't until I had Gracie Lynn that I understood the level of anxiety that plagued a mama's heart at all times. Fear of failing in one or all aspects of what was expected of a parent.

Maybe on some level, that's where Mama's moods came from. Was she regretting some of the things she'd done, or was she disappointed in the person I'd become? There was none of that attitude when she looked at Gracie Lynn, and for that I was grateful. But it still hurt my heart that she could be so dismissive of me.

Honor your mama.

It didn't matter what she said, God promised if we honored our parents, we would be blessed by it. I'd just keep trying to do what He asked of me, and maybe Mama would eventually grow to love me again.

I parked in front of the motel office and gathered up our things. The deli bag from the grocery store had to weigh a good ten pounds with the sandwiches and chips I'd gotten.

Once Gracie Lynn was out of the car, I handed her the cards. "You give these to Nana straight away, okay?" It might stop Mama's sour attitude before it could truly take.

First thing I noticed was Jazzy's empty crate. Had Mama taken her outside to pee? Then I heard Mama's voice coming from the kitchen. Did she have company? The only person other than Jenna who ever came by was Aaron. Couldn't be him; his daddy said he was working.

Gracie Lynn rushed ahead of me. "Hey, Nana."

I walked in as Mama wrapped Gracie Lynn in a big hug. "Well, goodness, chil', this is a surprise." Her eyes met mine over my daughter's head. "Thought y'all were goin' out to lunch with your friends." Was that joy I saw twinkling in her eyes?

I held up the sack. "We brought lunch home instead." Looking down, I saw Jazzy lying at Mama's feet. Must've been the puppy she was talking to.

Gracie Lynn pulled out of Mama's arms. "Here you go, Nana. Happy Mother's Day." She handed Mama the cards.

There was no doubt now—those were tears in Mama's eyes. I knew for sure, because a lump rose in my throat to match them. *Thank You, Jesus.* Even if this was a one and done deal with her, I was going to take what I could get, when I could get it.

Chapter 15

Aaron

The night air was heavy with humidity coming out of Atlanta. It was fixing to be a hot summer, and it was only mid-May. Maybe there was something to this global warming the media was always going on about. Of course, there'd been record highs every now and again for as long as people cared enough to keep track.

I'd gotten some used to my regular schedule, so things seemed a bit off taking the train back to Debutts at night. Maybe that's what had me feeling edgy. Or it could be that Cecil James was back after his heart issue. The doctors gave him the all-clear, but far as I was concerned, he didn't exactly look like the picture of health. His face was still a bit pasty.

We got ourselves situated in the Crew Holler that'd take us to the train, since it wasn't sitting at Inman station. I took a long look at Cecil's ghost-white face in the cab lighting. "You sure you're doin' okay?"

He shook his head with a snort. "What'd I say the last two times you asked?" *Fit as a fiddle.* But saying it didn't make it so.

As we bumped along the road, I reminded myself how to perform CPR just in case. Cecil came across as cantankerous as an old goat, but it was all bluff. I didn't want him dying on my watch. Why didn't he retire when he got the diagnosis instead of pushing for another year?

When we got to the train, I did the full inspection under the watchful gaze of a hoot owl high in one of the hackberry trees alongside the track. I'd forgotten how peaceful a night run could be, so why couldn't I shake this uneasiness that made my skin itch? It was like a cloud of doom pressing down on me. Was the Lord trying to warn me of something or was I just feeling edgy because of Cecil?

Within the hour, we were off. With my mind needing to focus on slow orders and upcoming signals, watching the board, and confirming everything with Cecil, I shoved everything else aside. That was the thing about crewing a freight train—it took every ounce of focus to keep things straight.

It was nearing dawn, and everything was smooth as could be. Cecil was doing fine, and the uneasiness of earlier was all but gone. Carried a bit of tension in my neck and shoulders, which a long, hot shower and a few hours of sleep would cure. I'd gotten worked up over nothing.

The sun was rising just as we passed through Cohutta and into Tennessee. "We're about home," I said.

"Yep." Cecil raised his arms over his head and stretched. "You were fussin' at me all this time for nothing."

I chuckled. "Just looking out for you, old man. Hope when I'm old as Moses, someone cares enough to fuss over—" I did a doubletake. Was something on the tracks ahead? A tree, maybe? No, too big. I squinted to block out the rising sun. A van. My heart rated doubled as my stomach dropped.

"We got trouble," I yelled, hitting the emergency brake. "Brace yourself." The brakes squealed something awful, but we both knew there was no avoiding a collision. It'd take a good mile before the train could come to a full stop. *Please, God, keep us on the tracks.*

I braced myself for impact. The high-pitched shriek nearly shattered my ear drums as smoke billowed up from the friction of the brakes on the tracks. I peered through the fog to assess what I could in mere seconds. Felt like slo-mo and hyper-speed all at once. We struck the van, and an explosive *boom* filled the car. Time stood still as we bounced off the tracks, mowing down a section of trees.

We finally stopped.

I was on my side, pain radiating from my right shoulder blade, heart thudding so hard, I couldn't draw a breath. *Cecil.* Disoriented, I pushed up with my left arm, twisting this way and that. "Cecil? You okay?" Cecil's empty seat was hanging over me. The train must've turned on its side. "Cecil!"

One-armed, I pushed myself up and balanced on my knees as a wave of nausea took hold. Head pounding, I took a deep breath and scanned the chaos until I spotted Cecil's still body crumpled in the corner behind my seat.

"Cecil, wake up." I scrambled over to him and felt for a pulse. Weak, but it was there. "Don't you die on me, you hear?" I crawled back to my seat and got hold of the **MIC**. After identifying myself, I let the dispatcher know we'd derailed due to a vehicle on the tracks, and we needed emergency crews dispatched. "Cecil James is unconscious. Weak pulse. It's not looking good."

"You okay?"

I tried to move my arm, but the pain tore through my body like I'd been speared clear through. Panting, I managed, "I'll live. But I'm not sure I can say the same for Cecil."

"Already called it in. Anyone in that vehicle you hit?"

Closing my eyes, I tried to remember what I saw just before impact. A young woman in the driver's seat. Was there another face in the back window? A child, maybe? Bile rose up my throat, and I took me a deep breath and swallowed. "For sure, there was someone in the driver's seat." Had she gotten stuck? Did her car run out of gas? Or was it a suicide? "Maybe a child." Couldn't help but picture Sarah Beth and Gracie Lynn.

It was my job to walk back to the place of impact and inspect the area. The thought of what I'd find was enough to make me weep. No one would fault me for bypassing that chore, since I'd been injured. But I needed to see for myself.

I dug my thumb and finger into my eyes to hold back the tears as the wail of a siren reached my ears.

The hours blended into one another. A blur of activity with emergency personnel, the train inspector, and even some in the community that showed up like a bunch of sick rubberneckers at the scene of an accident. I figured it was a God thing that the closest hospital was Parkridge East in Chattanooga. Turned out they were an accredited chest pain center, which was what Cecil needed since it appeared the accident precipitated a heart attack. He should've never been released to work, and I said as much to the inspector when asked.

I sat in the hospital emergency room with my eyes closed and tried to erase the image of what I found a half mile back of the where the train had been derailed. The driver couldn't have been any older than twenty, although I couldn't stomach taking more than a passing glance at her. Thank the Lord, there wasn't a child in the back seat. Not sure what I saw—maybe a shadow. All this would go into my Crossing Accident Form

Whether it was an accident or suicide, it was tragic. A life lost that could've been prevented. And maybe two, if Cecil didn't pull through. Thank God we weren't carrying hazardous materials. We wouldn't know more until the trainmaster finished his investigation, including downloading the event recorder located on the engine. And then there was the footage from the video camera on the lead engine—that would be downloaded and viewed. All this information would be made available to us—Cecil and me. The question was whether I'd want to know. Ignorance was bliss, wasn't that the old saying?

"Aaron."

I opened my eyes to find Mama bending over me, Dad right behind her. Even though I assured her I was fine when I'd called, her eyes were red, like she'd been crying.

"You haven't even been seen yet?" She ran a hand over my hair like she needed the connection. "How long are they gonna make you wait?"

Dad put an arm around her shoulders and guided her to sit beside me. "Don't make a fuss, Janice. The boy's gonna be just fine. Ain't you, son?"

Although my shoulder hurt like a son-of-a-gun, I was in better shape than Cecil—or the gal in that van. "Worse case, it's only a broken scapula. Bones heal." The young woman's crushed body flashed in my mind again. Would I ever be able to forget her thin frame and dark hair matted with blood?

"Aaron Cooper?" A nurse stood in the doorway between the waiting and exam areas, eyes roving the room.

"Right here," Mama said, jumping up and waving. "He's here."

I rolled my eyes and stood. "Y'all don't need to come back with me. I'm a big boy."

But there was no keeping Mama from walking me into the exam room and then asking Dr. Andrews a million questions. *How bad is the break? Will he need surgery? Just how long does it take for a broken scapula to heal? If it don't heal right, what's next? Will he need physical therapy? When will he be able to get back to work?*

By the time the doctor was done slinging my arm, I was exhausted from both the pain and Mama's incessant questions. Bottom line was I wouldn't be able to go back to work for at least six weeks. And it would put a definite kink in my remodel plans. But like I'd told Mama, bones heal. I'd be out of commission for a while, but that was the extent of it.

"Your private doc will be able to give you a better idea of when you can resume regular activity," Dr. Andrews said. "I'll give you a prescription for pain, but if you can manage it with ibuprofen after a day or two, that's what I'd stick with."

It was another hour before I was sitting in the passenger seat of Dad's car with Mama trying to convince me I should stay with them for a spell.

"I'll be fine on my own," I assured her. It was all I could do to keep my eyes open. The pain was easing up some after taking the Vicodin the doc prescribed, and I just wanted to lay down and sleep for a couple of hours.

"Your mama and me will collect your car from the railyard," Dad said. "We'll get it to you by tonight."

My eyes drifted shut, and I basked in the warmth of the sun pouring through the windshield. "No hurry. I can't drive for a few days anyway."

Mama piped up from the back seat. "That's why you outta stay with us, son. You can't even get yourself groceries with your shoulder like it is." There were worse things I'd have to deal with, considering it was my right arm slinged up. I wasn't about to tell her that, though.

Dad blew out a sigh. "Sweet pea, don't keep fussing at the boy. I'm sure Sarah Beth will be happy to look after him."

For once, Dad butting into my love life didn't grate on my nerves. Maybe him and God were conspiring to get me and Sarah Beth together. If that was true, I wasn't about to fight it.

Sarah Beth

Three days after running into Aaron's parents at church, I hadn't seen the smallest glimpse of my neighbor. I was itching to know if Aaron's daddy had done any snooping on my behalf, but I wasn't about to show up on his doorstep to find out. Just when I needed Jazzy to give me an excuse to go to his place, it seemed she'd kicked the habit of running off.

Gracie Lynn was settling in fine at preschool, although she came home plumb tuckered from all the activity. She expended a whole lot more in a classroom with nineteen other little ones than she did with Mama and me. It was all she could do to keep her eyes open long enough to eat lunch. After she finished off a PB&J and a bowl of grapes, I got her settled on our bed with Jazzy for a nap then went looking for Mama.

Found her in the office on the computer. She glanced up as I walked in. "There's some retro-style flooring on sale at Home Depot. Thought we could take us a look at it tomorrow morning if you got time."

I mulled over Mama's words, picking through each syllable for any hint of sarcasm or disdain, but couldn't find a one. She'd been little Miss Mary Sunshine since Mother's Day. Had I known it would've only taken a nice card and thoughtful gesture to switch her attitude, I would've done it weeks ago.

"That's fine, Mama. We can go right after carrying Gracie Lynn to preschool." I'd told Jenna a few weeks back that I was cautiously optimistic about Mama and me getting along. And that was true. It just seemed every time I started to relax a bit, she turned on me again. So, here I was tiptoeing through every conversation for fear I'd say the wrong thing.

"I'm gonna do some wallpaper stripping in Room 12 while Gracie Lynn's napping." Another day in there, and I'd be ready to paint.

"I'll keep a listen for her. You go on ahead and do what you gotta." Mama's focus was back on the computer.

It had to be near ninety in the sun. That meant the motel room would be stuffy as all get out, even with the windows open, making the chore more of a challenge. Still, I left the door open wide and made sure as much air as possible flowed through. I had me a fan situated in one corner and got it oscillating before I laid out all my equipment: Bottle of warm water, Diff gel, scraper, rubber gloves, and a large garbage bag.

I'd just poured a good amount of diff into the tray when a shadow fell over the doorway. With the sun pouring in the way it was, that's all I could see at first. My pulse kicked up a notch when I realized it was a very tall man. And when I recognized it was Aaron, it kicked up another notch. Only this time it was excitement rather than fear that had it racing.

"Hey, Aaron."

"Hey, Sarah Beth." First thing that struck me was there was a shade of dejection in his tone. Then he stepped inside, and I blinked the sunspots away. Was that a sling on his right arm?

"What happened?" I was at his side in an instant, my heart in my throat. "Did you have an accident?" Before he could answer, I took hold of his good arm and walked him to one of the retro chairs Jenna and me purchased at an estate sale and pointed at it so he'd sit.

"We were bringing the train up from Atlanta last night. About the time we were fixing to cross into Tennessee, we hit a van that was parked on the tracks. Derailed us." His words were matter of fact, which didn't align at all with the strain in his voice and features.

"Wait. What?" I knelt at his feet, struggling to find words. Fact was, there were so many questions bombarding my brain, I didn't know where to start. I looked into his pain-filled eyes. "Did you break your arm?" I ran my gaze over him to see if there were any other signs of injury.

"Scapula," he said. "It'll heal fine on its own. It'll just take a little time." Thank God for that. But there was something more. There had to be with that sadness in his eyes.

"Anyone else hurt?"

His gaze didn't meet mine. "Cecil James, the engineer on the train, had a heart attack."

"Oh, no. I'm so sorry. How bad is it? Will he be okay?"

Aaron rubbed his forehead. "I honestly don't know. He'd been off for weeks because he had bypass surgery. He didn't look too good when he reported last night, so I don't know if he wouldn't have had the heart attack anyway."

I touched his knee. "How bad was it, Aaron?" The idea of a train coming off its tracks was horrifying. It must have been terrifying to experience in real time.

He swallowed and shook his head. When he opened his mouth, nothing came out. Clamping it closed, he pushed out of the chair and turned his back to me—but not before I saw tears in his eyes. My own burned in reaction.

I slowly stood and crossed my arms. If he wanted to talk, he would. I wasn't about to push him before he was ready. But he'd showed up here for a reason. I'd just wait him out.

It was a full two minutes before he turned to me. "There was a car—an old van—on the tracks."

"You couldn't stop in time?"

He shook his head, pressed his finger and thumb into his eyes. "Most people don't realize you can't stop a train like you do a car. There's close to twenty tons of weight barreling down those tracks. Once we hit the emergency brakes"— he shrugged —"it takes a good mile to a mile and a half to stop it. Unless it derails, that is."

I couldn't even picture what a car would look like after being hit with that impact. Enough of a blow to take the train off its tracks. "Was there anyone in the van?" I held my breath. *Please, God, no.*

A tear broke free, and he swiped at it with a jerky move of his hand. "Yeah." He cleared his throat. "A young woman. Couldn't have been older than twenty or so. Just got a quick glimpse before impact."

I covered my mouth with a hand and closed my eyes as a wail rose up my chest and nearly escaped. What was going through her head? Wouldn't you think if you got your car stuck on the track, you'd do whatever you could to get out? Maybe there hadn't been time.

"I couldn't help but think of you," Aaron said. "I know whatever happened with your husband, it was bad. Maybe this woman—girl..."

My mind was racing. What did her death have to do with me? Unless... "You think she did it on purpose?" Tears sprang to my eyes, and I was helpless to stop them. Could her life have been so bad, she would rather end it than live? Suicides happened all the time, didn't they? My legs turned into limp noodles, and I eased into the chair Aaron had been sitting in only a few minutes before.

"I don't know." Aaron rubbed his face with his free hand. "There'll be an investigation. A dozen reports to fill out. A lot of questions that still need answering."

"But you saw her? This girl?"

He nodded. "Whenever there's an accident or the train is stopped, it's my job to do a thorough inspection. So, I walked back to where the van was struck. See if I could figure anything out that might help the investigation."

"It's not your fault," I blurted. "You're not in any trouble, are you?"

He shook his head. "No. But the FTA will still want all the facts, or as many as we can figure."

"FTA?"

"Federal Train Association. Anytime there's an accident and an injury, they get involved."

I stared at the sling holding his right arm to his chest and clenched my hand to keep from touching it. To keep from touching *him*. It was only natural to want to comfort him, wasn't it? "How long are you gonna be off work?"

"Depends." He blew out a breath. "Six weeks, at least."

It'd be hard to do life with one arm out of commission, especially if he was right-handed, which if I remembered correctly, he was. There were a lot of seemingly simple tasks that became near impossible with one arm literally tied up. If Aaron hadn't been anything more than a casual neighbor, I'd still return the favor he'd paid Mama keeping her fed when she didn't have anyone else.

But Aaron wasn't just a casual neighbor. He was a friend, at the very least. And the way I was itching to hold him in my arms and kiss away his hurts, I had me a feeling he was becoming a whole lot more.

Chapter 16

Sarah Beth

There were some that would use the tragedies in the world as an argument against the belief in God. How could a good God allow such evil if He truly loved His children? I'd heard it from time to time growing up—and I'd asked it for myself after a particularly bad fight with Jason. It's kind of a stretch to believe in a loving Father when you carry the marks of your husband's abuse—both physical and emotional.

When I thought about the girl who was killed by Aaron's train, other questions flooded my thoughts. Did she know Jesus? Was she now with Him in heaven? And if not... Well, it was too hard to think on for long. But it made me realize how important it was that I instilled that love for Jesus in Gracie Lynn.

It started with a verse the pastor shared on Sunday. It was out of the book of Matthew about the greatest commandment to love the Lord with everything we have in us. Then he said the second was to love our neighbor as ourselves. That's what I was fixing to teach Gracie Lynn—and I was hoping it'd rub off on Mama—when I planned out our meals for the week.

It was just as easy to cook for four as it was for three. I doubled up on the black-eyed peas I'd put in the crockpot first thing that morning and made a mess of fried chicken. At five that evening, I got Mama and Gracie Lynn's supper on the table, called them in to eat, and started bagging up some leftovers for Aaron.

While Gracie Lynn climbed into the chair at her place, Mama passed through the kitchen and peered over my shoulder. "What'cha you doin'?"

"I'm gonna take some food over to Aaron." I nudged her slightly so I could reach the sink to rinse my hands.

"He got himself a mama, don't he? I'm sure she'll look after him just fine."

"What's wrong with Mr. Aaron?" Gracie Lynn asked. "Is he sick?"

Wiping my hands on a towel, I ignored Mama and crouched in front of her. "Remember, I told you his train was in an accident?"

"Uh-huh." She picked at the crust on her chicken leg. "He hurt himself."

"Yes, he did. He's got one arm in a sling, so it's kind of hard for him to fix a meal."

Mama snorted. "Why're you makin' such a fuss? He can throw a frozen dinner in the microwave, can't he?"

Clucking my tongue, I glanced at Mama. "Did you forget how he tended to you before I came home? You'd have starved to death if it weren't for him." I fingered a strand of baby-fine hair from Gracie Lynn's cheek and waited until our eyes caught. "We're returning a kindness. Loving our neighbor as ourselves, like Jesus says to do."

Gracie Lynn smiled. "Can I come with you?"

I stood and kissed her head. "Not this time, baby girl. But maybe tomorrow after I collect you from preschool, you can help me take a couple meals to him. Right now, I want you to eat your supper, and I'll be home soon."

I grabbed the bag of food and left the kitchen, Mama right on my heels. "I won't be long. If Gracie Lynn finishes supper before I'm back, could you have her brush her teeth?"

Mama stepped around me and blocked my path, hands planted on her scrawny hips. "Is there somethin' goin' on between the two of you?"

I took a line from Aaron's playbook. "Just being neighborly."

"If that's all there is to it, why'd you change into a fancy blouse?"

It took all my control to keep from rolling my eyes. "I got a stain on the other and have it soaking, is all." I didn't own anything *fancy*, but this was the closest to it I had. Nothing wrong with putting my best foot forward.

She twisted her mouth like she'd sucked a lemon. "You keep this up, you're gonna get hurt."

I let out a sigh. "Honestly, Mama, I'm only trying to return the favor he paid you. If you're so concerned, maybe you should be takin' this to him." I offered her the bag.

Clenching her hands, she turned and marched back to the kitchen. No surprise there. Could be my kindness toward Aaron was enough to shift Mama back to her cantankerous ways.

When I stepped outside, the scent of summer brought a smile to my soul and eased the tension in my shoulders. Rich earth, wildflower blossoms, and the sweet scent of magnolias. I pushed my way through the bushes that had grown over the path between the motel and Aaron's place while birds twittered above me, harmonizing with the thrumming of cicadas. A cardinal swooped from one limb to another, its bright red body a stark contrast to the foliage in the trees. Never saw the likes of it when I lived in L.A.

The pathway ended at the back end of Aaron's yard. The patio he'd been working on with his daddy and brother appeared to be finished, if not a little stark. A few potted plants and maybe a couple of patio chairs would look real nice. I crossed it to reach the back door, and a sudden grip of shyness slowed my steps. What if he was sleeping? Or maybe he had company. The windows were open, and I strained to listen for conversation.

"You gonna stand there all evening or knock?" Aaron's voice had me nearly jumping out of my skin, and I fumbled the bag of food. Once I got a good hold on it, I peered at the shadow of him through the window screen to the left of me. "You scared the daylights out of me."

He moved out of sight for the brief time it took him to open the door. "You're the one skulking around in my yard." Opening the door wide, he said, "Come on in. Whatever you've got there smells good." He was wearing gray sweats that appeared a size too large, paired with a short-sleeve, button-up shirt. I'd only ever seen him in jeans and t-shirts, which would be near impossible to put on and take off with his shoulder the way it was. Of course, buttoning anything one-handed would be an all-day task for me. Especially with my *left* hand.

Stepping into his kitchen had my pulse racing a bit. Could he see it thrumming in my neck? "Fried chicken and black-eyed peas. Figured you could use a good home-cooked meal." He dwarfed the enclosed space. I glanced around to see if I could get a sense of his taste. Everything looked brand-spanking-new—white cabinets, black granite counters, and white herringbone backsplash. Aside from the pile of dishes in the sink, it was clean and somewhat sterile. But that was probably the 'in' thing these days. What did I know about décor?

"That's thoughtful of you." He took the sack and set it on the counter. "But completely unnecessary." He pulled the fridge door open and tilted his head, inviting me to look inside. It was stuffed full of casserole dishes. "And if this ain't a sight, the freezer's just as packed."

"You're mama?"

His crooked smile made his eyes twinkle. "Mama, sister, and a couple of their friends."

"I suppose you're set for food, then." I pointed to his sling. "How're you feeling? Does your shoulder still ache a lot?"

"Nah." He shrugged, then winced. "Unless I move it."

How in the world did he even dress himself? "Do you have someone coming to help with the basics?"

"I'm fine, really." He fingered open the bag of food I'd brought and peered inside. "You got enough here for an army."

"Apparently, more than you need." I hugged my chest, feeling awkward as a nerd at the cool kids' party. "You've been so kind to us—Mama, Gracie Lynn and me—I just wanted to return the favor. Guess I should've asked first."

"You wanna do something for me?"

"Anything." It would be a relief to pay him back even a fraction.

"Help me eat some of this food you brought and sit with me a spell. I feel like a caged animal with nothing to do and nowhere to go."

I might've told Mama I was just being neighborly, but the thrum of excitement that moved through my blood at the thought of spending time with Aaron said something different.

"Sure." My voice sounded a bit breathless on account of that pulse going crazy. "Have yourself a seat, and I'll get us fixed up in no time."

Aaron directed me as I collected plates and utensils. My stomach did a flip or two as I unwrapped the chicken. I would've thought it was hunger pains, except my fingers were trembling, too. I hadn't been this nervous since my first date with Jason, and look how that went sideways. *Get a grip, girl, he's nothing more than a friend.*

But Jenna was a friend, too, and I didn't get all fluttery when I was with her.

Aaron

Sarah Beth showing up at my back door was like a balm to my worn-out soul. It would be easy to fall into self-pity what with my bum shoulder making even the most insignificant chore a challenge. I'd taken simple things for granted—like being able to dress myself and brush my teeth without making a mess of it. But I was alive. And I reminded myself of that fact the second I got frustrated. The girl that got killed couldn't say the same. Still didn't know anything more, but it didn't lessen the tragedy any.

"How's your friend doing? Cecil is it?" Sarah Beth's question cut into my thoughts as she put a plate of food in front of me then sat down with her own.

A whiff of lavender hijacked my brain for a beat. Her shampoo, maybe? "Good memory." She had real nice hair—soft-looking and shiny. "He...uh...I mean, it looks like he'll pull through. Talked to his wife this morning, and she's gonna make sure he puts in for retirement first thing." Glancing down at my plate, I frowned. My meat was cut into bite-sized pieces.

"That's good, I was praying—is something wrong?" Sarah Beth's question sounded hesitant.

"You cut my chicken."

"Oh, I'm sorry." She jumped up and reached for my plate, blessing me with another whiff of lavender. "Guess I should've asked first. I'll get you a fresh piece."

"No, it's fine." I took hold of her wrist to stop her from taking the food away. "Surprised me is all." Her skin was soft and warm. It was a shame I had to let loose. "In a good way. A lot easier to eat like this." Even if it did make me feel like an invalid.

She stepped back and rubbed her wrist, her face flush. *Idiot.* I figured she'd been abused, so my touching her like that—well, it could've caused her to feel manhandled. That was the last thing I wanted.

"Now it's my turn to apologize." There was an elephant in the room, and one of us would have to point it out. "I didn't mean to scare you."

Her cornflower blue eyes went wide. "Scare me?" Frowning, she shook her head and sat back down. "Why would you think that?" Maybe because she was all of a sudden fascinated with the food on her plate.

"Your reaction when I touched you."

Shrugging, she let out a soft laugh. "It wasn't fear. It's just been a long time—" She bit her lower lip and lifted her eyes to mine. "You didn't scare me." Her gaze was unwavering, so I had to think she was telling the truth. Still, the heaviness of her past now filled the room.

"Am I wrong believing your husband was..." What would be the least offensive word? There wasn't one. "Did he abuse you, Sarah Beth?" The thought of it had my gut clenching. She was small-boned, delicate.

Sarah Beth pushed her plate of food aside and slumped back in the chair. "Guess you could say that." Her chin trembled, eyes wary.

I couldn't stomach *any* abuse, but for a man to overpower a defenseless woman—it was unconscionable. And a child? "Gracie Lynn?"

She scraped her hair back with a sigh. "No. But she was exposed to enough that I worry for her."

Questions ran through my brain. *Why did you stay? How bad did it get? Why didn't you press charges? How could you not see you deserved better?* My teeth were so tightly clenched, I couldn't get a word out. And maybe now wasn't the time to ask them. This was the first glimmer she'd given me into her past. If I started bombarding her with questions that might get her defenses up, I'd trample over what little headway we'd made.

When I could find my tongue, I focused on what appeared uppermost in her mind. "Kids are resilient. Leastways, that's what I've always heard." *Says the man who hasn't gotten past his own past.* "Gracie Lynn seems like a normal four-year-old far as I can tell. In fact, she's a whole lot more outgoing than my nephew, who's around the same age."

Sarah Beth leaned forward and rested her elbows on the table, her features relaxing. If she was anything like me, she'd rather discuss the price of soybeans than her own issues. "Since your brother's having his first, I'm guessing your sister has the little boy?"

I nodded. "Yep. Carrie and my brother-in-law Russell have a boy *and* a girl. Nelson is their son, and he's fixin' to start kindergarten in September. Then they have Katie, who turned three a couple months ago. Right before you came onto the scene, as a matter of fact." The change of subject eased the tension that had been hanging over us like a dark cloud since I touched Sarah Beth.

"Does your sister live nearby?" Sarah Beth slid her plate toward her and picked up a chicken leg.

"Chattanooga." I dipped my spoon into the black-eyed peas. Probably cold by now, but beggars couldn't be choosy. I would've eaten fried squirrel if it would keep Sarah Beth with me a little longer.

"That's nice y'all are so close together. I didn't even have me a cousin growing up. I used to dream about having a sister." She laughed. "I would've settled for a brother." Then her smile wavered. "And now Gracie Lynn's in the same way. No relatives to speak of. Except me and Mama, that is." The way she talked, her life was set in stone.

"You're young." I forked a piece of chicken. "You might remarry and have yourself a passel of kids still."

She shook her head. "I doubt it."

What if she found her dad, and he had a whole ready-made family for her? Would that be a blessing or a curse? Before I could ask, my cell blared from the kitchen counter. I scowled at it. There was no one I wanted to talk to more than Sarah Beth, but it wouldn't hurt to check the caller I.D.

Pushing back from the table, I crossed the kitchen in two strides and peered at the screen. Dad. Raising the phone, I glanced at Sarah Beth. "I gotta get this." Dad didn't usually call for no good reason. Now, if it was Mama, that'd be a whole different story.

"Hey, Dad. What's up?"

"Got myself a line on Sarah Beth's mystery man. Garrett Marshall." As if I wouldn't know who he was referring to.

"Yeah?" It wasn't coincidence that I'd been thinking of the possibility that very moment. Could it be Sarah Beth was right—God was in the middle of this?

"Yep. Lives down in Peachtree. Works for CSX railroad. Used to be he was with Norfolk Southern but quit some thirty years ago."

I riffled through my junk drawer to find a pen and something to write on. "You got an address?"

He rattled off the information, and I tried to scribble it down on an old Walmart receipt. With no way to anchor the scrap paper in place, it was like chasing a fly. "Hold on, Dad."

I turned to Sarah Beth and handed her the receipt and pen. "Can you take an address for me?"

"Sure." She wrote down what I repeated then showed it to me. "Is that it?"

"Yeah, thanks."

"Is that Sarah Beth?" Dad sounded pleased as punch.

"Yep. Listen, Dad, did you talk to the guy?"

A beat of silence, like he was put off. After a deep sigh, he said, "Nope. And my name's not to be mentioned, you hear? Don't need to get my wrist slapped after only bein' on the job a week."

"Promise. Thanks." I ended the call before he could ask any more questions.

When I sat back down, Sarah Beth pushed the receipt to me. "That have anything to do with Garrett Marshall?" Eyebrows arched, it appeared she was holding her breath. What if this turned out to be a wild hog chase? She'd had enough disappointment for a couple lifetimes.

"Yeah." I blew out a breath and studied her face. Eyes sparkling with excitement, cheeks flushed. Dad said the guy quit Norfolk about thirty years ago. "How old are you?"

Her mouth turned down. "Twenty-nine. Why?"

The timeline fit. "Are you sure you wanna open this can of worms?"

She hooked a strand of hair behind her ear and shrugged. "What do I have to lose?"

I could think of a few things. "I know you and your mama have a complicated relationship, but she's the only one you got." What if they butted heads over this and Sarah Beth left? The thought of it didn't sit well in my gut.

"That's true."

"And what if this guy turns out to be everything your mama said he was. Haven't you been hurt enough?"

She rubbed her face and let out a sigh. "Mama said he was dead." Her eyes caught mine. "I gotta know, Aaron. Maybe he turns out to be nothing more than a random guy who sent her a letter a long time ago. But if not—if he's really my daddy…"

I nodded. "Okay, then. Let me know when you wanna meet him, and I'll go with you."

Chapter 17

Sarah Beth

Life is unpredictable, which to some might be exciting. Never knowing what was going to occur could seem like an adventure. Growing up, I feared I'd die of boredom—the same ol' thing day in and day out. Nothing to look forward to.

What I wouldn't give for a little of that now.

When I was a senior in high school, my English class did a unit on Greek Mythology. I thought it was fascinating, although a few of the stories were enough to give me nightmares. Those gods had nothing on Freddy Kruger. One story in particular I thought about every now and again was the myth of Pandora's Box. I couldn't recall which god caused the ruckus—I think it might have been Zeus—but the moral stuck with me. *Be careful what you wish for.*

I learned that firsthand after I ran off with Jason. He was going to take me from my dull-as-dishwater existence. And boy, did he. But just like Pandora opening the box and letting loose all kinds of suffering and evil, marrying Jason did the same for me.

I'd told Aaron last night I had nothing to lose by meeting the man who might be my father. But I learned long ago things can always get worse. I jumped from the fire to the frying pan when I left Mama. And here I was, faced with another potentially life-altering decision.

Should I forget all about Garrett Marshall or take a chance that it might cause more pain? If it was only me that could be affected, it'd be an easy answer. But when I went to bed last night, my mind was spinning with how this could hurt Mama—probably would if this guy really was my daddy.

Then again, I was as certain God was opening this door for me. Of course, I could be wrong about that, too. Wouldn't it be great if the Lord handed us an answer clear as a text or email? Then there would be no guessing. *And no reason to be soaked in prayer.* It'd be real difficult to get close to God if we never spent time with Him.

Bleary-eyed from little sleep, I dragged myself out of bed before the sun rose on account of Jazzy's whining. After collecting her from the crate, I snagged the leash and took the both of us outside. The fresh air cleared the fog enough for me to look up at the half-moon that hung over the ancient magnolias tunneling the driveway. A few stars still twinkled in the indigo sky, and I drew in a deep, cleansing breath as I gazed at them. *Thank You, Lord, for Your creation.*

The tension of the long night eased from my shoulders as I clipped the leash to Jazzy and walked her to the side of the motel. Aaron had completed the playground project a couple weeks before, but I still got a little jolt of surprise when I saw it. The fenced pool beyond was still in disgraceful shape. Until we knew if the motel would survive, it didn't make sense to sink any more money than we needed to into it.

Jazzy yipped, and I looked down at her. "You all done, girl?"

She bounced up on her back legs—a sure sign she wanted to be picked up. I cuddled her soft neck as we walked inside. It had been enough that she brought Gracie Lynn joy, but I hadn't expected she'd grow on Mama and me, too. Not that having a puppy didn't come without challenges. She had an obsession with loose socks and still piddled on the carpet now and again.

I tiptoed into the bedroom, careful to not wake Gracie Lynn, and put Jazzy back in her crate. My Bible and devotional were sitting on the edge of my small desk, and I hugged them to my chest, intent on getting a little study time in before starting the day.

"Mama?" Gracie Lynn sat up and rubbed her eyes. "Is it time for school?"

So much for peace and quiet. I set the books back down with a sigh, crossed to the bed, and sat. "It's still early, baby girl." Fingering her hair from her face, I tried to make out her features in the dawn light coming through the window.

"But I'm woked up now." She pushed the blanket aside. "And I'm hungry."

Guess I'd have to put God on the back burner again, something I surely didn't want to make a habit.

Bound and determined to get another room painted before the day was out, I sweet-talked Mama into carrying Gracie Lynn to preschool for me. Most mornings, she was more than happy to oblige. This particular day she was in a mood because I wasn't home from Aaron's straight away last night. Mama always could carry a grudge to the point it came back to bite her.

The insects were becoming a nuisance, so I left the door closed but opened all the windows. Had me two fans blowing to get the warm air moving and help with fumes. Jenna had helped me pick out a beautiful shade of blue—called Palladian—that reminded me of the turquoise color popular in the fifties. I was itching to see how it'd transform the room from something time forgot to...well, I wasn't sure what.

It might seem silly, but I watched some YouTube videos to see the best way to paint. Jenna said it was nearly impossible to mess up this chore, but I wasn't taking any chances. I'd gotten everything taped off and was fixing to start with the edges when a shadow fell over the window. Aaron. He used his good hand to tent his eyes and had his face pressed up to the screen. Just seeing him there got my heart flipping every which way.

"Sarah Beth? You in there?"

"Yeah. Come on in." I was kneeling over the can of paint I'd just opened, a stir stick in my hand. "But watch your step." Last thing he needed was to trip over a drop cloth and injure his other shoulder.

He slipped inside, dwarfing the room, and smiled at me. "Hey."

"Hey, yourself." If I didn't get my heart rate settled, I'd have paint splotches everywhere. "How're you doing this morning?"

Mouth turned down slightly, he nodded and closed the door. "As long as I'm on this side of the grass, I'm good." His gaze homed in on the paint. "Nice shade of blue."

I dipped the stir stick into the can and swished it. Mostly so my eyes had somewhere to focus besides his bare legs. He was wearing shorts, and although they nearly went to his knees, what showed was still impressive. Muscled calves covered by a smattering of light hair. "You a paint-color expert?"

"Sure. When it comes to black and white."

I laughed and tilted my head to see him smiling. "Technically, I don't think those are actual colors."

He shrugged. "I like things simple." Which is what I assumed after seeing his kitchen last night. "Besides which, do you know how many shades of white there are?" He snorted. "It was enough to give me fits trying to pick the right one for my house." He gazed around the room "You need some help?"

I arched my brows. "I can make enough of a mess without you adding to it." If he couldn't button a pair of jeans with his left hand, it was anyone's guess how he'd do with a paintbrush.

"You worried I'll make a mess on your"—he frowned at the brown in-door/outdoor carpeting—"fancy flooring?"

Wrinkling my nose, I sighed. "It's awful, isn't it?"

"Even a color-blind fool like me knows it won't look good with that blue you picked out for the walls."

I brushed the stir stick clean and set it on the paint lid. "I'm gonna replace it. Eventually." One of those chores that would take elbow grease *and* money. "Found what I want at Home Depot. And I've been educating myself on the art of installation by watching YouTube." I started to drag the ladder to the corner where I planned to start.

"Ah." He edged me aside and picked up the ladder with his good hand. "Where d'you want it?"

I pointed. "Thanks."

He moved the monstrosity like it weighed no more than Jazzy. "You gonna do linoleum, tile, or carpeting?"

"Linoleum tiles." I picked up the paint can and my edging brush. "Found a great white and blue parquet that matches this paint to a T."

"I can help." The doubt must've been written on my face, because he laughed. "Okay, I can supervise. I've done a few floor installs in my time. And if you need a discount, I have a contractor-friend who gets me a good deal. You show me what you want, and I'll even get it ordered for you."

More favors. I could get used to this, and then where would I be? "Thank you, Aaron. You're very kind."

Was he blushing? "No problem." He cleared his throat. "So, any idea when you'd like to take a drive down to Peachtree?"

"What's in Peachtree?"

I turned to find Jenna standing in the doorway, a white bakery sack in her hand. "Hey, there. I didn't know you were stopping by." How had we not noticed the door opening?

"Brought some cronuts to give you energy." She glanced at Aaron. "Y'all planning a romantic getaway?"

I wish. The spontaneous thought had my face heating clear to my hairline. Where had *that* come from? Things were complicated enough without me losing my head over another man. Even one as sweet and cute as Aaron. And if him staring at the floor was a clue, he wasn't the least bit comfortable with idea, either.

That was good, right? So, why the tug of disappointment on my heart?

Aaron

I wasn't aware of any man who fully understood the perplexing species known as woman. I figured long ago that God had a sense of humor making us so different from one another, there were actually books written on the subject. An efficient translator would make a killing. I'd pay to know why Sarah Beth went beet red at Jenna's joke about us being romantically involved.

Of course, I had my own secrets that were hard to ignore with Jenna's appearance. When she wasn't around, I could forget there was still a lie between Sarah Beth and me, even if it seemed insignificant in the scheme of things. It would be simple enough to fix—just tell Sarah Beth that I'd been interested in buying the motel property. No biggie. Except with all the deceit she'd already been dealt, it could get blown way out of proportion.

"The two of you are awful serious for such a beautiful, spring day." Jenna opened the bag and waved it under my nose. The unmistakable scent of deep-fried cronuts made my stomach rumble. "You need yourself a little sugar." Then her gaze landed on my sling, and her eyes went wide. "What happened?"

To buy myself a slight reprieve from repeating the story *again*, I reached into the bag and pulled out a glazed pastry. "It's no big deal. Work injury."

Sarah Beth's mouth dropped open. "No big deal?" With a shake of her head, she blew out a huff of air. "His train derailed, Jenna. He broke his shoulder—"

"Scapula," I corrected.

"—his friend had a heart attack," she continued, throwing a glare at me, "and a girl was killed."

Jenna nabbed a cronut and handed the bag to Sarah Beth. "Seriously?" Brow furrowed, she looked at me. "Is your friend okay?"

"He will be." The sugary glaze covering the pastry was melting, so I took a bite. It was either that or find somewhere to stash it.

"When did all this happen?"

Sarah Beth dipped into the bag. "Sunday."

Jenna teetered across the room in ridiculously high heels and plopped onto a metal chair stashed in the corner. "And I'm only hearing about it now?" She picked off a piece of the cronut and popped it into her mouth.

"We haven't talked since." Sarah Beth wiped her sugary fingers on the seat of her jeans.

"We're friends, aren't we?" Jenna mumbled around a mouthful. "You should've called."

If I had anything better to do, and I do mean *anything*, I would've hightailed it out of there. My day was one, long snooze-fest. Besides, I'd planned to help Sarah Beth, and there was no way Jenna was going to be any good dressed like she was. She's what Carrie would call "high maintenance." I preferred Sarah Beth's ripped jeans and threadbare t-shirt. And unless I was mistaken, there wasn't even a smudge of war paint on her face.

"I've been a little busy here." Sarah Beth waved the paintbrush in the air. "Besides, with all your contacts, I'm surprised you didn't know about it before I did."

Jenna held a finger to her mouth and swallowed. "Actually, I did hear about the girl who was killed, but I didn't realize it was your train involved, Aaron." Her eyes teared as she gazed at me. "I'm so sorry. That must've been horrible."

I nodded. "Not for me as much as everyone else."

"Did the car get stuck on the tracks?"

I shrugged, then paid the price when pain radiated down my arm. "It's still under investigation."

Jenna blew out a sigh and was quiet for all of five seconds. "So, what's in Peachtree?"

Leaning against the wall, I looked at Sarah Beth. This was her story to tell.

"Maybe nothing." Sarah Beth dipped the brush into the paint then scraped most of it off on the side of the can. "Or, maybe everything."

Jenna scowled. "We're talkin' in riddles now?"

Crouching to the floor, Sarah Beth cut a swath of paint just above the baseboard. Did she know it would need to come out when she installed the linoleum? "Aaron's daddy found Garrett Marshall." Face averted like it was, she couldn't see Jenna's mouth-dropping reaction.

Jenna turned to me. "He's in Peachtree? Are y'all gonna go down there and confront him?"

I waited for Sarah Beth to answer, but she just dipped the brush into the paint can, lips tight.

"That's up to Sarah Beth," I finally said. "And just so you both know, we need to keep my dad's name out of this. It could cause him grief if anyone discovers he was snooping where he didn't rightly belong."

"Won't say a word." Jenna swiped her fingers across her lips like she was zipping them closed.

Sarah Beth set the paintbrush on the edge of the can with a sigh. "I'm not even for sure we should talk to him."

It was a relief to know she wasn't jumping in with both feet. Her meeting this guy could have a ripple effect. One small stone thrown into calm waters. Who knew where it might lead?

Jenna huffed. "I thought you said God led you to this guy. If that's true, wouldn't He want you to pursue it?"

She shrugged. "Maybe. But for all I know that envelope was from some random friend of Mama's."

"Then what's the harm in talking to him?" Jenna said.

Sarah Beth had that deer-in-the-headlights look about her. Whichever way she turned, she might be left with regrets. But she didn't need anyone talking her into something she clearly wasn't ready for.

"Don't push, Jenna," I said. "Give her the space she needs to figure this out for herself."

Sarah Beth offered me what I took as a grateful smile. Had she ever been free to make decisions for herself without a fight? Miss Pickett didn't strike me as the kind of mama who'd give her little girl the chance to think for herself. And it was a sure bet, Sarah Beth's monster-of-a-husband kept her on a tight leash.

"Whatever you decide, Sarah Beth, I'm here for you." Jenna stood up and glanced at her watch. "Right now, I have an appointment near Lookout Mountain, and I gotta get going." She hugged Sarah Beth real quick before turning to me. "You need anything? I make a mean tuna casserole."

Yuck. "Thanks, but I'm good." I gave her an awkward side hug before she slipped out the door.

The sudden quiet was deafening. Jenna showing up like she did disrupted the ease between Sarah Beth and me. I pointed to the three-inch swath of blue she'd applied above the baseboard. "It's a good color."

Her features relaxed into a smile. "Just what I pictured."

I rubbed my chin. "You do know the baseboard's gonna have to be replaced when you do the flooring, don't you?"

The smile disappeared quick as it came. "You mean I should've done the flooring *first*?"

I shook my head. "Not unless you wanna worry about spilling paint on it." Her crestfallen expression had me wanting to give her the moon. "We just need to pull up this old baseboard before you go any farther. We paint close to the floor as possible and cover it up with the new trim."

Scraping her hair back, she blew out a sigh big as the room. "I'm way over my head here, Aaron. I'm afraid I'm gonna make a mess of everything." Her shoulders drooped like she was carrying the world on them, and I had me a feeling she wasn't just talking about the remodel.

"It'll be okay." I put my good arm around her shoulders and squeezed them. Wanted to hug her real close, but I didn't want to spook her. "I'm here to help. Can't go back to work for another six weeks or more, and by that time, you'll be an expert."

She relaxed against me, laying her head on my shoulder. "It's not just the remodel," she whispered.

I dared to drop a kiss on the top of her head, that lavender fragrance overwhelming my senses. "I know. Either way, I'm here."

For the first time in my life, I meant it.

Chapter 18

Sarah Beth

Three days of wrestling with my past and praying for a hint of what God wanted me to do, and it was finally settled. He didn't shut any doors, and there was no peace in abandoning the notion. If I didn't at least meet Garrett Marshall, I'd regret it for the rest of my life. If he wasn't my daddy, then all I would lose was a day of travel down to Peachtree and back. Of course, Aaron would be losing the day, too, but he did offer to take me, so I refused to feel guilty over that. I had enough wearing down my heart as it was.

I texted Aaron about my decision, and he suggested we wait until Saturday so the traffic through Atlanta wouldn't be so heavy. His only stipulation was that we take his truck. Fearing my old car couldn't make the trip anyway, I agreed. It had been a while since I'd driven anything big as his vehicle, but it had enough dents and scratches that another one or two wouldn't make much difference.

The one snag in my plan was Mama. Lying to her didn't sit well with me, and it certainly went against the command to honor her. If I hadn't recommitted my life to God, I might could justify it. After all, if she hadn't lied to me about my daddy in the first place, I wouldn't need to sneak around behind her back. *If.* That little, two-letter word held a wealth of power.

I heard someone say once, "It's easier to ask for forgiveness than permission." I doubted Jesus saw it that way. A heart turned toward deception wasn't in line with His commands. But if (there was that word again) this trip to Peachtree proved Mama to be a liar, I'd come clean about my own deceit. Until then, I'd settle for a half-truth. That was the best I could do under these circumstances.

I got up before the sun on Saturday morning and put together some snacks for Aaron and me to get us through the day—a couple apples, granola bars, and a small bag of chips. Guilt had me up extra early, giving me time to whip up some pancake batter so Gracie Lynn and Mama would have a decent breakfast. It's what I was doing when Mama shuffled into the kitchen.

"Thought you and your friend was heading down to Atlanta early for them garage sales."

"Estate sales, Mama." How far I'd fallen to correct her about my lie. "And you know good and well her name is Jenna." Irritation with her poor attitude somehow made my shame a bit more bearable. "What have you got against her, anyway? She's been nothing but kind to you."

Mama snorted. "It's a cover. I done told you she was fixin' to talk me into selling this place to that neighbor you're sweet on." She hugged her thin housecoat closed. "You better watch your back."

Anger at her for misjudging Jenna and Aaron, and knowing she'd been right about Jason, warred within me like fiery arrows. "I'm not sweet on him," I mumbled.

She *tsked*. "Whatever you say. What time is she pickin' you up? If you're okay with me using your car, I thought me and Gracie Lynn would go to the park for a spell then to Crumpies for ice cream later this afternoon."

"I'm meeting her in town." Another lie. I couldn't take the chance Mama might see me sneaking to Aaron's or watching for Jenna's car, so I decided to drive over and pretend I was going into Rossville. *What a tangled web we weave, when we first practice to deceive.* Like Pandora's Box, this was another bit of knowledge from high school I could do without.

I kept my mind occupied getting Gracie Lynn up, Jazzy fed, and a batch of chocolate chip pancakes sizzling on the griddle. "There's a stack in the oven keeping warm," I told Mama as I handed her the spatula. "I should be home before supper." I hugged Gracie Lynn real quick and escaped while I could.

It was downright silly of me to drive next door and hide my car on the far side of Aaron's house. But if by some crazy chance Mama happened over, I didn't want her to see it. Maybe I should've come up with a better plan. Then at least I wouldn't have deprived Gracie Lynn of a rare outing with Mama. I wasn't cut out for deception. Never would've made it as an international spy, as if I could aspire to anything loftier than a motel proprietor.

Aaron's truck wasn't in the drive—instead there was a dark gray Acura. Not quite as fancy as Jenna's, but it still stirred up a little car-envy. Did he have himself a visitor?

"Hey, Sarah Beth." Aaron came out the front door, a key fob hanging off his finger, sunglasses perched on top of his head. Even with the sling on his arm, he was an adonis. Made me wish I was open to an entanglement after all. "Like the ride?"

Dragging my gaze from him, I focused on the car. "What's not to like? Is it yours?" Would I ever be able to afford something even half as nice?

"Nope. It's my dad's. I had him swap with me. Gets better gas mileage, plus, it's a lot easier to drive." He held out the fob.

Instead of taking it, I put my hand behind my back. "Oh, no. You said we were gonna take your truck." What if I scratched his daddy's car? Or worse, sideswiped someone with it? "I can't drive this."

His lips quirked. It was downright ungentlemanly of him to be amused at my discomfort. "Come on. We're wasting daylight." He dangled the key in front of my face.

What choice did I have? I blew out a breath and snatched it from him. "Fine. But if I wreck your daddy's car, it's on you."

Laughing, he opened the driver's door. "Your chariot awaits."

My face was warm as I got behind the wheel and fumbled around to put the bag of snacks and my purse on the floor in back. No one had ever opened a door for me before. How pathetic was it that I got all flustered over good manners? The black leather seat was as soft and comfy as a Lazy-Boy recliner. I might just be a motel-living girl, but I could get used to such luxuries.

Aaron slid into the passenger side and wrestled to get the seatbelt over his sling, challenged by one working arm. Without giving it a second thought I leaned across him, careful not to jostle his shoulder, and took hold of the buckle. My head scraped across his chin, my nose nearly buried in his chest. He smelled so good. No cologne for him—just a mixture of sunshine and laundry detergent with a hint of musk.

Heat climbed up my face as I snapped the buckle in place and pulled away. Either I was going through early menopause or his nearness caused spontaneous sparks inside of me.

"Thanks," he said.

Was it my imagination or was his voice was a little strained? Wishful thinking was all. He could have his choice of women, so the idea that I might could affect him the way he affected me was pure fantasy. And foolhardy. I'd vowed not to fall for another man as long as I lived. And here I was, only widowed for a few months, letting the first guy that came along get me all flustered. Foolhardy for sure.

Aaron

The truck might have been a safer option, after all. More space between Sarah Beth and me. Not that I was complaining. The way she pulled away after helping me buckle up was a sign she wasn't comfortable with me being so close. It wasn't easy for me, either. I'd never smell lavender again without picturing her.

I plugged the address Dad had scribbled down into the car's GPS as Sarah Beth reached behind my seat to retrieve her purse. She pulled out a pair of sunglasses and pushed them onto her nose so quick, I had to wonder if she was hiding behind them. Think it was Shakespeare who said the eyes are the window to the soul. Sarah Beth's were the color of the Mediterranean Sea. Beautiful and expressive. Maybe it was best she hid them from me. It'd be near impossible to stay focused on directions with her so close as it was.

When we were kids, our vacations consisted of road trips Mama and Dad thought would be educational. No Disney World for us. Dad was a history buff, so he was like a kid on Christmas when we visited Gettysburg. There were plenty of Civil War sites in the South, and I'd seen more than my share throughout childhood. Once I hit twelve, Mama decided I'd be the navigator. I'd wrestle with a roadmap—our directions highlighted in bright yellow—spread out across half the back seat. My eyes would be glued so hard on those squiggly lines, I never saw much out the window. Thank the Lord for technology. Now I could steal glances at Sarah Beth's pretty face and still get us to Peachtree without worrying over whether we missed a turn along the way.

"It's a little over two-and-a-half hours." I was telling Sarah Beth what she already knew, but with her sweet scent filling up the car, my brain went to mush.

"I remember." She cleared her throat and adjusted her glasses. "There's snacks in that bag if you get hungry."

Smart thinking, although I had other ideas. "Thought maybe we could stop for a bite somewhere along the way." Of course, that would require her to help with my seatbelt again. Win-win as far as I was concerned. I could get used to someone fussing over me.

"Oh, okay." She gripped the steering wheel so tight, her knuckles turned white.

It struck me right then I was pretty full of myself for believing her being all jittery had anything to do with me. This could turn out to be a life-altering day for her. "You nervous about meeting Garrett Marshall?" The early morning sun about blinded me when Sarah Beth took a turn. I plucked my sunglasses from the top of my head and put them on.

"I suppose." With a quick lick of her lips, she shrugged. "Haven't given it a whole lot of thought. He might not even be around, and this could be a colossal waste of your time."

"It's fine by me." I wasn't the least bit worried about the time. "I have more of it than I know what to do with until I can get back to work." My concern was leaning toward how it would affect Sarah Beth if she *did* meet the guy. What if he *had* abandoned her? After being raised by a less-than-nurturing mama and surviving an abusive marriage, it would be one more disappointment she didn't need to weather. And if he hadn't abandoned her, then it put her mama in a poor light. That was, if this man was even her daddy. Seemed like a longshot. A random envelope with nothing other than an address. What were the chances?

But since she believed God was showing her the way, I wasn't about to say different. I could do with a little more faith myself. It had been in the back of my mind since the derailment. Could be the train accident wasn't an accident at all, but a divine plan. That wasn't a comfortable place to land, though, considering a life was lost. Then again, who was I to question the ways of the Lord?

After we got onto the highway, Sarah Beth and me made idle chitchat about all sorts of things. Gracie Lynn's feats of fearlessness on the playground, Miss Pickett's recovery from her injury, and the plans Sarah Beth had for the motel. With each mile we covered, she seemed to relax enough that she smiled at me now and again. All was right with my world.

"You hungry?" We'd been driving for about ninety minutes and would be coming into the Atlanta area soon. If we were fixing to stop, it'd be a lot easier before getting into heavier traffic.

"Not really." She grimaced. "Guess I'm getting a little nervous now, and I don't think I could eat anything. But if you wanna stop—"

"No." I'd rather get to Peachtree sooner than later. "I'm fine."

She turned her head my way and maybe glanced at my slinged arm—hard to tell with her sunglasses covering her eyes. "You want something from my bag, I can pull over. There's no way you can reach back there like that."

"I won't starve to death."

Sarah Beth was so focused on the traffic as we drove through Atlanta, every question I asked got a one-word answer. Then again, maybe she was thinking about how this day would play out. Either way, I figured a little peace and quiet couldn't hurt.

It wasn't until we turned onto Kensington Drive, where Garrett Marshall lived, that Sarah Beth said anything. "I don't know if this is such a good idea."

She pushed her sunglasses on top of her head, scraping her hair back from her face in the process.

"Pull over," I suggested. "Let's talk about it."

She eased the car to the curb underneath an old oak and turned off the engine. "What if this is a mistake?"

I stared out the windshield. It was a nice neighborhood. Well-established with older homes and towering trees. The lots were spacious—maybe an acre or so. It would've been a whole lot better growing up here than a motel.

"We can turn right around and go back if you want, Sarah Beth." Either way, it had to be her decision. Maybe she needed a few more minutes to think on it before taking the next step. Or a few weeks. I kept quiet while the birds sang from the trees overhead and the gentle tinkle of wind chimes drifted from a nearby porch. *Help her, Lord. Whatever she does, protect her from being hurt again.*

A full minute later, her voice broke the silence. "Let's do this." She drew in a deep breath and let it out real slow.

I reached for her hand where it sat on her leg and squeezed it. It was the best I could offer given the circumstances. "The address we're looking for is just up here on the right." One quick glance at her ghost-white face, and I figured she could use some fresh air. "Why don't we leave the car here and walk?"

Outside, it was warm and humid. I got a whiff of a sweet scent of something blooming close by—jasmine, maybe. Not that I knew one flower from another. I took Sarah Beth's hand, and her long thin fingers entwined with mine like it was natural as breathing. With a slight tug, I led her down the block.

The single-story brick house was set back from the street a good bit. Its lush front lawn was the dream of every boy who ever spent a lazy Saturday morning playing tag football.

"This is it." We stopped in front of the house. "You want me to wait here?"

Sarah Beth shook her head and looked at me, her fingers tightening around mine. "Come with me. Please?"

In that moment, she appeared as small and fragile as Gracie Lynn. I couldn't have left her then if she'd begged me to.

Chapter 19

Sarah Beth

My heart was pounding against my chest so hard, it was a wonder it didn't jump clear from my body. There was a knot the size of Dollywood growing in my belly and somehow my legs wouldn't work. "Give me a minute," I whispered.

It was an ordinary house. Brick and vinyl, probably forty years old or more —nothing much different than where Jenna grew up. It was set back from a spacious front yard. A sturdy climbing tree in the middle, with thick gnarly branches perfect for a swing.

This could be my daddy's house.

Aaron tugged on my hand. "You okay?"

My brain must've disconnected from my voice, because all I could do now was nod. This was the sort of home I'd wanted growing up. A normal place where I could bring my friends and have slumber parties. Maybe a dog in the backyard and a garage where my daddy would work on his car or build things with wood.

"Are you sure you wanna do this, Sarah Beth?" Aaron's voice cut into my thoughts.

What if I discovered my reality—growing up the way I did with only Mama to care for me—was a whole lot better than the fantasy? If Garrett Marshall was really my daddy, then he abandoned us, just like Mama said. Meeting him wouldn't change the truth of it.

Oh, God, show me what to do. Had I imagined that the Lord led me here? Maybe I'd wanted it so badly, I used Him as an excuse.

I was fixing to tell Aaron we should forget the whole thing and leave when a car turned into the driveway and parked up near the garage. Like a rubber-necker at an accident, my attention locked onto it. The back door flung open, and a little boy hopped out. He ran toward the front porch as the driver's door opened while a little girl came around from the other side of the car.

"Come on, Gampaw. Gammaw's waitin' on us." She followed the boy as a man climbed out and peered our way.

My heart jumped clear to my throat, making it near impossible to draw air. Should I stay or should I go?

Aaron dipped down, his mouth close to my ear. "It's now or never."

"Can I help y'all?" The man called out. He was too far away to get a clear look at his features, and his medium build and height didn't give me any clues.

Aaron tensed, and his hand tightened around mine. "Let's just talk to him. Could be he doesn't even live here."

I drew in a deep breath and let it out real slow. "Okay."

"We're looking for Garrett Marshall," Aaron answered.

The older man started down the driveway. "That's me. What can I do for ya?"

Aaron slipped his hand from mine and gently nudged me forward. "You can do this."

My knees shook like wispy branches in a breeze as we drew closer to the man. He was maybe sixty, thinning white hair, narrow face. Attractive, but I wouldn't have looked twice if we'd met on the street. Unless I'd noticed his eyes. Gracie's eyes. My eyes. The color, the shape. Hadn't Mama said I took after him?

Aaron nudged me. "You wanna introduce yourself, Sarah Beth?"

But it was like I'd lost my voice again, because I opened my mouth, and nothing came out.

"I'm Aaron Cooper." He touched the small of my back. "This here is Sarah Beth McCallister."

Mr. Garrett glanced from Aaron to me, confusion clouding his eyes. "Nice to meet the both of ya." He hitched his thumb toward the house. "My wife's waitin' on me, so if we can make this quick."

He had a family. A wife, grandkids—and at least one child other than me. He walked out on Mama and me and had himself a whole new family. A zing of irritation straightened my spine and loosened my tongue. "Actually, my given name is Sarah Beth *Pickett*." Expecting to see some sign of recognition, I was taken aback when merely shrugged. "My mama is Georgina Pickett." Would he recognize Mama's name? I kept my eyes locked on his face for some sign.

Eyes widening, he stuck out his hand. "Well, I'll be, I didn't know Georgina had herself a daughter. It's nice to meet ya, Sarah Beth."

Instead of shaking his hand, I planted the both of mine on my hips. "So, you know my mama?"

He eased his hand back and wiped it on his jeans, a frown now fixed on his face. "Well, of course. Isn't that why you're here?" His gaze bounced between Aaron and me. "She's doin' okay, I hope."

"Garrett!"

I looked past Mr. Marshall to see a woman standing on the porch, his grandkids on either side of her.

"Everything okay?"

He turned and waved at her. "Give me a minute, Patsy. I'll be right there." When he faced us again, he let out a sigh. "What's this all about?"

Aaron slid his arm across my shoulders and squeezed. "Go on. Ask him."

Tucked against Aaron's side, I felt protected. And strong—or at least not so weak. "Were you married to my mama?"

Mouth turned down, he nodded. "I figured you knew that. I mean, you're here, aren't ya?"

Now I was the one who was confused. "And you walked out on her thirty years ago." The accusation had more heat behind it than I'd intended. But how could this man stand in front of me, knowing he was my daddy, and act like it was no big deal. Maybe it wasn't to him, but it surely was to me.

He lifted his hands, like he was stopping traffic, and took a step back. "Whoa there, that's not exactly how it happened. Seems like you got your facts mixed up some."

I folded my arms across my chest to keep from punching him in the nose. "You left her. That's a fact worth mentioning right there." Heat burning my cheeks, my voice rose with each word until I was nearly shouting.

Aaron tightened his hold on me. "Take a breath, Sarah Beth," he said. "Give him a chance to explain."

Closing my eyes, I rubbed my forehead. "I apologize for snapping at you. But you gotta understand how it hurts to know you don't even care." My voice cracked, tears burning my nose.

Mr. Marshall chewed on his bottom lip—just like I had a tendency to do when I was perplexed—and glanced back at the house. "I think there's been some...miscommunication between you and your mama. Maybe you should come inside where we can talk in private. The neighbors are nosy enough without giving them something to gossip over."

Aaron led me up the drive behind Mr. Marshall—Garrett. I didn't even know what to call him. Either way, were we really going to sit down with his wife and grandkids and talk about how he'd abandoned me before I was even born? It didn't seem to matter a lick to him, which fit right in with what Mama had said about him while I was growing up. Heartless, is how she'd described him. A no-good bum.

Except he didn't strike me as either. Of course, given enough time, some people changed.

When we stepped inside the front door, the temperature dropped a good bit. I hadn't even realized how warm it was outside until we were in the air-conditioned house. The entry hall was cozy with hardwood floors and an antique washstand—like one I'd seen at Dirty Jane's— beneath a tall, narrow mirror.

As we followed Garrett into the front room, his wife appeared. She was slender with short, dark hair and warm brown eyes. "Who do we have here?" Her smile was kind, and a pang of guilt had me wishing for her sake I'd never come.

Garrett tucked his wife to his side, natural as breathing. "Patsy, this is Aaron Cooper and Sarah Beth Pickett—Georgina's daughter." So, Patsy knew all about Mama and him being married. That was a relief. Did she also know he'd walked out on her when she was pregnant with me?

Patsy's smile wobbled some. "It's good to meet the both of you."

Garrett kissed her temple. "Why don't you take Kristy and Jake for an ice cream while I talk to these folks for a spell?"

She huffed out a breath. "They haven't even had lunch yet, Garrett. I've been waitin' on y'all to get back from the park."

He waved away her concern. "Then take 'em to Chic-fil-A."

Patsy opened her mouth like she was fixing to argue with him, then must've changed her mind. "Fine. You want me to bring you back something?"

He shook his head and swept his hand toward the couch. "Y'all have yourself a seat. Want something to drink?"

"Water'd be good," Aaron said as I shook my head.

Garrett followed Patsy out while we sat on the sofa. My stomach was knotted up something awful, and my hands were clammy as a dead fish. The kids' voices carried into the front room, although other than the high pitch of excitement, I couldn't make out what they were saying. Then a door closed, and it was silent.

It struck me right then that Gracie Lynn had herself some cousins. And I had a brother or a sister, just like I'd always dreamed.

The sound of ice tinkling into glasses reached my ears as Aaron took my sweaty hand in his. How could I be hot and cold all at the same time?

"It's gonna be okay." Aaron squeezed my fingers as I drew in a deep breath.

Garrett came out with a tray, carrying three glasses of ice water. There was a bowl of some kind of chips, too. If he thought this was a nice, little social visit, he was delusional. Every muscle in my body was stiff. I didn't know if I was fixing to fight or run. Neither would allow me to stuff the chaos I'd just unleashed back into Pandora's Box.

After setting the tray on the coffee table, Garrett picked up a water and sat on a chair across from us. "Now, let's see if we can't clear up a thing or two." He had a calmness about him that made me want to trust him. Then again, he could just be a smooth operator. "Your mama and me were married for a short time. That's true. I don't know what she told you, but I left because despite trying every which way to convince her otherwise, she decided we'd made a mistake." He appeared sincere, but how could I be sure he wasn't lying?

"When did you leave?" Could it be Mama had been with another man *after*? It didn't seem likely, but it was pretty clear I didn't know her at all, so anything was possible.

Pursing his lips, he glanced up like he was trying to remember. "Let's see. We were married in June of '94, and I believe it was somewhere around Memorial Day the next year she demanded I leave. Fact, she threatened to slap me with a restraining order if I didn't clear out."

My head was swirling with dates and counting out the months. "I was born October of '95." The words came out no louder than a whisper. If this man was telling the truth, Mama was four months pregnant when he left.

Garrett's face drained of color, and he fumbled with the ice water, nearly upending it in his lap. "That can't be," he said through stiff lips. Setting the glass down, he narrowed his eyes on me. "How could she..."

Oh, Mama, what have you done?

"You're my daughter?" He scrubbed his face with his hands and there were tears brimming his eyes. "Oh, Sarah Beth, if I'd known."

A lump grew in my throat, and my eyes burned. He was my daddy. Garrett Marshall was my daddy. But on the tail end of that thought was another—Mama had lied to both of us. All these years, she'd deprived us of a relationship. But why?

I must've muttered the question aloud, because Garrett shook his head and shrugged. "I can't rightly say. It was clear soon as we were married, she was struggling with something."

Aaron cleared his throat. "What d'you mean?"

Jumping up, he raked his hand through his hair. "Not sure how much I should share with y'all." His eyes caught hold of mine. "I'm sick about this, Sarah Beth. Truly sick. If I had known…" He held his hand in the air. "But maybe you should be talking to Georgina about the why of it all."

I didn't know whether to laugh or cry. So many emotions roiled around inside me, it was like a tornado was twisting up my belly. "I can't trust a word out of Mama's mouth. She told me from the time I can remember that you walked out on her when she was pregnant and didn't look back. Never said nothing about it being her choice." I barked out a humorless laugh. "Then when I asked her straight out to tell me about you, she said you were dead and gone. That if I had a notion to find you, I'd be wasting my time."

As I leaned forward and dropped my head into my hands, Aaron rubbed my back. The warmth of his hand soothed the anger coursing through my veins, and I let out a shaky sigh.

Garrett dropped back into his chair. "How *did* you find me?"

I hesitated to answer for fear he'd think I was nuttier than a pecan pie. "Would you believe God led me to you?"

Lips twitching, his eyes softened. "I would, yes. But maybe you could be a bit more specific."

As I reached for a glass of water, Aaron took his hand from my back. I handed him a glass before taking the last on the tray and sipping from it. "I was searching the closet in Mama's office and came across an envelope addressed to her. It had your name on the return label."

Garrett's eyes widened. "That's it?"

I shrugged. "It's a little more involved than that, but that's the gist of it." I didn't want to talk about how I'd prayed for God's guidance and direction. There were more important things to discuss—like what Mama was struggling with that would make her kick him out before they were even married a year. And I couldn't throw Aaron's daddy under the bus after he went out on a limb for me.

After taking a sip of water, I cradled the glass in my hands. "I really need to know what happened, Mr. Marshall. Otherwise, I have nothing to go on other than Mama's lies."

With a shake of his head, he snorted. "Mr. Marshall? I'd say the least you can do is call me Garrett, since it appears I'm your father."

It was mind-jangling enough to know this man was married to Mama without fixing on the fact he was my daddy. "Okay." I blew out a breath. "Marshall." Maybe someday I'd be able to call him 'daddy' without it sounding foreign as a pig-calling contest in a palace. "Can't you tell me what you know about Mama?"

Aaron patted my knee then stood. "Might be best if I give y'all a little time to yourselves."

"What?" I grabbed hold of his hand without thinking. "But where're you going?"

"Just gonna take a walk for a bit. Give you two a little privacy. If you're ready to go before I get back, just call me." He leaned down and planted a kiss on my forehead natural as if he'd done it a hundred times before.

Although my nerves jangled at the thought of him leaving, I appreciated him being sensitive to Mr. Mar—Garrett's feelings. And maybe Aaron didn't want to hear Mama's personal issues, seeing as how he hardly knew her.

As Aaron slipped out the front door, I settled back in the couch and tried my best to relax. My shoulders and spine were stiff and achy. I threw Garrett a hard look—or as hard as I could muster. A girl who allowed a husband to abuse her for years didn't tend to have much of a backbone. "I really need to know what happened."

Garrett sighed. "Well, your mama and me were married kind of fast."

"She said you met at a church picnic."

He nodded. "Your grandma introduced us, and I have to say, I was smitten from the time I laid eyes on her." He smiled and waved his hand toward me. "You favor her a good bit."

I quirked a brow at him. "She said I favored you."

With a shrug, he grinned. "I suppose maybe your eyes. But you got your mama's fine cheekbones and smile." He pushed back in the chair with a sigh.

"Either way, she was real pretty, and your grandma got it into her head your mama needed to get herself married. Not quite sure why she'd fixed her sights on me, but she did."

Even though I'd only been with him a short time, his calm demeanor and gentleness shone through. Maybe my grandma wanted some of that for Mama. Far as I could tell, she hadn't softened over the years, so there was no telling what she was like back then.

"Any rate, I fell hard for your mama, although I couldn't say why she agreed to marry me. Don't think she *loved* me, and the fact she never seemed to warm up to—" He clamped his lips tight like he thought better of finishing the thought, a flush creeping up his neck.

Never seemed to warm up to what? Him? If that was what he was about to share, there would've been no reason for his embarrassment. It struck me then he was talking about relations. Mama was uncomfortable with sex; was that what he wasn't willing to say? If so, I wasn't about to go there.

Instead, I summed it up nice and tidy for him. "So, she kicked you out, and y'all got divorced."

His mouth slid into a frown. "Not exactly." He rubbed his head. "Your mama wanted a divorce, but I fought it long as I could. Left Norfolk Southern and got me a job with the railroad here. It wasn't until I met Patsy a few years later that I finally caved. I called your mama every week and begged for her to give us a chance. Offered to go to counseling or whatever else it might take. Then she quit taking my calls. Since I sent a check every month, I started wrapping them in a letter. She cashed the checks but never responded to the letters."

If Garrett was telling the truth, and I didn't have reason to believe he wasn't, then he'd done everything he could to make things right with Mama. Not only had he not walked out, like she'd said, but he'd paid her alimony. If he'd known about me, I had me a feeling he would've moved heaven and earth to be part of my life.

This was one blow I wasn't sure I could recover from.

Chapter 20

Sarah Beth

If it hadn't been for Gracie Lynn, I would've stayed in Peachtree indefinitely. As it was, a part of me was left behind with Garrett, Patsy, and their grand-kids—Kristy and Jake. My niece and nephew. Kristy was only a year older than Gracie Lynn, and Jake was six. And it turned out I had myself two half-brothers, Chance and Caleb. Chance was Kristy and Jake's daddy. Caleb didn't have any kids yet; he'd only been married a year.

When Patsy returned, Garrett sent the kids out back to play and explained the situation to her. It had to be a shock to her, finding out Garrett had another child. I hadn't even considered how me dropping such a bomb on their family might come back to bite me. Patsy could've been resentful of me, but if she was, I didn't get even the faintest whiff of it.

"Why don't you call that boyfriend of yours to come back?" she'd suggested. "I'll put out some snacks, and we can get to know one another.".

"Oh, he's just a friend," I blurted, my face heating. *Boyfriend?* Well, why wouldn't they assume Aaron and me were together? My fingers shook a little as I texted him to come on back to the house. *Boyfriend.* I kind of liked the sound of that.

Once Aaron showed up, we spent another couple of hours getting acquaint-ed. Garrett talked about his railroad experience, and I told them all about Gracie Lynn, glossing over my marriage to Jason. That was a conversation for another time. He and Patsy appeared to be the perfect couple, and for the life of me, I couldn't imagine him with Mama. Couldn't picture him as my daddy, either, although there was pang of regret when it was time to leave.

Garrett walked Aaron and me down the block to the car. "I don't want too much time to pass before I see you again. And I wanna meet that granddaughter of mine." He wrapped me in a hug, and it was hard to step away. This was my daddy. The man I never thought I'd never meet. My childhood would've been so different with him in it. Where Mama was hard, he was soft. Where Mama was critical, he might've been supportive. Almost thirty years lost. The mere thought of it had tears burning the back of my eyes.

I couldn't promise him I'd be back soon, because my junker didn't even have one road trip left in her, but I nodded. I'd find a way somehow.

When Aaron and me climbed into the car, he fingered a strand of hair from my cheek, and it was all I could to keep from melting against him. "You alert enough to get us through Atlanta?" Commute traffic would be heavy, and there was no telling how long it'd be before we'd make it back to Rossville. "If I thought I could drive us with one arm, I'd do it."

My heart was full to bursting with all I'd learned the last few hours. "If God blessed me with wings, I could fly us home right now."

He glanced at the clock on the dash. "You think we should call your mama? She's expectin' you to be back in the next hour or so."

The mere notion of talking to Mama had my belly twisting in knots and suffocating my joy. That didn't last long. "I don't think I could keep a civil tongue right now."

He nodded. "Give me your phone, and I'll text her. I'll say you're heading into commute traffic and can't talk. And it'll be late before you get back."

I inhaled real deep and let it out slow. "Remember, she thinks I'm with Jenna." Appeared lying came as natural to me as it did Mama.

Aaron set up the GPS, and I drove down Kensington while he awkwardly texted Mama with his left thumb. "I don't know what I'm gonna say to her." Anger was flowing through my veins, and if she was with me at that moment, I'd surely explode.

"Wanna talk about it? Maybe if you bounce it off me, you'll figure out the best approach." He set my phone on the console between us.

I flicked the blinker and pulled up to the stop sign. "I knew the minute she told me my daddy was dead, she'd lied. So, why am I so angry over it? It's not like it's a surprise or anything."

As I turned the corner, Aaron flipped the visor down to block out the sun pouring through the windshield. "Did anything Garrett tell you about her help?"

I thought back to what he'd said—or rather *not* said—about Mama being uncomfortable with him. "Not unless Mama being frigid is a clue." Just saying the word *frigid* had me shuddering. It was an accusation Jason liked to toss around when I'd freeze up after a beating. Like I could flip a switch and pretend it had never happened. But I couldn't imagine Garrett abused Mama.

"He said that?"

Wrinkling my nose, I glanced at him. "Not in so many words. I had a feeling he was trying to be sensitive. But he did say he didn't think she loved him." I could judge her for marrying a man she didn't have feelings for, but it turned out the nut didn't fall far from the tree. Hadn't I done the same thing? Maybe Mama had been running from something just like I was when I took off with Jason.

"Even so," Aaron said, "that doesn't explain why she'd lie about him. I mean, if he was dangerous—" My phone buzzed, and he glanced at it. "Your mama's responding to the text. Want me to read it to you?"

"Not really." But that would just delay the inevitable. I groaned. "Might as well."

Aaron looked at the phone. "Huh. Maybe it's best if I don't."

"That bad?"

He slid the phone back onto the console. "Let's just say it's not going to do much to soothe your frustration."

I could only imagine.

Aaron picked up the conversation again. "I didn't get any dark vibes coming off Garrett. Did you?"

"No. In fact, he seems genuinely kind."

"Like father, like daughter," he quipped.

I snorted. "Yeah, right."

He grunted. "I'm serious. You don't think you're kind?"

I shrugged. "More like a doormat." Why did admitting to such a thing make me want to cry? "It's not the same thing." One was motivated by Jesus and the other by fear. I was tired of being afraid; it had motivated every decision I'd made for years.

Silence hung in the air, except for the occasional bird song and other cars on the road. The adrenaline that had fueled me for a good part of the day seeped from my body and left me limp as a dishrag. How would I ever stay alert enough to get us safely home?

"Listen, Sarah Beth." Aaron's voice broke the quiet. "Maybe we haven't known each other long, but I don't think for a minute you're a doormat."

The GPS direction-lady cut in, giving me a moment to absorb Aaron's words. Not a doormat? It seemed like the only time I ever made a decision for myself, it turned out bad. And how many years did I let Jason walk all over me? Abuse me? Aaron was either delusional or merely trying to make me feel better about myself. My eyes were wide open now, and I wasn't going to believe a lie anymore, even when the truth was hard to swallow.

"Did you miss the part where I told you my husband abused me?"

Aaron made a noise in his throat—somewhere between a growl and a cuss word. "Believe me, I'm not gonna forget it. But that doesn't define who you are now. You're here—"

"Letting my mama walk all over me." The pain-filled words hung in the air. "She's been lying to me my entire life. The only thing I ever wanted growing up was a daddy, like all the other kids had." The full impact of that landed on my chest, and it ached something fierce. "And I had one the whole time." Tears clogged my throat, and my eyes burned. *Don't you cry, Sarah Beth. It ain't gonna change a thing.* It was Mama's voice filling my head. Words she'd said so often, they were now ingrained in me. Words Gracie Lynn would never hear coming from my mouth.

Aaron touched my knee. "Let's pull over, Sarah Beth. There's a restaurant just up ahead."

I huffed out a breath. "We're already hours behind." Mama would be sure to point out every one of them, too.

"Another one's not gonna make any difference. We haven't had much to eat all day, and you need time to process without worrying over traffic."

That'd take a whole lot more than an hour, but it was better than nothing. The later we got home, the better chance Mama would be asleep. I couldn't face her tonight without ripping into her. Tomorrow, Gracie Lynn and me would go to church, and maybe I'd get enough of Jesus to weather the storm that was sure to come.

Aaron

It broke something inside me to know Sarah Beth was hurting and there wasn't anything I could do about it. Couldn't recall a time I cared enough about a woman to feel their pain. I'd always put a wall up before we could get to the point of discussing anything serious. Keep it superficial and no one gets hurt. That had been my motto.

Had me a feeling there was no chance of that with Sarah Beth at this point. If she walked away tomorrow, I'd be left with a scar or two.

Aside from an older couple in a corner booth and a family with three kids seated on the other side of the dining room, the coffee house was empty. Not a good sign. It wasn't like Sarah Beth and me were on a date, but it was a disappointment just the same. Mama still talked about where Dad took her the first time they went out. It stuck in a woman's head.

A waitress appeared. Gray hair, bags under her eyes. The brown and white uniform dress didn't do her any favors, either. "It's just the two of you?" Her enthusiasm was underwhelming.

"Yes," Sarah Beth said.

The woman waved us to follow her. "Right this way." When we were seated across from each other, she slapped plastic menus down in front of us. "We got us a fish special tonight. Fried cod with two sides. What can I get y'all to drink?"

"Sweet tea for me, please." Sarah Beth smiled at the waitress then focused on the menu.

"I'll have the same, thanks." I watched as she left to get our drinks, then shifted my focus to Sarah Beth. Head down, her hair fell forward, nearly hiding her face. I couldn't imagine the weight that was bearing down on her narrow shoulders. She was so much stronger than she appeared, but everyone had a breaking point. Would learning about all her mama's lies be it for her?

With a sigh, she slid the menu aside and looked up at me. There were dark circles beneath her eyes, and a frown marred her pretty face. "I'm not very hungry." She probably had a pit the size of Georgia filling her belly.

"That's good, 'cause I've got a feeling the food's not gonna be all that tasty." I had a brilliant idea. "However, there's no way they could mess up ice cream and French fries."

Laughter bubbled out of Sarah Beth. That was better. "I'd never let Gracie Lynn order that for supper."

I shrugged. "Then it's a good thing she's not here to see it."

The waitress didn't seem the least bit offended that we passed on the special—probably wouldn't eat it herself—and brought us each a sundae and a big plate of fries to split. "Will that be all?" There wasn't even a hint of a smile on her lips or in her eyes. Face set in stone, like the world had sucked all the joy from her. Kind of reminded me of Sarah Beth's mama.

"I think that'll do it." I offered up my best smile—the one Mama said always got me out of trouble when I was a kid. "Appreciate you bein' here to serve us."

She stood just a tad taller, and the faintest spark of life lit her eyes. "You let me know if you need anything else." She slid the tab on the table. "I can take care of this when you're ready. No need to hurry. You kids take your time."

Sarah Beth dipped her spoon into her ice cream and raised an eyebrow at me. "Look at you putting on the charm."

I leaned closer to her. "She remind you of anyone?"

"The waitress?" She licked the spoon and squinted like she was thinking about it. "I don't think so. Why?"

I hesitated. Maybe bringing up Miss Pickett wasn't a good idea. Sarah Beth didn't need any reminders of what waited for her at home.

"Well? You gonna tell me or keep me guessing?"

I snagged a French fry. "Your mama."

Her mouth turned down. "You really think so?" Twisting around, she glanced around the restaurant to get another look at the waitress until she spotted her in the corner with the other couple. "She seems wrung out to me. Mama's just downright cantankerous."

I laid my spoon aside and touched Sarah Beth's hand to get her attention. "They have the same look in their eyes. Kind of beaten down. You know what I mean?"

With a scowl, she snatched a napkin from the holder and swiped it across her mouth. "Mama has no one but herself to blame if she's feeling that way."

"You're not gonna find me sayin' different, Sarah Beth. It's just an observation." But I had to wonder why. Everyone had a story. What was hers? "How much of your mama's past do you know?"

Breaking a French fry in half, she shrugged. "Who knows? I mean, look at what we learned just today."

"What would make her throw your dad out like she did? Or marry him in the first place?"

Sarah Beth tossed the fry back on the plate with a sigh. "I don't have the first clue. Her whole life, far as I know it, has been one big, fat lie." Her eyes caught hold of mine. "Why do you care, anyway?"

Good question. Why *did* I care about Miss Pickett's past? It had nothing to do with me, aside from it hurting Sarah Beth. And right there was the answer. "Because I care about you." When Sarah Beth's eyes softened, I reached across the table and took hold of her hand. "Whatever happened in your mama's past affects you. You're a product of that." That wasn't true only for Sarah Beth. My parents past affected me, too. I could pretend what happened when I was little didn't have anything to do with who I was now. But it did.

After we finished our ice cream and I'd paid the bill, we stepped outside. The sun was dipping below the line of trees on the west side of the street, but the air was still warm. It would be past nine before we made it back home, and Sarah Beth was already dragging. I took her hand and walked her to the passenger side of Dad's car.

"I'm gonna drive the rest of the way. You look done in."

She leaned her back against the car. "You can't drive with one arm."

I grinned. "Sure, I can. I've even driven with my knees on occasion." I fingered a strand of hair from her face and got lost in her blue eyes. Pain, exhaustion, and a flicker of something that got my heart racing—passion. I leaned closer, and a whiff of lavender tickled my nose. "You smell real nice," I murmured. Her scent drew me closer, and her lips opened slightly, inviting me to kiss her. Unable to resist, I touched my lips to her softer ones. They were sweet and warm and pliant.

In that instant, I was sixteen again, kissing a girl for the very first time. My heart was racing as I deepened the kiss, fully aware of the limitations of one arm. I longed to pull her in close, to wrap her in a hug, to feel her body pressed close to mine. Her hands circled the nape of my neck, fingers buried in my hair.

The sound of a car horn reminded me where we were. I was kissing Sarah Beth in the middle of a parking lot, drowning in her warmth and lavender scent. Sarah Beth, who had only months ago been in an abusive relationship. Who had just that day learned the true depth of her mother's deception.

Pulling away, I drew in a deep draught of air and searched her face for signs of fear or disgust. But her eyes were half-closed, her lips soft and swollen. We both sighed at the same time, and a soft laugh escaped me.

"Wow," she sighed, eyes opening wide. "That was..." But she didn't finish.

It was what? Great? Scary? A mistake? "I'm sorry," I blurted. Which was a lie. I wasn't sorry at all. "You've been through a lot today, and I didn't mean to take advantage."

She let out a shaky laugh. "Yeah. I guess it's been kind of emotional." Fingers touching her lips, she slipped away from me and climbed into the car.

When I climbed behind the wheel, I turned to talk to Sarah Beth expecting we'd explore these newfound feelings, but she leaned her head back and closed her eyes. "Wake me when we get home, Okay?"

I'd been effectively shut out, which me left clueless and confused. A very uncomfortable combination.

Chapter 21

Sarah Beth

Playing possum was a phrase I'd heard when I was little, but driving home with Aaron the night before was the first I'd used that particular avoidance technique. Of course, after about ten minutes, I didn't have to fake it anymore. All the emotions of the day had me wore out, and I must've dozed off. It wasn't until we pulled into Aaron's driveway that I woke up. A quick thanks, see you later, was the best I could offer him before slinking to my car, praying Mama was asleep when I got home.

And she was. The apartment was dark as sin—not a single light left on—which was probably her passive-aggressive way to let me know she was put out with me. First having the audacity to take off for an entire day, and then being so inconsiderate, I didn't get home when expected.

Wait until she discovered where I really was.

I stared at the ceiling most of the night, still as could be so I didn't disturb Gracie Lynn. I was paying for the time spent snoozing in the car, leaving Aaron to do all the driving. Now all I had to process was bouncing around in my head like a silver ball in one of them pinball machines. Garrett—my daddy—and his family. Mama's lies and how they'd kept us apart. What I was going to do about it. And Aaron's kiss. How one little ol' kiss could make that earth-shaking list of events was a puzzle. It's not like he was my first.

But was there even the slightest possibility he'd be my last?

Hadn't I vowed to stay clear of entanglements? They only led to heartache. If my own personal experience hadn't made it clear enough, what Garrett went through with Mama surely clinched it. And I had Gracie Lynn to think about. If she got herself attached to Aaron—and there wasn't a doubt in my mind that she could—then she'd be hurt when things went sideways.

Why couldn't I get my brain to stop spinning long enough to pray? I'd start talking to the Lord, and then all the cares of my little world would crowd in again, like they had more power than God. This whole following Jesus thing was more complicated than I'd expected.

I finally fell into a fitful sleep near daybreak, only to be awakened by Gracie Lynn soon after. "Jazzy's gotta go pee, Mama." She leaned over me, her face only inches from mine.

Groggy, I dragged her on top of me for a hug and lots of neck kisses. Her giggles lifted the fog from my weary brain and pulled a grin from me. Snuggling her against my chest, I breathed in her scent—baby shampoo and Ivory soap. It was the only soap Mama ever allowed into her house, and just a whiff of it opened a flood of childhood memories—some I'd rather forget.

"Is your nana up yet?" When Gracie Lynn shook her head, I wrestled the both of us from bed. "I'll take Jazzy out to potty while you get your teeth brushed. If we get a move on, we can go by the donut shop before heading to church." Bribing her with sugar was for my benefit more than hers. I wasn't ready to face Mama yet, and I surely needed a dose of Jesus before I did.

I shrugged into a sweatshirt, took Jazzy from her crate, and slunk through the apartment. Didn't hear any noises from the kitchen, and Mama's bedroom door was still closed. She was partial to sleeping in on Sundays—or most days since I'd been back home. My entire childhood, she'd be up before the sun working on one thing or another. "No rest for the wicked," she'd say.

Just the week before, I'd used Mama's John Deere to knock down the weeds and set up a large kennel for the puppy out back where there was more shade than not. Cost as much as one of Dirty Jane's bargain dressers, but at least Jazzy had a safe place to play. Now, I freshened her water, filled up her food bowl, and left her with some toys before slipping back inside to get us ready for church.

God willing, Mama wouldn't wake before we left.

A half hour later, me and Gracie Lynn made our escape. My heart was racing like I had the hounds of hell after me until we got out of the driveway. It wasn't that I was afraid of Mama. Maybe afraid of how she'd react when I told her the truth—not that she had any right to be pointing fingers. Truth be told, I was some worried about whether I could keep a civil tongue once we got the conversation rolling. I needed to figure out a way to mind my heart. Wasn't there some such verse like that in the Bible?

During the drive from the donut shop to church, dark, ominous clouds blocked out the sun. One of the things I loved most about springtime in the South was the thunderstorms—but not when I was left without an umbrella. I'd lived too long in L.A.—where even the atheists were desperate enough to pray for rain—to remember such necessities. I'd have to be sure and get one in my car before the next downpour.

Although the rumble of thunder continued as I pulled into the church parking lot, there was no rain yet. It wasn't until we climbed out of the car, and I took hold of Gracie Lynn's hand, the first fat drop hit my arm. "We gotta run, baby girl, or else we'll be soaked." Head down, I nearly dragged her across the pavement as a deluge opened up. We didn't stop until we were under the alcove at the front doors where people were gathered in exuberant conversation.

"Whew." I scraped the wet hair from my face then did the same for Gracie Lynn. "Should've checked the weather before we left this morning." Not that it would've necessarily been accurate.

"Sarah Beth!"

I peered through the mingling bodies until I spotted Jenna and Chad, a wet umbrella dangling from his hand. We hadn't talked in a few days, and it struck me in that moment how much I'd missed her. All those years without a single friend, and now after such a short time, I couldn't imagine my life without her.

"Hey, Jenna. Chad." There was so much to tell her, but this wasn't the time or place. "Gracie Lynn, you remember Mr. Chad, don't you?"

Gracie Lynn tilted her head back and nodded. The girl could go from zero to sixty and back again in the blink of an eye. She needed as much socializing as Jazzy did.

"Can you say hey?"

Gracie Lynn shrugged, and Jenna crouched down for a hug. "Hey, sweet girl. How's that puppy of yours doing?"

A smile tugged at the edge of Gracie Lynn's mouth. "She's almost housebroken."

"Really?" Jenna's eyes were wide, like Gracie Lynn had just shared the most fascinating tidbit of news. "She must be really smart."

Gracie Lynn nodded then slid shy eyes toward Chad.

Jenna ruffled Gracie Lynn's damp curls and stood to give me a hug. "Feels like it's been ages. What've you been doin' with yourself?" Without giving me a chance to answer, she continued. "You about ready to get the flooring installed?"

Warmth bloomed inside when I connected her question to Aaron. After all, he said he'd help, didn't he? No sooner had that thought formed, a woman in my line of vision lowered her umbrella, and there he was. It was like I'd conjured him up out of thin air. What was he doing here? Didn't his mama and daddy say he hadn't been in church for years? As our eyes tangled, everyone else faded away in a romantic fog.

Oh boy, was I in trouble.

"Hey, Sarah Beth." His voice floated over me and his smile had me melting like peach ice cream on a hot summer day.

"I...This is a surprise."

Before he could respond, his parents came up behind him and broke the spell.

"Sarah Beth! What a pleasure it is to see you again." Janice nudged Aaron aside and hugged me. Caught up in greetings, the crowd shifting toward the doors, and keeping hold of Gracie Lynn, I lost track of Aaron.

Jenna looped her arm in mine as we moved down the church aisle, Chad tagging along behind. "What was that all about?" she murmured.

"What?" As if I didn't know. I couldn't fake my way out of a paper bag, so she wasn't about to buy the innocent act.

"Aaron. You. Staring at each other all googly eyed." She squeezed my arm. "I knew there was something between the two of you last time I dropped in. I made a little bitty joke about y'all booking a romantic getaway, and the both of you turned beat red."

She didn't know the half of it. Maybe I should've called or texted before Aaron and me took our trip the day before, but I didn't truly believe Garrett would turn out to be my daddy after all. If I was chasing rainbows like a fool, I didn't want Jenna to think less of me for it.

As I guided Gracie Lynn into a pew ahead of me, I leaned toward Jenna. "We need to talk."

Her eyes lit up and she silently clapped. If she'd yelled, "Goody," she couldn't have been more obvious. "My place, after church. I'll even feed y'all."

I hadn't yet been to Jenna's Northshore condo before. It was bad enough I had car envy, now I was going to have to contend with home envy as well. A modern two-bedroom in neutral colors with an open concept and high ceilings that made it feel bigger than it actually was. Nothing from Dirty Jane's in this place. Leather furniture, dark cabinets, actual artwork on the walls—no Hobby Lobby knockoffs. It was clean and stylish, although not *my* style. Working to remodel the motel, I'd come to appreciate retro colors and patterns. Unable to picture living in such luxury softened the edges of my envy some.

I was grateful Chad didn't join us at Jenna's. I wanted to get to know him better, since she was clearly infatuated, but me airing my dirty laundry in front of him? TMI and all that. As it was, I had Gracie Lynn's little ears to worry about. Bless Jenna's heart, she had that figured out, too.

"We'll just get her settled in the living room with PB&J, and I'll stream *Gruffalo* for her to watch. That ought to give us at least a half hour."

I winced. "Peanut butter and white leather aren't the best combo." She'd have a lot to learn if she was fixing to have kids.

"No worries. It's easy to wipe up." She got Gracie Lynn taken care of then slipped back and started pulling salad fixings from the fridge. "Now, what's goin' on with you and Aaron?"

It would be a whole lot easier to talk with her if I wasn't sitting in her kitchen like a useless lump. "Why don't you give me something to do? I'm too antsy to sit still."

She pulled a glass bowl from an upper cabinet and handed it to me. "How 'bout tearing lettuce?"

I washed my hands at the sink while organizing my thoughts. "So, just to give you an update, Aaron and me went down to Peachtree yesterday." I let that hang in the air long enough for Jenna to catch up.

Eye's widening, she stopped working on a tomato mid-slice. "Did you see him? This Garrett Marshall fella?"

I drew in a deep breath and nodded. Before saying more, I glanced across the room to be sure Gracie Lynn was focused on the cartoon rather than us. "I was right about him, Jenna. He's my father."

She dropped the knife and her jaw all at once. "Get out. You're sure?"

"Without a doubt."

"That's amazing." Her voice rose then she snapped her mouth shut as we both glanced at Gracie Lynn to be sure she didn't hear. At a near whisper, Jenna continued. "Was it weird? Does he seem like a good guy? Why didn't you tell me you were going?"

I closed my eyes and took a breath. "Yes, yes, and it's complicated."

She snatched up a dish towel, and wiping her hands, drew close enough to me I could see the gold specks in her green eyes. "This is unreal." She nudged me with an elbow. "Does he have a family?"

A knot of emotion grew in my throat, and I had to swallow before answering. "A wife. Patsy. She's totally cool." I let out a bitter laugh. "Nothing like Mama. They have two boys and two grandchildren."

Jenna leaned against the counter. "Wow. Did you meet them? The boys, I mean."

I shook my head. "No, but they had the little ones with them. Not much older than Gracie Lynn." Just talking about it undid all the grace I'd filled up on in church. I'd have to be in the presence of Jesus 24/7 to get through this without pitching a full-on hissy fit on Mama.

"You have brothers." Jenna sounded as awestruck as I'd been. "When are you gonna meet them?"

I ripped into a piece of lettuce like it had offended me. "I don't know. Soon, I hope." If I could get a ride back down to Peachtree. Maybe I could borrow Aaron's car. Then again, hadn't he already done enough?

"You're looking a little green, Sarah Beth. You feeling okay?" Jenna placed her wrist on my forehead. "No fever."

"It's a little malady called fear." I tried to lighten my mood with a chuckle, but it came out sounding more like a growl.

"Huh." She folded her arms across her chest. "You haven't said nothing to your mama yet, have you?"

Wrinkling my nose, I sighed. "Am I too old to run away from home?"

She clucked her tongue. "What've you got to be afraid of? You're not the one who lied, Sarah Beth. Your mama outta be ashamed of herself."

She was right, but it didn't change how my heart pounded at the mere thought of telling Mama what I learned. It reminded me of all the times I stood up to Jason, knowing I was in the right. Hadn't done me a lick of good in the end. Narcissists always had a way of turning the tables, so the victim was the one apologizing.

Jenna lightly backhanded my arm. "That doesn't explain the googly-eyes you and Aaron were sharing when he showed up at church."

Even though I focused on tearing lettuce like it was my life's work, I could feel Jenna's eyes boring into me.

"Y'all were alone in the car all the way down and back from Peachtree. Or did you have Gracie Lynn with you?"

I shook my head. "Mama kept her for me." Since I was sharing Mama's sins, it was only fair I shared one of my own. "Told her you and me were going to Atlanta to check out a couple estate sales." I pulled a grimace.

"Well, if you're worried I'll tell her different, don't be. It's not like she's given you a choice." That wasn't exactly true; everyone had a choice when it came to speaking truth or spouting lies.

"So, all those hours sitting alongside Aaron with nothing to do but talk." She grinned. "And today, you practically swooned when he showed up at church."

I threw her a scowl. "Don't be ridiculous." Because the idea that Aaron could have feelings for me was just that—ridiculous. That kiss was merely a combination of things that didn't add up to anything more than a natural response. Wasn't that how guys operated? They didn't need an emotional connection to act on a physical attraction. Of course, that would mean he was at the very least *attracted*. Then again, so was Jason, and I wasn't looking to repeat that mistake.

"Earth to Sarah Beth." Jenna waved her hand in front of my face. When I blinked and focused on her, she said, "Where'd you go?"

Unless I wanted to stumble along this rocky road alone, I'd have to confide in someone. It's not like I could talk to Aaron about it, and Jesus wasn't likely to have a sit-down with me.

"He kissed me," I finally blurted. "We stopped for something to eat right after leaving Peachtree, and when we got back to the car, he just kissed me."

Jenna giggled like I'd shared a romantic secret. All sweet and new and shiny. Except with the darkness of my past, it could easily become tarnished and scary. Just like Mama and Jason.

The grin slid from Jenna's lips as lines formed between her brows. "You don't like Aaron?" My face must've betrayed my thoughts.

Huffing out a breath, I shrugged. "What's not to like?"

She tilted her head slightly. "Then why don't you look happy about him kissing you? I know he's got feelings for you."

I couldn't hold back the snort. "He tell you that?" Which wouldn't have made a lick of difference. People said things they didn't mean all the time.

"Not in actual words. I mean, it's not like we've had the opportunity to talk about it." She slid the salad bowl over to the cut-up tomatoes and scooped them onto the lettuce. "But it's pretty obvious. You can see it written all over his face when he looks at you."

Entanglements. Everywhere I turned, there they were.

Jenna squeezed my hand. "What's goin', Sarah Beth? If I didn't know better, I'd think you got the troubles of the whole world sitting on your shoulders."

Tears bit at the back of my eyes. That's exactly how it felt. Was that warped or what? Garrett was a good man who wanted a relationship with me. Aaron...well, Aaron wasn't the least bit like Jason—all hat and no cattle. He had substance and goodness. He had a sweet family and was hard-working. And attractive. There was no denying that. What was *wrong* with me?

"I'm scared," I finally confessed. "There are too many feelings coming at me, and I don't know how to process them."

Jenna wrapped an arm around my shoulders and tilted her head to meet mine. "You've been through a lot. Give yourself a little time."

Stepping away, I rubbed my hands over my face. "When am I supposed to do that? I can only avoid Mama for so long. And who knows what she'll do when I fess up."

"True. But if you and Gracie Lynn need somewhere to go, you're always welcome here."

"Ha! You're nuttier than a pecan pie."

"I'm dead serious, Sarah Beth. I got an extra bedroom, and this place can feel downright lonely sometimes. I'd enjoy having y'all here."

I laughed, partly because she was crazy and partly because there was relief knowing I wouldn't be left living on the streets of Chattanooga when Mama kicked me out.

Chapter 22

Aaron

It had been weeks, maybe months, since I'd attended church, and I hadn't clocked many hours in God's Word, either. That didn't mean I'd forgotten the lessons taught when I was a kid. Take Adam and Eve, for example. Sin entered the world the moment Eve let that slippery serpent talk her into eating the forbidden fruit. Then Adam, being the sucker he was, let her talk him into it as well. Ever since, women had been confounding men.

I spent the better part of the night trying to make sense of Sarah Beth. Had to do something, since I wasn't able to sleep. Maybe I wasn't an expert where women were concerned, but I would've bet my last nickel Sarah Beth had enjoyed that kiss. I sure did.

So, why'd she fake sleep most of the way home and brush me off the minute I pulled into my driveway?

Then our eyes tangled outside the church this morning, and I was even more confused. She appeared every bit as affected as me, with her flushed face and deer-in-the-headlights gaze. I'd never been in love before, and I wasn't about to claim I was then. I mean, it was just chemistry, right? She was beautiful and kind and funny. She was a wonderful mama to Gracie Lynn. She was loyal to her own mama, even though the woman was prickly as a porcupine. I'd have to be dead to not be attracted.

But what if it was more than that? What if this knot in my gut was God's early warning system, letting me know it was time to man up?

Only people I trusted to talk to about it was Mama and Dad. You'd think when I invited myself to their house for lunch, I'd just handed them the winning ticket for Publisher's Clearinghouse. Church *and* lunch? Just proved what a loser-son I'd been lately. Couldn't remember the last time I hung out with them on a Sunday afternoon. Shame on me. I could blame it on work, but that dog won't hunt. Found myself plenty of time to work on the house. It seemed my family had gotten the short end of the stick for quite some time. If I was fixing to get serious about Sarah Beth—and that was a big *if* seeing as how she was so squirrely—I'd need to change my priorities.

Church was good. Might've gotten a bit more from the sermon if I hadn't been focused on Sarah Beth sitting across the sanctuary. Either she was completely unaware of my eyes on her, or she was choosing to ignore me. Confounding females were God's sense of humor. Looked for her as we left, but the only view I got was the tail end of her car leaving the parking lot.

"You gonna follow us over to the house?" Mama narrowed her eyes on my sling. Could practically see the wheels of doubt turning in her head.

"Yes, ma'am. Drove most of the way home from Peachtree last night and here this morning. I think I can manage a few more miles."

Dad wrapped his arm around Mama's shoulders and turned her toward their car, throwing a grin at me while he did so. "He's a big boy, sweetie. He'll be right behind us."

Growing up, mid-meal on Sundays was always a mishmash of leftovers, but Mama always sweetened the pot with her orange fluff. Mandarin oranges, marshmallows, and Jell-O—and probably a load of sugar. Turned out, nothing had changed. I dished up a healthy portion to go alongside the cold chicken and asparagus salad. Was a whole lot more appealing than the fish special at the restaurant last night.

"You wanna say the blessing, son?" Dad laid his napkin across his lap—one of Mama's requirements—and I did the same. The other two were no elbows on the table and no talking with a mouth full of food. Her small contribution toward civility.

I was about to pass the honor of praying over our meal back on him, then I thought better of it. Saying the blessing could be *my* small contribution to drawing closer to the Lord. "Yes, sir." Took me a deep breath and bowed my head. "Lord in Heaven, we thank You for the abundance that You have given us. We truly appreciate how You care for us. Please, nourish our bodies with this food so we may be better able to serve You. In Jesus' name we pray. Amen." It wouldn't win any theological awards, but it was a start. If the Devil could take advantage of a small foothold, the Lord could surely do more with less.

Mama scooped a portion of the sweet Jell-O salad onto her plate and passed the bowl to Dad. "This is nice, Aaron. It's too bad Linc and Carrie were already busy, or we could've had ourselves a little family reunion."

Answered prayer. Hard to discuss anything more than kid-stuff with them around. "Next time." I took a bite of chicken and chewed slow enough to organize a thought or two. What the heck? I might as well jump into the deep end. "Thought y'all can give me some advice."

The way their eyes popped, and forks stopped mid-lift, you'd have thought I'd just grown two horns. Dad was the first to rally. "Advice?" He set his fork down and broke Mama's rule when he folded his elbows on the table. "You read the trainmaster's report of the accident?"

So focused on Sarah Beth, it took me a beat to switch gears. "No." I drew in a breath. "Plan on doing that sometime this week before I stop by Cecil's and see if there's anything his wife needs." Knowing the stubborn old coot, he'd be itching to disregard doctor's orders and tend to chores he had no business doing. "I've had a few other things on my mind lately." That was only partially true. It was easier to focus on Sarah Beth than to face the report. As long as I didn't see it for myself, I could pretend the derailment was more dream than substance.

"Then maybe it has to do with Sarah Beth?" Mama grinned, her eyes sparkling. Ever the romantic. And generally two steps ahead Dad and me.

My throat went dry as dust, and I took a gulp of sweet tea. "Truth is, I have feelings for her, but y'all are aware my struggle. I mean, getting close and shutting down on account of...well...you know."

A wrinkle formed between Mama's brows. "You're not gonna let that nonsense hold you back now, are you?"

"Nonsense?" Talk about switching gears. "Y'all practically beat me over the head with how being separated from you as a kid messed me up. Now that I'm agreeing it's a problem, you're calling it nonsense?"

Dad raised his hands. "Hold on there, son. You're gettin' all riled up. Let's take it down a notch and talk about it."

I shoved my fingers through my hair. "Fine."

"We only wanted you to be aware," Mama said. "You said yourself you have a habit of shuttin' down."

I nodded.

"Well, now that you know where it comes from, you can work through it."

Before I could respond, Dad cut in. "We talked about this some weeks back. You remember what I told you?"

It wouldn't have mattered if I hadn't—Dad's solution to everything was the same. Guess I'd heard it so much, it went in one ear and out the other. "Pray." Then the hypocrisy of it hit me between the eyes, and I looked at Mama. "But you're the one who suggested counselin' might be the answer."

She reached over and patted my hand. "Sweet boy, that's not what I said at all. I said it wouldn't *hurt* you none to have someone to talk to who isn't all wrapped up in it. But your daddy's right—prayer is the best place to start. Only Jesus knows what's goin' on in your heart. Probably better than you do."

They made it sound so easy. Pray about it and the problem would disappear.

Dad sighed. "Look, son, every one of us has something to work through—it's just part of livin' this side of heaven. You think when your mama and I got hitched, we had it all figured out?" He snorted. "Not by a long shot. I was a workaholic slob who didn't consider her feelings as much as I should've. Traipsed dirt over the house, acted like I didn't know how to wash a dish, and sometimes said hurtful things before thinking."

Mama's chuckle got her eyes to dancing. "And I could nag a body to death, given half a chance. And I didn't make it easy for your daddy to apologize.

Marriage is work. And there isn't a one of us who can do it well without Jesus in the middle."

Dad nodded. "We men can be real good at compartmentalizing. I've seen you do it with this accident." He flicked a hand toward my shoulder. "We don't wanna think about something, we shove it into a box to deal with later. But the Lord? You can't shove Him in a box. Give Him control over all of it and see if that doesn't change things for you."

Until that moment, it hadn't occurred to me how much tension I was carrying around. But the fact remained, that wall I tended to put up was still an issue. It wasn't like I could hand it over to Jesus like a big ol' rock and everything was fixed.

"What's goin' on in that head of yours?" Dad's voice cut into my thoughts.

"I get what you're sayin', but I have Sarah Beth to consider. She's been through too much as it is"—and I hadn't even told them yet about Garrett Marshall being her father—"I just don't want my...issues, for a lack of a better word, to be her problem."

He picked up his fork and pointed it at me. "There's a verse in the Book of James about how God provides wisdom when we ask for it. But we can't be wishy-washy about believing He'll give it. Says doubt's like a ship tossed around on waves—nowhere to land."

Mama cut in, "Marriage is a package deal, Aaron. If you're serious about this girl, and I think you'd be plumb crazy *not* to be, then your problems become hers and hers become yours. It's how it works. Iron sharpens iron."

Sarah Beth

After leaving Jenna's condo, I sat in my car and pondered what to do for so long Gracie Lynn fell asleep. I was only half-kidding when I asked Jenna if I was too old to run away from home. It was downright tempting to take her up on the offer of a place to stay. I wouldn't even have to go back to the motel. It's not like we'd be leaving anything of value behind.

But that'd be the easy way out of this whole mess, which is what landed me right smack into the last one. I was going to have to face Mama, so I might as well get it over with. Besides it might be a toss-up whether Gracie Lynn would choose me or Jazzy. I even played with the notion of sneaking back after Mama went to sleep to snatch the puppy. It just showed how desperate—or crazy—I was.

Like a bolt of lightning, it struck me on the way home that I hadn't even bothered to pray. Talking to God didn't come natural. I was a nobody who hadn't bothered to even think of Him until I was in trouble. It was hard to figure why He'd even listen to little ol' me. In the pastor's message just that morning, he'd made a point of reminding us that God was infinite. The One we prayed to is the One who parted the Red Sea for the Israelites and wrote the Ten Commandments on stone tablets with is His finger. It was a hard concept to wrap my head around.

Since Gracie Lynn was still sound asleep, and I wasn't in a hurry to face Mama, I pulled the car onto a quiet side street and parked under an elm tree. It didn't seem right to multi-task when praying to the Lord. Maybe since I *was* a nobody, giving God my full attention might could soften His heart toward me a bit.

The rain had stopped, and when I looked ahead at the sky, my breath caught. A ray of sunlight poured down through a fluffy white bank of clouds. God's spotlight. Was He doing that for me? Oh, how I wanted to believe it was so. A knot of emotion took hold of my throat while tears burned at the back of my eyes.

I clasped my hands like I'd been taught in Sunday School all those years ago and bowed my head. *Oh, Heavenly Father, I don't even know where to start. I've failed You more times than I can count, but You're still here watching over me. I just know it. I wanna do right by You, Father. I wanna live the way You call me to. But I'm so angry with Mama. All the hurt she's caused over the years and the lies.* Tears leaked from my eyes and trickled down my cheeks.

Sniffling, I swiped them away then refolded my hands. *I know You love her, too, even if she's dismissed You like I have. It seems downright selfish of me to ask for another miracle. You saved me from Jason's abuse. You led me to my daddy. And I don't know that Aaron's not another miracle You're working out for me. But I need help dealing with Mama. Curb my tongue when I want to lash out. Help me to see her the way You do. Be with me when I confront her about all the lies. Please help me, Jesus. Help me be pleasing to You.*

Opening my damp eyes, I took a breath deep enough to stretch my lungs and let it out real slow. The clouds had parted enough that the sunlight no longer resembled a holy painting. Was that a good sign or a bad one? This whole communicating with God thing was more complicated than I'd expected. If I'm the only one doing the talking, then how would I get any answers?

Ten minutes later, I pulled into the motel driveway, and my heart was no longer wrestling with my head. That right there could be an answer, couldn't it? Wasn't peace one of those fruits of the Spirit?

Gracie Lynn didn't rustle until I unhooked her seat belt. "Are we home?" she mumbled, rubbing her eyes.

"We are, baby." I helped her out of the car and fingered some flyaway hair from her face as she blinked up at me. "Why don't you go out back and check on Jazzy while I see what your nana's doing?"

That miraculous peace took a bit of a hit as I watched Gracie Lynn skip around the side of the motel. I wasn't about to let her witness a confrontation between Mama and me. The child was extremely well-adjusted considering. *Another miracle?* It was like God was reminding me that Gracie Lynn and me had never been alone. *Thank You, Jesus.*

Tucking my bag under one arm, I walked into the apartment and left the door ajar for Gracie Lynn. Mama wasn't in the front room or the kitchen. There wasn't a sound other than the ticking of an old clock that hung on the wall across from Mama's recliner. Had she gone out? If so, with who? She'd done a fine job alienating what few friends she once had, so it wasn't likely someone picked her up.

I stepped back outside as Gracie Lynn appeared with Jazzy in her arms. The puppy started squirming and shaking when she spotted me.

"She wants to say 'Hi,' Mama." Gracie Lynn handed Jazzy up to me, and I held her against my chest while she wriggled and bathed my chin with kisses. How could I have considered, even for a brief moment, leaving this little bundle of joy behind?

Rubbing the puppy's soft ears, I glanced down the row of motel rooms. There was still a lot of work to get done, but—was the door on the end open? I was sure I'd locked it up last time I was in there, which was a couple days ago.

I looked at Gracie Lynn. "Can you go get Jazzy's leash? It might be good for the both of you to spend some time outside on the playground." Although the child had been stuck inside all day, fresh air wasn't my main reason for sending her to the swings. Mama missing and the motel room left open? No telling what was going on, and I didn't want Gracie Lynn near it.

I made my way past the several units that still needed work, sweat pooling at the low of my back as I neared the last one. A combination of humidity and nerves. Since all the furniture was stored in another room until the flooring got done, there wasn't much to steal if someone had broken in. When I reached the open door, I peered into the dark interior—or dark compared to the bright sunlight.

It took a moment for my eyes to adjust, and when they did, I spotted Mama coming from the bathroom. Her arms were folded across her thin chest and her gaze was fixed on the walls like she was inspecting them for flaws. How many times had I asked her if she wanted to see what I'd been doing, and she declined? Well, at least the mysteries were solved, even if my heart was now racing at the thought of confronting her.

"Mama?"

She jerked like I'd startled her. Pressing a hand to her chest, she scowled. "You could warn a body, Sarah Beth. Took a dozen years off my life."

"Sorry," I managed through the pounding of my heart. Why'd I have to be such a big chicken? Why couldn't I be self-confident like Jenna? I bet she wouldn't cower at the idea of confronting her mama. Although she did everything she could to avoid mine. "I didn't know you were down here. I saw the door open and thought maybe someone had broken in."

Mama opened her mouth like she was fixing to say something then snapped it closed. I stiffened in response like one of those dogs I'd learned about in high school science. Pavlov, I think it was. Then with a shake of her head, she closed her mouth and took herself a breath. "You did a real nice job paintin' this room and number Eleven." *Wait for it.* She was sure to add some caveat to ruin the compliment. "I saw a bunch of furniture crammed into Room Nine. Guess that's what you and Jenna's been pickin' up at those estate sales."

A rare, pleasant conversation? Not even a hint of an attitude. It would be so easy to smile, nod, say, "Thank you," and pretend there wasn't a lie between us. But it would only prolong the inevitable and give me an ulcer in the waiting.

Straightening my back—which proved I wasn't spineless—I licked my lips. "I didn't go to an estate sale yesterday, Mama." A calm flowed into my spirit as my eyes caught and held hers. "I went to Peachtree to meet Garrett Marshall."

If I had even the slightest doubt about who Garrett was, Mama's face draining of all color at the mention of his name would've clinched it. "Wh...Who?"

Folding my arms across my chest, I shook my head. "My daddy. You know, the man you said was dead and buried years ago?"

Swaying slightly, she reached a hand to the Palladian-blue wall. Her shoulders rounded like a boulder weighed them down—or maybe a boulder-sized lie. "Who says he's your daddy?" Was she really going to carry on this charade?

"It's a simple math equation, Mama." A hard edge accompanied my words, but I considered it a win if I kept hold of my tongue and didn't lash into her like she deserved. "The thing is, he was as unaware of me as I was of him."

Head down, she rubbed her brow like it would miraculously give her the answers she needed. "I'm not gonna talk to you about this, Sarah Beth. You had no right to—"

"No right?" My words seemed to reverberate off the walls. So much for keeping my tongue. "How could you do this to me? To him?" I clenched my fists when what I wanted to do was pummel her. "You've been lying to me my whole life."

The fire in her eyes as she looked at me was hot enough to burn. "I ain't gonna discuss this, so you can just forget it." She stormed past me like she was running for her life.

Chapter 23

Sarah Beth

Even in my darkest hours with Jason, the silence between us didn't hang as heavy as what I experienced with Mama over the next couple of days. She poured every smile and kindness onto Gracie Lynn and turned a blind eye on me—like I didn't even exist. This wasn't the answer to prayer I was hoping for, and I had to wonder if God and me got our wires crossed.

Then again, maybe I wasn't meant to stay on with Mama. She hadn't kicked me out, but that probably on account of Gracie Lynn. And if I was going to be brutally honest, I only came home because I had nowhere else to go, and Mama knew it. It wasn't a love for her that brought me here—it was a love for self. And for Gracie Lynn, of course. At least it seemed to be working out well for one of us.

I'd already spent a good portion of Jason's life insurance on the motel renovations, which made it hard to walk away. The cost and labor would be all for nothing if I didn't see it through. But if I continued, it might be no different than throwing the money into a pit and lighting it on fire. The plan Jenna and me put together for making it prosperous would tank the minute I left. For sure, Mama wouldn't bother to finish what I'd started.

The boxes of linoleum tiles were sitting in Room Eight just waiting for me to get to them. I had Aaron to thank for that. He'd gotten the flooring ordered and delivered as promised, and I hadn't even paid him yet. But I'd take care of it this week since he was supervising the installation. It didn't matter that

I had no experience except what I'd learned on YouTube. What started out as a nerve-wracking jaunt into the unknown world of construction was now insignificant compared to everything else.

Aaron had agreed to come over and help on Wednesday morning, so I dropped Gracie Lynn off at preschool and started moving the linoleum into the unit where Mama and I had our showdown, pathetic as it was. I'd found a little wagon in the shed down by the garden, and although the wheels were a bit wonky, it worked well enough to carry a few boxes of flooring at a time. Just being in the room got my blood boiling again. *Let it go.* I didn't know if the command came from me or God, but either way, it was good advice.

I was stacking the last of the boxes into the corner when I glanced out the window and spotted Aaron's truck pull into the lot. Immediately, my heart took to skipping—another Pavlov-dog-reaction. If I didn't know better, I'd have thought I had a murmur or some other malfunction. While he backed up to the door, I took some breaths to get my nerves settled before stepping outside.

He jumped from the truck and inspected me from head to toe with a grin. "We're gonna make a construction worker out of you yet." Even when I had dressed to impress Jason, his eyes never lit up with the admiration I caught in Aaron's.

I wrinkled my nose at the knee pads buckled over my faded jeans. "I feel ridiculous."

Opening the tailgate, he chuckled. "I think you look sexy." Wow, was he a charmer or what?

I moved to the truck to help unload the tools. "Is this it?" Aside from a gallon can, everything was packed in one mid-sized Amazon box.

"I told you it's an easy job." He slid the box to the edge of the tailgate and tried to muscle it with one arm.

"Let me," I said, nudging him out of the way. While carrying it inside, I took stock of the contents—some sort of trowel, a measuring tape, a metal ruler... a utility knife and a roller. "This really is all we need?" I turned to see him with the can.

He held it up and my eyes locked on his lips when he said, "Adhesive."

My face flamed. How embarrassing. You'd think I was a schoolgirl with her first crush. One kiss. It was just one, little kiss. If I was more sophisticated, I could brush it off as a flirtation and not give it another thought. Instead, I couldn't seem to take my eyes off him as he set the glue next to the boxes of tiles.

"Have you talked to your mama about Garrett yet?"

It took a moment for me to process his question. *Mama*. That certainly brought me back to my sense. I moved around him and set the box down with the other supplies. "I did. Or at least I tried." I swiped at a strand of hair that had escaped my ponytail. "She refuses to discuss it." I looked at the stuff in the corner. "All this is most likely a waste of money." I grimaced. "Which reminds me I need to pay you for everything."

He waved it away, like we were talking about a Sonic burger instead of a thousand dollars, and frowned. "I'm in no hurry. We got us eleven more rooms to do after this one."

I huffed out a bitter laugh. "I don't think Gracie Lynn and me can stay here, Aaron." I knew it was true as the words left my mouth. No more wavering. "When I said Mama won't talk about it, I mean she won't talk. Period. It's like I no longer exist." I rubbed my forehead. "I should've never come back here," I whispered. Of course, I wouldn't have ever known about Garrett or Jenna—or Aaron.

"You don't mean that, do you?" Maybe I had a hard time believing Aaron had deep feelings for me, but even I couldn't miss the hurt that shadowed his eyes as he touched my cheek.

There went my heart again. He didn't do more than look or touch, and I wanted to melt into his warmth. But I knew better than to trust my fickle feelings. "I don't know." I couldn't think clearly with him so close, so I stepped back. "I came here for all the wrong reasons. Maybe it would be best if we went down to Peachtree. I could find myself a job and a place to stay. At least I have family there."

Aaron planted his hands on his hips and blew out a breath. "You have family here, Sarah Beth. I know you're upset with your mama right now, but she'll come around. And even if she doesn't, why go down there? You can find a job in Chattanooga."

I couldn't imagine living so close to Mama with things bad between us. "I have brothers down there and—"

"You've never even met them." He scraped his hand through his hair with a growl. Was he *angry* with me?

"Hey, are you okay?" *Please don't be angry. I can't take anymore animosity coming at me.*

His eyes softened, and he managed a chuckle. "Yeah, of course. Just a lot goin' on right now."

Here I was, thinking about myself again. Poor Sarah Beth. Aaron was in physical pain, still dealing with the accident, and his friend was in the hospital. "I'm sorry. You have enough on your plate without me whining about Mama."

Going around me, he moved toward the supplies. "If I had your mama, I'd be whining, too." Then he spun around, his eyes wide. "That came out wrong." He reached his arm toward me with a grimace that had me fighting a grin. "I mean, you're not whining, but if you were, you'd have every right."

He was so cute stumbling through the apology, the grin won. "Don't worry about it; I'm not the least bit offended. Truth is, I'm kind of sick of myself. Always fussing but never doing anything about it." Like letting Mama off the hook. I couldn't make her talk, but I didn't have to lay down like a rug mat and let her walk all over me, either.

"I don't see it that way at all." Aaron unloaded the box, one item at a time. Should I help or keep my distance? Every time I got close to him, I lost my head a little. "You've been working to get this place fixed up, raising up a sweet little girl, and handling your mama all at once." He raised the metal ruler and pointed it at me. "And"—he drew the word out —"solved the mystery of who your dad is."

"Ha." His praise warmed me clear through. "Your daddy was the one who solved the mystery. I just found an old envelope stuffed at the bottom of a drawer." I crossed to the box and fished out the only two items left—the trowel and measuring tape. "Guess we outta get started." When I stood up, Aaron was so close, I could see light stubble on his strong chin. He brushed his fingers over my cheek, and my eyes drifted closed. Was he going to kiss me again? Did I want him to?

When his lips touched mine, it was all I could do to hold back a sigh. They were soft and gentle, just like the last time. Hesitant, like he wasn't sure if I would bolt. But that was the last thing on my mind. Instead, I wanted more of him, so I pressed closer. It was all the encouragement he needed to deepen the kiss. Warmth spread through my body as the scent of him filled my senses.

When he lifted his mouth from mine, I opened my eyes slowly, like waking from a dream, and looked into the green depths of his. "Don't go, Sarah Beth," he whispered.

Aaron

The words escaped without thought. "Don't go, Sarah Beth." But I didn't regret them. It could be thinking too much was my problem. Worrying over what might or might not happen and putting up barriers to protect myself. What was I afraid of, anyway?

Wrinkles formed between Sarah Beth's brows. "What'd you say?" She was giving me an out. With anyone else, I might've been tempted to take it, too.

Cupping her chin in my hand, I looked her straight in the eyes. "Don't go running off to Peachtree. Give us a chance."

Her mouth dropped open, and she blinked. "Oh." Her hand was splayed across my chest. Could she feel my heart beating like a bass drum? Drawing in a deep breath, she let it out real slow and stepped back. "This is kind of sudden." She smoothed a strand of hair from her face, and a host of emotions shadowed her eyes.

It was too bad I was illiterate when it came to reading women. Fear, excitement, passion. I couldn't tell. But since she didn't respond with an immediate,

"Yes," then it was anyone's guess. I should be grateful she didn't say, "No," either.

She huffed out what might've been a laugh. "You've been through an ordeal of your own, lately. I mean, with the train accident and the death of that girl." Her voice petered off at the end, and a shadow of pain crossed her eyes. Maybe I wasn't so illiterate, after all, because I knew right then what she was thinking.

"Kind of puts things into perspective, doesn't it? Our petty problems looked mighty small when stacked up against that accident." Or suicide. I'd been too wrapped up in how the report would hit me to find out.

"Yes, they do." She touched my arm, a light sweep of her fingers. "Have you heard anything yet? About the girl, I mean."

I shook my head. Sarah Beth was carrying a load on her thin shoulders, but she'd still found the strength to face her demons. Whoever said men were the stronger sex didn't have a clue. "The reports are done, though."

She frowned. "No one's told you the outcome?"

"I haven't asked," I admitted, toeing a smudge on the floor with my shoe. "Guess I'm not as brave as you."

"Brave?" She shook her head so hard, her ponytail slipped. "Hardly." Raising her gaze to mine, she said, "I like you, Aaron. A lot. But I don't know if I'm brave enough to take a chance on getting hurt again."

Honesty. How refreshing. Maybe I should try it. "Are you afraid I'll turn out to be like your husband?"

"Not really." Folding her arms, she shrugged. "He was a product of his lousy upbringing. No family to speak of, so it's no wonder he became so hateful. I know in my head you're nothing like him. You're kind and thoughtful and loyal." Sounded like she was describing a Golden Retriever.

"There are plenty of good people who weren't brought up in a loving home." Like her, although I wouldn't point it out. "And plenty of others who had a family like mine and still turn out ugly." I reached out and brushed a knuckle down her baby-smooth cheek, which immediately flushed pink. "Would it help to know I'm kind of scared, too?"

She grinned, little lines crinkling around her eyes. "You're not either."

Fingering a loose strand of hair from her face, I nodded. "God's honest truth. You're not the only one worried about being hurt, Sarah Beth." It was time to man up and be as honest as she was. "I've always kept distance between myself and whoever I was seein' for fear I'd be rejected."

She quirked a brow. "You're kidding, right?" With a snort, she swept a hand to encompass my body like I was on display. "I bet you could have just about any woman you wanted. You're the whole stinking package." Guess she was partial to Golden Retrievers.

Laughter erupted from me when her face went immediately red, and she clamped a hand over her mouth like she wanted to stuff the outburst back inside. Kind of like closing the pig pen once the hogs got out.

"You give me way too much credit, but I appreciate it anyway." I rubbed the side of my nose, stalling long enough to grow a spine. "My parents tell me it's on account of when I was a baby."

Folding her arms, she jutted out a hip. We sure weren't getting much work done today, but it was more important we cleared the air some. "Did they drop you on your head or something?" The twitch of her lips told me she thought I was making a joke. I could stop right here and play it that way. But where would that get us?

The forced chuckle fell flat. "Nope. Nothing quite so cliché." I cleared my throat. "I was put in foster care for about five months."

Her eyebrows drew together as she frowned. "You're *not* kidding, are you?"

I shook my head.

"What happened? I mean, if you don't mind me asking."

Scraping my hand through my hair, I shrugged. It was going to sound ridiculous. Because it sort of was. "When I was only a few months old, Mama got pregnant with my sister Carrie. There were complications right from the get-go, and halfway through the pregnancy, her doctor put her on complete bed rest."

"That must've been hard. Can't imagine having to stay like that for months, but couldn't your daddy care for you?"

"He'd only been with the railroad a couple years, and he worked the Extra Board. If he didn't work, they'd have no money or insurance. Mama had a sister they were hopin' would take me, but she had three little ones—the youngest born only a month before. So, they didn't have much choice but temporary foster care."

Sarah Beth appeared lost for words as she lowered herself onto the stack of floor tiles.

"I know what you're thinkin'."

Squinting up at me, she said, "You do?"

"What does one have to do with the other, right? I mean, so what? I spent a few months living with someone other than my parents." I huffed out a laugh.

"That's not even close." She'd gazed up at me. "You ever hear of RAD—Reactive Attachment Disorder?"

"Uh-huh." Sounded like a fancy psychology term Mama's counselor might've shared with her.

"It's what can happen to a child when they're not given enough nurturing as a baby. It's kind of extreme, and not what you're talking about, but it helps to understand how babies can be affected early on."

I narrowed my eyes on her. "How d'you know about this stuff?"

"When I was in high school, I was fixin' to become a teacher, so I did a lot of research. It kind of scared me. That's one of the problems teachers face with kids in the classroom. But I remembered it mostly because my own mama wasn't exactly Mary Poppins."

I tapped my heart. "But you don't think that's what this is."

A smile softened her mouth, and she shook her head. "Of course, not. The thing is, anytime a baby's dealt a trauma like what happened to you, it has repercussions. That's one of the reasons I worry over Gracie Lynn so much. She saw and heard more than any kid ought to."

Massaging my sore shoulder, I looked at Sarah Beth. "Okay, Doctor McCallister, what's the cure?"

The tinkle of her laughter eased the heaviness of our conversation. "Don't rightly know, since I got my degree by way of the Internet. But I'd say your prognosis is pretty good."

Considering she had me wanting a lifetime with her, I had to agree.

Chapter 24

Sarah Beth

Aaron Cooper was a dangerous man. With only a couple kisses, he had me dreaming of happily-ever-afters. I blamed it on my weakened emotional state. If not for this business with Mama and finding out my daddy was alive and well, I would've been able to keep my fickle heart under control.

That was a lie, of course. All Aaron had to do was swipe a finger down my cheek, and I melted like cheap wax. And his kisses. Whew, he sure knew what he was doing. Then again, who was I to judge? Aside from a peck on the cheek from Billy Blankenship when I was in the third grade, my experience was limited to Jason.

Things were less complicated when it was just me and Gracie Lynn. If Aaron wasn't in the picture, I'd take myself down to Peachtree and start fresh. I wouldn't have to worry over his feelings—or mine. But if I was fixing to stay, I needed to get some answers out of Mama whether she was of a mind to give them or not. And if she refused? Well, I guess I'd have to take Jenna up on her offer of a place to live until I could find me a job.

After I dropped Gracie Lynn at preschool, I sat in the car for a good long time praying for Mama to have a softened heart and for me to stay calm—basically, a miracle. It didn't keep my palms from sweating on the drive home or for the pit in my belly to go away. What did I have to be nervous about? It's not like I'd lose anything if Mama refused to answer my questions. Jason's blood money, maybe, but nothing of any real importance.

I parked the car at the end of the lot in front of the room that was now finished—thanks to Aaron's help with the linoleum. I poked my head inside and sighed. It turned out real nice with the floor and walls having a coordinating color. It smelled new, too. We'd hauled some of the pieces Jenna and me got at the estate sales, and it set the room off perfectly. Exactly as I'd imagined. It'd be a shame for it to go to waste because Mama was obstinate.

No point in stalling any longer. I walked past the other rooms while the birds in the magnolia trees chirped away. It was mating season, and they did it up right. The sun was warm on my face and the air smelled of flowers blooming and rich earth. I soaked it all up. *Thank You, Jesus, for this moment. Help me to walk through this with Mama in a way that honors You.*

The motel apartment was dark as night after being in the bright sunlight. I blinked until my eyes adjusted and listened for where Mama might be. A pot clanked from the kitchen, and I drew in a deep breath and let it out real slow. Ready or not.

Sun poured through the window and bathed Mama in stark light. Thin as she was, the skin on her upper arms was loose and wrinkled, and her face was etched with deep grooves. Summers working in the garden, and maybe whatever anger seemed to lurk in her heart, had aged her quite a bit. Anyone who didn't know her birthdate might think she was ten years older than she was.

So focused on taking her in, I didn't notice she'd seen me until she spoke. "What d'you want?" A loaded question. I could think of a dozen things, but I'd settle for answers.

"We need to talk, Mama." I'd wanted my words to exude confidence, but instead they came out weak—breathless.

Mama scowled and turned her back to me. "You wanna talk about Gracie Lynn or the weather or what's next on your to-do list, fine. But I ain't gonna talk about your daddy."

Clearing my throat, I pushed back my shoulders. "Then we got a problem." There was the confidence I'd been praying for. "If you refuse to talk to me about this, I got no choice but to leave here."

She turned quick as snake. One hand gripping the counter, she placed the other against her chest and glared at me. "After all I done for you and Gracie Lynn?" Her eyes filled with hatred as she narrowed them on me. "You ungrateful, spoiled—"

"No!" She was echoing the exact insults Jason had hurled at me when I dared to question his behavior. "I'm not gonna stand here and take your abuse, Mama." My throat ached with tears, and I had to swallow before they choked me. "God knows I've not been a perfect daughter to you, and I'm sorry for that. But you've been ugly toward me since I can remember. If you treated me with half the kindness you show Gracie Lynn, I wouldn't have run off with Jason in the first place." The accusation hung heavy between us, and Mama sagged against the counter.

Afraid she'd collapse, I rushed to her side and wrapped an arm around her, half expecting she'd push me away. "You need to sit." I walked her to a kitchen chair and helped her ease into it. Maybe it was an act. Play the frail old lady, and I'd back off. Instead, I got her a glass of water then pulled out another chair and sat so close, our knees nearly touched.

"What did I ever do to make you so disappointed in me?" It wasn't until the words tumbled from my mouth that I knew it was the heart of all our battles. Years of trying to win Mama's love when I didn't have the first clue how. I couldn't help the tears that swam in my eyes or the pain that laced my question. I was so tired of being a failure. I failed as a daughter, failed as a wife. And I feared I'd fail as a mama, too.

Mama's chin wobbled, and it appeared she was doing all she could to hold onto her composure. I'd never seen her cry. Didn't even think she was capable. "You've never been a disappointment." The words seemed as if they were pulled from her, one painful syllable at a time. Then she hung her head, like the admission had taken every ounce of energy.

A tightness in my chest I'd never recognized before eased. It wasn't a declaration of motherly love, but it was a start. "Then why have you been so angry with me my whole life?"

She rested her elbows on the table and peered up at me. "It's not you I been angry at, Sarah Beth."

When she didn't say more, I pushed. "Garrett?"

Shaking her head, she sighed. "None of this is his fault. Fact is, he's been good to me all these years."

All these years? "But y'all haven't seen each other since before I was born." That *was* what he'd said, right? Had he lied, too?

Mama reached across the table to snatch a napkin from the holder then swiped it across her eyes before she took to folding and unfolding it. "You fussed at me a couple times, wantin' to know how I was making ends meet with business so slow." Slow? It was dead as could be. "Garrett"— she cut a quick glance at me—"your daddy, he's been sending me money every month. Didn't matter that I kicked him out before you were born, he just kept sending those checks."

I wasn't sure what it proved more—that Garrett was a merciful man or Mama took advantage. Either way, she had no call to divorce him. "If you didn't wanna be with him, then why get married?"

Eyes focused on her hands, Mama started shredding the napkin with shaky fingers. "Thought I could do it. My mama was pushing me to get hitched, and Garrett—well, he was ever'thing a woman could want in a husband. But I was too broken."

"Broken how?" Mama didn't answer, and a knot fisted in my belly as the truth dawned on me. "Were you assaulted?" Even though I whispered the question, Mama winced as if she'd been struck. "Who, Mama?" I clenched my hands and rested them on my knees.

"Don't matter who, Sarah Beth. Fact is, I couldn't..." She shook her head. "Garrett deserved better. He was a good man, and he needed someone who could love him proper."

That explained why she'd kicked him out, but there was still something that didn't make sense. "So, why didn't you tell him you were pregnant? If he was the man you thought he was, he would've done everything he could for you—for me."

Mama lifted tear-filled eyes to me. "You're all I had, Sarah Beth. He would've been right to take you away from me, and I didn't think I could survive it." Swallowing, she blew out a sigh. "You asked who I was angry at all these years. It was me. I been angry at myself for lettin' what happened that one time steal what life I had to give. And I been angry at the man who took it from me."

There was a part of me that wanted to close the distance between Mama and me and wrap her in my arms. She was hurting, that was clear as could be. But I'd been hurting my whole life, and she could've fixed it. Instead, she'd been so caught up in herself, she couldn't see what it did to me. How she pushed me away and into the arms of a man most likely as vile as the one who abused her.

All sorts of edgy, I jumped up. I needed to get some air, to think. To pray.

"You gonna take Gracie Lynn and leave here?" Mama's voice stopped me halfway out the kitchen door.

I couldn't look at her—not yet—so I didn't bother to turn. "I don't know, Mama." Without waiting for a response, I walked out the door.

Aaron

Kylie Hinson. That was the name of the girl who'd been killed by my train. Or rather had committed suicide by train. Sarah Beth's the one who convinced me to look at the report, even if she wasn't aware. She thought I was kidding when I told her she was brave, but it was the God's honest truth. A lot braver than I'd been. Not only had she survived the abuse from her husband, but she came home to help out her mama who didn't seem to appreciate it at all.

Sarah Beth was every bit the Golden Retriever she'd accused me of being. Kind, thoughtful, and loyal.

It turned out that Kylie, a distraught twenty-year-old, parked that old van onto the tracks and waited for death to snatch her up. Cecil and me were cleared of any wrong doing, which came as no surprise. There was nothing we could've done to prevent it from happening.

So why did I feel so guilty?

Once I read the report, I couldn't get Kylie Hinson out of my mind. Maybe it was none of my business, but I wanted to know why she chose to die like she did. Basically, a child who had her entire life ahead of her. And if I was going to be completely honest, I wanted compassion for her to override my anger. Even though Cecil had been released from the hospital, he almost died. A train derailment was a serious incident. What if we'd been carrying hazardous materials or the derailment took out another vehicle or person? More deaths because one person wanted to end her life.

Every railroad man heard of the Waverly train derailment of 1978—sixty miles north of Nashville on the way to Memphis. The Louisville and Northern Railroad was carrying 92 cars, some with propane. Unseasonable warmth the day after the derailment caused the tanks to expand while crews worked to clean it all up. By the time someone realized vapor was leaking from one of the cars, it was too late. The explosion killed sixteen people. Debris was found more than 350 yards from the scene. So, yeah, I needed to dig a little to find grace.

Kylie Hinson's address was in Cleveland, north-east of Chattanooga. It was an easy drive—physically. No telling how it might tax me emotionally if I actually made contact with any of her kinfolk, not that I expected to. According to the report, she wasn't married. Her address was a matter of record, and a Google search told me it was a large apartment complex.

I'd invited Cecil to go with me, but his snort of disapproval came over the line clear as if he'd been standing in front of me. "You ain't gonna get anything but wasted time playing Sherlock Holmes," he'd said. "You work on the railroad long as I have, you grow a thicker skin."

He made it sound like a good thing. I didn't want a thicker skin; I wanted a softer heart—not that I'd ever confess as much to him. If I was going to get myself hitched, I wanted to be the kind of husband God would call me to be. The Bible said a husband was to lay his life down for his wife, love her like Christ loved the church. A thick skin wouldn't do me a whole lot of good.

It was nearing the first week of June, and spring had already given way to summer. By the time I'd pulled my truck into the apartment complex parking lot, my shirt was sticking to my back and sweat had popped up along my neckline. It didn't help the air conditioning was on the fritz, and I had a severe case of nerves.

The building had two levels, the doors lined up so close together they looked more like motel rooms than living areas. There were a few kids playing kickball in the parking lot and a few more huddled together looking at something on a tablet. No adults around, which nicked at some latent protective instinct in me. Shouldn't someone be watching the little ones? A couple of them were no bigger than Gracie Lynn.

I climbed the outside stairs on legs heavy as cement posts and moved halfway down until I reached the right apartment. Taking a deep breath, I knocked on the door and could hear a baby crying from inside. Surely, Kylie didn't have herself a baby? She was just a kid herself. After about ten seconds, I was fixing to leave when the door was wrenched open.

A young man, couldn't be older than mid-twenties, had a baby tucked under one arm. His head was shaved near bald and both arms were tatted clear to his t-shirt sleeve. "Yeah?"

Frowning, I glanced at the address I'd written down to be sure I got the right place. "Is this Kylie Hinson's place?"

He shifted the baby, his eyes narrowing. "Yeah. Or leastways, it was. Who're you?"

My heart sunk along with my nerve. "Aaron Cooper." I cleared my throat. "You kin to Kylie?"

"Not exactly." The baby let out a wail, and he cradled it against his chest and patted its back. To look at the dude, you wouldn't think he had a paternal bone in his body. Guess that's why we weren't called to judge. You never knew the depth of a person from looking at the outside. "Kylie and me was gonna get married." He might've had a hard edge, but there was a sheen of tears in his eyes. "Why? What's it to you?"

A young couple came down the corridor, arguing over someone named Heather. I tilted my head toward the apartment. "You mind if we go inside?"

His jaw flexed. "Not 'til you tell me why you're here."

Adjusting the sling on my arm, I sighed. "I work for Norfolk Southern, and I was on the crew—" Snapping my mouth closed, I shook my head.

"It was your train that killed Kylie." His face drained of color leaving him a ghostly white. The walking dead. Most likely, it's how he felt. A fiancé who was gone, left with a baby to raise.

"Yeah. I'm afraid so."

I tensed every muscle in my body, waiting for a blow to the face or gut, but instead, he stepped back and opened the door wide. "Come in."

Relief had me nearly sagging as I stepped inside. I wasn't wrong about it looking like a motel unit. The studio apartment was crammed with a couple chairs and a bed—all of which were covered with clothes or baby paraphernalia. The counters in the kitchenette were covered with food boxes, and the sink was overflowing with dirty dishes.

The kid balanced the baby with one arm and swept the chairs of clothing with his free hand. "It's kind of a mess. I could say it's on account of Kylie bein' gone, but it's been like this since we moved in two months ago." The baby started fussing, and he bounced it up and down against his chest rather than sit.

"Is there something I can do?" Inept was the best word to describe me in that moment. I'd be better suited to teaching chemistry, and I'd barely passed high school science.

"Nah." He nodded toward one of the chairs. "Sit if you want. I'm just gonna get Faith her bottle."

It didn't feel right to sit while he wasn't, so I leaned my hip against the cluttered counter, awkward as a pimply kid at his first dance. "How old is your daughter?" Faith, he said was her name.

"Goin' on three months." He grabbed a bottle from the fridge and frowned at it. It didn't take but a second for me to see his dilemma. With one working arm, I'd found myself in similar situations multiple times a day.

"Can I open that for you?" I pointed to the bottle.

He hefted the baby. "Actually, you mind holding her?" Before I could answer, he handed Faith to me. What could I do but take her? As I cradled the wriggling body against my chest, he unscrewed the bottle and put it in the microwave. 'How'd you hurt your arm, anyway?"

Would it be thoughtless to tell him I got injured when the train derailed on account of Kylie? "A little accident is all. And it's a broken scapula. The sling's to keep me from moving it too much."

"You okay holding her?" He pointed at the baby.

"Sure." I glanced down at the little girl who was looking at me with wide, blue eyes. There was a smattering of peach fuzz on her head and dimples in her cheeks when she smiled at me. Being an uncle, she wasn't the first baby I'd held, but it was the first time it drew a yearning for my own from me. Was this what Gracie Lynn looked like when she was just a baby?

The microwave's beep broke Faith's hold on me, and I looked up to see Kylie's boyfriend test the temperature of the liquid on his wrist. "I didn't catch your name," I said as he screwed the top onto the bottle.

"Connor Baxter." He set the bottle down and took Faith from me. "If you don't mind, I gotta feed her."

As he sat down, I settled into the only other chair. "You have any help with the baby?"

Tempting Faith with the nipple of the bottle, he shrugged. "I got my mom and Kylie's sister." When Faith latched onto the bottle, he focused on me. "If you came here 'cause you blame yourself, don't. I mean, Kylie was havin' a hard time ever since the baby was born. I tried to get her to see a doctor..." He looked down at Faith, but not before I caught the tears again. "Anyway, she woulda done it one way or another." His words sounded casual—almost cold—but the sagging of his shoulders and pain etched in his face told me how much he was hurting.

"If there's anything I can do..." Like what? Babysitting duty? Hardly. Maybe slip him a couple hundred bucks to help out?

Connor shrugged. "Unless you got a line on a job."

That might be something I could do. "How do you feel about workin' for the railroad?" Wouldn't that be a strange twist?

Chapter 25

Sarah Beth

Ever since I'd run off with Jason, I blamed Mama for it. If only she'd treated me better, if only I hadn't been so needy. It seemed to me those two little words—if only—were the saddest combination ever. How many people looked through the rearview mirror with those words on their lips, steeped in the bitterness of lost dreams? Apparently me, for one.

I was coming to realize a better lens to look through life was "but God." I mean, wasn't He the one who could take our messes and make something beautiful from them? Take Gracie Lynn, for example. If not for Jason, I wouldn't have my precious daughter, and I wouldn't trade her for anything in the world.

So, why was it so hard for me to get past Mama's lies and be thankful for what it brought me rather than what it took from me? Why was I so gracious with my own failures and so critical of hers? I knew it wasn't fair, but that didn't change it any.

And then there was Aaron. He claimed to have feelings for me. I wasn't blind, so I saw it coming. Sort of. And, oh, how I wanted to tell him I felt the same. I didn't bother responding to his texts, even though I was itching to. If only. If only I hadn't been hurt by a man and fearful of trusting another. If only I was sure my feelings for him were real and not based on a heart that desperately needed to be loved.

I surely hated those two, little words.

So, what's a girl to do when she can't make heads or tails out of her life? Most would go running to their mamas for advice. That wouldn't do me a lick of good. Instead, I was running to my daddy, hoping he would help me get a little clarity and a much-needed escape from Mama's influence. If Aaron hadn't basically declared his intentions and asked me not to move to Peachtree, I might've invited him to come along. It sure would've been safer to take his truck instead of my clunker. Instead, I decided to trust God to get me and Gracie Lynn down and back without my car dying on me.

I didn't bother to hide the trip from Mama, either. I was done lying to her if for no other reason than to see how she'd react—which was not at all. She merely shrugged and sighed. Guess she figured her opinion no longer mattered, which it didn't. I wasn't proud of how I was feeling, but I wasn't ashamed, either. And God must not have been too disappointed in me, because He made sure we got down to Peachtree without a single incident.

It was a stunning day with plenty of sunshine and a few puffy clouds overhead. It took us a little more time than when I'd gone there with Aaron on account of needing to stop for potty breaks for Gracie Lynn and Jazzy.

I'd called Garrett ahead of time to be sure he'd be around. It would've been foolish to drive all that way only to find he was gone for the weekend. Aaron and me just got lucky when we went down the first time. Garrett had asked when I called if I wanted to meet my half-brothers, but I told him the two of us needed some time to talk first. I didn't want to be grilling him on personal things in front of two men—and maybe their wives—who I didn't even know.

It was nearing noon when I pulled my clunker into Garrett's driveway. His neighbors were going to think their poor kin had shown up. My car was a blight on their picture-perfect front yard, but there was nothing I could do about that. Gracie Lynn was fast asleep in her seat with Jazzy curled up beside her. I climbed from the car and stretched, my gaze moving up to the top of the huge tree thick with leaves to search for the mockingbird chattering away.

"You're here." When I turned, Garrett was walking down the porch steps. "How was the drive?"

A sudden bout of shyness struck me. It was so strange to think this was my daddy—and I'd spent all of three hours with him. "It was good. We had to make a few pitstops for Gracie Lynn and Jazzy."

"Jazzy?" His brows drew together. Before I could respond, he held up a finger and smiled. "Gracie Lynn's puppy. I remember now." He closed the distance between us and pulled me in for a hug. That shyness I was feeling melted away. It was like our hearts were bonded even if our minds had not.

Stepping back, I waved to the car. "Let me get Gracie Lynn." He was going to meet his granddaughter for the first time. What would he think of her? What would Gracie Lynn think of *him*?

When I opened the back door, Gracie Lynn opened her eyes. "Are we there yet?"

I brushed my finger down her cheek. "We're here. Are you ready to meet your granddaddy?"

Nodding, she wrestled with the car seat straps, pushing my hands aside when I tried to help. "I can do it." While she unhooked herself, I reached across to pick up Jazzy and snapped her leash to her collar. I wasn't about to let her loose in Patsy's house until she'd emptied her bladder.

Walking the two of them around the front of the car, Gracie Lynn looked up into Garrett's twinkling eyes and broad grin. "Gracie Lynn, this is your granddaddy."

Garret crouched down to eye level and opened his arms. "Well, aren't you the spittin' image of your mama. You mind if I give you a hug?"

Expecting Gracie Lynn to shrink against my legs, I was pleasantly surprised when she ran into Garrett's arms. Then again, she'd done the same with Mama. How that child could be so *normal* was a testament to God's favor.

Gracie Lynn hugged Garrett, and when he stood, her eyes followed him. "Are you Mama's daddy?"

"Yep, I sure am. And you have some cousins here that are excited to meet you, too."

A pang of disappointment had my smile slipping. If Chance and Caleb were here, I wouldn't be able to ask Garrett all those questions that had been crowding my mind for the last couple days.

"They're out back with your... my wife, Miss Patsy." He took one look at me and read my mind. "Don't worry. The boys dropped them off and will be back for an early supper. That should give us plenty of time to talk. And Gracie Lynn will have someone to play with while we do." Bless his heart. He'd thought of everything.

Rather than go in the front door, Garrett led us around to the backyard, which I hadn't seen on my previous visit. There was a large lawn area with a swing set much like Gracie Lynn's in the middle, and a climbing tree like the one out front. Except this one had a tire swing and a treehouse. How perfect was that?

"Y'all out here?" Garrett called.

Kristy and Jake popped their heads through the two windows in the treehouse. "We're here," Jake said. "Do you wanna come up and play?" He asked Gracie Lynn.

Garrett waved them down. "You come here and say hello to your aunt Sarah Beth and meet your cousin Gracie Lynn, first. Then y'all can play."

The kids scrambled down the ladder as Patsy came out with a tray of drinks and food. "Hey, Sarah Beth." As she placed the tray on the table beneath the patio cover, Jazzy barked and ran up to her, tail wagging. Patsy squatted down, scooped up the puppy, then smiled at Gracie Lynn as the kids gathered around. "Hey there, Gracie Lynn. I'm Patsy, and it sure is a pleasure to meet you."

Gracie Lynn leaned against my leg but returned Patsy's smile. "That's Jazzy. She's my puppy."

Kristy's eyes widened. "She's sure cute. Can we play with her?"

Gracie Lynn nodded, and the three of them took off, Jazzy running and nipping at their heels while the giggled and squealed. As I watched them romp around, pure joy filled my spirit. Gracie Lynn had cousins and grandparents. A family, just like I'd always wanted for her.

"Y'all must be hungry," Patsy said, breaking into my thoughts. "I know you two wanna talk, so I'm gonna take the kids out to lunch and to the park, if that's okay with you." She arched her brow at me and waited for my answer.

Would Gracie Lynn go willingly with people she'd never met before? I turned to see how she was taking to Kristy and Jake. The three of them were huddled together like they'd already become fast friends. "If Gracie Lynn's okay with it, I am."

Once they were gone, Garrett and me were alone. Other than the birds chattering in the trees and Jazzy barking at a squirrel hanging from a limb.

"Have a seat. I think Patsy poured us sweet tea, but if there's something else I can get you...?"

"No, thanks. This is perfect." As I sank into one end of the L-shaped sofa, it struck me that the patio furniture was nicer than Mama's living room set. No faded and tattered cushions or nicked up frame.

"We've got some veggies and dip. You like hummus?" He fussed with the trays, like he was as nervous as me.

The way my stomach was flip-flopping, food was the last thing I wanted. "I'm fine with the tea for now." Leaning toward the tray, I got me a frosty glass, if for no other reason than to have something to hold while we talked. Otherwise, I'd take to wringing my hands like a Nervous Nellie.

Garrett picked up his glass of tea and settled into the chair closest to me. "You said there's somethin' you needed to talk about. I figure your mama's none too happy about our connecting like this."

I took a sip of tea and set the glass back on the table. "Let's just say things have been a bit tense since I told her about seeing you." But that wasn't what I'd wanted to discuss. There wasn't anything he could do about it, and even being mad at Mama like I was, I wasn't fixing to be ugly about her to Garrett. "Maybe what's between you and Mama isn't any of my business, but I'm curious why you've been sending her money all these years. I mean, she treated you poorly, but you've still supported her."

Garrett rubbed his hand down his thigh and frowned. "She told you that, did she?"

"Yes, sir. Not without a little badgering on my part, though." Did he know Mama had been assaulted before the two of them met?

"I suppose these days, most young people don't take marriage seriously. Soon as things go sour, they walk away." He huffed out a humorless laugh. "Even heard a couple gals talkin' a few weeks back about what they're lookin' for in their *first* husband. Like tradin' in a car when it gets too many miles."

"Except Mama said she made you leave. Isn't that true?"

"It is. Doesn't matter, though. I still made a commitment, even if your mama thought otherwise. She might've divorced me, but I still had to do right by her." He shrugged as his eyes slid from mine.

"Did you know about Mama's past? That she'd been assaulted?"

He twisted his mouth. "Suspected. It made sense the way she was with me. There was nothin' I could do to change her mind. She wasn't willin' to get help. I'll admit, after I left, I struggled with anger a good bit." The feeling of betrayal must've run deep as the Mississippi River.

"So, I guess you forgave her. I mean, why would you send money all these years later if not?" Far as I was concerned, that went beyond forgiveness. Maybe that's what Jesus meant in the Bible about how we were supposed to treat those who hurt us.

"I came to realize holdin' onto bitterness wouldn't accomplish anything but cause grief for myself." Shaking his head real slow, he sighed. "But I have to say, I'm havin' a rough time forgivin' your mama for not telling me about you. It's like she punished me for someone else's sins twice. And you and me...well, we were made victims of her abuse, too."

I hadn't thought of it like that, but it was true. One person's evil actions had a ripple effect that might could go on for generations if someone didn't break the cycle. I just didn't know if I was strong enough to be the one to do it.

Aaron

No one would ever accuse me of being a patient man, but I waited two days for Sarah Beth to come by or call. Considering I'd poured my heart out to her, it was an interminable amount of time. I'd left no fewer than three messages for her with not so much as a thumbs-up emoji. It was time we talked, and it was going to be face-to-face.

Meeting Connor and seeing how Kylie's death affected him cemented my decision to try and make a go of things with Sarah Beth. She was the only woman I'd ever met that had me thinking about my future—and I didn't want it to be without her and Gracie Lynn in it.

I'd kept a wide berth around Miss Pickett, but if I was fixing to marry Sarah Beth someday (soon, I hoped), her mama and me would have to find a way to get along. With that thought in the forefront of my mind, I decided to march myself over to the motel with the boldness of David facing Goliath. Miss Pickett might not be a giant, but she sure had the attitude of an angry Philistine at times. Still, I refused to let her bully me from seeing Sarah Beth.

Too worked up to worry over chiggers and ticks, I barreled my way through the thicket-covered trail. When I stepped out onto the motel property, first thing I noticed was the absence of Sarah Beth's car. She could've been at the store or on some jaunt with Jenna, which made me pause. Maybe I should check back later. Send another text message. *Chicken.*

"She ain't here." Miss Pickett's cranky voice drew my attention. She stood outside the unit Sarah Beth and me had installed linoleum in the other day. It took a moment for me to process what she'd said.

"You know where she is?" *Please don't say she's moved out.*

Miss Pickett sniffed and folded her arms across her thin body. "Peachtree." Then she headed off toward the apartment like she hadn't just punched me in the gut, which is where my heart sank to.

"Hang on a sec." I took advantage of my long legs and crossed to her in about ten strides. To her credit, she stopped and turned to wait for me. "Did she move out?"

She tented her narrowing eyes with a hand and peered up at me as I drew close. "Thought the two of you was thick as thieves." Her lips pursed tight, like she'd sucked a lemon. "You know better than me what she's up to." If she worked at it, she couldn't be less likable. If Sarah Beth did move out, I could hardly blame her. Even if doing so without so much as a word to me would prick my pride some.

Gritting my teeth, I took me a few breaths. If I'd prayed for patience, the good Lord couldn't have tested me more. "Haven't spoken to her for a couple days." Didn't want to betray Sarah Beth's confidence, but I was bordering on desperate. "Did she just go down for a visit?" Although, I couldn't see her trusting that piece of junk she drove with Gracie Lynn in tow all the way past Atlanta and back. If she wanted to visit Garrett, why didn't she ask to borrow my truck?

"Still got clothes in her closet, so I s'pect she'll be back." If Miss Pickett was checking out Sarah Beth's belongings, she must've been worried. "She didn't bother tellin' me one way or the other. Just that she was headin' down to see...her daddy." Miss Pickett's eyes clouded over as she started off toward her apartment.

If I had half a brain, I would've hightailed it back to my place, but the droop of her shoulders and shuffle of her steps tugged at me. Could've been the Lord pushing me to practice grace or maybe I'd been weakened by events of the last day or so. Either way, I called out to her before I thought better of it.

"Can we talk?"

Turning, she frowned at me. "'Bout what?" Good question. One I had to scramble to find a plausible answer to. Could hardly admit I pitied her. That and five bucks might get me a fancy coffee at Peet's.

"Sarah Beth," I finally blurted. That subject alone could cover a whole lot of territory. I'd just have to find a way to avoid the landmines.

A furrow creased her brow as she tilted her head toward the apartment. "Come on, then." It was a toss-up whether her invitation was a blessing or a curse. Guess I'd find out quick enough.

I hadn't been in the motel since the last time I'd dropped off food for her three months ago. Ever since Sarah Beth had come home, Miss Pickett wouldn't let me past the threshold. Where before there'd been clutter on the reception desk and clothes strewn about the furniture in the front room, everything was now tidy. Not even a hint of dust. Appeared Sarah Beth kept a clean house, not that it mattered a lick to me. I'd been on my own so long, I was downright efficient with a dust cloth and vacuum. Didn't need myself a live-in maid, although having someone to cook would be a nice change from frozen dinners.

Miss Pickett didn't bother with social niceties but pointed to the couch like I was Jazzy and she was giving a command. I sat just the same. No sense poking the bear.

She eased herself into the recliner and frowned at me. "I'm listenin'."

My palms sweated like I was standing in front of a firing squad. "Look, I know you don't like me, but—"

"Thought you wanted to talk about Sarah Beth." She tossed a glare sharp enough to cut.

Wiping my free hand on my jeans, I glared right back. "I'm gettin' there, if you'd let me finish." How was it Sarah Beth hadn't pulled every bit of hair from her own head dealing with this woman?

Miss Picket crossed her arms. "Go on, then." Swallowing a groan, I adjusted my sling, and her gaze homed in on it. "Sarah Beth said you got yourself hurt in a train accident."

I nodded once. "We derailed when we hit a van parked on the tracks. Wasn't exactly an accident, though. The girl who parked there...well, she was intent on ending her life."

Her eyes snapped up to meet mine. It was clear Sarah Beth hadn't shared that tidbit of information. "Suicide?" It was the first time I'd heard compassion in her tone. "How old a girl was she?"

"Twenty or so." This wasn't what I'd wanted to talk about, but it beat listening to her snipe at me. "She had a baby, too. A three-month-old named Faith."

She cocked her head. "You get all that in a report?" I'd forgotten she had some knowledge of how the railroad worked.

"No, ma'am. I wanted to offer my condolences, so I went to her place up in Cleveland. Had herself a fiancé. Connor's his name. He's pretty broken up about it, as you can imagine."

Whatever I'd expected, it wasn't her sudden agitation. She rubbed her forehead and mumbled, "Just a child. Hard to figure. So young, and with a little one, too." Then her eyes caught hold of mine. "Do you reckon...?" Her question flitted away as she ran a trembling hand across her chin.

I shifted to the edge of the couch. "Miss Pickett, you okay? Can I get you some water?" Didn't know how it would help, but it was the only thing I could think of.

She waved the offer away like shooing a pesky fly. "Never mind." With a shake of her head and a deep breath, her focus returned. "What is this about Sarah Beth?"

I straightened my spine, and a sharp pain reminded me I was injured. "I care about her, Miss Pickett. And even though you don't like me, I—"

"Don't trust you," she cut in. "Most ever' man I've come across had himself a selfish streak a mile wide." That was not only unfair, I had a feeling it wasn't true, either.

"Just so you know, I was the one who drove Sarah Beth down to meet Garrett Marshall."

Her scowl aged her a good five years. "So?"

Thrusting out my chin, I pinned her eyes with mine. "So, I don't guess he was the sort who cared only about himself. Struck me as a decent guy. More than decent, in fact."

She shrugged one shoulder. "That might be true; he wasn't around long enough to know." Yeah, because she kicked him out.

But if I was going to point out the speck of dust in her eye, I'd need to admit to the plank in mine first. "Sarah Beth told me you suspected I was bein' nice to you on account of wantin' to buy your land."

She glared and sniffed like a queen looking down her nose at a peasant. "You sayin' different?"

"No, ma'am. You were right about me." Her eyes about bugged out of her head, and she started sputtering. Before she could get a word out, I held up my hand. "Sort of. I was ponderin' the idea but ditched it the minute Sarah Beth showed up. And I wasn't tryin' to cheat you out of anything, I was just hopin' that if you chose to sell, you'd give me a chance to make a pitch."

Pursing her lips, she crossed her arms. "Since you're of a mind to be truthful, maybe you can answer me somethin' else." Was there the tiniest bit of respect in her eyes when she looked at me now?

"What's that?"

"You said you care about my daughter. Like a friend, maybe, or are you sweet on her?"

Guess that was a fair question, and since she might could be my mother-in-law some day, I owed her an honest answer. "Yes, ma'am. And I'm gonna do my best to convince her to marry me."

First time I'd ever seen Georgina Pickett speechless.

Chapter 26

Sarah Beth

The trip down to Peachtree was exactly what I'd needed to get the stuffing out of my head. Garrett…Daddy…helped me to put most everything into perspective. My brain told me I needed to forgive Mama, or I'd end up just as bitter and ugly as her. My heart wasn't quite on board yet. Daddy said forgiveness was a process—like peeling an onion. One layer at a time. But I was afraid it wouldn't happen unless I put some distance between us. Maybe find me a job and get Gracie Lynn and me an apartment in Chattanooga.

I met my half-brothers, Chance and Caleb, who looked so much alike, they could've been twins. It was hard to say if they resembled Daddy or Patsy more. Their wives, Jasmine and Eva were precious. They were all so kind and welcoming, the awkwardness I expected never came. As we all sat down to supper, I got so choked up, I had to excuse myself for a few minutes. I couldn't get over the fact that Gracie Lynn and me had an honest-to-goodness family.

And Mama kept me from them. Knowing how much I'd missed out added another layer to that onion.

Gracie Lynn and me didn't get home until late, and I prayed the whole way my car would make it. Daddy wanted me to borrow his SUV, but I couldn't. Even though I appreciated his concern, I was some worried how it would appear to the family. A gold-digging daughter come looking for a handout.

Since Mama was in bed when we got home, there was no drama. Gracie Lynn fell right to sleep, but even exhausted, I laid awake half the night thinking about my day—about my newfound family. Worrying over how it would be with Mama in the morning. And Aaron. He was always hovering somewhere in the back of my mind like a dream too good to be true.

Somewhere around seven the next morning, the dinging of my phone pulled me from my groggy state. I didn't have to look at it to know it was Aaron. He and Jenna were the only ones who ever texted me, and since I'd talked to her on the phone most of the way home, I figured it had to be him. And I was right.

Are you home? Can we talk?

Two little questions, and my heart started skipping like he'd declared his undying love. *Yes and yes. Meet me out front in five.* I climbed out of bed, careful to not wake Gracie Lynn, and slipped into the bathroom. There wasn't time to do more than brush my teeth and splash water on my face. For all I knew, he'd changed his mind about me and wanted to let me down gently. I'd dangled that ol' carrot in front of his nose long enough, and he was done. Done with my fears, done with Mama's ugly attitude, just plain done.

Oh, please, Lord, don't let that be how he's feeling.

My heart was pumping so hard as I tip-toed through the apartment so as not to wake Mama. I wasn't ready to see her quite yet. And when I glanced out the window to find Aaron waiting next to my car, I forgot to breathe until I stepped outside. He was so handsome, kind, and tall. Boy, was he tall. He appeared capable enough to fight back whatever demons were plaguing me, even with one arm in a sling.

"Hey," I whispered, tucking a strand of hair behind my ear.

His smile alone assured me he wasn't fixing to walk away quite yet. "Hey, Sarah Beth." His eyes drank in my face and the smile wavered. "Don't take this as an insult, but you look tired. You okay?"

I glanced over my shoulder, suddenly fearful Mama was lurking in the background. "Can we take a walk?" Then I remembered I was wearing flip-flops. "Maybe down the street a piece?"

"Sure." He offered his hand, and with a sigh of relief, I took it. "Is Gracie Lynn still sleeping?"

I nodded and laced my fingers with his larger, stronger ones. Somehow, we fit together just right. "We got in pretty late last night." I peered up at him. "We went down to Peachtree to see Gar—my daddy." I huffed out a light laugh. "It's gonna take a long time to get used to calling him that."

"You should've told me you were goin'. I would've loaned you my truck. Hate to think of you breaking down between here and there."

Guilt at ignoring his texts had my face warming some. Or maybe it was the heat of the sun peeking through the magnolia trees. "I know. I'm sorry."

He squeezed my hand. "No need to be sorry. I was just worried about you is all. Did you have a good time?" His question was quiet-like, and he didn't fix his eyes on mine. Made me think he wasn't sure he wanted to know the answer. Probably thought I was fixing to move, like I'd talked about last time we were together.

"Yeah, I did. I met my half-brothers and their wives." My chest tightened at the picture of us all sitting around the table. "Mama's taken so much from me, Aaron." My voice broke, and I took a deep breath. "I'm trying to find a way to forgive her." I combed a hand through my hair as we turned off the gravel drive and onto the street. "I *need* to find a way to forgive her. Garrett—I mean, Daddy, did. Do you know he's been sending her money every month? I mean, she kicks the poor guy out, and he *still* takes care of her. Of course, knowing that she'd kept the two of us apart put him back some."

Aaron didn't say anything, just squeezed my hand. When I dared to glance up at him, he appeared deep in thought, his eyes straight ahead. I figured he'd have plenty to say about Mama, seeing as he wasn't her biggest fan—with good reason. Maybe he was tired of my drama and needed a break. But when we'd walked a quarter mile or so without a word between us, uneasiness knotted my belly.

"You okay, Aaron?" A car rumbled down the street, and we moved to the scruffy grass along the edge to give it plenty of room to pass.

As we stepped back into the road, Aaron said, "You know the girl who died in the train accident...or whatever you call it?" That was random, but at least he was talking.

"Kylie, right?"

"Yeah, Kylie. Anyway, I met her fiancé the other day."

I was still wrapping my head around the change of subject, and the pieces weren't quite fitting. "I thought you didn't know anything about her. Last you told me, you hadn't even seen the report."

He grunted. "Guess a lot's happened since then."

"Guess so," I murmured. It was only a few days. Maybe if I'd bothered to answer his texts. Instead, I was so wrapped up in my own stuff, I'd pushed his aside. "So, you read the report?"

"Yep. Kylie Hinson. Twenty years old, and she committed suicide by train."

Even though it was expected, I couldn't hold back the gasp. "Twenty?" She was a child. "And she was engaged?" I wasn't much older when I ran off with Jason, but now it sounded so young.

"Not only engaged, she also had a three-month-old baby."

In my darkest moments, I might've briefly entertained how much easier death would be. But after Gracie Lynn was born, I would've done anything in my power to be there for her. This poor girl, Kylie. She couldn't have been in her right mind.

I blinked away the sudden tears. "How'd you meet her fiancé?"

"Her address was in the report. Tell you the truth, the only reason I decided to follow up was because I was angry with her and was searching out a way to humanize her some. What she did, parking herself on the tracks, put a whole lot of people in danger. Cecil could've died, and if we'd had hazardous material..." He shook his head. "It doesn't really matter why I went. But this kid, Connor, has himself a baby to raise without a mama."

"Does he have family that can help?"

"Yeah. His mama and Kylie's sister." He huffed out a breath. "The thing is, I expected he'd be angry with me—or rather the railroad company—for takin' Kylie's life. But he wasn't. Said she's been dealing with deep sadness since their baby was born."

"Post-partum depression." Common enough that I knew about it. Common enough someone should've recognized it. "How'd Connor seem to you?"

Aaron shrugged. "About as you'd expect. I'm gonna see what I can do to get him trained to work for the railroad. He sounded interested when I brought it up."

"That's kind of you." But not unexpected. "You're a good man, Aaron." The truth of it warmed me clear to my pink-painted toenails.

He stopped walking and tugged on my hand until I turned to look up at him. "There's something I need to tell you." Eyebrows drawn together, he frowned. My stomach clenched at the seriousness of his expression.

"What's wrong?" Was he done with me, after all?

"Nothin's wrong, exactly." He nodded toward a downed log on the side of the road. "Let's sit for a minute."

Aaron

Before texting Sarah Beth that morning, I spent a good bit of time praying for the Lord to guide my steps. There were so many layers to the woman, so many past hurts, it seemed her emotions were like a house of cards. One wrong move, and the whole mess would come tumbling down around us.

Honesty. That word kept poking at me the whole time I was praying. Sarah Beth was afraid to trust because she'd been handed one lie after another. If I was going to have any chance with her, I had to be a man of integrity. No lies, no matter how trivial they might seem to me.

I tugged her hand until she sat next to me on the thick log. Her knees poked through the holes in her faded jeans—holes I had no doubt came by hard work and lots of wear. No fancy, designer clothes for this girl.

Sarah Beth swirled a frayed thread around her finger and sighed. "If you're fixin' to let me down easy, I'd rather you didn't. Just rip off the Band-Aid. I have a lot to do today."

Should I be amused or insulted? Decided it'd serve me better to choose humor. "Guess I'm not all that high on your checklist, huh? Get a load of laundry done. Check." I drew a check mark in the air with my finger. "Give Jazzy a bath. Check. Dump the lovestruck boy next door. Check."

It must've worked, because when I glanced down at her, she was biting her lip against a smile. "So, I haven't scared you off yet?"

Huffing out a laugh, I nudged her shoulder with mine. "You hang out with me long enough, you'll find out I don't scare so easily." Although, that wasn't true in the past. Something about Sarah Beth made me want to be strong. I never cared for the idea of being someone's hero—a knight in shining armor—until she came along.

"Then what do you need to talk about?" Her shoulders tensed up like she was preparing for a hit.

"I saw your mama yesterday. Did she tell you?"

"I haven't seen her since I got home last night. She was already in bed, and I snuck out to see you before she got up." She wrinkled her nose. "Was she ugly toward you?" Then before I could answer, she huffed out a humorless laugh. "I suppose that's a silly question. Mama's never treated you good. I know I've said she's just being herself, but it still makes me crazy. Why does she have to be that way?"

I covered her hand with mine and took a leap onto that flimsy card house. "She has her reasons, Sarah Beth. When you told me she didn't trust me, I should have admitted it then."

Frowning, she shifted so there was space between us. "Admitted what?"

Even though it seemed so trivial now, it wasn't easy to voice. "That I was interested in her property. I thought maybe I could build a spec home on it. But as soon as you showed up, I let go of the idea."

Chewing on the corner of her lower lip, she pulled her hand from mine and stood. I could practically see the wheels turning in her head as she tried to put the pieces together. Then her eyes homed in on mine. "Jenna was your realtor. Mama said she came sniffing around trying to buy the property for a client of hers. That was you." The accusation stung, even if it was true.

"Yes." I reached out to take her hand again, but she stepped back. "This all happened before you came home, Sarah Beth. Like I said, once you showed up, we ditched the idea." What seemed so easy to explain now sounded deceitful and clandestine. At least that's how a person who'd been betrayed over and over again might see it.

She started walking backwards, like she was fixing to take off. "This is what you wanted to talk about? How you and Jenna lied to me? I've been defending you to Mama since I got home, but she was right all along." Her face was red, and tears shimmered in her eyes.

I blew out a breath. "It wasn't like that. And that's not all I wanted to tell you." How had this gone so bad so fast? "If you'll sit down, we can talk this out."

She shook her head. "You lied to me. Why should I believe anything else you have to say?" She flounced down the road, tension in her every step.

Every muscle in my body strained to run after her. She'd be easy enough to catch, but the last thing I wanted was for her to feel threatened. Now what? I looked up to the sky as if I'd see God sitting on a cloud staring down at me. So much for honesty. *Okay, Lord, that didn't go as planned.* Closing my eyes, I repeated the question over and over again—*now what?* Mama always said when asking for answers, it's best to stay real quiet. Wait for God's still, small voice.

With everything in me itching to race after Sarah Beth, I forced myself to stay put. Wait for God to speak to me. But how was I supposed to hear a thing over the ruckus the birds were making overhead, dogs barking in the distance, and my own voice clanging in my mind? *Why didn't I share how I cared for her first then ease into the lie? Because it didn't seem like such a big deal. It wasn't a lie. Not really. More like an omission. Okay, a lie of omission is still a lie. So, what do I do now?*

Wait.

One word, the same as when the Lord planted the demand for honesty on my heart. I didn't rightly know what I was supposed to wait for, and I wasn't sure it came from God and not my own thoughts, but what choice did I have?

Chapter 27

Sarah Beth

Everyone lied. Mama. Aaron. Even Jenna. How could I be such an idiot? Heart pounding, I nearly ran back to the motel. Didn't slow down even when my toe caught on a tree root. I was going to pack up everything Gracie Lynn and me owned and drive us down to Peachtree. It didn't matter that I'd lose all the money I'd dumped into Mama's business or that I didn't have me a job.

As I neared the door to Mama's motel apartment, I slapped the tears from my cheek and took a deep breath. It wouldn't do for Gracie Lynn to see me riled like I was. And even if Mama had been right about Aaron all along, I couldn't stomach another "I told you so" coming from her.

Why'd this have to happen, God? I'm having a hard enough time figuring out how to forgive Mama. Now Aaron, too?

I could hear Mama and Gracie Lynn talking in the kitchen as I opened the front door. Jazzy's high-pitched bark sounded the alarm before she tore across the room to launch herself at my shins. I scooped her up to keep from tripping over her.

"That you, Sarah Beth?" Mama's voice carried over the commotion.

I was feeling ugly enough to respond with a sarcastic, "Who else would it be?" but I managed to hold my tongue. Gracie Lynn would learn enough bad habits from me; sarcasm didn't need to be one of them.

"Yes, Mama." I carried Jazzy into the kitchen. Gracie Lynn, still in her PJ's, was slurping down a bowl of sugary cereal while Mama nursed a cup of coffee.

"Where you been this early?" There wasn't even the slightest edge to her question. Maybe me taking off for Peachtree yesterday took some of the fight out of her.

I set the puppy on the floor and looked at Gracie Lynn. "You best go get ready for school, baby girl."

Mama clucked her tongue. "She don't got school today. It's Thursday." She narrowed her eyes on me like she was trying to see into my soul.

With no anchor to my week, it was no wonder I lost track of the days. Or maybe it was the emotions piling one atop the other making my brain foggy. "Go get yourself dressed, Gracie Lynn. Then take Jazzy out back for a spell. Your nana and me need to talk."

Gracie Lynn dropped her spoon into the bowl with a shrug, milk splashing onto the table. "'Kay." She slipped off the chair and ran from the room, calling Jazzy to follow her.

I took Gracie Lynn's bowl to the sink and ran some water over a dish rag. While Mama eyed me, I scrubbed the table clean.

"You wanna tell me what's got you in such a tizzy?" Like I didn't have reason enough with what we'd been going through.

"Doesn't matter." I tossed the rag into the sink and turned to her. "Me and Gracie Lynn are moving out just as soon as I can get our stuff packed up."

Aside from Mama clutching the coffee cup so tight her knuckles went white, she didn't react. No twist of her lips or hardening of her eyes. Guess we both knew it was for the best.

"This on account of your daddy?" Her words were steady. Calm. Resigned, maybe? If she could act like an adult, I could, too.

I dropped into the chair Gracie Lynn had been sitting in. "Partly." I swiped my hand through my hair before resting my elbows on the table. "I don't know how to forgive you, Mama."

Her gaze was steady. "You think runnin' away's gonna change that?"

A snort broke from me before I could stop it. "I'm not running away. I'm moving."

She shrugged her thin shoulders. "Same difference."

"No, it's not." I clenched my jaw against the surge of emotion I wanted to spew at her. Wouldn't do a bit of good to lose my temper. I was no match for Mama. "There's nothing here for me. I need a job. And a family for Gracie Lynn would be nice, don't you think?" Despite me wanting to stay calm, bitterness was woven around each word.

Mama pursed her lips, moved her coffee cup aside, and rested her elbows on the table. "You and me ain't so different, Sarah Beth." I opened my mouth to argue, but she held up a hand. "Hear me out, chil'." When I shut my mouth, she leaned forward. "I been pushin' ever'body away on account of my hurts. You run instead."

There wasn't any point arguing with her, so I didn't. But she was wrong. When had I ever run away? *When I left Mama for Jason. Left L.A. when Jason died, even though I could've had a job easy enough. Now I'm running from Mama again. Or maybe, I'm running from Aaron. And Jenna. And the pain of their lies.*

"Thought you and Aaron were sweet on each other." I'd never heard Mama call him by his name—or talk about him without souring up like a lemon.

"There's nothing between us." Now I was the liar. "Not anymore, anyway." When she didn't say anything, I decided to lay it all out. "You were right about him, okay? He admitted to wanting to buy your motel, just like you said. And you were right about Jenna, too. She was in on it."

Mama nodded. "So he tol' me yesterday when he came lookin' for you."

"He did?" Didn't matter. Too little, too late.

"What're you afraid of, chil'?" Mama's eyes held mine. "Me? I was afraid I'd lose you. Figured if I jus' kept a wall between us, I wouldn't get hurt when you took off, like your daddy did." She sighed. "It don't work, Sarah Beth. You leavin' like you did nearly killed me, even knowin' it was my fault. *'Specially* knowin' it was my fault."

A lump rose in my throat. "Daddy didn't leave. You kicked him out."

"Don't make much difference. End result's the same." Rubbing the rim of the cup with her thumb, she smiled real sad. "You wanna make the same mistakes I did, Sarah Beth, or you wanna do some better?"

She pushed up from the chair with a grunt. As she passed me, she reached out and laid her hand it on my shoulder. Unaccustomed to her touch, I stiffened. "This thing with Aaron? You're makin' a mountain outta a mole hill. Lookin' for reasons to run 'cause you're afraid you're gonna get hurt. Don't make the same mistakes I did."

Mama was an enigma. I think that was the word I was looking for. She didn't beg for my forgiveness. Didn't even try to make an excuse for her lies, except to admit it was fear that drove her. Never in my wildest imagination would I have said the two of us were alike.

Don't make the same mistakes I did. First time she'd ever given me motherly advice that didn't come with an attitude. I wasn't ready to follow it with Aaron. That was too big a fear I needed to nurse for a while. Jenna would be some easier, especially since she didn't know I had me a bone to pick with her. Rather than give her fair warning, I decided to show up at her office and catch her off guard. No time to concoct a lie to cover a lie.

Simon & Wright Realtors was in downtown Chattanooga. We'd stopped in there a time or two when she'd had to pick up paperwork before heading off for an estate sale. I parked on a side street so she wouldn't see me coming—if she was even there. That was the one possible hitch in my plan to confront her.

It was really too perfect a day to be in an ugly mood. Summer was nudging into spring with warm weather, lots of brightly colored flowers spilling over the planters along the curb, and wispy clouds in the sky. A mockingbird sat atop a streetlight, singing its heart out. I supposed if my mind latched onto these simple things, there was hope for me. I hadn't quite morphed into Mama yet.

That was a sobering thought.

I stepped into Jenna's office and goosebumps skittered up my bare arms. It was at least ten degrees cooler—or maybe I'd had an attack of nerves.

"Can I help you? Oh, hey, you're Jenna's friend." Rosie, one of Jenna's colleagues, stood in front of a tall file cabinet. I'd met her the last time I was there. "Sarah Beth, isn't it?" She pushed the drawer closed, and it latched with a heavy *thump*.

"Yes." Shame heated my cheeks. *Jenna's friend*. And here I was showing up unannounced, fixing to light into her for a lie that suddenly seemed like the mole hill Mama claimed it was. "But if she's not here or if she's busy—"

"Oh, not at all." Rosie waved me to follow her. "Right this way."

I glanced at the door and fought the urge to run. *I been pushin' ever'body away on account of my hurts. You run instead.* Maybe Mama wasn't so far off, after all. Straightening my shoulders, I followed Rosie down the hall and stepped into Jenna's office behind her.

Jenna glanced up from her desk, and the moment she spotted me, her face lit up. "Hey, Sarah Beth. You must have some sort of ESP, 'cause I was just this moment thinkin' about you." She came around her desk to hug me as Rosie slipped out. Her big hair tickled my nose along with whatever expensive perfume she was wearing. Guilt over my intentions had me stiffening.

Stepping back, she patted my arm. "You wanna go over to Puckett's for an early lunch?" She lifted her wrist and glanced at her watch. Gucci or Rolex or whatever designer timepiece she wore. "I got an hour before my next appointment."

Folding my arms across my chest, I took a deep breath. "Can we talk for a minute?"

A wrinkle formed between her brows, and she frowned. "Of course." She sat on the edge of her desk and waved toward one of the fancy, leather chairs facing her. "Everything okay?"

I didn't bother sitting but stood stiff as a board instead. No sense beating around the bush. "I just found out this morning that you and Aaron were fixin' to buy Mama's property."

Her smile wavered, and confusion clouded her eyes. "Well, yes, but that was before you came home." She fingered a wayward strand of hair from her forehead. "You already knew this. We talked about it." Trivial or not, what she said wasn't technically true.

I raised my eyebrows and kept my gaze fixed on her until she broke eye contact. "Okay, I didn't tell you that Aaron was my client, but I didn't think it was relevant." When I didn't respond, she blew out a breath and spread her arms wide. "This had nothing to do with you. I thought we put this to rest, Sarah Beth. I mean, both of us have been helping with the remodel, haven't we?" Like I didn't know that. Except I worked it out in my mind on the way over and decided their help was a guilt offering.

"Why didn't you just tell me the truth from the beginning? Why the lies?"

Jenna rolled her eyes. "Because of this right here. When you got upset with me for bringing it up right after you came home, I told Aaron I couldn't work for him. And I was the one who suggested we not tell you. No sense adding to whatever pain you were carrying around already. If that makes me a bad person, so be it." She planted her hands on her hips, tears shimmering in her eyes. "I consider you my best friend, Sarah Beth. I'd do just about anything for you, but you gotta learn to give people the benefit of the doubt. Not everyone is out to hurt you."

Unless she was a world-class actress, the pain in her expression was real. Guilt wouldn't have anyone putting in the time Jenna had to carry me to estate sales. And Aaron spent his own money to make sure the playground was safe for Gracie Lynn. And hadn't he helped me with installing the linoleum, which I'd plumb forgot to reimburse him for?

Shame heated my cheeks, which I covered with my hands as I sank into the chair Jenna had offered a few minutes before. Jenna was right. Mama was right. Daddy was right. If I let the hurts of the past forever color my future, I'd become just like Mama. I could choose to live a life of fear, pushing aside everyone who cared about me. Or I could live life to the fullest, and trust that the Lord was keeping a watch.

If Aaron wasn't finished with me before, he surely would be now. "What have I done?" The groan came from deep inside and nearly cut off my breath. "You must think I'm crazy as a June bug." Tears flooded my eyes faster than I could bat them away. I was a fool, and it shamed me.

Jenna sank onto her knees in front of me and pulled my hands from my face. "We're all of us crazy as June bugs, Sarah Beth. We each have our own baggage from past hurts that we insist on luggin' around."

How was it possible that perfect Jenna, with her designer clothes, upscale condo, and fancy car, could have any wounds? But there was something lurking in her eyes when I looked real close that told me different. Maybe if I hadn't been so wrapped up in my own troubles, I would've taken notice of hers.

"I've made a real mess of things, Jenna." I squeezed her hands before letting go.

She patted my knee and struggled to stand on those ridiculous three-inch heels. Resembled a flamingo who'd gotten drunk on bad shrimp. "You haven't done any such thing." She dropped onto the matching chair next to mine. "We'll forget this entire conversation. Reboot."

Scraping my hands through my hair, I sighed. "I appreciate you taking that attitude, but I'd rather not forget. There's some important lessons sprinkled among all the crazy." Mainly that I needed to be the friend to Jenna that she'd been to me. "And I didn't just make a mess of things with you."

If only I could do a reboot with Aaron.

Chapter 28

Aaron

Twenty-four hours and counting. That's how long it'd been since Sarah Beth marched herself down the street in a huff. And I was still waiting. Never before had I trusted the Lord more than I did in those seemingly interminable hours. It helped that I'd spent a good part of the night hanging around at the hospital waiting on Ashley to have her baby girl. Caroline Elizabeth Cooper was born at 3:42 am, making Linc the happiest daddy since Abraham had Isaac.

You'd think Mama and Dad would be satisfied with having themselves three grandchildren and another on the way—thanks to Carrie and Russell making good on their threat to try for a third kid. But the moment I walked into the waiting room, they were giving me the look. Could practically hear the question running through their collective minds, "When are you gonna get yourself hitched and start makin' babies?" I didn't have the heart to tell them Sarah Beth had pitched herself a hissy fit and wasn't talking to me right then. No sense throwing a wet blanket over the celebration.

The sun was streaming through the leafy branches of the trees when I got home. Too tired to worry over Sarah Beth, I stripped off my jeans and climbed into bed. A few hours of sleep, and I'd be right as rain. Or at least coherent enough to function. Seemed like only minutes before a pounding woke me from a dead sleep. Took a good bit for me to realize it was coming from the front door. A quick glance at the clock and I realized it'd been a few hours rather than minutes since I'd laid down.

Sarah Beth.

I jumped from bed and wrestled one-armed into my jeans, nearly falling on my face a time or two. "I'm coming," I shouted. My heart raced with the fear that she'd give up and leave.

Stumbling to the door, I raked my hand through my unruly hair and blinked the sleep from my eyes. But when I yanked the door open it wasn't Sarah Beth standing on the porch—it was Billy Jones. A lesser man would've cried at the disappointment.

"Hey, Billy." I glanced past him, just in case. *Idiot.* "What're you doin' here at the crack of dawn?"

Frowning, Billy glanced at his watch. "It's after nine, Bro. Bein' off work's made you lazy." He chuckled at his own joke. "You gonna let me in or what?"

Turning away, I shuffled toward the kitchen. "I need coffee." Heard the door close and then Billy following close behind me.

While I filled the kettle with water, Billy pulled out a chair and sat. "You've done a lot with this place. Still plannin' on selling it?"

Good question. If he'd asked a week ago, I would've known the answer. Had it all planned out in my head. Sarah Beth and me would get married and live here with Gracie Lynn. She could still run the motel with her mama, if that's what she wanted. Only thing that'd be missing was the white-picket fence. Of course, God wasn't done with this story, so anything was possible.

Billy tapped the table with his fist. "Hey, you okay?"

Turning on the burner, I grunted. "Was at the hospital till early this morning. My brother and his wife had their baby." I tried to wrangle the lid from the coffee canister, awkward as an elephant doing the tango. You'd think after weeks with my arm out of commission, I'd have it down.

"Let me help you." Billy crossed over to me in two strides and took over. "How long are you gonna have that sling on your arm?"

"Don't know." I collected mugs from the cabinet and slid the ceramic cone over to Billy. "Another week or two, maybe. Should be back to work a week or so after that. Soon as the doc clears me for duty, I'll be there."

Billy fit the paper filter into the cone. "Well, just thought you should know I'm turning in my papers." He wasn't facing me, so I couldn't read his expression. But he didn't sound elated.

"You're quitting?" Couldn't say it surprised me. Every conversation we'd had about the work, he was riddled with anxiety.

Tilting his head toward me, he grimaced. "It's that or my marriage."

"Missy's handing you an ultimatum?" A year ago, I'd have scoffed at the idea. But now, I saw things a little clearer. Hearing Mama's take on basically being a single parent. Coming to understand the hierarchy of how things ought to be—God first, family second, work third. A tough lesson for a workaholic like me.

"Nah. Missy ain't like that. But I keep putting work ahead of everything else, my marriage is gonna suffer." He shrugged. "And my kids."

The kettle whistled, and I turned off the burner. "Kids? But you only have Kyle." The grin on Billy's face reminded me of Linc's right before he announced Ashley was pregnant. "You're fixin' to have another baby?"

Crossing his arms, he nodded. "She's due right before Christmas. We're gonna have us a girl this time."

I slapped him on the back. "Congratulations. That's great news." First Carrie and now Billy. Everyone was moving on with their lives, and I was stuck in limbo. A purgatory of sorts. "What're you gonna do for work?" I set the coffee cone on one of the mugs and poured the hot water over it. The rich scent of French roast wafted up in a cloud of steam.

"I got an uncle who owns a construction company. The pay won't be as good, and insurance might be a problem." He shrugged. "But I don't have to put in as many hours. We'll figure it out." He glanced around the kitchen. "You ever wanna leave the railroad, I'm sure he'd give you a job. You do good work."

"Thanks. I—" A knock on the door cut me off, and I froze. *Sarah Beth?*

"You expectin' someone?" Billy carried the mug with the cone on top to the sink. "Guess I should've called first."

I combed my hair with shaky fingers and headed for the door. "Probably my mom or sister dropping off food." But it wasn't either of them standing on the other side of the door when I opened it.

Sarah Beth appeared nervous as a cat in a roomful of rockers. Hands tucked into the front pockets of her frayed jeans, eyes wide, chewing on the corner of her full lower lip. Her blond hair was a messy pile clipped to the top of her head, and her cheeks were an attractive shade of pink. From embarrassment or the sun, it didn't matter. Looked beautiful either way.

"Hey." She yanked her hands from the pockets of her jeans, folded her arms, and shuffled her feet. "Can we talk?"

"You drink your coffee black?" Billy's voice called from the kitchen.

Sarah Beth leaned sideways and peered behind me. "You got company."

"Just Billy." As if she'd know who that was. "A guy I work with. Or rather, *worked* with. Came by to let me know he put in his papers." She couldn't care less, and I was rambling.

Billy showed up and saved me from making a bigger fool of myself. "Hey, there. Didn't mean to interrupt anything." He stuck out his hand. "Billy Jones."

Sarah Beth shook it. "Sarah Beth McCallister. Pleased to meet you."

"Pleasure's mine." He threw me a cocky grin and patted me on the back. "I'll just be goin' now. You give me a call if you need any help. Missy and me will find a time to have y'all over for a barbeque." He tipped an imaginary hat at Sarah Beth and side-stepped past her. "See ya."

Sarah Beth crossed her arms again. "I came to apologize for yesterday." *Thank You, Jesus.* Her eyes darted around, seemingly unable to land on one particular thing, and I could take a full breath for the first time since she'd walked away.

"In that case, come on in. You want some coffee? Just made it fresh." I opened the door wide and stepped back so she could enter.

"I'm jittery enough without adding caffeine to the mix."

I'd been waiting long enough to clear things up between us, and I didn't want to waste a minute of it. Instead, I led her into the front room. "You wanna sit?"

Had me a feeling this conversation right here would be one of those pivotal moments in my life.

Sarah Beth

Faith is a funny thing. On the one hand, it was pretty clear God created every living thing. "Let there be light," and there it was. All the animals and plants and birds and fish. *Everything.* Then He breathed life into Adam and used his rib to create Eve. The Bible even says that He knit me together in Mama's womb. How crazy was that?

And yet, I sometimes forgot He had an excellent plan for my life—beyond my mistakes. I liked to think God was fixing to make Aaron a part of it, but that meant I needed to eat a whole lot of crow. I'd practically perfected the art of an apology since I'd done more than my fair share. I even tended to apologize for other people, like Jason and Mama, as if my association to them made me guilty of their behavior.

It was clear since talking to Jenna the day before, I had some fences to mend, but it took me until that very morning to get up the nerve. God and me talked off and on throughout the night, which is when He reminded me I could count on Him. Always. No matter how many times I made a mess of things.

So, there I was, sitting on Aaron's sofa with my heart in my hands—figuratively speaking, of course. He looked downright adorable in scruffy jeans and a wrinkled, white shirt. His hair was going every which way. Had just gotten out of bed? Did his shoulder pain make it hard to sleep? Or maybe he hadn't slept on account of me being ugly the day before.

So wrapped up in my thoughts, it hadn't occurred to me Aaron was literally on the edge of his seat, tapping his thumb on his knee, like he was waiting on me to say something. Maybe to offer the apology I owed him. But my tongue was suddenly all twisted up, and I couldn't seem to form a single word.

"You sure I can't get you something?" He ran his palm up and down his thigh, sort of like wringing his hands when he only had but one. Interesting. What did he have to be nervous about? I was the one who walked away without giving him a chance to explain—not that he needed to.

"I messed up." Me blurting those three little words opened up a floodgate of emotion. My throat went tight with the threat of tears as my face heated. "You have every right to be angry with me after the way I treated you yesterday. I'm forever waiting on people to disappoint me, which you didn't, of course. But it's like Mama said, I'm always looking for reasons to run. And I know that's crazy." I threw my hands up. "I mean, seriously crazy. What kind of a life is that for Gracie Lynn? I'm no different from Mama, really. All these years, I've been holding her accountable for the bad choices I made, when the whole time it was my own fault." My voice got louder and louder, until I was practically shouting. I'd have gone on, too, if I wasn't out of breath.

Aaron's lips twitched like he was fighting back a grin. Probably afraid if he let it loose, I'd take offense and go off again. "Was there an apology tangled up somewhere in all those words?" I opened my mouth to respond, but he held up his hand. "I hope not. Because you have nothin' to be sorry about."

Even though I'd known in my head he was nothing like Jason, right there was when the truth of it anchored into my heart. "You're wrong, Aaron." A knot of regret made it hard to talk without my voice cracking. "You've been nothing but kind, and I assumed the worst. I should've listened when you tried to explain yesterday." Like I had Jenna.

Aaron crossed to the sofa and sat close enough he could tuck me under his arm. I rested my head on his shoulder with a sigh and let my eyes drift shut. If only for the moment, everything was safe and right in my little world. *Thank You, Jesus.* He couldn't hold me that way and still be mad, could he?

"Let's forget about yesterday." The rumble of his voice vibrated against my ear. "We'll start fresh right here. Right now."

"A reboot," I mumbled.

He chuckled. "Yeah. A reboot." He ran his hand up and down my arm, soothing all my fears away. "So, what I was fixing to tell you yesterday before we got interrupted by—"

"Me stomping off like a spoiled brat?"

"Your righteous indignation."

A laugh erupted before I could stifle it. "Yeah, let's go with that."

He kissed the top of my head. "I love you, Sarah Beth." So simple and unexpected, I wasn't sure I heard him right.

Pulling back, I looked up into his eyes. Steady. Sincere. "What'd you say?"

His mouth turned up. "I love you." Slipping his arm from around my shoulders, he ran a finger down my cheek. "In case you're thinking I'm loose with the words, I've never told another woman that before." He grimaced. "Guess that's not exactly true. I did tell Janie Reynolds I loved her in the fourth grade, but only 'cause Kyle Martin dared me to. *And,* since she was only nine, she wasn't technically a woman."

He loved me. Aaron *loved* me.

The grin slipped from his face. "I don't expect you to feel the same." He tucked me under his arm again. "But I'm hopin' you'll at least let me take you on a proper date. Lots of proper dates. I mean, something more romantic than layin' linoleum. And maybe in time, you'll trust me enough—"

"I do trust you." I put some distance between us so I could look him in the eyes. "I do." And I loved him, too. Or at least I *thought* I loved him. I'd never actually experienced the romantic, gushy, out-of-my-head sort of love I'd heard about. But whatever this was with Aaron, it was close. "I know it didn't appear that way yesterday, but I think I was reacting to old wounds."

"I get that. But wounds...they take time to heal. The thing is, Sarah Beth, somewhere along the way, I'll disappoint you again. I'm only human. I wasn't kidding about never telling another woman I loved her. You're the first. And I pray you'll be the last. That doesn't mean things are gonna be easy."

I didn't expect easy. "I have a lot of baggage." As if he didn't already know that. "Unpacking it all might get a bit messy."

He shrugged. "None of us get through this life without having some hurts. But if you give us a chance, I pray that over time, you'll come to see I'm *always* on your side. I might put my foot in my mouth or fail to say what I should or misinterpret your feelings. I promise you, it'll never be intentional. I'm just a lamebrain with my own issues."

I reached up and pressed my hand to his cheek, a little rough with stubble, and stared into his serious, green eyes. "I think I love you, too, Aaron. I've never felt this way about anyone, so it's new and a little scary." My heart was racing fast enough to give proof to that.

He took my hand and kissed the palm, the warmth of his lips sending a shiver up my spine. "I'm right there with you, Sarah Beth. It's scary for me, too. But I think if we keep our eyes on Jesus, everything else will tend to itself."

I wasn't one to take initiative, but such joy bloomed in my chest, I couldn't help but reach up and kiss him right on the lips. With a soft groan, he slipped his hand to the back of my head, his fingers tangling in my hair as he drew me in deeper. When he pulled away, it took a full five seconds for my eyes to drift open. If I could only stay in this fog where all my issues with Mama and the motel reno and my pathetic insecurities could be forgotten.

A slow grin lit his face. "You keep this up, we might need your mama to chaperone us." That was a sobering thought. "Do I need to ask her permission to date you? 'Cause if that's the case, I better figure out how to worm my way into her good graces." Then raised his hand. "Kidding. I'm not gonna make that mistake again."

Laying my head on his strong chest, I breathed in the scent of laundry soap, bleach, and his unique scent—one I'd love to get to know real well in the future. "You don't need to worry yourself over that; I think she's already softening toward you."

"Well, I'd say that's a miracle right there." We snuggled together, and after a few minutes, my lack of sleep the night before had me drifting into that dreamy, halfway state. "So, did you and your mama talk?"

I sighed. Guess no one could truly hide from their problems. "We did. Nothing's gonna get fixed over night, but like you said before, if I keep my eye on Jesus, everything'll work out eventually."

For our good and His glory. Wasn't what the Bible said? And I was fixing to hold Him to it.

Epilogue

One Year Later

Sarah Beth

The arch of turquoise, cotton candy-pink, white, and black balloons swayed in the slight June breeze alongside the newly painted *Pickett's Mill Motel* sign. A beacon to welcome what few people might show up for the Grand Reopening. Jenna assured me we'd have a crowd that would far surpass my low expectations. Growing up like I did, it was taking some heart-to-heart Jesus-time to overcome my tendency towards such. And I had to take into account we'd actually completed what we'd started, so that right there exceeded my hopes.

I stepped through the arch and glanced along the motel grounds with new eyes, trying to experience what our guests would in the next little bit. The building had a fresh coat of white paint, trimmed with the same vintage turquoise in the balloons. Mama had planted honeycup, sparkleberry, Georgia basil and sweetshrub in the beds out front of the twelve units—showy bursts of color that added depth and beauty. The playground had been spruced up with a few fancy additions, thanks to Aaron. Although I couldn't see it from where I was standing, the pool had also been resurfaced and tiled in keeping with the retro theme.

Food trucks offering hotdogs and Coke, fried pies, popcorn, and cotton candy lined the perimeter facing the motel along with a couple face-painting booths for the kids. The coolest feature, far as I was concerned, was a pink and white, 1957 Chevy Corvette photo booth. And, of course, a bouncy house in the middle of it all. Gracie Lynn, Kristy, and Jake had been testing it out since it'd been set up an hour before.

Caleb, Chance, and Daddy were putting up some tables and chairs while Jasmine and Eva finished them off with plastic turquoise covers and darling centerpieces they'd made—jukebox candy holders filled with Pixie Sticks, Hot Tamales, and Turkish Taffy.

Mama, dressed in her Sunday best, chatted with Patsy by the registration office. She kept fussing with her hair, like she hadn't yet accepted the new cut and color, even though we'd all assured her it was perfect. And it was. She looked ten years younger than when I'd arrived a year ago March. A lot had changed, actually. The fact she even bought herself a few dresses for church was a miracle on par with parting the Red Sea. Then she went and got herself baptized the week before. Just remembering it got me all choked up again.

Movement from the edge of the property drew my eyes, and Aaron came into view. Married a whole two months, and my heart still melted whenever I saw him. The pathway between the motel and his house—*our* house—had been cleared and groomed for easy access. Good thing, too, since he was hauling two seven-pound bags of ice.

Rather than standing around like a bump on a log, I speed-walked past the food trucks to help him. "Let me take one of those for you."

He skirted around me with a grin. "No, ma'am." Then he leaned in for a lingering kiss that about made my toes curl. Would I ever get tired of his kisses? Surely not. "This is your party." He scanned the parking lot. "Jenna or Connor here yet?"

"Nope." I'd been on the lookout for both of them—Jenna because she needed a hug and Connor because he'd have Faith with him. That baby girl was sweet enough to eat, although she was giving her daddy fits now that she was walking.

"There's Jenna now." Aaron nodded toward the magnolia-covered drive. Jenna was having a time of it walking the gravel path in killer shoes. May not be the wisest choice, but it sure set off her skinny jeans and gold-colored tank. I figured she'd show up wearing confidence-building armor since Chad had dumped her the night before.

I met her halfway and wrapped her in my arms, while her big hair and perfume nearly suffocated me. "You're better off without him." I'd only said it five times during our hour-long conversation when she called to break the news. An hour I would've rather spent snuggled in bed with Aaron. But it's what friends did for one another.

Jenna's chin wobbled. "That's a year I'll never get back." She blew a breath out through pouty lips. "Meanwhile, my biological clock is tickin' away."

Now wouldn't be the time to tell her I was pregnant. Especially since I hadn't had a chance to tell Aaron. By the time I got off the phone with Jenna, he was sound asleep. And this morning, we were in a rush to wrap up all the loose ends for this shindig. Sharing news that important deserved a special delivery. Romantic and memorable.

"You got plenty of time to have babies," I assured her. The problem was pinning down a daddy for him or her. Maybe Jenna was too picky. I knew for certain Chad was a fool to let her go.

"Doesn't matter now. There's work to be done before the crowd arrives." Jenna's job, along with Mama, was to give tours of the newly renovated rooms. If anyone bothered to come. Didn't matter either way, because we were already booked a month out. I would have sent Jenna home to wallow in her sorrows if I didn't think the distraction would be better for her.

Wasn't a half hour later, she was busier than a moth in a mitten. The crowd she'd predicted arrived along with a couple newspaper reporters. The grand opening of Pickett's Mill Motel had created quite a buzz in town, which told me right there nothing much happened in our sleepy community. Connor had a time of it directing cars where to park, so I supposed it was best he left Faith with his sister for the day. I'd get my baby time soon enough.

Five hours later, the motel parking lot was littered with popcorn, cardboard cotton candy tubes, soda lids and a plethora of other trash. Looked like the carnival had come to town and left a mess in its wake. But it didn't matter one whit, because the event was a success. While Aaron walked Connor to his car, Mama took Gracie Lynn to the house to give her a bath and feed Jazzy.

I wanted nothing more than to climb into bed and sleep for twelve hours. Instead, I got me a trash bag and started picking up the garbage scattered among Mama's plants. I'd just plucked a cotton candy tube from a honeycup plant when Aaron came up from behind and hugged me to his back.

His mouth was warm against my ear and his kisses sent a shiver up my spine. "Let's leave that for now and go to bed. You've worked hard enough." Oh, how I wish we could.

I turned and wrapped my arms around his neck. "Can't. We got church in the morning." Tucking my head beneath his chin, I sighed. If I could stay right here in this exact spot for a bit, I might could muster enough energy to finish what I'd started.

"Connor's gonna bring Faith to church tomorrow." That drew a smile from me, although it didn't come as a surprise. Aaron had been mentoring him since he'd gotten on with Norfolk Southern, so I knew it was only a matter of time. "Before you know it, we're gonna have to expand our little group to two pews."

"That's a good thing," I murmured, half asleep. *I don't remember being quite this tired when I carried Gracie Lynn.*

Aaron took hold of my shoulders and crouched down so he could look me in the eyes. "What'd you say?"

I blinked. "Said it's a good thing. Expanding to a second pew."

"After that." He was laser-focused on me.

"I didn't—" *Oh. Had I said that part about carrying Gracie Lynn out loud?* Feeling limp as a rag doll, surrounded by carnival-like trash, wasn't exactly the memorable scene I'd pictured for this news. Guess the good Lord had other ideas. "I was fixin' to tell you over a romantic supper."

His eyes were nearly bugging out of his head. "Tell me what?" We hadn't really talked about having a baby, except in generalities. Would he be happy about it? *Oh, please, let it be so.*

"I'm pregnant."

His grin answered that question right quick. "We're gonna have a baby?" Was that a rhetorical question or had he not heard me?

"Yes. If the home pregnancy test I took yesterday was accurate."

He whooped loud enough to be heard clear to Chattanooga then picked me up like I weighed no more than Gracie Lynn and twirled me around. "This calls for a celebration."

When he set me down, I had to grab hold of his hand until the dizziness subsided. "We'll do that, but right now, we gotta get this mess cleaned up. It's getting late, and—"

"Nope." He gathered me in his arms. "*I'm* gonna clean up the trash after we get you home. I'll send your mama on her way so you can take yourself a bath and climb into bed." When I opened my mouth to argue, he stared me down. "Please, Sarah Beth." Were those tears shimmering in his eyes? "You've blessed me beyond anything I'd hoped for in this life." Who could argue with that?

As we walked down the path between the motel and our home, Aaron tucked me close to his side as our footsteps fell into sync. "I know you were nervous about today. I was, too." He'd never once let one.

"Really?" I snuggled closer. "But we did it. We actually pulled it off." With a whole lot of help from the Lord.

"We're a team, you and me." He kissed the top of my head. "As long as we remember that, and we keep our eyes on Jesus, there's nothing we can't handle."

   * * *

Acknowledgements

First off, I have to give a huge shout-out to the inspiration for this series. Thank you, Kenny Barnes, for bringing the railroad to life through your stories and experiences from your lifelong career. I also appreciate your willingness to answer all my questions through numerous texts, emails, and chats.

I also have to thank friend and Street Team member Kathy Bumgardner for help with creating the title *Train-Wrecked Hearts*. Creating titles is always a challenge for me, so I appreciate your input.

None of my books are written in isolation. I have two amazing critique partners! Thank you Katie Shands for keeping me Southern and Wendy Cunningham for making sure I have the proper "beats" within the story.

And my wonderful Jen's Street Team. You ladies my be small in number, but you are mighty in faithfulness, support, and encouragement. I couldn't do this without you.

Also by Jennifer Sienes

About the Author

Jennifer Sienes holds a bachelor's in psychology and a master's in education but discovered life-experience is the best teacher. She loves Jesus, romance and writing—and puts it all together in inspirational contemporary fiction. Her daughter's TBI and brother's suicide inspired two of her three novels. Although fiction writing is her real love, she's had several non-fiction pieces published in anthologies including four in *Chicken Soup for the Soul*. She has two grown children and one very spoiled Maltese. California born and raised, she now lives in Middle Tennessee with her real-life hero and husband.

Visit her at www.JenniferSienes.com

www.ingramcontent.com/pod-product-compliance
Lightning Source LLC
Chambersburg PA
CBHW061236310726
48971CB00007B/2095